STORMFALCON!

Driven and desperate, Taen flung herself against the ship's rail. Hard hands caught her, yanked her back. The little girl flailed wildly and the sea breeze caught the feather the sorcerer had given her. It skimmed upward, out of reach.

Through blurred eyes, Taen watched Anskiere's feather whirl on the wind. It shimmered, exploding with a snap into a tawny falcon marked with black. A triple halo of light circled its outstretched wings.

"Stormfalcon!" a sailor cried. Wind gusted suddenly, screaming through the rigging.

Taen smelled fear in the ship—and lightning on the air.

JANNY WURTS

Stormwarden

BOOKS BY JANNY WURTS

Sorcerer's Legacy

THE CYCLE OF FIRE
Stormwarden*
Keeper of the Keys
Shadowfane

The Master of Whitestorm

THE WARS OF LIGHT AND SHADOW
Curse of the Mistwraith
Ships of Merior*

With Raymond E. Feist
Daughter of the Empire
Servant of the Empire
Mistress of the Empire

*Available from HarperPaperbacks

JANNY WURTS

Stormwarden

Book One of the
Cycle of Fire

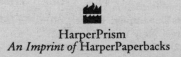

HarperPrism
An Imprint of HarperPaperbacks

This is a work of fiction. The characters, incidents, and dialogues are products of the author's imagination and are not to be construed as real. Any resemblance to actual events or persons, living or dead, is entirely coincidental.

HarperPaperbacks   *A Division of* HarperCollins*Publishers*
10 East 53rd Street, New York, N.Y. 10022

A mass-market paperback edition of this book was published in 1984 by Ace Books.

Cover illustration by Janny Wurts
Frontispiece and map by Janny Wurts

First HarperPaperbacks printing: February 1995

Printed in the United States of America

HarperPrism is an imprint of HarperPaperbacks. HarperPaperbacks, HarperPrism, and colophon are trademarks of HarperCollins*Publishers*

10 9 8 7 6 5 4 3 2 1

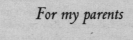
For my parents

ACKNOWLEDGMENTS

With special thanks to those painters within the field of fantasy and science fiction illustration whose advice and encouragement contributed to my career as an artist. And for those special friends who provided my "home away from home" in New York.

to Shadowfane

Northsea

Wrecker's Bay
Clover's Warren

Felwaithe

Kierkforest

Murieton

Canyon Lake

Cliffhaven

Riftwater

Eastplain

Kisburn

Royal Palace

Mainstrait

Elrinfaer Tower

Merk's Point

Terin Sea

Elrinfaer

Telshire

Cael's Falls

Mhored Kara

Deshforest

Prologue

WRITTEN IN THE RECORDS OF THE Vaere is the tale of the binding of the Mharg-demons at Elrinfaer by the wizard of wind and wave, Anskiere. He was helped in his task by Ivain, master of fire and earth, for the skills of a single sorcerer were insufficient to subdue so formidable a foe. But at the moment of crisis, when the peril of the Mharg-demons was greatest, legend holds that Ivain betrayed his companion out of jealousy.

Yet, Anskiere survived and the Mharg-demons were bound. The major wards are sealed still by Anskiere's powers. And though neither Ivain nor Anskiere ever spoke of the dissent which arose between them on a lonely isle at Northsea, so potent was the magic in the words spoken by Anskiere to his betrayer, sailors who have visited the rocky spread of beach claim the winds there repeat them to this day.

Your offense against me is pardoned but not forgotten. This geas I lay upon you: should I call, you, Ivain, shall answer, and complete a deed of my choice, even to the end of your days. And should you die, my will shall pass to your eldest son, and to his son's sons after him, until the debt is paid.

On a nearby ledge, battered by tide, lies a stone with an inscription believed to be Ivain's reply.

Summon me, sorcerer, and know sorrow. Be sure I will leave nothing of value for your use, even should my offspring inherit.

CHAPTER I

Stormwarden

The fisher folk clustered in a tight knot before the cottage door. Wind off the sea tugged their home-woven trousers into untidy wrinkles, making the cloth look awkwardly sewn. One man, tougher, uglier, and more sunburned that the rest, finally knocked loudly and stepped back, frowning.

The door opened. Dull pewter light from a lowering sky touched a figure in shadow beyond.

"Anskiri?" The fisherman's tone was rough, aggressively pitched to cover embarrassment.

"I am Anskiere." A quiet voice restored the name's foreign inflection. "Has there been trouble?" With the dignity associated with great power, the Stormwarden of Imrill Kand stepped over the threshold, a thin, straight man with sculpted features and harsh gray eyes. Sea wind whipped white hair about shoulders clothed simply in wool.

"Ye're wanted, sorcerer, at Adin's Landing."

"Then there has been trouble, yes?" Anskiere's light eyes

flicked over the men confronting him. No one answered, and no one met his glance. The breezes fanned the fishermen's weathered cheeks, and their sea boots scuffed over pebbled stone and marsh grass. Their large, twine-callused hands stayed jammed in the pockets of oilskin jackets.

The Stormwarden's gaze dropped. He laid a slim capable hand on the door frame, careful to move slowly, without threat. "I will come. Give me a minute to bank the fire."

Anskiere stepped inside. A low mutter arose at his back, and someone spat. If the sorcerer noticed, he gave no sign. The distant sigh of the breakers filled the interval until his return. A gray cloak banded with black hooded his silver head, and in his hand he carried a knotted satchel of dyed leather. Somehow he had guessed his summons might be permanent. No one from Imrill Kand had seen either satchel or cloak since the sorcerer's arrival five winters past.

A tear in the clouds spilled sunlight like gilt over the shore flats. Anskiere paused. His eyes swept across the rocky spit of land he had chosen as home and fixed on the ocean's horizon. The fishermen stirred uneasily, but a long interval passed before Anskiere recalled his attention from the sea. He barred the cottage door.

"I am ready." He moved among them, his landsman's stride sharply delineated from the rolling gait of the fishermen. Through the long walk over the tor, he did not speak, and never once did he look back.

Angled like a gull's nest against the cliff overlooking the harbor, Adin's Landing was visible to the Stormwarden and his escort long ahead of arrival. Towering over the familiar jumble of shacks, stacked salt barrels, and drying fish nets was a black crosshatch of rigging; five warships rode at anchor. A sixth was warped to the fishers' wharf. The town streets, normally empty at noon, seethed with activity, clotted here and there by dark masses of men-at-arms.

Anskiere paused at the tor's crest and pushed his hood back. "King's men?" A gust of wind hissed through the grass at his feet, perhaps summoned by him as warning of his first stir of anger. But his voice remained gentle. "Is this why you called me?"

The ugly man clenched his hands. "Anskiere, don't ask!" He gestured impatiently down the trail.

The sorcerer remained motionless.

"Mordan, he has a right to know." The other's outburst sounded anguished and reluctant. "Five years he has served as Stormwarden, and not a life lost to the sea. He deserves an answer at least."

Mordan's lips tightened and his eyes flinched away from the sorcerer. "We cannot shelter you!"

"I did not ask shelter." Anskiere sought the one who had spoken in his behalf, and found he knew him, though the boy had grown nearly to manhood. "Tell me, Emien."

The young man flinched unhappily at the mention of his name.

"Emien, why do King's ships and King's men trouble with Imrill Kand?"

Emien drew a shaking breath and stared at hands already deeply scarred by hours of hauling twine. "Stormwarden, a Constable waits at the Fisherman's Barrel with a writ sealed by the King."

Anskiere contemplated the sky's edge. "And?"

"Kordane's Blessed Fires!" Emien's blasphemy was laced with tears. "Warden, they call you murderer. They tell of a storm that arose from the sea and tore villages, boats, and cattle from the shore of Tierl Enneth. Your doing, they said." The boy faltered. "Warden, they say you watched, drunk with laughter, as the people screamed and drowned. And they carry with them a staff marked with the device you wore when you first arrived here."

"A falcon ringed with a triple circle," Anskiere said softly. "I know it well. Thank you, Emien."

The boy stepped back, startled into fear at the sorcerer's acceptance. The penalty for malign sorcery was death by fire. "Then it's true?"

"We all have enemies." Anskiere stepped firmly onto the trail, and around him, the wind dwindled to ominous stillness.

Market square lay under a haze of dust churned up by milling feet. The entire village had gathered to see their Stormwarden accused. Taciturn, a unit of the King's Guard patrolled the streets off Rat's Alley. Foot lancers clogged the lanes between the merchants' stalls, and before the steps of the Fisherman's Barrel Inn a dais constructed of boarding planks and pickling vats held a brocaded row of officials.

"We've brought him!" Mordan shouted above the confusion.

"Be still." Anskiere bestowed a glare dark and troubled as a hurricane. "I'll go willingly, or not at all."

"Just so ye go." Mordan fell back, bristling with unease. Anskiere slipped past. Though his storm-gray cloak stood out stark as a whitecap amid a sea of russets and browns, no one noticed him until he stood before the dais. A gap widened in the crowd, leaving him isolated in a circle of dust as he set his satchel down.

"If you have asked for me, I am Anskiere." His pale, cold eyes rested on the officials.

The villagers murmured and reluctantly quieted as a plump man in scarlet leaned forward, porcine features crinkled with calculation. "I am the Constable of the King's Justice." He paused. "You have been accused of murder, Anshiri." A syrupy western accent mangled the name. "Over four thousand deaths were recorded at Tierl Enneth."

A gasp arose from the villagers, cut off as the Constable

sighed and laced ringed fingers under his chin. "Have you anything to say?"

Anskiere lifted hands capable of driving sea and sky into fury. The crowd watched as though mesmerized by a snake. Yet neither wind nor wave stirred in response to the sorcerer's gesture. Gray cloth slipped back, exposing slim veined wrists, and Anskiere's reply fell softly as rain.

"I am guilty, Eminence."

Stunned, the onlookers stood rooted, unable to believe the Stormwarden who had protected their fishing fleet from ruin would meekly surrender his powers. Anskiere stayed motionless, arms outstretched. He did not look like a murderer. All of Imrill Kand had trusted and loved him. Their betrayal was ugly to watch.

The Constable nodded. "Take him."

Men-at-arms closed at his command, pinioning the accused's shoulders with mailed fists. Three black-robed sorcerers rose from the dais, one to shackle the offered wrists with fetters woven of enchantment. The others fashioned a net of wardspells to bind Anskiere's mastery of wind, wave, and weather, and sensing security in his helplessness, the crowd roused sluggishly to anger. As people surged toward the dais, the foot lancers squared off and formed a cordon, jostled by aggressive hands. Anskiere spoke once, mildly. One of the men-at-arms struck him. His hood fell back, spilling silver hair. When he lifted his face, blood ran from his mouth.

"Kill the murderer!" someone shouted. The mob howled approval. Kicked, cuffed, and shoved until he stumbled, Anskiere was herded across the square. Thick as swarming insects, the King's Guard bundled him away from the crowd, across the fishers' wharf, and onto the decks of their ship. His light head soon vanished into the depths of the hold.

The crowd screamed and stamped, and dust eddied. Striped with shadow cast by a damp fish net, Emien bent and shook the shoulder of a small girl who lay weeping in the dirt. "Taen, please."

The child tossed back black hair, her cheeks lined with tracks of tears. "Why did they take him? Why?"

"He killed people. Taen, get up. Crying won't help." Emien caught his sister's hand and tugged. "You'll be kicked or stepped on if you stay here."

Taen shook her head. "Stormwarden *saved* lives. He saved me." She curled wet fingers tightly around her brother's wrist and pulled herself awkwardly to her feet. With one ankle twisted beyond all help of a healer's skills, she limped piteously. "The fat man lied."

Emien frowned, sickened by the child's naïvete. "Did Anskiere lie also? He *said* he killed people. Could you count the mackerel in *Dacsen*'s hold yesterday? That many died, Taen."

The child's mouth puckered. She refused to answer.

Her brother sighed, lifted her into his arms, and pressed through the villagers who jammed the square. Taen was unlikely to accept the sorcerer's act as evil. Anskiere had stilled the worst gale in memory to bring a healer from the mainland when an accident with a loading winch had crushed her leg. Since that hour, the girl had idolized him. The Stormwarden had visited often during her convalescence, a still, tall presence at her bedside. Taen had done little but hold his hand. Uncomfortably Emien recalled his uncle's embarrassed words of gratitude, and the long, tortuous hikes across the island with the fish and the firewood they could not spare. But his mother had insisted, though the Stormwarden had asked for nothing.

A sharp kick caught Emien squarely in the kneecap. The past forgotten, he gasped, bent and yelled through lips whitened with pain. "Taen!"

Despite his reprimand, his sister squirmed free of his hold and darted into the crowd. Emien swore. When Taen wished, she could move like a rabbit. Angrily he pursued, but the closely packed bodies thwarted his effort. A fishwife cursed him. Flushed beneath his tan, Emien sat on a nail keg and rubbed his sore leg. The brat could get herself home for supper.

But night fell without her return. Too late Emien thought of the dark ship which had sailed from the fishers' wharf that afternoon, to anchor beyond the headland.

"I'll find her," he promised, wounded by his mother's tears. He took a sack of biscuit from the pantry shelf and let himself out onto the puddled brick of Rat's Alley.

The moon curved like a sail needle over the water at the harbor's edge. Emien cast off the mooring of his cousin's sloop *Dacsen*, fear coiled in his gut.

"Taen, I'll kill you," he said bitterly, and wept as he hauled on the halyard. Tanbark canvas flapped sullenly up the mast. Emien abruptly wished he could kill the Stormwarden instead, for stealing the child's trust.

The black ship *Crow* rolled mildly at her anchorage, tugged by the rhythmic swell off the barrier reefs. Gimbaled oil lamps swung in the tight confines of her aft cabin, fanning splayed shadows across the curly head and fat shoulders of the Constable where he sat at the chart table. He had shed his scarlet finery in favor of a dressing robe of white silk and he reeked of drink.

"You disappointed the Guard Sergeant," he said. "He expected the villagers to fight for you, and he wanted to bash heads. How very clever of you to plead guilty, Anshiri. Blessed Fires! Instead he had to protect you from them." The Constable crashed his cup, empty, onto the chart locker. He stroked his stomach. "The Sergeant cursed you for that."

A fainter gleam of white stirred in the dimness beside the bulkhead, accompanied by the clink of enchanted fetters. "But I am guilty, Eminence." Anskiere spoke with dry irony. "Had I not spared your mistress's life, Tierl Enneth would not have drowned at her hand."

The fat man chuckled. "Tathagres richly enjoyed your performance, you know. It was entertaining to hear you confess in her place, just to spare an islet of shit-stinking fisher folk. Or were you truly eager to escape their gull-splattered rock?"

Anskiere sat with his head bent. The oil lamp carved deep shadows under his eyes and tinted his skin as yellow as an old painting.

"I forgot." The Constable belched. "You love fish stench and poverty and, oh yes, a boy whose sister has a twisted leg. Tell me, was he good?"

"Innocent as you are foul." Anskiere spoke softly, but his glance held warning. "Why mention the boy?"

The Constable smiled and bellowed for more wine. He licked wet lips, and his hands stilled on his belly. "Ah, it was touching, Anshiri. The forecastle watch caught the boy climbing the anchor cable. He claimed his sister had stowed away, for love of you, and he came to fetch her home in a fish-reeking little boat. He was angry. I believe he hates you."

The Constable's chuckle was clipped by Anskiere's query.

"What? The girl?" The official blinked, then sobered. "We searched, of course, but didn't find her. Perhaps she fell overboard." Planks creaked under his bulk as he leaned forward, slitted eyes intent on the prisoner's face. His features oozed into another smile. "You lied, Anshiri. You said Tathagres had no means to force your will. But I think now that she does."

Taen woke to her brother's sudden shout.

"No!" His words carried clearly to her hiding place in the ship's galley. "I beg you! Without *Dacsen*, my mother and cousins will starve."

Emien's protest was answered by the drawl of a deckhand. "Cap'n said cut her adrift, boy." Laughter followed.

Taen shivered. The chilly rims of cooking pots gouged her

back as she pressed her face against a crack in the planking to see out. Torches flickered amidships, casting sultry light over the naked shoulders of the sailors. Black armor gleamed in their midst. Taen saw her brother hoisted in the grip of a foot lancer. The boy struggled as a rigging knife flashed in a sailor's hand. A rope parted under its edge, and the whispered flop of *Dacsen*'s sails silenced as wind swung her bow out of the dark ship's shadow.

"That was unjust." Emien's desperation turned sullen with anger. "I've done no wrong."

The foot lancer shook him. In the pot locker, Taen flinched, and her fingers twisted in the cloth of her shift.

"Cap'n don't like flotsam dragglin' aft." The sailor sheathed his knife and nodded toward the open hatch grating. "An' he won't have shore rats messin' his deck, neither. You'll go below."

Helplessly Taen watched the foot lancers drag her brother away. The sailors clustered round the hatch, grinning at Emien's curses; aft, the deck was deserted. Taen bit her lip, hesitant. Earlier she had seen the Constable push Anskiere through a companionway left unguarded. Abruptly resolved, the girl crept from the cranny which had sheltered her and slipped from the galley, the drag of her lame foot masked by the slap of wavelets against the hull. She paused, trembling, by the mainmast. Torches moved up forward. A deckhand said something coarse, and a splatter of laughter followed. The white crash of breakers on the reef to starboard was joined by a hollow scream of splintering plank.

Taen blinked back tears. *Dacsen* had struck. Through wet eyes she saw sailors crowding the forecastle rail to watch the sea pound the small sloop to wreckage. With a restraint beyond her years, Taen seized her opportunity while their backs were turned. She crossed the open deck into the dark gloom of the quarterdeck.

The latch lifted soundlessly in her hands. Beyond lay a

narrow passage lit dimly by the glow which spilled from the open door of the mate's cabin. Taen heard voices arguing within. She peered through, and saw the two sorcerers who had bound Anskiere's power leaning over the mate's berth. Bright against the woolen blanket lay a staff capped with a looped interlace of brass and counterweighted at the base. Beside it rested Anskiere's leather satchel.

"Fool!" The sorcerer robed in red gestured with thin splayed fingers at the man in the braid. "You may know your way about a ship, *Captain*. You know nothing of craft. Anskiere's staff is harmless."

The captain moved to interrupt. Fast as a cat, the sorcerer in black hooked his sleeve. "Believe him, Captain. That staff was discharged by Tathagres herself. How else could she have raised the sea and ruined Tierl Enneth? You don't believe the power was her own, do you?"

"Fires, no." The captain fretted uncomfortably and tugged his clothing free. "But I'll certainly have mutiny, a bloody one, unless you can convince my crew that Anskiere can work no vengeance."

"That should not prove difficult." The sorcerer in red caught the satchel with a veined hand, and in the doorway Taen shrank from his smile. "An enchanter separated from his staff seldom goes undefended. Anskiere will not differ." The sorcerer loosened the knots of the pouch, upended it, and spilled its contents with a rustle onto the blanket.

Taen strained for a glimpse of what lay between the men.

"Feathers!" The captain reached out contemptuously, and found his wrist captured in a bony grip.

"Don't touch. Would you ruin us?" Disgustedly, the sorcerer released the captain. "Each of those feathers is a weather ward, set by Anskiere against need. You look upon enough force to level Imrill Kand, captain."

The dark sorcerer lifted a slim brown quill from the pile.

Taen recognized the wing feather of a shearwater. She watched with stony eyes as the sorcerer tossed it lightly into the air.

As the feather drifted downward into a spin, it became to the eye a blur ringed suddenly by a halo of blue-violet light. From its center sprang the sleek, elegant form of the bird itself, wings extended for flight. Damp salt wind arose from nowhere, tossing the lamp on its hook. Shadows danced crazily.

The red sorcerer clapped a hand to his belt. A dagger flashed in his fist. He struck like a snake. The bird was wrenched from midair and tumbled limp to the deck, blood jumping in bright beads across the oiled wood. The bird quivered once, and the breeze died with it.

Taen shivered in the grip of nausea. The red sorcerer wiped the knife on his sleeve while the dark sorcerer picked another feather from the bed. Before long the hem of his robe hung splattered with scarlet. A pile of winged corpses grew at his feet, and blood ran with the roll of the ship. At each bird's death there was a fleeting scent of spring rain, or a touch of mellow summer sun, and more than once the harsh cold edge of the gales of autumn. At last, sickened beyond tolerance, Taen stumbled past the door. Preoccupied with their slaughter, the men within did not notice.

Beyond the chartroom door, Taen heard the wet bubbly snores of the Constable. The lamp had burned low. Her eyes adjusted slowly to the gloom. Past the chart table and the Constable's slumped bulk, Anskiere sat with his head resting on crossed arms. Enchanted fetters shone like coals through tangled hair, and his robe was dusty and creased.

Taen stepped through the door. At the faint scrape of her lame foot, Anskiere roused, opened eyes flat as slate, and saw her in the doorway. He beckoned, and the chime of his bonds masked her clumsy run as she flung herself into his arms.

"The soldiers took Emien, and *Dacsen* wrecked on the reef." Her whisper caught as a sob wrenched her throat.

"I know, little one." Anskiere held her grief-racked body close.

Taen gripped his sleeve urgently. "Warden, the sorcerers are killing your birds. I saw them."

"Hush, child. They've not taken the one that matters most." Anskiere flicked a tear from the girl's chin. "Can I trust her to your care?"

Taen nodded. She watched gravely as the Stormwarden made a rip in the seam of his hood lining. He drew forth a tawny feather barred with black and laid it in her palm.

The girl turned the quill over in her hands. The shape was thin, keen as a knife, and the markings unfamiliar. Anskiere touched her shoulder. Reluctantly she looked up.

"Taen, listen carefully. Go on deck and loose the feather on the wind."

The girl nodded. "On the wind," she repeated, and started at the sudden tramp of feet beyond the door. Fast as a rat, she scuttled into the shadow of the chart table. The Constable snored on above her head, oblivious.

Men entered; the captain and both sorcerers. Blood-streaked hands seized Anskiere and hauled him upright, leaving Taen with a view of his feet.

"Where is it?" The red sorcerer's voice was shrill.

Anskiere's reply held arctic calm. "Be specific, Hearvin." Somebody slapped him.

The black sorcerer advanced. His robe left smears on the deck. "You have a stormfalcon among your collection, yes? It was not in the satchel."

"You'll not find her."

"Won't we?" The black sorcerer laughed. Taen shivered with gooseflesh at the sound, and gripped the feather tightly against her chest.

"Search him."

Cloth tore and Anskiere staggered. Taen cowered against the Constable's boots as the sorcerers ripped Anskiere's cloak and robe to rags. Near the table's edge, mangled wool fell to the deck, marked across with bloody fingerprints.

"It isn't on him," said the captain anxiously. "What shall I tell the crew?"

The red sorcerer whirled crossly. "Tell them nothing, fool!" Taen heard a squeal of hinges as he yanked open the chart room door. "Confine the Stormwarden under guard, and keep him from the boy."

The stamp of feet dwindled down the passage, underscored by the glassy clink of Anskiere's fetters. Taen shivered with the aftermath of terror, and against her, the Constable twitched like a dog in his sleep. The smell of sweat and spilled wine, and the impact of all she had witnessed, suddenly wrung Taen with dizziness. She left the shelter of the table and bolted through the open door. With the feather clamped in whitened fingers, she turned starboard, clumsily dragging her twisted foot up the companionway which led to the quarterdeck.

A sailor lounged topside, one elbow hooked over the binnacle. Taen saw his silhouette against the spoked curve of the wheel, and dodged just as the sailor spotted her.

"You!" He dove and missed. His knuckles barked against hatchboards. Taen skinned past and ran for the taffrail.

"Fires!" the sailor cursed. At her heels Taen heard a scuffle of movement as he untangled himself from the binnacle.

Torches moved amidships. At the edge of her vision, Taen saw the black outline of a foot lancer's helm above the companionway stair. Driven and desperate, she flung herself upward against the beaded wood of the rail. Hard hands caught her, yanked her back. She flailed wildly, balance lost, and the sea breeze snatched the feather from her fingers. It skimmed upward out of reach.

Taen felt herself shaken till her teeth rattled. Through blurred eyes she watched Anskiere's feather whirl away on the wind. It shimmered, exploded with a snap into a tawny falcon marked with black. Violet and blue against the stars, a heavy triple halo of light circled its outstretched wings. Taen smelled lightning on the air. The man above her swore, and below, a crowd began to gather in the ship's waist.

"Stormfalcon!" a sailor cried. His companions shouted maledictions, threaded through with Anskiere's name, as the bird overhead took flight. Wind gusted, screaming, through the rigging. Half quenched by spray blown off the reef, the torches streamed ragged tails of smoke.

Smothered by the cloth of her captor's sleeve, Taen heard someone yell for a bow. But the falcon vanished into the night long before one could be brought. The sergeant rounded angrily on the girl held pinioned by the deckhand.

"Is that the brat the boy came looking for? I'll whip the blazes out of her. She's caused us a skinful of trouble!"

But the voice of the black sorcerer cut like a whip through the confusion. *"Leave the child be."*

Startled stillness fell; the wind had died, leaving the mournful rush of the swells etched against silence. The onlookers shifted hastily out of the sorcerer's path as he approached the sergeant who held Taen in his arms.

"The harm is done." The sorcerer's voice was as brittle as shells. "The stormfalcon is already flown. The girl, I'm told, is valued by Anskiere. Give her to me. He will soon be forced to recall his bird."

Taen was passed like a bundle of goods to the sorcerer. The touch of his bony wrists, crisscrossed still with bloodstains, caused her at last to be sick.

"Fires!" The sergeant laughed. "Take her with my blessing."

"Go and tell Tathagres what has passed," said the sorcerer, and the sergeant's mirth died off as though choked.

Below decks, a guard twisted a key in a heavy padlock. With a creak of rusted hinges, a door opened into a darkness filled with the sour smell of mildewed canvas. The black sorcerer pushed forward and swore with impatience. Nervously, the boatswain on his heels lifted the lantern higher; light flickered over a bunched mass of folded sails and the gaunt outline of a man chained to a ring in the bulkhead. A deckhand's cotton replaced the captive's ruined robe and the gleam of enchanted fetters on his wrists was buried under baggy cuffs.

The black sorcerer studied Anskiere with contempt. "I've brought you a gift." He threw back a fold of his robe and set Taen abruptly on her feet.

The girl stumbled into Anskiere's shirt and clung. The Stormwarden locked his hands over her quivering back.

The black sorcerer smiled. "Stormwarden, you are betrayed." He added sweetly, "Earlier you claimed you would rather burn for the murders at Tierl Enneth than bargain with Tathagres. But for the child's sake perhaps you will reconsider."

Anskiere did not speak. Presently, muttered oaths and a scuffle beyond the doorway heralded a new arrival as two sailors brought Emien, trussed and struggling, between them. The black sorcerer stepped aside to avoid being jostled. Given a clear view of the sailroom, the boy caught sight of his sister, then the Stormwarden sheltering her.

"Taen!" His outcry held despair mingled with anger. "Taen, why did you come here?"

When the girl failed to respond, her brother spat at the Stormwarden's feet. One of the sailors laughed.

"Do you find hatred amusing?" said a new voice from the darkness behind.

The sailor who had laughed gasped and fell silent, eyes widened with fear.

"Or did I arrive too late to share some jest?" Preceded by a faint sparkle of amethyst, a tall, slender woman stepped into view. Silver-blond hair feathered around a face of extraordinary beauty; beneath a masculine browline her eyes were thickly lashed and violet as the jewels which trimmed her cloak at collar and hem.

The black sorcerer bowed. "Tathagres."

The woman slipped past the boatswain's lantern and entered. She placed an elegant hand upon the bulkhead, leaned on it, and bent a bright gaze upon the Stormwarden and the girl he sheltered.

"You are brought low, Anskiere of Elrinfaer." Her accent was meticulously perfect.

The Stormwarden cradled Taen against his chest. "Not so low."

"No? You'll do the King's bidding." Tathagres fingered the hilt of the dagger at her waist, serene as a marble carving. "Stormwarden, recall your falcon."

Anskiere answered with grave courtesy. "The bird is beyond my present powers." He lifted his hands from Taen's shift, and cotton sleeves tumbled back, unveiling the sultry glow of fetters. "Dare you free me? I'll recall her then."

Tathagres' fingers flinched into a fist around the dagger hilt. The skin of her neck and cheeks paled delicately. "You presume far too much. Do you think your stormfalcon concerns me? She is insignificant, and you are less. If you value that little girl's life, you'll go to Cliffhaven and ward weather for the Kielmark, by royal decree."

Anskiere stirred. Gently, he covered Taen's head with crossed palms. Her black hair streaked his knuckles like ink as he spoke. "Do you threaten?"

"Have you never heard a child scream?" said Tathagres. "You shall, I promise."

Behind her, Emien struggled violently; the sailors cuffed him until he subsided. Tathagres resumed as though no disturbance had occurred. "Aren't you interested enough to ask why?"

Yet Anskiere showed less regard for the royal intentions concerning the Kielmark, who ruled an empire of outlaws, than for the girl beneath his hands.

Irritated by his silence, Tathagres straightened and folded

her arms. "The King promises you legal pardon for Tierl Enneth."

Without moving, Anskiere said, "Providing I free the frost-wargs," and at Tathagres' startled intake of breath added, "the Constable couldn't resist telling me that the King desires their release so he can break the Free Isles' alliance. What did he offer for your help? Wealth, or the Kielmark's power?"

Tathagres stiffened. A flush suffused her cheeks, yet only triumph colored her reply. "Nothing so slight, Cloud-shifter. I asked for the Keys to Elrinfaer Tower itself."

At that, Anskiere looked up, still as the calm before a terrible storm. His fingers tightened over Taen's ears. "Be warned, Tathagres. The King will never command my actions, even should children be made to suffer."

Which was more than Emien could stomach. He lunged against the sailors' hold, thin face twisted with horror. "Kordane's Fires consume you, sorcerer!"

Tathagres met the boy's outburst with disinterested eyes. "Be still."

Emien quieted as though slapped. He glared sullenly as Tathagres tilted her head. Her hair glittered like frost against her gem-collared throat where the pulse beat visibly, giving an impression of vulnerability. Unaware his emotions had become her weapon, Emien was moved by a powerful urge to protect her. He swallowed, and his hands relaxed against the sailors' grip. Tathagres smiled.

"Boy," she said huskily. "Should your Stormwarden refuse the King's command, will you help me break him?"

It was Anskiere's fault Taen had endangered herself. Anskiere's fault the sloop was lost. As the son of generations of fishermen, the offense was beyond pardon. He spat on his palm, then raised his fist to his forehead. "By my oath." His voice grew passionate with hatred as he met Tathagres' glance. "Misfortune and the Sea's curse claim me should I swear falsely."

"So be it." Tathagres signaled the deckhands who held the boy. "He has sworn service to me. Free him."

The men's hands fell away. Emien shivered and rubbed reddened arms, eyes fixed on his mistress. "I think," he said, then hesitated. "I think you are the most beautiful lady I have ever known."

And Taen suddenly comprehended her brother's change of alliance. "You shame your father!" she shouted. Anskiere's touch soothed her.

Emien lifted his chin with scorn. "He'll kill you, sister."

But Taen turned her face away, into the Stormwarden's shoulder, and refused to move. The boatswain pulled her, screaming, from his arms.

"Let me have charge of her." Emien raised his voice over her cries. "I'll make her understand."

But Tathagres only gestured to the boatswain. "Lock the girl in the hold."

Believing she tested his loyalty, Emien made no protest, though the brave new oath he had sworn ached in him like a burden. He waited while Tathagres and her entourage left the sailroom. As the torch was carried past, light cast an ugly distorted profile of his face against the bulkhead. Emien hid his eyes. The sting of his raw wrists reminded him of the shackles which still prisoned Anskiere, and he longed for the simple awe he had known for the Stormwarden of his childhood. Shamed, he lingered, expecting sharp rebuke for the rebuttal of his upbringing on Imrill Kand.

But Anskiere offered no reprimand. Neither did he plead. When he spoke at last, his words held sad and terrible understanding.

"The waters of the world are deep. Chart your course with care, Marl's son."

And Emien realized he had already been weak. "Murderer," Emien whispered. "Sister-killer." Driven by feelings beyond his understanding, he banged the door shut, leaving darkness.

CHAPTER II

Cliffhaven

THE WIND, WHICH USUALLY BLEW from the west in summer, dwindled until the sails hung limp from the yards. *Crow* wallowed over oil-sleek swells, her gear slatting and banging aloft until Emien wished he had been born deaf. The deckhands cursed. The captain grew sullen and silent and watched Tathagres' sorcerers with distrust. No one mentioned the stormfalcon. No one dared. Yet archers were stationed in the crosstrees with orders to watch for her return.

Emien paused for a drink at the scuttlebutt, but bitter water did nothing to ease the knot in the pit of his stomach. All his life he had lived by the sea; in the oppressive, unnatural calm he read warning of a savage storm. He squinted uneasily at the horizon. No quiver of air stirred. The ocean lay smooth as pewter. Day after day the sun rose and blazed like a lamp overhead until the sky seemed to have forgotten clouds, and the oakum seams between planks softened and blistered underfoot.

"Deck there!" the mate's shout roused the sailhands who

idled in the few patches of shade. "Turn out both watches to shorten sail. The captain's called for oars."

Emien joined the crew at the ratlines with trepidation. Uncovered oar-ports could become a hazard in open waters. A sudden squall could drive the waves high enough to let in the sea. Yet the risk seemed less than the prospect of lying motionless at the mercy of the storm every soul on board believed Anskiere's falcon would unleash. And though Emien had not seen Tathagres since the night he had sworn her service, her impatience could be felt the length and beam of the galleass.

Yet even under the strong pull of her oarsmen, three more days passed before the lookout sighted land. The moment the call came from aloft, Emien joined the crowd at the rails, unable to contain his curiosity. All his life, he had heard tales of the stronghold of the pirates; this would be the first time he set eyes on it.

Cliffhaven jutted upward from the sea, black as flint against the sky. The slate roofs of a village glinted between jagged outcrops of rock, and above them, like a battered crown, lay the battlements of the Kielmark's fortress. Emien shivered. No man had ever challenged the Kielmark's sovereignty and won. If the tales were true, beneath the galleass' keel lay the bones of scores of ships his fleet had sunk to the bottom. Here even Tathagres was obliged to move with caution.

Crow entered the harbor beneath a white flag of neutrality. No royal ensign flew from her mizzenmast. On deck, her hands worked quickly, and without chanteys, aware their vessel would receive questionable welcome if she lingered.

Emien helped the sailors sway out the longboat which would carry Anskiere ashore. Beyond the rail, the sun threw a blazing reflection upon waters glazed with calm. Emien licked sweat from his lips and felt strangely chilled. Never had he seen such weather, not in fourteen years of fishing. The sooner the Stormwarden was offboard the better.

Blocks squealed overhead and the boat struck with a smack,

scattering ripples. Emien made fast his slackened line and glanced toward the companionway just as Anskiere was brought on deck. Two sorcerers stood guard at his side and fetters still gleamed on his wrists, but there all semblance of captivity ended. Emien gasped. Anskiere stood newly clad in indigo velvet adorned with gold. He carried both staff and cloak, and his silver hair lay trimmed neatly against his collar.

Surprised by such finery, Emien knew resentment. "They treat him better than he deserves."

A nearby soldier spat and shook his head. "No, they condemn him. Anskiere wore those same robes when Tierl Enneth was destroyed."

Emien blinked perspiration from his lashes. "He looks like a king's son."

The soldier grinned outright. "You didn't know? He *is* a king's son."

Unsure if he was being gulled, Emien fell silent, brows puckered into a scowl. If his ignorant upbringing on Imrill Kand amused people, one day he would find means to end their laughter. Resolved and bitter, he gripped the taffrail while Anskiere descended the side battens and stepped into the boat. Both sorcerers went with him. Hooded like vultures under ebony cowls, they settled in the stern seat.

Emien cast off the line, and felt a hand on his back. At his shoulder, Tathagres called out.

"Stormwarden!"

Startled by her voice, Emien turned, still frowning. Her scent enveloped him, and his ears rang with the fine jingle of gold as she leaned past him over the rail.

"Anskiere, remember the King's will." Tathagres closed her fingers over Emien's wrist in warning.

Below, the oarsmen threaded their looms, and the boat rocked slightly in the glassy calm. At last Anskiere looked up.

Tathagres' grip tightened. Her nails dug into Emien's flesh.

"Lest you be tempted, remember those you have left in my care."

Anskiere's gaze shifted to include Emien, and lingered. The boy broke into sweat despite Tathagres' presence. Chills prickled his skin, for that searching look seemed to weigh the balance of his very soul.

"Mistress," said the Stormwarden, "should you gain entry to Elrinfaer, you will be doomed."

Tathagres tossed her hair, and ornaments and amethysts flashed in the sunlight. "Your threats mean nothing. If I win access to the seat of your powers, Cloud-shifter, the ruin shall be yours."

Anskiere ran lean fingers over his staff. "Your plan is flawed. Elrinfaer does not, nor ever did, contain the foundation of my power. For that you must search elsewhere."

"If the Keys of Elrinfaer fail me, I will," Tathagres replied. She released Emien and addressed the captain briskly. "Deliver the Stormwarden to the Kielmark. We sail the moment he is ashore."

The oarsmen leaned into their stroke, and the longboat sheared out of *Crow's* shadow, water curling at her bow. But Emien did not linger to watch Anskiere's departure. He left his place at the rail and bowed before Tathagres.

"Lady, with the Stormwarden gone, will you permit me to fetch my sister from the hold?"

"The girl is a hostage, and valuable." Tathagres studied the boy's face as though assessing the set of his jaw. Suddenly she smiled. "You may visit her. But wait until the longboat returns, and *Crow* is back underway."

Speechless with gratitude, Emien bowed again. When he rose, Tathagres had gone, and shouted orders from the captain dispersed the crowd at the rails. Yet despite the bustle of activity, the interval before the longboat arrived passed slowly. Emien paced from the rail to hatch grating, consumed by impatience. The moment the deckhands threaded pins into the capstan, he bolted for the hold.

He stood, blinking in darkness, and the clank of chain through the hawse reverberated painfully in his ears as the anchor rose from the seabed.

"Taen?"

Light flickered overhead. A guardsman descended with a lantern. Emien picked out the dim outlines of baled cargo, and the flash of reflection from a pan of water. A rat raised luminous eyes and darted away from a lump of sourdough biscuit nearby.

Emien shivered. "Taen?" The sight of abandoned food left an uneasy feeling in the pit of his stomach. Raised plainly, the girl was not one to waste. Nothing moved in the shadows. Emien glanced up at the guard. "She's not here."

"Impossible." The man wheezed, stepped off the bottom rung, and swung the lantern onto a hook in the beam overhead. With a final clang the anchor settled and the echoes faded.

"She didn't eat." Emien's voice sounded loud in the sudden stillness.

"No?" The guard glanced at the bread and sighed. "She's probably hiding. But she won't have gotten far. Her hands were tied."

"Not any more." Emien bent, pulled a frayed bit of line from the sharpened twist of wire which bound a wool bale. The strands were stained dark with blood.

The guard gestured impatiently. "Well, search for her, then!"

Emien stumbled into blackness, nostrils revolted by the smell of bilge and the rotted odor of damp and brandy casks. He tried not to think about the rats. "Taen?"

His call dissolved into silence, overlaid by the bump of oars being threaded overhead. And though he searched the hold with frantic care, he found no trace of his sister. The guard left reluctantly to inform Tathagres.

Soldiers were sent to assist. For an hour, the hold resonated with men's curses and the squeal of startled rats. But they found nothing. Desolate, Emien wiped his brow with a grimy wrist and sat on a sack of barley flour. Helpless anger overcame him. If harm had come to Taen, the Stormwarden would be made to pay dearly.

"The girl could not have escaped," said Tathagres clearly from above. "If she's hiding, hunger and thirst will drive her out in good time. Until then let the vermin keep her company."

Beyond the shops and houses which crowded against the wharves of Cliffhaven, a stair seamed the face of a rocky, scrub-strewn cliffside. The walls of the Kielmark's fortifications crowned the crest, black and sheer above the twisted limbs of almond trees. While *Crow* rowed from the outer harbor, Anskiere climbed the stair.

The bindings had been struck from his wrists, and noon shadow pooled beneath the gold-trimmed hem of his robe. He used his former staff as a walking stick. The metal tip clinked sourly against risers so ancient that grasses had pried footholds between the cracked marble. Summer's sun had bleached their jointed stems pale as the bones of fairy folk; and like bones, they crunched under the bootsoles of the two sorcerers sent as escorts.

"You will ask directly for audience with the Kielmark," reminded the one on the Stormwarden's left.

Anskiere said nothing. Except for the rasp of crickets, the hillside seemed deserted and the town beneath lay dormant. Yet none were deceived by the stillness. Renowned for vigilance, the Kielmark's guards had surely noticed them the moment *Crow*'s longboat reached shore; as strangers, their presence would be challenged.

Anskiere paused on the landing below the gate, staff hooked

in the crook of his elbow. The cloak on his forearm hung without a ripple in the still air.

"Well?" The sorcerer on his right gestured impatiently. "Move on."

But Anskiere refused to be hurried. That moment, the rocks beside the stair seemed to erupt with movement, and the three found themselves surrounded by armed men with spears held leveled in a hostile ring.

"State your business," said the largest soldier briskly. His tanned body was clad in little but leather armor. He carried no device. Only the well-kept steel of his buckles and blade, and the alert edge to his voice, bespoke disciplined authority.

Anskiere answered calmly. "Your weapons are not needed. I wish only words with the Kielmark."

The guard captain studied the Stormwarden with unfriendliness, but he lowered his spear. "By what right do you claim audience, stranger? The Kielmark dislikes intruders. Why should he honor you?"

Before Anskiere could reply, one of the sorcerers pushed forward. As one the weapons lifted to his chest.

"Slowly," the captain warned. "Your life is cheap here."

Livid under his hood, the sorcerer placed a finger upon the steel edge closest to his throat. "Take care. Do you know whom you threaten? You point your toys at Anskiere of Elrinfaer, once Stormwarden at Tierl Enneth."

The captain sucked in his breath. Sudden sweat spangled his knuckles, and his bearded face went a shade paler.

Anskiere smiled ruefully. "To me, your weapon is no toy. I bleed as readily as any other man."

The captain withdrew his spear, jabbed the butt ringingly onto stone. "Are you . . ." He jerked his head at the elaborate gold borders which patterned the blue robe at cuffs and hem, eyes narrowed with wariness.

"I am Anskiere, once of Elrinfaer, come to speak with your master. Will you tell him?"

The captain turned on his heel without another word. Hedged by skeptical men-at-arms, the two sorcerers in black exchanged quiet sighs of relief. It seemed Anskiere intended to see the Kielmark willingly. Even with his arcane powers bound and the children from Imrill Kand as hostage, the Storm-warden made an unpredictable charge. The mortal strength he still possessed could yet make their task difficult.

The sorcerers waited nervously in the heat while the looped metal at the head of the staff cast angular lines of shadow across the Stormwarden's face. They watched as he stared at the horizon, and his very stillness fueled their unease.

"The weather doesn't seem to bother him," one sorcerer whispered to his colleague in the language of their craft. "He almost seems part of it."

"Impossible." The other blotted his brow with his sleeve. "He can originate nothing with a spent staff, and the major bindings hold."

"Stormfalcon . . ."

"Nonsense. She never returned."

A spear flashed in the nervous grip of a guard, checking the discussion abruptly. The tense interval which followed passed uninterrupted until the captain's return.

He emerged in haste from the gatehouse, whitened beneath his tan and dripping sweat. "Put up your weapons."

The men complied with alacrity. To Anskiere, the captain said, "The Kielmark will see you at once."

Stormwarden and escort resumed their ascent of the stair, accompanied by the dry slap of sandaled feet; the men-at-arms moved with them.

For this the captain shrugged in taut apology. "The men must come along. No one has ever entered the Kielmark's presence armed. With you he makes an exception."

Anskiere paused beneath the stone arches of the gatehouse. "I would surrender my staff, should the Kielmark ask," he said, but his offer did not reassure.

The captain's manner became sharply guarded. "He's not such a fool." Any man with experience knew the touch of a sorcerer's staff caused death. The captain's face reddened in memory of the Kielmark's curt order: "A sorcerer at Cliffhaven is just as dangerous to my interests as one standing in my presence, with one difference. Here I can watch his hands. Bring him in directly."

The Kielmark waited beneath the arches of a great vaulted hall. There the richness of Anskiere's robes did not seem misplaced, for the chamber was ornamented, walls and floor, with the plunder of uncounted ships. Gilt, pearl inlay and jewels adorned everything, from tapestries to rare wood furnishings; the Stormwarden and his escort approached the dais across a costly expanse of carpet.

Except for a single seated man, the chamber was empty. The Kielmark chose to meet them alone. Tathagres' sorcerers were not beguiled. Their sharp eyes missed nothing. Amid the cluttered display of wealth, they discovered a mind geared toward violence: the great hall of the Kielmark was arrayed in strategic expectation of attack, its glitter a trap for any man fool enough to challenge the Lord of Cliffhaven.

Seated in a chair draped with leopard hides, the Kielmark returned the scrutiny of his visitors in icy detachment. Except for the tap of a single nervous finger, he seemed unimpressed, even bored by the fact Anskiere's name was linked with four thousand deaths. Outlaws came to Cliffhaven to serve or they died there, for the King of Renegades tolerated no disloyalty, and his judgment was swift.

And strangely, the sovereign who reigned in such gaudy splendor was himself the note that jarred, the piece which did not fit. As the sorcerers drew near, they saw, and redoubled their wariness. Beyond a torque set with rubies, the Kielmark wore plain leather armor like his men. But there, comparison ended, for his frame was stupendously muscled, and his brow reflected intelligence untempered by gentleness. Dark hair shadowed eyes blue and intent as a wolf's. The man had all the stillness of a weapon confident of its killing edge.

The sorcerers glanced at Anskiere, and found him calm. Untouched by the tension which ringed him, he stopped before the dais and waited for the Kielmark to speak.

"Why have you come here?" The sudden question was an open challenge.

The Stormwarden answered quietly. "I plead sanctuary."

"Sanctuary!" The Kielmark closed massive fists over the arms of his chair. His eyes narrowed. "Sanctuary," he repeated, and his gaze moved over the blue robes and gold embroidery which made the request seem like mockery. "So. You present yourself as supplicant. Yet you do not bow."

The sorcerers struggled to conceal rising apprehension. The interview had not opened in accordance with Tathagres' plan. And subtly Anskiere extended his appeal. He raised the heavy staff from his shoulder, laid it flat on the dais stair, and stepped back, empty hands relaxed at his sides.

"I do not bow."

The statement met silence cold as death. Shocked by the symbol of a sorcerer's powers relinquished, the men-at-arms all but stopped breathing. But the staff on the stair roused nothing but calculation on the Kielmark's florid face. His attention shifted to the sorcerers, and in their bland lack of reaction found discrepancy. His lips tightened. "Warden, your colleagues seem strangely unimpressed by your gesture."

Anskiere shrugged. "These?"

The sorcerers shifted uneasily as his simple gesture framed them.

"They are none of mine, Eminence," said Anskiere softly.

The Kielmark sat suddenly forward, brows arched upward. *"Not yours?* Then why are they here?"

Anskiere met his glare. "Let them speak for themselves."

"Ah," said the Kielmark. He settled back, keenly interested, and laced his knuckles through his beard. Almost inaudibly, he said, "What have you brought us, Sorcerer?"

The Stormwarden made no effort to answer. The sorcerers, also, chose silence. For a lengthy interval, nothing moved in the chamber but the flies which threaded circles through the single square of sunlight on the floor.

"What happened at Tierl Enneth?" said the Kielmark. His manner was guarded, and his voice dangerously curt.

Anskiere stayed utterly still, but something in his attitude seemed suddenly defensive. Although at Cliffhaven his reply would be judged with no thought for morality, he answered carefully. "I was betrayed."

The Kielmark blinked like a cat. "Only that? Nothing more?" When he received no answer, he tried again. "Were you responsible?"

Anskiere bent his head, and his long, expressive fingers clenched at his sides. "Yes."

A murmur stirred the ranks of men-at-arms, silenced by the Kielmark's glare. Tathagres' sorcerers fidgeted restlessly, disquieted by the turn the interview had taken. Anskiere's request for sanctuary had initiated an exchange whose outcome could not be controlled. And with lowered spears at their back, they dared not intervene.

The Kielmark shifted in his chair, muscles relaxed beneath his swarthy skin. "I accept that," he said, and abruptly reached a decision. "You are welcome to what safety Cliffhaven can provide, if you will ward the weather in return."

Anskiere looked up. "There are limits to both." Without explaining how severely his powers were curtailed, he added, "I will do all I can."

The Kielmark nodded, rubies flashing at his neck. "I understand. You may take back your staff. Now what would you suggest I do with the two who came with you?"

"Nothing, Eminence." Anskiere retrieved the staff and

straightened with an expression of bland amusement. "For them I claim sole responsibility."

One sorcerer hissed in astonishment. The other whirled, openly affronted by Anskiere's presumptuous boldness. And on the dais, the Kielmark awarded their shattered composure a sharp bellow of laughter. "So. The hyenas have not forgotten their spots," he observed. He sobered in the space of a second, strong fingers twined in the leopard fur. "I will allow you their fate, Stormwarden, but with one difference. I mistrust the intentions of anyone who claims no convictions, be they sorcerers or men. I wish this pair gone from Cliffhaven in three days' time."

The sorcerers settled in smug satisfaction. The Kielmark had cornered Anskiere neatly; with his powers bound and the lives of two children at risk, he could never complete such a promise. Eager as hounds on fresh scent, the sorcerers waited for Anskiere to confess his helplessness, and appeal to the Kielmark's mercy.

But to their surprise, Anskiere executed the bow he had refused the Kielmark earlier. "Lordship, I give my word." No gap was discernible in his assurance, but his gesture carried the haunted quality of a man who has just signed a pact with death.

Confident Anskiere's lie would ruin him, the sorcerers stepped back in anticipation of dismissal. But the Kielmark gestured and the men-at-arms raised weapons, stopping their hasty retreat.

"Wait."

Without moving from his chair, the Kielmark stretched and caught a sword from its peg on the wall behind him. The basket hilt glittered in the sunlight as he extended the weapon to Anskiere. "You may have need of this."

A startled twitch of one sorcerer's cheek immediately justified his impulsive action. And when Anskiere reached to grasp the hilt, his sleeve fell back to expose a livid line where a fetter had recently circled his wrist.

Shaken by such blatant evidence of abuse, the Kielmark tugged gently on the sword as Anskiere's hand closed over the grip. He spoke barely above a whisper. "Come here."

Anskiere mounted the steps.

The Kielmark bent close, so no other could hear. "I see I did not misjudge, old friend." He inclined his head toward the sorcerers who waited, rigid with annoyance. "Could they ruin you?"

The Stormwarden drew a long breath. Through the weapon held commonly between them, the Kielmark noted fine tremors of tension Anskiere's robes had concealed until now. Yet the Stormwarden's eyes were untroubled when he spoke. "I think not."

"Your difficulties are beyond me. I have no choice but to trust you." The Kielmark's huge wrist flexed, twisting the sword against Anskiere's palm. With greater clarity, he said, "Then you can rid us of this accursed heat?"

Anskiere smiled. "That would require violent methods, Eminence."

Below the dais, the sorcerers twitched as though vexed.

"Koridan's Fires," swore the Kielmark, and he chuckled. "Your puppets seem displeased. Be violent, then, Cloud-shifter, with my blessing. After that we'll talk again." And he released the sword with a broad wave of dismissal.

Escorted only by sorcerers, Anskiere left the Kielmark's fortress without delay. Once past the gatehouse, urgency left him. He paused on the terrace at the head of the stair and began an intent inspection of the harbor. The view was creased with heatwaves. Below, the town reawakened; he could hear the crack of shutters as shopkeepers opened their stalls. The ocean lay flat as burnished metal, and the air smelled like an oven. Anskiere shifted his grip on the staff.

The sorcerers watched his restlessness with impatience of their own. Apparently Anskiere did not find what he sought so keenly. And although the Kielmark had granted him freedom of Cliffhaven, he passed up the shade and refreshment of a tavern. He left the stair. Careless of his velvet finery, he set off into the scrub on what seemed to be a goat track.

Like shadows, the sorcerers followed. By custom of sanctuary, they could use no force to stop him, except in defiance of the Kielmark's law. The sword added inconvenience to nuisance. Anskiere's acceptance of mortal steel reflected an independent turn of mind they dared ignore no longer.

The hillside offered wretched footing. The taller sorcerer stumbled on a loose rock. Brush clawed his clothing. "Fires!" he swore, and grabbed his companion for balance. Awkward as the maneuver appeared, it was timed to allow Anskiere to pass beyond earshot. The sorcerer spoke softly in the ear of his comrade. "Tathagres misjudged him."

The other sorcerer considered, a frown on his face. "Perhaps. But Anskiere seems to have chosen isolation. If so, we have him secure. The Kielmark's edict of sanctuary will be little help to him in the hills."

"Didn't you notice?" The first sorcerer gestured angrily and strained to maintain a prudently lowered voice. "The Kielmark *knew* him. And asking sanctuary instead of service was a master stroke. Anskiere will have a reason." Briskly, he started forward.

His companion hustled to keep up. "I'd thought of that." A thorn branch snagged his sleeve. He yanked clear. Sweat trickled at his brow, and his soft boots were unsuited to hiking. Yet the Stormwarden showed no sign of slackening pace. Well ahead of his escort he began to ascend a defile. He moved easily, despite the difficult terrain.

The sorcerers pursued, unable to guess his purpose.

"He could be bluffing."

"You're a fool to think so. And Tathagres is a fool to wish the wards on Elrinfaer Tower broken. I don't think the

Stormwarden lied when he said the foundation of his powers lay elsewhere."

The second sorcerer stopped midstride; disturbed pebbles clattered down the hillside, rousing thin spurts of dust. He said quickly, "What is Elrinfaer to you?"

The first sorcerer shrugged. "A pile of granite, no more. But if the frostwargs are not released on schedule, the Free Isles will not fall." He glared at his companion, breathing hard. "Hearvin was misinformed. *Never* has Anskiere of Elrinfaer been known to use guile. He's not bluffing. The stormfalcon will return. Mark me. Then we'll have trouble."

The other sorcerer pondered this, then glanced at the Stormwarden, who stood outlined in sky at the crest of the rise, staring out to sea yet again.

The sorcerer sighed. "Very well," he said. "We'll separate. You follow Anskiere. Challenge his intentions. Then watch him carefully."

"And you?"

"I will proceed to the cave of the frostwargs. If Anskiere breaks our control, I can rearrange the wards which bind him. His own release shall rouse the frostwargs. They will break from sleep in a rage, and ravage Cliffhaven, with Anskiere alone to blame." A smile creased the sorcerer's face, revealing broken teeth. "After Tierl Enneth, do you suppose the Kielmark would forgive him?"

The other sorcerer smiled also. "Anskiere is guileless. He would loose the frostwargs himself rather than ruin an ally." With the smile still on his lips, he left to follow the Stormwarden.

Above the fortress, the climb steepened and the goat track faded, lost among jagged outcrops of shale. Anskiere toiled upward. Weather-rotted stone crumbled loose under his boots and bounced in flat arcs down the slope.

Chafed by sweat-drenched robes, the sorcerer tripped and stumbled on the Stormwarden's heels, pelted by pebbles from above. He cursed the land, the suffocating heat, and the wizard he guarded, but he followed with the diligence of a madman. When Anskiere at last reached the summit, he was only half a pace behind, and not much wiser than he had been earlier. Anskiere's intentions were still obscure, though the sorcerer had sifted possibilities until his head ached from thought.

On the crest of the crag the Stormwarden paused. He leaned on his staff and bent a searching gaze toward the far horizon, his features expressionless. At his side, the sorcerer looked also, but saw nothing in the scenery to warrant such close attention. The afternoon was spent. Below, a spread of hills quivered in the heat haze. A gull flapped above a pale stretch of sand, and the beach plums and dune grasses lay still, untouched by a ripple of breeze. The bleached vault of the sky hung empty and at the edge of the sea, like massive bruises, lay the headlands of Mainstrait, key to the Kielmark's power; for every ship which passed the strait to trade with the eastern kingdoms, Cliffhaven exacted tribute. Yet no vessel moved in the dense calm.

To the sorcerer, the earth's own vitality seemed locked behind the Stormwarden's silence. The thought was irrational. Irked at himself, the sorcerer said, "You cannot keep your promise to the Kielmark."

Anskiere stared out over Mainstrait, utterly still.

"Well?" The sorcerer spoke sharply. "Do you believe yourself capable of warding weather?"

Anskiere glanced briefly at his adversary, and his reply held no rancor. "No."

"Then what have you gained, Cloud-shifter, except enmity in the one inhabited place left open to your presence?"

Anskiere regarded the ocean as though searching for something lost. He did not speak. And that quiet lack of response unsettled his escort as nothing had before. The sorcerer longed to lay rough hands on his charge, and shatter the stillness which clothed him. In a tone stripped by malice he said, "What bard will sing of you, with the blood of Tierl Enneth on your hands?"

"What bard would have liberty to sing, should the Free Isles' Alliance be broken?" Anskiere removed his attention from the sea to the sorcerer. "Hear me," he said softly. "Not once did I promise to free the frostwargs."

Tathagres' henchman reddened beneath that steady gaze. "Beware. The little girl will be made to suffer for your treason."

Anskiere laughed. *"Treason? Against whom? Tathagres?"*

"Against the Kielmark, Cloud-shifter. And against your sovereign lord, the King of Kisburn."

Anskiere gestured impatiently. "I am no vassal of Kisburn's, to be called to heel like a dog. His ambitions will ruin him without any help from me."

"What of the Kielmark?" The sorcerer reached out, and delicately plucked a tern's feather from a cranny in the rocks. "If you defy my liege and the frostwargs are not freed by your hand, recovery of your powers will rouse them to riot. To alter the weather, you must bring about destruction upon Cliffhaven. Your promise is now linked to your demise."

"So is your threat." Anskiere stood straight as an ash spear. Dying sunlight glanced through the interlaced metal which capped his staff, unaltered by any trace of resonant force. Yet his assurance seemed complete as he said, "Dare you tell your mistress?"

"Dare I?" The black sorcerer stiffened, and the quill crumpled like a flower petal between his fingers. "Tathagres is the King of Kisburn's tool. As you are." And he released the feather, letting it drift, broken, to the ground.

Anskiere caught it as it fell. He turned its mangled length over in his hands, then slowly smoothed it straight. Without another word, he set off down the slope toward the sea.

The pace he set was recklessly fast. Angrily the sorcerer followed. If Anskiere would not be ruled, his will would be broken by force, however distasteful the method. The sorcerer plunged down an embankment, flailing his arms for balance as the footing crumbled under him. Over a rattle of pebbles he said, "You have until dawn. After that, I have no choice but to inform Tathagres. When the child cries out in agony perhaps you will reconsider."

Anskiere's knuckles whitened against the wood of his staff. But that was the only sign he heard the words at all.

CHAPTER III

Tempest

Fuzzed by heat haze, night fell over Cliffhaven, and a reddened quarter moon dangled above Mainstrait, mirrored by ocean unmarred by waves or current. At the crest of a bluff overlooking the beach, Anskiere waited on a cluster of rocks, his staff against his shoulder. He had stood watch since sunset. Close by, the black sorcerer sat among the dune grass, irritably keeping his vigil. The heat had not lifted. The surrounding land seemed poisoned, throttled by a hush which silenced summer's chorus of crickets. Even the gnats were absent.

The sorcerer blotted his sweating face, nagged by the feeling that the simplest of motions somehow violated the unnatural quiet. He shifted uncomfortably to ease cramped limbs. Grasses pricked through his robe, making him itch, and his flesh ached for rest and for the meals he had neglected. Yet while Anskiere remained on the rocks, the sorcerer had no choice but to stay with him.

The moon set well after midnight. Overhead, the stars

wheeled with imperceptible slowness until dawn at last paled the sky above the mountains.

The sorcerer stirred stiffly. He shook the dew from his robe as day brightened around him. "Stormwarden," he said. "Give me your decision. Will you consent to the royal command, or shall the village girl be made to suffer?"

Anskiere raised his head and closely studied his adversary. "I chose on the night I left Imrill Kand." He smiled, and a slight cat's paw of breeze stirred his hair.

Wind. The weather was changing. The sorcerer noticed a chill against his skin, and his stomach knotted with apprehension. A second puff stirred the cloth around his knees. Uncomfortably, he felt as though something stalked him from behind. He whirled, and that moment discovered how Anskiere had manipulated him.

Low in the northwest, a black anvil of cloud rolled above the crags of Cliffhaven; nightlong, Anskiere had directed his attention to the east, a ruse of such simplicity it had not been challenged. The sorcerer had never thought to watch his back. Appalled by his error, he licked whitened lips and tried not to overreact.

"Stormfalcon," he said accusingly. "This shouldn't be possible. What object could possibly key the bird's return? Your powers were bound well before her release, and Tathagres had you stripped of everything you brought from Imrill Kand, even your clothes."

A gust slammed down from the north, flattening the dune grass. Anskiere's cloak streamed like a flag. He raised the staff, and the sorcerer understood with a jolt. *The staff itself had been the object of the falcon's homing,* a provision set up well in advance of Anskiere's imprisonment; and a risk no responsible adept could justify. That power of such magnitude should be linked to an object possessed by an enemy was unthinkable. Yet Anskiere had dared.

The gale rattled through the beach plums, wrenching off

dead leaves. With only seconds to act, the sorcerer sprang at the Stormwarden. Anskiere gave ground. Steel chimed from his scabbard, and he blocked his attacker's rush with the Kielmark's weapon.

The sorcerer checked, and escaped with a torn sleeve. His wrist trickled blood, penalty of an instinctive reflex to ward off the blade which thrust at his heart.

"Fires consume you!" he shouted. "Do you think steel can save you?" And quivering with outrage at the insult, for his prowess went well beyond mortal weapons, he raised both arms and began to shape a spell which would bring Anskiere to his knees.

Light arched between his fingers as the binding took form. But sword in hand, Anskiere paid the spell little heed. His face stayed set like a rock beneath tumbled hair. Suddenly he whistled and lifted the staff.

The sorcerer tensed with the spell only half complete, and at the edge of vision glimpsed a black-and-yellow shape which knifed the air like a scimitar, haloed in blue-violet light. He spun around, saw the stormfalcon rise, feathers parted by wind, her target Anskiere's staff. The sorcerer altered tactics to suit. He snatched up his knife, and with a word redirected his spell. The light he had conjured arced with a snap and joined with the blade in his hand. He then flung the knife at the falcon.

Anskiere shouted. His sword fell, ringing onto stone, as the knife flashed toward the bird's soft breast. She cried shrilly. The sorcerer laughed in triumph. Desperately the stormfalcon banked, talons upraised. And the halo of force around her suddenly split into the brilliant triple aura of a defense ward.

The knife struck a starred pulse of light. Energy whined on the wind. The sorcerer's laughter changed pitch, transformed to a scream of terror. Unbelievably, the falcon carried all the safeguards of the power Anskiere had once invested in his staff. It was reckless folly, all the more unbelievable after what had gone before, that an adept should ever bind such force into a form a stranger could trigger. Incredibly, Anskiere had done so.

Trapped by miscalculation, the sorcerer saw his enchanted knife tumble, charred, to the ground. Before he could invoke a countermeasure, the terrible power his attack had released ripped across the spell which linked him with his weapon, and tossed him limp to the ground.

Anskiere steadied the staff as the falcon alighted. Her aura transferred with a crackle of sound, restored to its rightful center amid the interlaced metal. He could not damp the force, which was wasteful. Although shielded by the resonance of his own conjuring, the Stormwarden could direct none of the energy. One enemy now lay dead, but the sorcerer who remained still held sway over his powers.

Anskiere coaxed the falcon to his wrist. He had to recover his weather sense and quickly, for linked inextricably to the falcon's presence was the fiercest tempest ever to rage across the northeast latitudes. Already the sky churned, blackened by clouds. The ocean tossed, ripped into spume, and waves crashed against the shore, hurling fountainheads of spray. Storm and tide would shortly break with unmanageable violence over Cliffhaven. Gripping his staff for balance, Anskiere hoped the Kielmark had heeded the warning he had tried to deliver; any ship caught beyond sheltered waters would be pounded by nature's most merciless fury. Until Tathagres' remaining sorcerer could be found and dispatched, Anskiere was helpless to save them; and the sorcerer certainly would be found in the worst possible location. Anskiere jabbed his staff into the earth, and bent his steps toward the cave of the frost-wargs.

The storm struck with the violence of a crazed man's nightmare. Daylight lay smothered under sooty combers of cloud. Rain mixed with hail battered Cliffhaven with a rattle like enemy bowfire. In the town the street lanterns were quenched by the torrent, and folk huddled around darkened dripping chimneys and shivered as the wind tore the slate from their roofs.

The gale raged across the headland, screaming through the rocks above the cave which imprisoned the frostwargs. Although the entrance was narrow, the tunnel plunged steeply downward, doubling back upon itself; the walls carved the gusts into a hollow dirgelike wail. Far down, beneath the level of the seabed, the passage opened into a stone cavern. Even there, the storm caused drafts which rippled the robe of Tathagres' remaining sorcerer and teased his upraised torch until it guttered and hissed in complaint.

Even underground he felt the stormfalcon's return. He also knew his companion was dead, since the spell which confined Anskiere's powers had partially linked their awareness. Rather than pause for mourning, the sorcerer who survived plotted vengeance with the neatness of a spider spinning its web. He lifted the torch higher, and at last discovered what he came to find.

Close to a century before, the Firelord Ivain had employed his command of flame and earth to fashion a prison for the frostwargs. In the flickering spill of light, the King's sorcerer saw a circular pit incised into the cavern floor. He made his way cautiously to the brink. The torch revealed no bottom. Below lay darkness so thick it bewildered the senses. A man who gazed too long into those depths could became dizzied by vertigo and fall headlong to his death. The sorcerer did not look down. Instead he jammed the torch in a niche. The draft extinguished the flame. He made no move to restore it. Rigid with concentration, he drew upon his craft, and soon a small blaze of illumination arose between his fingers.

He bent, anchored the light at the edge of the drop with a word of mastery. Reflections glazed the sweat on his brow as he stepped back, then loosed the spell with a gesture.

The spark drifted across the abyss, scribing a thin, violet

line across the deep. The sorcerer rounded the pit. He fielded the spell as it reached the far side, and flicked it out, leaving the glow of its passage bridged like a needle across the expanse. The sorcerer stepped widdershins to the side. Another spell flashed in his hands. Presently a second line crossed the pit. Patiently, the sorcerer moved again, creating a third, then a fourth line, until the mouth of the frostwargs' prison lay masked in meshes of light. Restless currents of air sighed around his head as he stood back, gazing contentedly upon his handiwork.

Far beneath the starred eye of his spell slept the frostwargs. At one time, the sorcerer knew, the creatures had roamed the lands above, ravaging forests and farmlands from the first chill of autumn until spring. Come summer, they burrowed into the ground to sleep until the cold returned to color the leaves. In Landfast's records, the sorcerer had read accounts of wasted acres and dismembered settlements; from Hearvin, who trained him, he learned the secret of the frostwargs' confinement. The arrangement was so simple that he laughed.

Temperature change keyed the frostwargs' awakening, and warm weather kept them comatose. Ivain, who was both Earth-master and Firelord, had merely sunk a shaft for them below reach of winter's cold, where the air stayed constant from season to season. In the years since their entombment, the creatures had never roused.

The sorcerer smoothed his robes, congratulating himself for cleverness. He stood at the brink of the pit and let his consciousness conjoin with the horrors who slumbered below. Their dreams were restless. Aware they had been cheated of their seasonal rampage, the frostwargs emanated viciousness like lust. Their eight-legged forms twitched, claws clicking against stone; spiked tails thrashed, and between hornlike mandibles slim tongues flickered in memory of the taste of blood and torn earth. Stirred by the creatures' subconscious desires, the sorcerer shivered in anticipation. For the passage of years had unbalanced the rhythm of the frostwargs' slumber; any shift in the air would disrupt their fragile dreams. Warmth, instead of further prolonging hibernation, would stir them to ungovernable rage.

Delicately the sorcerer disengaged his contact. With the finesse of a man courting a reluctant lover, he summoned forth the framework of the wards which locked Anskiere's powers. They flamed across his mind's eye, a maze of convoluted force, once sealed into a structure Anskiere could not break. But now the death of one of its creators had spoiled the symmetry. Gapped interstices and torn angles showed where the spell was vulnerable. This the sorcerer changed.

He balanced the breaks with a linkage to the net woven across the pit. The principle was artlessly simple; should Anskiere attempt to exploit the advantage he had gained by murdering Tathagres' warden, his aggression would transfer to the web and dissipate into the pit as heat. The plot made the sorcerer smile.

"Try to escape," he mocked, wishing his adversary were present. "Just try. Your efforts will free none but the frostwargs." And his smile dissolved into laughter until the grotto bounced with echoes. Confident of the trap he had wrought, the sorcerer groped among the rocks for his torch. Once it was lit, he started up the shaft.

The weight of sodden velvet bowed Anskiere's shoulders like mail as he traversed the cliffs where Ivain had secured the frostwargs. He had discarded the cloak long since. Knotted in a sling of rags torn from the lining, his staff glowed at his back. The stormfalcon circled above, held by the geas of homing even as the storm was bound still to her flight path. Anskiere toiled over rocks glazed by rain, beleaguered by gales his own hand had once controlled; the sensitive instincts which enabled him to bend weather into harmony with his will were absent. Unaccustomed to the hostility of the elements, Anskiere felt like an artist gone blind in the midst of a masterpiece. The predicament might have hurt less had his adversaries not captured the children.

A breaker smoked over the reef, needling Anskiere with spray. His skin had long since gone numb. Shivering, he crossed a narrow ledge, unable to gauge when the storm would peak, or estimate the high tide mark. The waves were still building. Foam smothered another almost under his boot, and spindrift stung his eyes. The ledge was certainly unsafe.

Ivain had designed the frostwargs' prison above reefs which slashed the tides into boiling currents of whitewater; waves threatened to dash Anskiere like flotsam from the path. Forced to give ground time after time, still, when the water receded, the Stormwarden always pressed on. He had no choice but to cross at once, before the storm rendered the ledge impassable.

But progress was painfully slow. Morning was nearly spent when Anskiere began the final approach to the cave. Tormented by the conviction that his enemy had used the delay to his disadvantage, the Stormwarden began the ascent of the final precipice. There, with the cave entrance an arm's reach overhead, he heard the sea rise at his back.

Anskiere leaped, grabbed a handhold. The foaming maw of the breaker thundered into his shoulders, slammed him against rock. Water pummeled the breath from his lungs, dragged cruelly at his limbs. Grimly he clung. His palms tore on the stones. His body slipped slowly seaward. The surf would kill him, bash him over and over against the coral until his flesh was a mangled rag. Tathagres would laugh, and Taen . . .

Anskiere grimaced, consumed by the need to survive. He gathered himself, driven by the roar of another larger wave. With a heave that taxed every sinew in his frame, Anskiere clawed his way through the tumble of receding water. He rolled, gasping and disheveled, into the shaft.

Pebbles scored his skin. The staff clanged against close stone walls and wedged in a fissure. Caught by the sling,

Anskiere tumbled onto a mild incline. He lay prone, blinking salt from his eyes, content at first to be still. But the chill soon made him shiver. Bruised, abraded, and wrenched in every joint, the Stormwarden rose to his feet. Outside the gale battered the cliff face, blocking his retreat; and below, if his assessment was correct, an enemy awaited with plans to ruin him.

Anskiere shook the water from his hair, spat out the taste of salt. He reached for his staff. Sodden knots loosened reluctantly under his fingers as he freed the wood from the sling. The sea had inflamed the marks on his wrists, but their sting was overlaid by the sharper memory of Taen's fists clamped in his shirt. Distressed, he started down the shaft, scattering droplets from his robe. Now he was glad the dead sorcerer's aggression had kindled the wards in his staff, for their bright radiance lit his way like a beacon.

The path was smooth at first. Deeper, Anskiere recalled, tunnels twisted with angles and buttresses of slagged stone. Below, the prison fashioned for the frostwargs was as black and tangled as the character of its creator.

Ivain had originally melted the rock with wizardry of fire, but the acrid smell Anskiere remembered from the shaft's forming had faded long since, replaced by musty odors of roots, earth, and moist granite. Except for the echo of his own steps the cave was silent. Bats sought other roosts than the arched ceilings overhead, and wildlife avoided the place, instinctively shunning the evil which hibernated below. The Stormwarden rounded a bend, and the terrain under his boots roughened. Beneath stretched a series of terraces hedged with crystals like swords. Here amid the dazzle of refracted light a misstep could cripple the unwary trespasser. Anskiere trod carefully, unsurprised to discover human bones tumbled among the cave's bewitching beauty. The Ivain he knew had always been careless, even disdainful of life. Uneasy, the Stormwarden proceeded with every sense alert for danger. The din of the storm receded above, dampened by baffles of stone;

far ahead, a polished vein of agate threw back a reflection the color of blood.

The Stormwarden noted, and froze. Cloaked in the frosty gleam of his staff, he looked closer, and saw the crimson flicker brighten slowly into orange. He identified flamelight as its source. Someone with a torch must be ascending the shaft from below and presumably no one had interest in the frostwargs except Tathagres' henchman.

Fenced by the razor edges of thousands of crystals, Anskiere was in a poor position for confrontation. The staff could not be quenched to glean any cover from darkness, and by now the brilliance of the wards might have warned the enemy sorcerer he was not alone in the shaft. Before the sorcerer caught him, Anskiere chose retreat, hoping to reach the narrow place where the corridor crooked, barely a hundred paces higher. Anguished by thoughts of a small child's tears, he hurried, and barely felt the sting of a crystal against his calf, or the blood which welled above the top of his boot.

"Why run?" said a voice from below. "By now the tide will have sealed off the entrance."

Anskiere leaped the last tiers of crystals and whirled, panting, beneath the curve of the upper tunnel. Outside the radiance of the staff lay darkness. The sorcerer had not rounded the corner below; he possibly had yet to notice the wards stood complete, a piece of luck Anskiere had wished for but dared not assume. He seated himself on an outcrop just past the place where the tunnel narrowed. The staff's confined aura bathed him in a raw light. Under similar circumstances, Anskiere recalled, Ivain would have smiled.

Slowly the orange glow in the distance brightened and acquired the harsh edges of open flame. Light danced up from below, trapped in the hearts of a faery forest of crystals.

"Fires!" swore the sorcerer. He had at last sighted the wards. Picking his next steps with care, he said, "So that's how you killed Omer." And he paused and cursed for a minute and a half.

Ivain perhaps would have chuckled. Positioned at the mouth of the tunnel, Anskiere derived little satisfaction from his enemy's predicament. Blocked by solid stone, the sorcerer could not force the Stormwarden out of the shaft without direct contact with a staff whose aura was instantly fatal to anyone unattuned to its forces.

"You can't win," said the sorcerer. He raised his torch, haloed by a haze of reflections. "The staff will eventually burn itself out."

Anskiere did not state the obvious, that well before it dimmed the staff could be reduced to safer levels if only his powers were freed. Aware he was protected, he waited for his enemy to reveal whatever plot had drawn him into the cave.

The sorcerer stopped. He threw back his hood, exposing features polished like a skull's. "The girl will suffer well for this."

"Can you contact Tathagres through rock, then?" Anskiere said mildly. But his voice missed its usual note.

"Fires!" The sorcerer gestured angrily. "That ward won't block me forever. I'm not fond of patience. Perhaps we could settle things more quickly."

Anskiere did not reply.

The sorcerer impaled his torch on a crystal and gazed upward, his attitude one of regret. "I think you should be taught a lesson, Cloud-shifter."

He lifted his hands, and light blossomed, firing the crystals into a thousand pinpoint reflections. The cavern blazed, suddenly lit by a pattern delineated in the air. Spread before him, Anskiere saw the spell which confined his powers revealed in geometric splendor. And his trained eye noted, like sour notes in a counterpoint, the gaps one sorcerer's death had torn through the structure, weakening it.

The display was a blatant invitation to challenge; and also a fully baited trap. Anskiere's hand jerked once against the wood of his staff. Without weather sense, or magic, he could not explore the dangers any resistance might unleash. He rose slowly, burdened by responsibility for the children from Imrill Kand whose loyalties brought them to share his fate. Bound, he could not save them. Free, he had a chance, if a slim one, to counteract the threat his aggression would spring. The marred pattern taunted him. One sorcerer had underestimated him; he had no choice but hope that the second had done the same. "By the Vaere," he murmured. "Let me be right."

"Won't you bid for your powers?" the sorcerer urged. He pitched his confidence to antagonize.

Anskiere gathered his will and calmly thrust his consciousness into the spell which spread like a web across the dark. He thought he heard laughter in the moment before his mind caught in the strands. But whether the sound arose from the sorcerer or from an older memory of Ivain, he could not tell. Power snared his awareness like birdlime; fierce opposition blocked all effort to fathom the forces aligned against his inner control. Anskiere never hesitated. The forces which held him were flawed. Poised on that knowledge, he condensed his consciousness to a pinpoint and darted through a gap. The move triggered a sharp blaze of heat. The trap had sprung. Anskiere had no choice but discover the sorcerer's intent swiftly, and try to unbalance his enemy through brash action. Since the threat had been left linked through each break in the spell, Anskiere embraced the pattern's entirety and rammed thoughts like hot needles across every weakness he encountered. Then he withdrew.

Aware once more of the cold illumination from his staff, he shivered, gripped by the distinct impression he had raised a holocaust. Seconds later, when a high, keening wail arose from the bowels of the tunnel, he understood why. The dead sorcerer's threat had been a real one.

"Fires," the Stormwarden said softly. "Between us we've

roused the frostwargs." And where Ivain would have laughed outright, he felt only terrible calm.

Below, his enemy stirred from a pose of taut concentration, and the spell's bright pattern faded. Though pleased by the success of his plot, Anskiere's lack of response startled him. Only the insane would linger to face a frostwarg. The sorcerer masked uncertainty with scorn. "Fool. You've accomplished nothing but Tathagres' bidding after all."

A second ululation issued from below, reverberating eerily through the cave. A faint click of claws followed. Anskiere sat down on his rock. "I see that."

The rattle of horny carapaces echoed up the shaft; the frostwargs scuttled wildly toward freedom. They moved with horrifying speed, Anskiere recalled. He watched his antagonist's face turn pale, triumph transformed to dismay. The only available exit was still blocked by the aura of an active staff.

The sorcerer snatched up his torch. "I'll not set you free. You must flee. You have no other alternative."

The staff burned steady as a brand in Anskiere's hands. He did not move.

The scrabble of the frostwargs drew nearer. Their frenzied whistles rose, braided into a shrill crescendo of harmonics. A crystal shattered into slivers.

The sorcerer started forward, careless of sharpened edges under his boots. "Fly! Is your memory gone? No ward can stop a frostwarg."

"I hadn't forgotten." Anskiere stood solidly in the tunnel.

The sorcerer checked. His mouth opened, speechless, and his hands fluttered in an imploring gesture he already guessed was futile. The Stormwarden evidently intended to meet the frostwargs, and die.

Furious, the sorcerer shouted over the rising clatter of claws. "You have lost, Cloud-shifter! The frostwargs are released, and no Firelord remains to control them. The Free Isles will fall, and Cliffhaven also." He spat. "You're a suicide, unmanned by a child's tears and a mother-clinger's principles. Were you worthy of your training, you'd not lie down for death."

"Have I?" said Anskiere.

A ringing clash underscored his words. Armored by heavy shells, the frostwargs spilled around the lower bend in the shaft. Mustard and black by torchlight, mottled bodies hurtled over the bottom rung of crystals, tumbling them like glass. The sorcerer glanced down, saw a row of glowing purple eyes, and horny mandibles glistened with curved spikes. Nimble as centipedes, the frostwargs swarmed through the cavern, arched tails rattling behind.

The sorcerer gasped. He dropped his torch, whirled and fled. A crystal bit like a blade into his calf. He fell. Terror overwhelmed him and he screamed aloud. In the corridor above, Anskiere felt the barriers imposed on his powers suddenly dissolve.

His mind rang, no longer numb to the energies thrown off by the staff; and reawakened weather sense deluged his inner vision with information governing the storm which raged topside. Freed, Anskiere seized control. Without pausing to watch the sorcerer's demise, he quenched the staff's aura and ran. Only seconds remained before the frostwargs tired of the corpse and tasted his scent.

Daylight glimmered ahead. Too far ahead; Anskiere knew he could not reach the cave mouth. He stopped. From his sleeve he pulled the tiny feather Tathagres' sorcerer had used to taunt him. The quill glowed blue in his hand as he tossed it into the air.

"Fly," he said, and placed his will upon it.

The feather shimmered into light. From its center flew a living tern, fragile and white as porcelain in the darkness. The bird darted on spread wings for the opening above. The moment it cleared the cave, Anskiere plunged his awareness into the raging heart of the storm. The tempest answered. Wind shrieked like a chorus of hags, funneling down the shaft.

Anskiere shouted, conscious of the frostwargs' whistles at his back. The gale struck. His clothing tore, flogged into tatters. Hair lashed his face. Flattened against the tunnel wall, Anskiere drew breath and called the rain.

Water cascaded into the cave, a wrathful, rampaging torrent. It bounded from rock to rock like a demented animal, capped by slavering jaws of foam. Anskiere spoke, even as the water blinded him, and the temperature dropped at his command. Spray fell, rattling, transformed to pellets of ice. Anskiere spoke again, and the cold intensified. Waterfalls froze, arrested in midflight, and the current which curled over his knees crystallized, locking his boots in a grip of iron. Yet the Stormwarden did not relent. He drove the temperature down, and down again, until the stone snapped and sang, shackled by bands of frost. Ivain's tunnel became choked by a glassy, impenetrable bastion against which the frostwargs' razor claws scraped in vain. Sealed in by a solid mass of ice, they howled and gnashed their mandibles.

Above, enmeshed in the effects of his own defenses, Anskiere heard their enraged cries, and where Ivain might have cursed in self-reproach, he smiled. As the ice encased his limbs, he engaged the last of his resources.

Past the blocked mouth of the cave, the stormfalcon lifted barred wings and exploded into flight. Rising swiftly on the wind, she circled and turned eastward, away from Mainstrait, for the staff no longer ruled her homing. In her wake fluttered a tern whose form contained a ward of safety for a certain small girl. And lastly, locked living in a tomb of ice, Anskiere invoked the geas he had placed upon Ivain at the time of betrayal. The act was born of desperation, for, better than any, Anskiere knew his only hope of release lay in a Firelord's skills. And between the crisp crackle of frost and the shrieks of the frostwargs, he thought he heard someone speak.

"Truly, now I have triumphed," mocked a well-remembered

voice, and the laughter which followed seemed to last a long time. . . .

Exhausted by wind and rain, a guard captain banged at the entrance of the Kielmark's study. The door opened. He entered and saluted, dripping water.

Surrounded by his staff, the Kielmark straightened from a table draped with charts. Wet hair lay plastered against his cheekbones and the skin of both hands was abraded from shortening docklines against the gale.

"Well?" he said sharply.

"The storm is lifting." The captain leaned wearily against the wall. "The wind has dropped forty knots in an hour and the tower watch reports visibility to Mainstrait."

"By Kor." The Kielmark sat heavily in a chair, uncharacteristically withdrawn for a commander who had lost six moored vessels to the tide, and whose domain sustained an untallied toll of damages. "The Cloud-shifter kept his word then."

Relaxed by his apparent unconcern, the men burst into excited talk.

The Kielmark's great fist slammed into the charts. "Fires! Are we as impressionable as fresh maids? I want this entire island surveyed by nightfall and a list of losses, wounded, and dead, accurate to the last drowned hen. Am I clear?"

As the captain moved toward the door, the Kielmark's voice pursued them. "I don't want one of you back until your report is complete. And send a company to me at the south wharf warehouse. I'm going to clear it of tribute for use as a mercy shelter. Direct the homeless there."

Despite the severity of the Kielmark's orders, scarcely an hour passed before a rider clattered to a halt at the dockside with a dispatch. Summoned from the warehouse, the Lord of Cliffhaven heard the message and after a moment of silence dismissed the courier with savage discourtesy. The remainder of the afternoon passed without incident. By sunset each of the captains had reported, and were excused from duty with the praise they had earned. Only after the last one left did the Kielmark's attention return to the earlier message. He saddled a horse and set off across the twilit dunes toward the island's northern headlands.

The heavy clouds had parted. A star shone against the cobalt of the zenith, and angered, storm-whipped surf slammed beaches tumbled and darkened with sea wrack. The Kielmark reined his horse beside the bluffs overlooking the sea. Wind brushed his hair, his cloak, and the stiff mane of his mount. In silence, alone, the Lord of Cliffhaven beheld the phenomenon the courier had described, and confirmed every word to be true.

Spread before him, in high summer, stood a cliff ridged with ice. Gulls wheeled and called above perches silvered with frozen cascades. They did not alight.

The Kielmark shivered, gripped abruptly by intuition. Bitterness tightened his throat. Since Ivain Firelord's death, no sorcerer remained who could achieve Anskiere's release. "Old friend," he said to the air. "You spared us. Could you not also spare yourself?"

He sat in the saddle and waited. No answer came. But long after dark, when he turned his horse to leave, the wind ruffled his hair like a brother.

CHAPTER IV

Summons

FAR NORTH OF CLIFFHAVEN, IN the copychamber of Morbrith Keep, a scribe's apprentice suddenly shivered. Though summer sunlight beat strongly across the trestle where he sat hunched over parchment and open books, Jaric was cold. His pen felt clumsy as a stick in fingers gone peculiarly numb. The boy hugged ink-stained hands close to his body and thought wistfully of the woolens packed into chests lined with cedar.

"Jaric!" Master Iveg rose from his desk and padded stiffly across the library. Stooped as an old bear, his shadow fell across the parchment Jaric had been lettering. "Are you dreaming again, boy?"

The master's tone was not unkindly. Yet Jaric flinched, and his thin frame shuddered afresh with chills. Immediately the master's manner changed from gruffness to concern.

"Jaric? By Kor, if you spent the copper I gave you on drink or women, I'll have you branded misfit."

Had he felt better, Jaric would have smiled. Unwatered

wine made him fall asleep; and the coarsest trollop in Stal's Tavern invariably treated him with matronly kindness. Although he was nearly seventeen, he had the build of a sickly child.

Master Iveg leaned over his assistant, nearsightedly squinting. At length, he clicked his tongue. "Are you ill, then?"

Jaric blinked, suddenly dizzy. "Maybe." Through blurred vision he tried to read the line he had been inking, and saw his pen had dripped on the parchment. The blotch annoyed him. Unskilled at athletic pursuits, his sole passion was neat copy.

Iveg sighed. As Master Archivist to a busy court, he was reluctant to spare his most diligent pupil even for an hour. But the boy was obviously unwell. Long since resigned to his apprentice's delicate constitution, Iveg pushed a book away from Jaric's stained fingers and said, "Go outside. Sit in the sun for awhile. Perhaps a break and some fresh air will clear your head."

Jaric rose obediently. Careful not to trip, he caught the doorframe with evident unsteadiness. Aware the boy resented coddling, Iveg stayed by the copy table, his droopy hound's features lined with worry. "If you want, I'll send for a healer."

Jaric shook his head. "No need. I feel a little faint, that's all." And he passed quickly into the hall, fearful if he delayed longer his legs might fail him.

His boots echoed unexpectedly on stone. The carpets had been rolled aside, and a serving maid knelt industriously beside a bucket brimming with suds. She peered into Jaric's face as he approached.

"You going ta puke?" She gestured, and her sodden brush spattered soap against his shins. "If so, go elsewhere, d'ya mind?"

Jaric eyed the plump flesh which quivered beneath her blouse and said nothing. Dizzy though he was, nothing ailed his stomach. Accustomed to taunts, he crossed the puddle left by her scrubbing and marked unsteady footprints the length of the corridor.

"Kor," yelled the woman at his back. "Ya messed my clean floor with yer blighty feet, ya daisy."

With a grimace, Jaric caught the latch of the postern. The woman's insults failed to provoke. He was wise enough to understand she intended no malice. The fact he was small and awkward with weapons did not make him any less a scholar; if some women felt his dark eyes and fine hands should have been paired with more manly attributes, he refused to cloud what gifts he did possess with bitterness over his shortcomings. All the same, he longed to slam the door as he let himself out. Yet even so slight a rejoinder proved beyond his strength.

Shaken by sudden vertigo, Jaric barely managed to avoid being struck by the heavy iron-bossed panel as it swung shut. He stumbled down the steps into sunlight. The apothecary's herb gardens were snugly tucked in a courtyard between the outer battlements and the west keep. Jaric often came there in times of trouble. Today light-headedness transformed the gravel paths into a shimmer of glare, and the close high walls buckled crazily before his eyes. He felt inexplicably menaced. The rich scent of poppies seemed to choke him. Disoriented, Jaric sat gasping on the bottom stair. Sun-warmed stone shocked his flesh like a brand, yet he continued to shake with chills. He frowned. Lank mouse-colored hair fringed his wrists as he rested his head in his hands. *What was the matter with him?*

His cheeks tingled. The sage brush by his knee rippled as though stirred by current. Then his vision blurred and slid sickeningly into darkness.

Afraid he might faint, Jaric chafed his arms, unaware his nails gouged flesh. Though immersed in the heat of midsummer noon, cold clamped like a fist in his chest. He could not breathe. Trapped in a morass of confusion, he felt a compulsion rise up to smother his will. Desperate with panic, he resisted.

"Mercy!" The plea emerged as a pinched croak. Aware the force he wrestled was another's, Jaric tried again. *"Let me be. I am blameless!"*

But no quarter was granted. The alien power gained intensity, stripping away his identity like flame-seared wax. Words died on his tongue. He felt himself falling, not into the familiar fragrance of sage leaves, but into icy, limitless space. Another reality flooded his inward eye, carved into ruthless focus. Like a scene viewed through a ship's glass, Jaric saw a promontory exposed to a thunderous clamor of surf. A vibrant red-headed man crouched against the rocks. His face contorted with hatred toward a second man, a gale-whipped figure with silver hair and ragged blood-stained clothes. Had Jaric been able to move, he would have shivered. But the image held him frozen as the second stranger raised his head. His features were as battered as the rest of him, yet he spoke with inhuman calm. And his words tore into Jaric with the fury of the wind, shackling his spirit bondage as absolute as death.

Your offense against me is pardoned but not forgotten. This geas I lay upon you: should I call, you, Ivain, shall answer, and complete a deed of my choice, even to the end of your days. And should you die, my will shall pass to your eldest son, and to his son's sons after him, until the debt is paid . . .

"No!" Jaric shouted.

But, inexhaustible as the elements, the stranger's powers sealed him within ringing nets of force. Terrified, Jaric knew if he yielded, that other will would consume him. His entire existence would plunge into change. Ill-prepared for the world beyond Master Iveg's study, he took refuge deep within his mind, where no light, no sound, and no sensation could reach him. Sprawled across the stair by the apothecary's herb garden, Jaric lay as though dead.

* * *

The night *Crow* made rendezvous, the King of Kisburn's war fleet lay becalmed fifty leagues from Islamere, easternmost archipelago under the Alliance's charter. Tathagres at last granted the crew reprieve from the blistering pace she had demanded since leaving Cliffhaven, and *Crow*'s company rested gratefully. Crusted with the dried sweat of exertion, the rowers slept beside oar-ports left unsealed in the heat. The helmsman drowsed against the binnacle with the wheel clamped in the friction brake as the galleass drifted under the limp billows of her staysails. She scribed barely an eddy in the smooth face of the sea.

Curled in a berth in the forecastle, Emien lay awake, eyes fixed sullenly on the hammocks of his crewmates. Each morning he visited the hold, but Taen had not answered his call; two days without water or food should by now have driven her from hiding. Miserably, Emien recalled his promise to bring her safely home. He could send his mother and cousins the silver he earned to pay for the wreck of *Dacsen*, yet even Tathagres' largest amethyst could not atone for the loss of a sister. Emien stirred restlessly. Although the sorcerer Hearvin had recently forbidden him to enter the hold, he decided to try one last time. With no guards present, surely he could coax Taen to come out.

Emien rose grimly. He would lie, even bribe his sister with promises of Anskiere's release. Once she was found he would make her understand; the Stormwarden would be forgotten.

Emien's bare feet made no sound as he slipped through the rows of sleepers in their hammocks. The running lamps at bow and stern crosshatched the decks with shadow. Beyond the rail, the lights of the fleet were scattered like fireflies beneath a sky featureless and black as a pit. But Emien did not notice the absence of stars. Intent upon stealth, he slipped down the companionway. The sailor on watch lounged by the port capstan, cleaning his nails with a marlinspike. He raised no alarm as the boy crept past the galley and lowered himself through the hatch which led to the oar deck.

Emien descended the ladder, progress masked by the noisy snores of a slave. Dizzied by the odor of confined humanity, the boy waited for someone to raise an outcry. But the officer on duty had his back turned and the lantern guttered on its hook, nearly out of oil; the sooty flame barely glimmered through the glass. Emien groped in the gloom, caught the slide-bolt which secured the lower hatch. He spat on the metal, careful to work the bolt gently before drawing the pin. The hinges smelled of grease. Sweating, Emien raised the grating, eyes clenched shut. But the hatch opened soundlessly. Damp sour air wafted from the hold.

Sails ruffled topside; *Crow* shuddered and nosed a ripple in the sea as Emien swung himself onto the ladder. But he had no chance to notice the fact that the terrible calm had ended.

Something scraped overhead, followed by a flurry of sound. Emien froze just as a white object plummeted from the beams of the oar deck. He waited, breath locked in fear. But the disturbance was caused by a bird. Feathers brushed past his cheek. Emien recoiled bruisingly into the ladder.

Though the hold was a cavern of darkness, he saw the creature clearly. Traced by a faint halo of blue-white light, it drifted on slender wings. Emien felt blood leap in his veins. The bird was surely Anskiere's. Certain it had come for Taen, the boy hooked an elbow over a rung. No longer concerned with silence, he snatched the dagger from his belt, clamped the blade in his teeth, and hurled himself downward.

That moment, wind arose over the sea like a howl of outrage. Someone shouted topside. The sails jibed, then crashed back onto starboard tack with a bang that rattled the chainplates. Over-canvassed, *Crow* rolled violently on her side. Emien was tossed backward into the ladder. The fall spared him; a crate overbalanced and tumbled across the deck where he had stood a moment before. It crashed heavily into the timbers between the galleass' ribs.

Emien heard a sickening splinter of wood. Water fountained through the breach. Above decks, another gust shrieked through the rigging. The headsails flogged and thundered taut, and stressed lines whined as *Crow* heeled, oar-ports pressed remorselessly to the waterline. Mired by the broad yards of her staysails, the galleass began to drink the sea.

Emien grabbed the ladder and took the knife from his teeth. "Taen!" His shout blended horribly with the screams of oarsmen chained helplessly to their benches. Emien heard a mounting roar. Water dashed like a spillway into the bilge. Across the bulk of stacked cargo, he saw the tern alight with a flutter on the rim of a cask.

The ship lurched. Emien knew fear. If the galleass pitched any further, her ballast would shift. Iron bars would tumble like battering rams, slivering the contents of the hold to wreckage. Desperate, Emien shouted again.

"Taen!"

A snap sounded aloft, followed by the whipcrack report of torn canvas. Emien swore with relief. A bolt rope had broken. One sail, at least, would spill the murderous burden of wind which held the vessel pinned. Emien clung to the ladder as the galleass ponderously answered the helm. Water sloshed. *Crow* began to head up.

Emien peered across the hold. The tern still perched on the cask, wings outstretched for balance as the ship slowly righted. The halo shone like ghostlight on frail black-tipped feathers. Carefully Emien gauged the distance and aimed the knife.

Abruptly the aura around the bird brightened to a hard-edged ring of force. Emien tensed to throw. The tern cocked its head and regarded him with a bright unwinking eye. All at once the bird seemed to contain everything he had loved and left behind on Imrill Kand. Arrested by a sense of poignant loss, the boy hesitated. He forgot his hatred of Anskiere. His impulse to murder withered before a beauty so clean it made him ache.

Emien's hand trembled. The weapon suddenly burdened his arm past bearing. He longed to cast the steel aside to follow the bird toward a destiny that rang bright as music in his ears. But the memory of his oath to Tathagres left echoes which spoiled the harmony.

Slapped by the waves of a roused sea, *Crow* rounded into the wind. Water sloshed coldly over Emien's ankles. He felt nothing. Oblivious to the shouts of the officers and the storm-ridden chaos aloft, the boy stood torn by indecision, his mind wrung by promises of laughter and life, and his cheeks drenched with tears. He did not see the lanternlight which struck down from above. Neither did he notice the sorcerer who descended the ladder, robes the red of new blood in the flamelight.

"Boy!" Hearvin's voice was curt with annoyance. "Boy!"

Emien did not budge. Shadow flickered across his face. Absorbed by the tern, he let his hand loosen. The knife dropped into the bilge with a splash. "Taen?" Bemused as a dreamer, Emien stepped forward.

Hearvin sprang from the ladder and grabbed the boy's wrist. "Idiot! Are you mad?"

He jerked Emien back. The boy stumbled clumsily. Hearvin yanked him around, and the lantern lit the shining streaks of tears on a face unnaturally fixed in tranquillity. The sorcerer understood the cause. Anskiere had engaged the power he had recovered, and tried to form a geas to summon the children. Hearvin's fingers knotted savagely in the boy's sleeve. The girl was still missing, but apparently the attempt had found the boy susceptible; Tathagres was going to be distinctly displeased.

"Kor's Fires!" Hearvin slung the lantern on a peg and traced his hands swiftly before the boy's eyes. A symbol glowed in the air where it passed. The sorcerer muttered a counterspell; the glyph flashed scarlet and faded. Emien blinked. He shuddered, and his peaceful expression crumpled into horror as the illusion which called him dissolved into a nightmare of storm-tossed darkness. He drew breath and cried out.

Hearvin shook him. "Forget Imrill Kand! Forget your family! Your loyalty belongs to Tathagres, and she has summoned you."

Wind screeched above his words. *Crow* heaved awkwardly, dragged into another roll by the swirling gallons which flooded her hold. Emien staggered and shrugged free of Hearvin's grip. The deck tilted. Steel rattled and clanged overhead as terrified rowers struggled to tear free of their chains. Their panic might prevent the seamen from sealing the oar-ports, Emien thought dully. *Crow* was in peril of sinking. Strangely, he did not care.

Hearvin caught the lantern from its hook, and the hold fell into darkness, loud with the enclosed splash of the bilge. "I forbade you to come down here." He started up the ladder. "Why did you?"

Emien followed, sullenly silent. Just before he reached the hatch, he glanced back, but could not recall what had drawn him to leave his berth in the forecastle. Hearvin noted the boy's confusion with satisfaction. The spell of binding he had crafted was sufficient; Anskiere's meddling would trouble Emien no further.

The sorcerer did not perceive the tern which perched on the rim of a certain brandy cask in the depths of the hold. The binding he had used to secure Emien had also blinded the boy to its presence, since the shimmer of the bird's aura was invisible to hostile eyes. The one child Anskiere's ward still guarded would not be sought until she was delivered to safety.

Caught by a rising wave, *Crow* pitched, and the wheel clattered with a rattle like old bones as her helmsman strove to hold her bow to windward. Although Tathagres was land bred, she braved the quarterdeck on braced feet, white hair lashed into tangles by the gale. The cling of sodden velvet shamelessly accentuated her femininity; but the captain who confronted her had little appetite, no matter how alluring her curves. His gesture of protest withered under her scornful regard, and his mouth gaped speechlessly open.

Tathagres laughed. The oath she uttered belied her delicacy, as did the command which followed. "Slaughter them, then, but get those oar-ports *closed.*" Her violet eyes narrowed angrily. "They're only slaves. If they drown, they'll be just as dead. So will we all, if you don't act quickly."

A gust slammed into the spanker, which men still labored to furl. The captain lost his balance. Testily, he grabbed a stay, and barely missed jostling Tathagres. He began a plea for temperance. "Lady—"

The woman returned no threats. Yet the captain felt a quiver in his knees. "I'll see it done," he said quickly, though he had intended different words. Reduced to subservience on his own vessel, he hastened toward the companionway and almost collided with Hearvin, who had just arrived topside with the boy.

Tathagres transferred her displeasure to the sorcerer. "By the Great Fall," she exclaimed fiercely. "You owe me an explanation, Hearvin. Anskiere's possessions were scuttled, you said. How in Kor's Name could that stormfalcon get a homing fix on us?"

A wave smacked *Crow* onto her beam ends. The quartermaster wrestled the helm, and Tathagres slammed into the rail, knocked breathless. As Hearvin fetched up beside her, she noticed that Emien seemed strangely passive in the sorcerer's grip. She began at once to comment, but Hearvin interrupted.

"I did tell you. At the time I knew of no means by which the stormfalcon could track anything other than its original key of return." He regarded the woman without apprehension. "I also counseled caution, which you unwisely ignored. My two colleagues are dead."

Tathagres flung her head back, drenched by spray as *Crow*

wallowed, lee rails awash in the waist. The galleass recovered
sluggishly. An officer shouted frantic orders; the deckhands
abandoned the spanker and slashed the halyards. But not even
the pandemonium and canting decks disrupted Tathagres' obsession.

"Anskiere? Has he defied me?"

Hearvin's mouth twitched. "He has escaped. At what cost, I
cannot guess. But this much I promise: the frostwargs are
roused, but not free, and the stormfalcon circles Kisburn's fleet.
Your plans are balked."

"Not balked." Tathagres released the rail as the galleass
swung level. "Never that. We have the boy." She detailed two
deckhands to ready *Crow*'s pinnace for launch, intending to sail
directly and confront Anskiere at Cliffhaven.

Hearvin watched her until rain fell in sheets and quenched
the stern lantern. Familiar with her temper, he had prudently
avoided telling Tathagres how close she had come to losing the
boy. Neither did he mention the fact that he guessed the pinnace would not make landfall at the Kielmark's isle. *Crow* quivered, battered by ever steepening waves. The wind skirled like
demonsong through her masts. Hearvin heard its violence, and
was not fooled. Unlike his dead companions, he did not underestimate the threat Anskiere's falcon had unleashed. The Free
Isles might condemn the Stormwarden whose powers had leveled Tierl Enneth; but Anskiere's loyalty would never change.
Kisburn's warships would be smashed like toys.

The gale worsened. Towering whitecaps tumbled across the
galleass' decks, sweeping gear and human life into the sea with
equal abandon. The effort to launch the pinnace soon became a
struggle for survival. Awash up to her oar deck, *Crow* plowed
clumsily into the waves, unresponsive to the helm. Despite the
efforts of her crew, the galleass could not be saved. Hoarsely,
the captain ordered the longboats unlashed. But no man would
board until the King's officers were away in the pinnace. Beaten

and tired the captain left the quartermaster at the helm and sought Tathagres.

Thigh-deep in the foam-laced flood of the waist, Crow's best seamen labored with the pinnace. The sea sucked and thudded, and the masts traced dizzy circles against the sky. The captain found Tathagres with her sorcerer, clinging to the companionway rail. He touched her shoulder even as the pinnace jerked, freed at last from her cradle. Tathagres returned a slitted glare of annoyance.

The captain was too pressured to be cowed. "Get to the boat. If the seamen panic, I cannot ensure your safety."

A gust shivered the rigging, and something gave way aloft, streaming a snarl of lines to leeward. Tathagres' reply was obliterated by a sailhand's shout and the booming crash of a fallen yard. She made no move toward the pinnace.

Hearvin caught her arm. "Go at once."

Tathagres resisted. "Where is the Constable?"

Exasperated, the captain shouted warning. "You'll lose your chance!" He pointed forward.

A great sea reared above the galleass' bows. For an instant, the bowsprit rose, a glistening spear aimed at a sky which smoked with spindrift. Then the wave broke, avalanching water across the forecastle. A thunderous cascade of foam spun the pinnace in the waist. The seamen strove to hold her but the sea unravelled their grip like crochetwork. The boat struck the rail. Beaded wood exploded into wind-borne fragments. The next wave would likely tear the pinnace loose, empty of passengers.

"Go!" Hearvin thrust Tathagres and the boy headlong down the companionway. Moving hard on their heels, he shouted, "It's too late for the Constable!"

The sea swirled up to receive them. Belted chest-high by cold water, Tathagres stumbled. A seaman caught her. The deck tilted; he lost his balance and shoved her roughly into the arms of another man. Tathagres was lifted and dumped rudely onto the floorboards of the pinnace.

The next wave struck. Spray geysered overhead. Kicked by bare feet as the seamen tumbled into the boat, Tathagres had no chance to struggle upright. The pinnace slewed. Water bashed and hissed under the keel, and a gust tore the shouts of the seamen into unintelligible scraps. Then with a bump that knocked Tathagres against a thwart, the pinnace broke free.

"I have the boy," cried Hearvin from the stern.

A sailor lost his footing and fell, clutching desperately to the gunwale. The boat rolled under his weight and threatened to capsize. Another seaman pulped the man's knuckles with an oar. His screams were quickly lost astern as the pinnace lifted like a chip over storm-maddened crests. The seamen fought her steady. They bent over the oars. Spray slashed their backs and washed stinging runnels into their eyes. If the pinnace broached, even once, all her passengers would drown.

Tathagres pushed her hands against the boards, and curtly demanded the heading. Hearvin explained that the storm drove them southwest, toward Innishari and the lower reaches of the Alliance. Cliffhaven lay in the opposite direction, and until the weather improved, the pinnace could hold no better course. Tathagres accepted the reverse with steely practicality. She reviewed her assets, beginning with the boy from Imrill Kand who sat in the stern, an oddly wooden expression on his face.

Tathagres studied him carefully. A fisherman's son whose past actions had been impulsively, even violently, brash, would never sit passive while his boat was endangered by heavy seas.

"Emien," she said sharply.

The boy responded as though drugged. Tathagres frowned. "Hearvin." Reprimand edged her voice. "You've placed a stay-spell on the boy. Why?"

The sorcerer leaned with the motion of the pinnace, his hood pulled over his head and his features in shadow. "You'd have lost him to Anskiere, had I not. The falcon's return forestalled any chance to involve you."

"*What!*" Tathagres stiffened. She struck the seat with her fist, and gold jangled through the rush of the gale. "Do you tell me Anskiere sent a summoning aboard *Crow*, and you saw fit not to inform me? Koridan's Fires! *I'd like to see you flayed.* Because of your misjudgment, that foolish little girl will probably survive." She stared crossly over waters wracked by spume. "We won't recover her now, that's certain."

Hearvin said nothing. What he thought could not be guessed as Tathagres spun back to face him, her wet hair twisted into snake locks.

"It *is* a stay-spell?" She paused only for Hearvin's affirmation. "Then release him. I want the boy aware his sister's death was caused by that cloud-shifter's stormfalcon. Convince him, if he asks, that Taen perished in the hold of the galleass."

Hearvin obediently traced a pass in the air before the boy. A symbol glimmered red, framed briefly by the black surge of a wave before the sorcerer snapped his fingers. The glyph faded. Emien blinked, started, and his blankly disoriented expression transformed into a desperate survey of the pinnace's passengers.

Tathagres awaited her opening. With narrowed, predator's eyes, she absorbed every nuance of the boy's expression as he realized his sister was absent. He did not speak. But his body convulsed with a savage flare of rage.

Plotting for the future, Tathagres sought a way to exploit that anger; and in the seawater sloshing under her knees, found inspiration. She yanked a bucket from the pinnace's locker and thrust it between the boy's hands. "Bail," she urged softly. "Your life, and mine, depends upon keeping this craft seaworthy."

Emien seized the handles with a grip that blanched his knuckles, his eyes already hardened. He would live, Tathagres saw, expressly to avenge his sister. She smiled in the darkness.

The boy was tough as sword steel and charged like a thunderhead with passion. Under her guidance he would become a magnificent weapon. Settled by the thought, Tathagres leaned against a thwart and shut her eyes.

Of the survivors of the pinnace, Emien alone searched astern for a glimpse of the vessel left behind. *Crow* reeled in her death throes. Thrashed like flotsam, she listed in the spume, the corpses of her slaves streaming from the oar ports. As Emien watched, rain alone wet his cheeks. Once, he would have wept for the sister he had lost. Now his grief was eclipsed by hatred so pure it burned his very soul. If he lived, Anskiere would die. Mechanically, Emien continued to bail.

The abandoned galleass settled slowly to her deep water grave. No living man remained to observe as, tickled by a trail of bubbles from the hold, a brandy cask rose like a cork to the surface. Perched precariously on the rim, a tern spread wings haloed by the blaze of an enchanter's craft. Though gusts hammered the surrounding waves into a churning millrace of foam, the cask bobbed gently, girdled by calm only one sorcerer could command. Dry inside, Taen slept. Anskiere's ward drew her scathelessly through the gale-ravaged wreckage of Kisburn's fleet and westward into the open sea.

CHAPTER V

Ivain's Heir

IN THE CLOSE HEAT OF EVENING
Jaric lay limp on his cot in the loft above Morbrith Keep's
smithy. Although more than one healer plied him with remedies, he had not regained consciousness since he had fallen
senseless in the apothecary's herb garden two days past. Sightless as an icon beneath his blankets, he did not respond to the
flare of light beneath the dormer by his head; nor did he stir as
the tramp of booted feet shook the ladder which led to the loft.
Far beyond reach of physical senses, the scribe's apprentice remained unaware his illness had earned him the attention of the
Master Healer, and oddly, the Earl of Morbrith himself.

A liveried servant raised a lantern over the cot, revealing a
profile now sharp-edged and sunken. Flamelight accentuated
the boy's bloodless lips, and the fingers splayed on the coverlet
seemed as fragile as the fluted shells washed in by the tide.

"He seems dead," said the Earl. Emeralds flashed as he bent
and lifted Jaric's wrist. The limb was icy, and slender as a
maid's in the man's callused grip. The Earl swallowed, moved

to pity for the boy. Raised by the Smith's Guild, Jaric had proved too slight for the forges; he had been forced to repay the cost of his fostering on a copyist's wages. The Earl chafed the boy's skin, startled to discover blisters. He turned the hand he held to the light. "Did you see this?"

The Master Healer clicked his tongue. "Severe sunburn," he said gruffly. "The boy lay unprotected for several hours before anyone noticed him. The other side of his face is marked also. Except for that, he shows no trace of injury. I found no bruises, and if he's sick, his symptoms match no affliction I have ever known. I tell you, Lord, I believe him stricken by sorcery."

The Earl smoothed Jaric's arm on the blanket. He settled on his heels, remembering Kerain, the smith's son, who had hung for murdering his betrothed. Under oath at his trial, Kerain had sworn he had done nothing except prevent the girl from slaughtering her newborn child. The young man claimed to have snatched the infant from under her knife, and she had promptly turned the blade against herself. The earl winced in recollection. Condemned to the scaffold, Kerain had voiced his death wish; he claimed the orphaned baby as his own. Morbrith Keep's archives recorded the boy child as Kerainson Jaric, assigned as ward of the Smith's Guild. Sixteen years later, the Earl studied the delicate features of that same boy, now certain the burly, black-haired Kerain had not been the father. If Jaric was a sorcerer's get, his mother's attempt at murder became plausible; a wizard's heir inherited the enemies of his sire, and terrible misfortune often befell those who surrounded him.

The Earl blotted sweat from his temples. Had he guessed the truth at the trial, he would have spared Kerain, and put the child to the sword instead. But hindsight was useless. The present offered options considerably less favorable. Unhappily, the Earl made his decision.

"I want the boy moved to the sanctuary tower behind Koridan's Shrine."

The healer gasped, startled. "That's not wise." The tower

lay outside the walls, on the other side of the summerfair. The crowded alleys beyond the gates were no place to be carrying a sick boy after dark. "Jaric's condition is most serious, my Lord."

The Earl straightened angrily. "You'll move that boy quickly and without any fuss. I'll send guardsmen to help. Am I clear?"

"Very." The healer bowed with evident distress. "But you risk the boy's life."

Pressured by concern he had no wish to explain, the Earl said nothing. What healer could understand that this boy might be better dead? For should Jaric prove to be other than Kerain's get, the consequences might threaten all of Morbrith.

Jaric never felt the hands which lifted his blanket-wrapped body from the cot above the smithy. Fretful from worry, the Master Healer oversaw the guardsmen as they hefted the boy down the ladder. More guards waited below. Even with the doors open, the forge was stifling with the smoky heat of banked embers. Yet Jaric stayed chill to the touch, and his eyes glinted, pupils widened and black in the glare of the lamps.

"Kor," said one guardsman. "He's cold as a fish. You sure he's not dead?" Watched uneasily by his companions, he lowered the boy onto a litter.

"If he were dead, none of us would be missing sleep," snapped the healer. He snatched up his satchel of remedies and stalked out of the forge. The men-at-arms followed more slowly with the boy.

"Damned summerfair's no place to go with a litter," muttered the guardsman in the lead. His complaint was just. The nomads who gathered on Morbrith Heath each solstice were clannish and temperamental; though merchants bartered goods with them during the day, no townsman lingered outside the keep walls after dark. To cross the festival with a helpless boy was to invite violence; but no Morbrith man dared gainsay the High Earl's command.

In the shadowed security of the gatehouse, the guardsmen checked their weapons. The valley below was patterned like patchwork with wagons, colored lights, and the flimsy wooden booths of the summerfair. Shouts and laughter and the scraping notes of fiddles blended raucously on the night air. The guardsmen formed up. With the healer and the boy sheltered inside a ring of mailed bodies, they set out.

From the moment the gates clanged shut, the crowd enveloped the small party like the surge of a breaker. The guards struggled to maintain position, aware steel would be little deterrent should they encounter trouble. Jaric never stirred, though he was shoved, fingered, and jostled by painted clansmen who reeked of sweat and spirits. He knew nothing of the noise, the discomfort, or the dust as the Earl's men-at-arms labored to clear a path through the closely packed revelers. By the time they reached the far boundary of the summerfair the men were tired, white with the strain of handling clansmen who were drunk, and often quick to draw knives.

As the noise and lights fell behind, the healer permitted a short pause by the river at the edge of the heath. The men rested the litter on the stone buttresses of the bridge. In the wind-tossed light of the lantern, the boy's eyes seemed as glazed as a corpse's. One guardsman whispered apprehensively and another disguised a shiver by dusting the grit out of his tunic.

"He sure looks dead."

The healer overheard. He jammed his hat over his ears until his hair stuck out in bristles, and gestured toward the summerfair. "Want to go back? No? Then he's alive and that's the end of it."

The men moved reluctantly forward. The path to the sanctuary tower laced between a stand of pines, dim and gray by starlight. The healer lifted Jaric's wrists from the blankets. The boy's pulse was erratic, and much too fast. If Jaric was going to die, let it happen in the High Lord's presence, the healer thought vindictively. He urged the men to increase their pace.

The land rose sharply, eroded into gullies made treacherous by roots and loose shale. The lantern swung, and cast bewildering shadows over the footing which steadily worsened. The guardsmen stumbled and swore until exertion robbed them of breath. The trail steepened. Jaric jounced on his litter, raked by branches and bruised against rocks. The poles which bore his weight dragged against the scrub, and weaponry clanked. Night birds startled into flight almost under the guardsmen's boots as they toiled through narrow clefts of rock.

Finally lights glimmered ahead and the spire of the sanctuary tower reared in silhouette against a starry arch of sky. The men quickened pace, anxious to reach the stone-paved security of Koridan's Shrine.

Just before the gates a figure on horseback cut them off.

Certain that he faced an outlaw, the healer started back and slammed painfully into a litter pole. The men-at-arms reached for weapons.

"Desist at once!" commanded the Earl of Morbrith, his voice overlaid by the dissonant ring of steel. "Fires!"

He dismounted irritably. His horse sidled, oddly noiseless; its hooves and bit had been muffled in flannel, and it smelled of sweat. The Earl had brought no escort, and his cloak, tunic, and the harness of his mount were bare of ornaments. Whatever his intentions, he had taken care to travel without attracting notice.

"How is the boy?"

The healer framed his reply with resentment. "He lives, but barely." His insolence was ignored.

The Earl lifted lathered reins from the horse's neck, and offered no explanation for his appearance. He turned immediately with instructions to his guardsmen. "Remain here. Let no man enter the shrine." His tone softened. "You've done well.

The flask of wine in my saddlebag may be shared among you, but keep the celebration quiet. I want no priests awakened before I return."

The Earl tossed his reins to the guard captain. Then he bent over the litter, gathered Jaric in his arms and started for the gates. The healer moved after, determined to protect his charge; through thirty years of practice, he had never known the Lord of Morbrith to behave so callously.

The Earl paused and blocked his path. "Your services are no longer needed," he said coldly.

The healer's muscles knotted with outrage. "You're unaware of the risks. Would you sanction murder? I'll stay only if you swear no harm will come to the boy."

The Earl answered in a tone of ringing authority. "I'll swear to nothing. Consider yourself excused, or I'll have the guards tie you like a felon."

"You've gone mad." The healer groped for words to argue, and lamely shook his head. "Stark mad."

The Earl said nothing. Unwilling to linger under the healer's accusing stare, he spun on his heel and bore Kerainson Jaric out of the circle of lamplight.

The healer watched with a leaden sense of foreboding. The haste, the secrecy, and the Earl's curt manner were reasons enough to fear for Jaric's safety. The boy had no family but the Smith's Guild; who would ask questions on his behalf should he fail to return? Spurred by self-righteous concern, the healer decided to follow.

The Earl had proceeded in the direction of the sanctuary tower, but darkness, rocky footing, and the need for silence hampered the healer's progress. By the time his eyes had adjusted to the dark, his quarry had already reached the postern of the tower. The Earl was no longer alone. The healer saw a tall figure muffled in gray standing beside him. From the shadow of its cloak hood gleamed lidless orange eyes, too widely spaced to be human and with pupils slotted like a serpent's.

The healer gasped. Sweat sprang along his spine and his hat seemed suddenly too tight against his brow. The creature he beheld was surely of demonkind, a Llondian empath; its presence within shrine grounds became a breach of natural law. The healer strove to quell his fear, without success. Surely as tide, the Earl intended to investigate Jaric's affliction through contact with the accursed being's mind. Such practice was unthinkable, heresy beyond the pardon of any decent man.

Without pausing to review consequences, the healer ran forward, hands interlocked in a gesture to ward off evil. "I cannot sanction this!" he shouted.

The pair ahead froze and looked back. Startled, the Llondel whistled and ducked into the arched doorway of the tower. Its eyes shone like coals in the dark.

"Be still, you fool." The Earl shifted the unconscious boy against his shoulder and faced the healer with an expression of rage. "Waken the priests, and I'll see you burn with me. If a member of my household is struck down by a sorcerer, I'll know who, and why, no matter what methods are required. I'll not endanger all of Morbrith for the sake of a single boy."

"This is irresponsible." Trembling, the healer considered the powers of the Llondelei, and the accounts of humans driven mad from their effects. "Have you no thought for your guardsmen? They lie well within range of Llondel's imaging, and you left them without warning."

The Earl stood stiffly as the wind tumbled Jaric's hair against his collar. "You're wrong," he said at last. "The wine is drugged. The men-at-arms will sleep soundly until dawn. Either accompany us or go back and share the flask with them."

But the healer held his ground. "What of the priests in the shrine?"

"That was less easily arranged." The Earl sighed. "But I can promise they will suffer no ill effects from this night's work."

The Llondel glanced around, orange eyes ablaze with un-friendliness. It copied the healer's earlier gesture with seamed, six-fingered hands, and stalked after the Earl. The healer straightened his hat and watched as its dusky cloak blended into the dark. For all his concern, this time he was unable to proceed.

The Earl waited, circled by the intricate mosaic work which patterned the anteroom of the sanctuary tower. The Llondel barred the door, its movements liquidly graceful.

"I'm sorry," the Earl said softly, aware the being he ad-dressed could follow his emotion, if not his words. "Few of my kind understand."

The Llondel trilled a treble seventh. It touched the Earl's shoulder, trilled again, and extended long arms toward the boy.

Muscles aching, the Earl surrendered Jaric's weight with a grateful sigh. Moments like this always made him wonder why Kordane's Law held all demons alike. Most types were danger-ous, it was true; the Llondelei were no exception. But their em-pathic sensitivity made them gentle, even retiring, and they spun harmful images only when threatened. The Earl of Morbrith started up the stair, knowing stone walls made the Llondel ill at ease. Yet the creature had come without hesita-tion earlier when he had relayed the plight of the boy.

'Sorcerer,' the Earl thought, and recognized the mind-touch of the Llondel by the way the concept formed; the creature must have picked up his inner reflection. It stopped on the stair, shifted Jaric's limp form into the crook of one elbow, and repeated the healer's gesture to ward off evil. 'Must,' it sent ur-gently, then consolidated its disjointed attempt at communica-tion into a single image.

And the Earl frowned, for the concept the demon pressed against his awareness implied the evil to be averted constituted danger to the *sender* of Jaric's affliction. Exasperated, he sighed. The Llondel was surely mistaken.

'No.' Orange eyes flashed up out of the gloom. *'Not wrong.'* Frustrated with word symbol images, the Llondel stamped a clawed foot on the stairway, bitterly offended.

"I'm sorry." The Earl was desperate to know the cause of Jaric's distress. He pushed open the door at the head of the landing and held the carved panel wide. "Humans have difficulty believing what they cannot see. Will you show us?"

Light flooded from the chamber beyond, illuminating a gray-brown alien face. The creature hesitated. Crescent nostrils quivered, and its bone-slim fingers tightened on the blanket-wrapped boy.

"We need your help," the Earl coaxed softly.

The Llondel returned a sour chirp. It moved forward, but not, the Earl understood, for the sake of Morbrith. As the demon crossed the threshold, he again received the impression of a sorcerer endangered; but this time he held his opinion. He closed and barred the door, and a voice called querulously from the shadows.

"You took eternity to get here."

"I know." The Earl bent and stuffed a length of felt into the crack beneath the door. "I had to wait for the guardsmen. Would you want to cross the summerfair with a litter?"

A grunt answered him. The Earl straightened and regarded the wizened countenance of Morbrith's Master Seer by the light of the cresset which blazed in an iron bracket close by.

The old man glared back, chin jutted outward from a nest of untrimmed hair. His mouth pursed deeply with displeasure. "Better that than the saddle at my age. You'd never, were you seventy. My bones ache."

But spry movements belied his complaint as he rose and shuttered the chamber's single window. The Llondel seated itself in the center of the floor with Jaric cradled in its lap. Then it fixed its sultry gaze upon the Earl and pointed to the cresset.

'End the light,' it sent.

The Lord of Morbrith lifted the torch and plunged it into a

water bucket beneath. The chamber went dark with a crackling hiss of steam. The man settled himself beside the seer, and waited as the last airborn spark flurried and died, leaving blackness punctured by two burning red-gold lamps which were the Llondel's eyes.

Suddenly uneasy, the Earl clamped damp palms on his sleeves. "You will reveal to us the sender of this boy's affliction," he said to the Llondel. "No harm will come to any human here."

The eyes vanished, eclipsed by the cloak hood as the Llondel bowed its head. No image arose in reply, and no sound intruded but faintly labored wheezes from the seer. But as the Earl strained to see form in the darkness, a spark of yellow appeared suspended in the air. It flared brighter, acquiring the flowing edges of live flame, then widened into a ghostly wheel of fire which shed no light on any of the surrounding objects. The apparition sent a thrill of fear down the Earl's spine. The Llondel and the boy appeared to have vanished.

Through a gut-deep hollow of dread, the man understood that he gazed directly upon Jaric's nightmare, and he longed suddenly to be outdoors, surrounded by summer's chorus of crickets. But door and window were barred, and every chink battened with felt. The Llondel's empathic imaging smothered the Earl's wish, pitched his awareness through the spinning heart of the flame, into the boy's mind. . . .

. . . Fog, wind, and the icy sting of spray. Surf hammered into rocks scant yards below the ledge where Jaric huddled, arms clasped tightly around his knees. The elements battered his unprotected body with cruel force. Though soaked and chilled, he did not care. His face remained hidden behind hands rigid as carved ivory, even when he sensed he was no longer alone. The sorcerer from his earlier vision stepped out of the mist and paused on the ledge before him. But Jaric did not look up.

"I call you, Firelord's Son." The sorcerer gazed down at the boy. The wind tossed his silver hair, his staff glowed with a brilliant aura of power, and the air tingled with the resonance of terrible forces held in check.

Yet Jaric made no move. If he acknowledged the sorcerer's existence, he might forfeit control of his destiny forever. His will would be crushed, scattered like the ashes of the dead, and he would lose all that was dear to him.

"In the name of Anskiere you are summoned," said the sorcerer, and he raised the staff over the stiff figure of the boy.

Jaric felt the power around him shift, align like a spear to pierce his innermost self. Dread locked his limbs. His thoughts raced, and something, no, *someone* jabbed him with the realization that he *would* die, should he continue to reject the fate the sorcerer had decreed for him. But Jaric ignored the warning. Heedless as the moth which flies into candleflame, he chose oblivion; and was blocked. Two slit-pupiled eyes appeared, etched like coals against his retinas.

Jaric screamed. *His own eyes were closed.* Yet hotly as Kor's Fires, the demonic gaze trapped him. His mind was possessed by a nightmare vision of shame and guilt and the horrid certainty that his denial would eventually condemn his entire race. "Let me be!" shouted Jaric. But the eyes melted into smoke, replaced by an image of Master Iveg chained amid a blazing pyre of books while demon forms danced in silhouette. Their shapes were black as ink, pooling into darkness. Jaric found himself thrust into the streets of Morbrith Keep, a torch clutched in sweating hands; and the bleached skeletons of dead men snapped like sticks under his feet as he walked. Then out of the shadowed sockets of a skull, the demon's red eyes reappeared and focused accusingly upon him.

'You alone can prevent this.'

He cried aloud in denial, but his heart betrayed him. He could never let Morbrith be destroyed.

The demon's dream rippled like fabric and left him.

Beaten to his knees, Jaric looked up at last, beheld the weather mage who had called him. He had no spirit left to resist. Empty of passion, he stared into features troubled as storm sea. Just then the staff descended in a blistering arc of light.

It struck with a blast of energy. Gale wind screamed. The sea rose, towered into boiling crests which broke over the ledge with a roar. Foam-laced tons of water hurled Jaric from his perch.

He shouted in panic as he tumbled over and over. Then darkness drowned him in yet another dream. Ice snapped and sang like harpstrings in his ears, overlaid by the cries of creatures imprisoned, yet lusting hotly for blood and killing. Jaric shivered, shaken by the knowledge that those cries would echo for centuries yet to come were nothing done. Then an arching flare of sunlight struck his face. He squinted, saw a cliff armored with prisms of ice. Waves boomed beneath, splintered into diamond drops of spray and the wind crooned in a minor key. Tragedy had occurred here, Jaric understood, and he knew unconsolable grief. Tears traced his cheeks. Then the scene upended, replaced by the stinging prod of Anskiere's geas. Direction aligned like a compass within his mind; he knew he must travel southeast. The sorcerer's command intensified, became a compulsion no protest could deny.

Then Jaric knew only darkness, threaded by a far-off echo of voices. Fuzzily, he attempted to orient himself. His eyes seemed clotted with shadow and his limbs weighed like lead. Confused by the return of his senses, Jaric stirred in the Llondel's embrace, then sighed and lifted his head. An elderly man with rumpled hair lifted a freshly lit torch from a bracket in the wall. Jaric recognized the Master Seer of Morbrith but the chamber was unfamiliar, decidedly not part of the castle. The walls were strangely polished and incised with geometrical carvings. Jaric blinked, confused, and the voice which droned in his ears slowly resolved into speech.

". . . Must be Ivain Firelord's son," said the seer in a tone of misgiving. No sorcerer's name was more feared, except that of Anskiere, who had leveled Tierl Enneth; and Anskiere himself had called the boy into thrall.

"Kor's Blessed Fires!" The Earl leaned sharply forward, clenched both hands into fists, and crossed his wrists in a gesture to avert malign sorcery.

Jaric felt someone's arms tighten around him. He looked up, startled by the creature who held him, surely a demon with hideous glowing eyes. The boy gasped in fear. *This was the sender of images who had forced his submission to Anskiere.*

He appealed at once to the Earl. "Have mercy. My Lord, I beg you. Have the demon release me."

But the Earl acted as though Jaric had never spoken. He stared at the Llondel, his expression like iron in the torchlight. When he spoke, his reply was for the demon alone. "I'm sorry. I cannot permit the boy to live."

The Llondel hissed. Paralyzed with terror, Jaric saw the Earl draw his knife. The seer shouted, and dropped the torch. Flame streaked as it tumbled to the floor. Amid a mad whirl of shadows, Jaric saw a blade flash, quickly eclipsed by the Llondel's body. The creature rolled, bearing Jaric with it. The boy heard a thump, felt the quiver as steel struck flesh. He knew no pain. The Llondel had taken the thrust intended for him just below the shoulder.

The Earl cursed. Jaric gasped as the demon's good arm tightened around him. His face was crushed into cloth which smelled of sweetgrass. He struggled but could not break loose. The Llondel lifted him, fumbled the door open, and dragged him into the landing beyond. Jounced and half suffocated by blood-soaked fabric, Jaric fought to tear free. But the Llondel bundled him toward the stairway with a grip like wire. Jaric panicked. He wrenched against this captor, pulled clear long enough to manage a glance behind.

The Earl had not pursued. He crouched, bloodied to the

elbow, over the sprawled body of a boy with pale hair. With a jolt, Jaric recognized himself. The handle of the knife stuck through the blankets, piercing his heart.

Jaric screamed. The Llondel yanked him forward, sent him crashing down the stairs. Stone risers bruised his bare heels. They were solid, *real*, as the corpse in the room could not be.

'Image,' assured the demon, picking up his distress. It jabbed him between the shoulder blades with a spurred palm, driving him downward. *'I show your kind what would happen should they kill you.'*

Jaric tripped, caught the railing to prevent himself from falling. "Why do you care?" His voice cracked with emotion. Already he could feel Anskiere's geas tug at his mind, urging him southeast with the wretched persistence of a headache.

Calmly the Llondel framed a reply. *'I act for the sorcerer.'* A steel crossguard gleamed beyond the curve of the cloak hood; the Earl's knife was embedded still in the demon's back. Jaric felt his skin crawl. Surely the creature was in agony. A man had wounded it, yet it stood patiently, its luminous gaze unpleasantly dispassionate.

"You're hurt." Jaric pointed to the weapon, wrung by revulsion. "Why should you suffer for the sorcerer who massacred all of Tierl Enneth?"

The demon hissed in anger. It grabbed the boy's wrist, tore him away from the railing, then spun him, reeling downward. *'Fool,'* it sent. *'Tierl Enneth fell at Tathagres' hand. And now, in ignorance, she seeks to free the Mharg-spawn as well.'*

But fear and trauma, and the ache of Anskiere's geas, had driven Jaric far beyond rational understanding. Half blinded by tears, he stumbled across the anteroom and struck the door with such force the breath slammed from his lungs. The Llondel arrived just behind him. Spurs clicked like dice against metal as it raised the bolt. The portal swung, pitching Jaric headlong into the night. He fell, tumbling over and over, clawed by weedstalks and dew-drenched grass. But the Llondel permitted no respite. It jabbed an image into his mind. Flat on his back, Jaric saw the stars obliterated by a clearly focused scene outside the gates of Koridan's Shrine. Six of the Earl's guardsmen lay asleep in the scrub. A horse browsed in their midst, saddled, bridled, and equipped with a sword in a sheath beneath the stirrup.

'Now go,' sent the Llondel. 'Take the animal and flee, for your own kind will surely take your life.'

Cornered by Anskiere's geas and the Earl's intent to murder, Jaric had no other option. Horses intimidated him. A sword in his hands was so much dead weight. Yet with a throat tight with grief, he rose to his feet and ran.

The Llondel watched him go with burning eyes. Satisfied the boy would not turn back, it clutched its hurt shoulder and sank slowly to the floor. There it lay still. Warm blood pooled, darkening the mosaic in a widening puddle. Aware its wound was mortal, the Llondian shunned communication with its own kind. Instead it clung to consciousness, spent its last strength spinning thought-forms; and images bloomed like opium dreams in the minds of the humans in the chamber above.

In the baleful flicker of torchlight, the Earl watched the blood he believed to be Jaric's drip down his wrists. Prisoned by the Llondel's imaging, he felt as if the knife he just used for murder had also severed the threads of natural progression. Chaos remained. Violence echoed on the air with the dissonance of a snapped harpstring, and the stains on his hands darkened, dried, and blew away as dust. A woman's face appeared, circled by braided coils of hair the color of frost. She was lovely beyond description, but behind amethyst eyes shone an inhuman lust for power. The Earl felt his stomach tighten in recognition of evil. The image shifted, showed the woman kneeling while the occupant of a jeweled throne handed her a cube of black stone which contained Keys to a sorcerer's ward. A smile touched her lips; and the Llondel's vision of the future shattered into nightmare.

The woman rose, *uncontested because Jaric had died of a knife thrust*, and armies marched. Towns blazed like festival lanterns, and corpses bloated in the parched soil of ruined fields. The woman laughed. The cube in her hand went molten, blazed whitely, and became a wheel of fire. A sorcerer's defenses burst with a white-hot snap of energy and winds rose, smashing maddened waves upon a desolate stretch of shoreline. Nearby a tower of granite tumbled and fell. Demonkind spewed forth, hideous beyond any the Earl had ever known. Fanged, taloned, and patterned with iridescent scales, they swept skyward with a thunder of membranous wings. Where they passed, their breath withered flesh, curdled the fruit on the trees, and left the stripped veins of leaves blowing like cobwebs in the breeze. The earth rotted and knew no spring. The oceans spewed up dead fish. And at Morbrith Keep the streets lay reeking with a tangle of human remains.

"No!" the Earl's scream tore from his throat in near physical agony, but the images kept coming. He saw a forest dell tangled with the white flowering vine which often grew on gravesites. There a black-haired fisherman's daughter dragged a silvery object which contained a wardspell to stay the escaped demons. But she was slain, cut down by a brother's sword, and soldiers turned the box's powers against their own kind. The snow-haired woman whispered praise, and her voice became the croak of ravens feasting on dead flesh.

Weeping now, the Earl beheld a headland scabbed with dirtied drifts of ice. A ragged band of survivors set fire to stacked logs, while other men chipped through the resulting slush with swords and shovels. They hoped to release a weather mage believed to be trapped inside, for legend held his powers might subdue the horrors which blighted the land. But where the sorcerer had been, they discovered bones wrapped loosely in a bundle of rags. Exhausted from their labor, the men abandoned the place in despair; and through a rift in the ice, a quavering whistle echoed across the lonely face of the sea. The snow-haired woman laughed. And the Earl saw his civilization plunge into a well of darkness, all for the murder of a Morbrith boy in the sanctuary tower at midsummer.

"No! Koridan's Fires, *no!*" With his throat still raw from screaming, the Earl opened his eyes. Daylight spilled brightly through the casement. The seer crouched trembling in the sunlight, his white head familiarly rumpled. No bloodied corpse marred the floor.

The Earl buried his face in his hands. *He had only dreamed the boy's death.* But the Llondel's prescient images left a deep and lingering warning of danger. Preoccupied, the Earl did not notice the rich blue robes of the men who arrived in the doorway until after the Archpriest had addressed him.

"My Lord, it is unavoidable. You must be tried for heresy."

The Earl swore tiredly and leaned back against the wall. He did not immediately respond. The seer watched him in naked alarm, but said nothing.

The priest mistook his silence for regret. "Perhaps you may not burn for the crime. Your men claim the knife which killed the Llondian demon is your Lordship's. If you can prove you dealt the death blow, you may be judged more leniently."

From the doorway, the healer broke in with vindictive satisfaction. "Jaric has escaped. He stole your horse."

"Don't pursue him," the Earl said quickly. He stared down at the floor, stung to a flurry of thought. Jaric must not be stopped. He added in a hoarse whisper, "The horse was a gift."

The Earl did not resist as the priests drew him to his feet and placed fetters on his wrists. His own dilemma seemed of small importance beside the warning of the Llondel's death image. For it appeared the fate of Morbrith rested on the shoulders of a small sickly apprentice whose sole talent was penmanship.

"Kor protect him," muttered the seer, and the priests, misinterpreting, bowed their heads in earnest prayer for the man they had taken into custody.

CHAPTER VI

Gaire's Main

THE GALE SET LOOSE BY Anskiere's stormfalcon raged across the southwest latitudes and finally spent itself, leaving skies whipped with cirrus and air scoured clean by rain. Emien woke in the pinnace to a cold fair morning. Bruised after days of battling maddened elements, he raised himself from the floorboards. Bilgewater dripped from his sleeves as he stretched and rubbed salt-crusted eyes. The pinnace wallowed through the troughs, her helm lashed and her oarsmen sprawled in exhausted slumber across their benches; but the craft's other two occupants seemed strangely unaffected by fatigue. Hearvin and Tathagres sat near the stern, involved in conversation.

Emien gripped the gunwale. Seasoned fisherman though he was, his palms had blistered at the oar; waterlogged skin had since split into sores. Yet the boy noticed no sting, obsessed as he was with his desire for vengeance. Of those on board only Tathagres hated Anskiere as he did. She had promised the Stormwarden's demise, and for that the boy had sworn an oath no fisherman's son would betray. Though weary and starved, his first thought was for his mistress.

Emien stood cautiously. Dehydration had left him light-headed, and the roll of the pinnace made movement without a handhold impossible. Unsatisfied with the boat's performance, he ran a critical eye over the canvas set since the storm relented. The mainsheet needed easing, and the headsail drove the bow down because the halyard was too slack. Instinctively, Emien started to adjust lines.

The sound of raised voices carried clearly from the stern as he worked. Hearvin and Tathagres openly argued, and Emien paused to listen.

". . . Failed to accomplish your purpose," Hearvin said bluntly. He sat as he always did, straight as chiseled wood against the curve of the swells.

Tathagres responded inaudibly but her gesture bespoke annoyance.

"What else have you achieved?" Hearvin jabbed a hand into the wet folds of his cloak. "Your liege expected the release of the frostwargs and a Stormwarden on Cliffhaven who would subvert the Kielmark's sovereignty. Thus far you have delivered two dead sorcerers, a smashed war fleet, and a boy you would have lost had I not intervened."

Absently Emien reached for the mainsheet. Although a gust masked Tathagres' reply, her expression became haughtily angry.

Hearvin stiffened, no longer impassive. "And I say you've meddled enough!"

This time Tathagres' voice cut cleanly across the white hiss of spray. "Do you challenge me? How dare you! You fear the Stormwarden, that much is evident. And you speak of the Kielmark as more than a mortal man, which proves your judgment is dim as an itinerant conjurer's. I'm disappointed. Kisburn promised me better."

Hearvin jerked a fist from his robe and made a pass in the

air, as if he thought to retaliate with sorcery. Concerned for his mistress, Emien cleated the line in his hand and hastened aft. But Tathagres met the sorcerer's threat with a scornful laugh.

Hearvin abruptly recovered control. "I warn you, Lady. Don't underestimate me as you did Anskiere." The sorcerer stopped, forced to brace himself as a wave lifted the stern.

The pinnace lurched. Emien stumbled noisily against a thwart. Hearvin started around. The wind snatched his hood, unveiling pinched cheeks and an expression of annoyance. Tathagres seemed to welcome the interruption. She tilted her head and smiled sweetly at the fisherman's son from Imrill Kand.

"Boy, were you taught navigation?" She raked tangled hair from her brow and smiled with girlish appeal. "Do you know enough to sail this boat to land?"

Close up, Emien saw the marks Anskiere's storm had inflicted on the mistress he had chosen. Her fair complexion was chapped from salt water and sun, and weariness had printed circles dark as bruises beneath her eyes. Emien swallowed, momentarily overcome by the urge to protect her beauty from further ruin. Embarrassed by his flushed skin and knotted muscles, the boy answered self-consciously.

"My Lady need not have worried. I took sights last night while the polestar was visible. The isles of Innishari could be reached in a fortnight with good wind. If Kor grants us rainfall for water, I could get you there safely."

Tathagres tumbled the bracelets on her wrists with elegant fingers and bestowed a vindictive glance upon Hearvin. "Then let us sail directly. At Innishari we can engage a trader bound for Cliffhaven. Have you any more objections? Do tell me. I'm certain Emien would welcome the entertainment."

She waited, poised like a cat toying with helpless prey. But the sorcerer refused to be baited.

He raised his hood over his head, apparently content to let the quarrel lapse. Only Emien glimpsed wary anger in the sorcerer's eyes before shadow obscured it. The boy distrusted Hearvin's intentions, but he was canny enough to keep silent. He could serve Tathagres best if the sorcerer remained unsuspecting; and dedicated less to intrigue than to practicality, he applied himself to the task of sailing the pinnace to Innishari.

His responsibility was not slight. The following days would bring hardship enough to tax the endurance of the toughest man on board. Tathagres' slim build left her perishable as a woodland flower. Without nourishment she would be first to weaken.

Brooding, Emien considered his priorities. The pinnace held course decently enough with the tiller lashed, but her heading would be more accurate if the helm were manned. With the self-reliance gained while fishing aboard *Dacsen*, the boy began to strip the rope from the whipstaff. The knots were barely loosened when he noticed Tathagres watching him, her lips curved with disdain.

Emien frowned. "Does my Lady disapprove?"

Tathagres braced herself against the gunwale, aware the backdrop of empty sky accentuated her femininity. "I gave you charge of the pinnace. Does a captain stand watch like a common seaman?" Carefully judging her interval, she raised violet eyes and regarded the boy from Imrill Kand.

Caught staring, Emien reddened. Shamed by an adolescent rush of desire and stung by scorn from the woman who inspired it, he responded awkwardly. "Is that what you wish?" He abandoned the lashing, charged with frustration he dared not express. "If I establish watches among the seamen, I'll require a log to maintain dead reckoning." He did not belabor the fact he could not write.

Tathagres neatly eliminated the need. "Then Hearvin will act as your secretary."

Nervously Emien glanced at the sorcerer. But Hearvin made no protest; left no course but one which did not defeat his pride, the boy licked dry lips and faced his mistress.

"Well?" prompted Tathagres.

Balked by conflicting emotions, Emien could not answer. He turned on his heel and made his way forward. He did not see Tathagres' smile of approval when his reluctance transformed into rage. He jabbed the nearest seaman awake with his toe, and anger lent him authority beyond his years.

"You! Take the helm, and steer southwest."

The sailhand stumbled to his feet, too startled to protest. Emien felt the power of command surge through him, sweeter than fine wine and far more intoxicating. Never again would he grovel as an ignorant fisherman before his betters. In time, he too would be master. Tathagres would see she had chosen well by asking him into her service.

Emien braced his legs against the roll of the pinnace, brow drawn into a scowl. "You will stand watch until noon. I will send a man to relieve you."

Accustomed to discipline, the seaman obeyed. And on a reckless wave of daring, the boy decided to explore the limits of his discovery. He turned aft and bowed respectfully to Tathagres.

"My Lady, for the good of the vessel, I require the jewelry you use to fasten your cloak."

Tathagres stared at him with a calculating expression. Sweat sprang along Emien's temples. Yet he did not tremble or back down, and at length, Tathagres unpinned the two gold brooches. She handed them over to Emien and asked no explanation.

The exchange was not lost upon the seaman at the helm. As the boy made his final bow and moved forward, he viewed Emien with fresh respect. The boy's confidence swelled. He felt himself a man for the first time since the accident with the net which had caused his father's death. On Imrill Kand, he had been called bungler, a child bereft of common sense and shamefully slow to learn. Now he knew otherwise. With his chin lifted haughtily, Emien cupped the brooches in his torn palms, and chose a place where he could work and still keep an eye on the helmsman.

Hearvin watched as, skillfully, the boy began to twist the jewelry into lures and hooks to catch fish. "Well, at least there's a chance we won't starve, even if our meals are dearly bought," the sorcerer commented. He leaned back against the gunwale and blandly faced Tathagres. "That boy learns remarkably fast. Perhaps too fast."

Tathagres said nothing. Her attention seemed absorbed by the flash of the gold between Emien's fingers. But the thoughts reflected in her amethyst eyes had a hungry quality which left the sorcerer uneasy.

Just past noon on the day following his flight from the sanctuary tower, Jaric rode into the village of Gaire's Main. Both nose and throat were gritty with dust. The insides of his knees were raw from the saddle, and his ankles bruised repeatedly against the stirrups, which dangled too long from his feet. Jaric had not paused to shorten the leathers. Though his flight had taken him through several settlements, he dared not stop, even to water his horse, in any town subject to the Earl's authority.

But Gaire's Main lay outside the borders of Morbrith. The site had once been sacred to the tribes who gathered for the summerfair, but now only the name remained as a reminder of less civilized times. Jaric reined his mount down a lane lined by sleepy cottages, whitewashed and neatly roofed with thatch. The horse stumbled with exhaustion. Lather dripped from the rags used to muffle the bit. The animal's sides heaved, each breath labored, and the low-pitched clink at each stride made Jaric suspect a loose shoe. If he did not find a smith, he risked laming the horse. Travel afoot frightened him more than Morbrith's retribution; with no mount, he would be helpless.

Jaric rounded a crook in the lane. Ahead, a wide crossroad sliced Gaire's Main into quarters; there also lay the spring where the tribes had once held rites. But the traditional ring-stones of slate had been pulled down for shingles. A brick trough replaced them, and the run-off trickled into a chain of muddy puddles presently foraged by tame ducks, and a sow tended by a boy with a stick. They too stared at the strange rider who entered the square.

The horse sensed water and raised its head. Jaric gave it rein. Children rushed out to run beside his stirrup and their excited chatter made his head ring. A woman with a bucket paused in a doorway to point. As the horse plodded tiredly across the square, Jaric felt as though all the folk of Gaire's Main had stopped their work to watch him.

He was too weary to care. The horse splashed through a puddle, scattering fowl. The sow raised herself from her wallow with a grunt, as Jaric dropped the reins and permitted his mount to thrust its muzzle into the trough.

"Why, the rider is barefoot!" exclaimed the pig-boy, and the other children giggled.

Jaric sighed. They seemed enviably carefree. Any other time, he would have been cheered by the laughter of children; but now Anskiere's geas throbbed like a wound in his chest, and he had no inclination to smile. Beyond the spring lay a tall, sprawling structure with a shingled roof. A board hung on chains from the gables. Faded letters identified the building as a tavern, but the sign was unnecessary; Gaire's Main offered little else but peasant cottages. Jaric knew from keeping accounts that the folk traveled to Morbrith for goods. He could not recall whether the village boasted a smith. He would have to inquire.

The horse snorted loudly, and resumed drinking. Summoned by the noise, a weathered man in dusty coveralls emerged from the wing which held the stables. His hair was white and his cheeks sunburned. He braced sinewy arms on the lip of the trough, and regarded Jaric suspiciously.

"Ridden all night, have you?" His voice was rusty, with an

inflection as quaint as the town. "What brings you to Gaire's Main?"

Jaric reddened. A ragged woman shambled out of the stables and joined the old man. Ancient and gnarled as treebark, she peered at Jaric with eyes turned pearly white by cataracts. Assuredly she was blind; yet she stared as though she were sighted. Jaric shivered with apprehension. Resigned to the fact the entire village was listening, he answered in the cultured accents learned at court.

His voice came out hoarse, as though he had forgotten the use of it. "No doubt you think me childish. I wagered my cousin that I could ride fifty leagues in my nightshirt and still defend my honor without weapons. The contest was made in drunken folly. Do you wonder, now I'm sober, that I chose to ride at night?"

Intrigued, the children clustered closer. The ragged woman pinned him with eyes like fish roe, and the man stared pointedly at Jaric's soft hands and blistered knees. He grimaced in contempt.

"Your horse needs a shoe," he said carefully. "Shall I see to it?"

Jaric nodded, his throat too tight for speech. The folk had not believed his lie, but apparently no one present chose to question it. Relieved, he slid from the saddle, but to his dismay, his knees buckled the instant his feet struck ground. The pain of tortured muscles made him gasp.

The beggar woman caught his shoulder with gnarled hands and steadied him. Her grip felt like ice. Jaric flinched, startled by the chill. Through a wave of dizziness, he saw she was wizened and small, and clothed not in rags but in knotted leather skins like the hill tribe's dress. Not every inhabitant of Gaire's Main was civilized; with a jolt, Jaric recognized what he had been too tired to notice earlier: the woman could only be the Lady of the Well. Blinded by ritual as a maiden and dedicated to oracular vision, she would tend the shrine until death, though the place had probably changed much since she was a girl. She smelled of the byre. Nevertheless, she deserved respect. The boy drew breath to offer thanks.

But his words were blurred by a cry as eldritch as the mystery which surrounded the spring. Jaric's spine prickled horribly. Darkness arose in him, and his senses reeled.

"Fire!" said the woman clearly. "I see thee a man, ringed with the living fire. The ravens of discord fly at thy heels."

She added more in the tongue of the clans. But Jaric heard none of her warning. Lost in a rushing tide of faintness, he collapsed, and even his slight weight was too great for the Lady. She staggered against the stable master, who caught the boy in his arms.

Shaken by the upsurge of the old powers, the stablemaster lifted a pale, uncertain face to the blind priestess. For years she had been senile and helpless, little more than a beggarwoman who slept in his hayloft. "What shall I do with this boy?"

The woman blinked, relapsed into the blankness of advanced age. But her reply was lucid. "Do all that is needful for him, as well as his mount. You'll find silver in his saddlebag. Take what fee you earn, and set him on his way. He must not be delayed." She subsided into muttering. The children who had lingered to observe scattered suddenly and ran.

Alone by the spring, the stablemaster left the gelding with its reins trailing. The animal had been ridden to exhaustion; it would not stray while he carried the young master inside to the innkeeper's wife.

Jaric revived, coughing, to the sharp taste of plum brandy. He swallowed, stinging the membranes of his throat, and opened his eyes. A plump middle-aged woman with blowsy hair bent over him. When she touched the flask to his lips for a second draught, he shook his head, momentarily unable to speak.

"What's wrong? Can't you hold a man's drink?" The

woman set the flask on a trestle by her elbow. Out of habit, she wiped damp hands on her skirt, her manner softened by the matronly kindness Jaric's frailty invariably inspired. "You'll stay scrawny, lad, if you don't learn to handle your liquor."

Jaric sighed and wished the advice was true. In the copy-chamber his delicate stature had been no disadvantage. But alone on the road, he was unable to avoid the fact that he was unfit to survive the rigors of his own culture. For the first time, the thought shamed him. He could not meet the woman's eyes.

"Drink the rest if you can," she urged gently. "I'll send my daughter Kencie out with a meal."

She passed through the doorway to the kitchen with the comfortable self-possession accumulated through years of hospitality. Jaric studied his surroundings uneasily. He sat in an armchair built of plain wood which was dwarfed by an immense stone fireplace. No logs burned, but a tallow candle on the table illuminated a beamed ceiling, whitewashed walls, and trestles and benches well-polished with use. Except for a man whittling by the tap, the common room was deserted. For all the notice the elder gave the boy, he might have been deaf.

Presently Kencie appeared with a tray of food. Large-boned, blond and close to Jaric's age, she set her burden on the table, and regarded the boy with curiosity. Startled by her likeness to her mother, Jaric stared back.

"Quit gawking and eat." Kencie rubbed knuckles still damp with dishwater on her apron. Her cheeks dimpled faintly with disdain. "By your looks you need to. Got wrists so thin I'd suspect you'd have trouble lifting a fork."

Jaric plucked a roll from the tray and bit into it, as though to blunt the taste of bitterness. Accustomed as he was to taunts from the women at Morbrith, Kencie's comments cut him; her brisk observation granted no respect, even for a stranger who shared the inn's hospitality. Jaric tasted the stew, and even in Kencie's presence could not keep his hand steady.

Hoping to soften her contempt, he said, "The food is quite good." But exhaustion left him barely able to eat.

Kencie shrugged. "You look half dead. I'll wrap what you can't finish. You can take it in your saddlebag." She wrinkled her nose and smiled. "At least they can't make me polish your boots."

Her banter appeared friendly. But as she swept the floor beneath the trestles, Jaric caught her staring when she thought he would not notice, and once, from the corner of his eye, he saw her raise crossed fists in the sign to avert evil sorcery. Plainly, the wise woman's prophecy had marked him; the townsfolk of Gaire's Main treated him well because they wished to be rid of him. Unhappiness raised a lump in Jaric's throat. How could he possibly manage, without Morbrith's walls and the sanctuary of the library? Kencie's teasing made Anskiere's geas seem bleak and hopeless as exile. Caught by fresh terror, Jaric felt his stomach clench.

He set the spoon aside, afraid he would drop it, afraid Kencie would notice his weakness and laugh anew. Jaric shoved his hands into his lap to hide their trembling. "I can't finish any more," he said desperately.

Kencie propped her broom against the bar. "Come along, then. Mother asked me to show you to the front room."

Jaric stumbled to his feet. "You're very kind."

"No. You're paying." Kencie fetched a candle from her apron pocket and touched the wick to the one already alight on the trestle. "Mother saw you carried only silver. She said she'd charge you half, since the Lady spoke for you. But you can't stay more than a night."

Relieved to discover the Earl's saddlebags had at least contained coins, Jaric limped stiffly toward the stair. The villagers need not have worried. Hounded by the sorcerer's geas, he doubted he could linger in Gaire's Main an hour longer than necessary.

*   *   *

Jaric slept dreamlessly through the afternoon. Fully clothed and dusty from travel, he lay crumpled across the bed exactly as he had fallen when Kencie closed the door to his chamber. He never stirred, even at sundown when the innkeeper's wife brought him hot water to wash. She left the steaming basin on the stand by the window, and quietly departed, convinced the boy would rest until morning. Left to himself, he might have; but the sorcerer whose summons had claimed him seemed to permit no allowance for weakness. Jaric was jabbed out of sleep by restlessness which brought him fully and instantly awake.

The room was dark. Beyond the window, the moon drifted, yellowed as old ivory above the hills. Though a full hour remained before dawn, Jaric could not stay in bed. The geas goaded his muscles into aching knots of tension. His skin tingled as if the very air might scald him if he stayed still any longer.

Jaric rose, groped blindly for candle and striker. He bashed his wrist into the basin. Water slopped over the side, wetting his fingers, but its coolness did nothing to ease the discomfort which increased steadily with each passing minute. Jaric endured only long enough to rinse his face, and bolted for the door.

Movement brought respite. Shivering with relief, Jaric hurried down the corridor. He would have to find his horse quickly and settle his account with the inn before uncertainty and the cruel effects of the geas overwhelmed him.

The common room was deserted. Outside, Kencie leaned over the spring with a yoke and two buckets, drawing water for the kitchen. As the main door to the inn swung open, she glanced up, surprised by the sight of Jaric on the steps.

"Leaving?" She set her burden down and approached him, careful to avoid the puddles which gleamed in dull silver patches on the ground. "You're early. The stablemaster isn't up yet."

Irked that she should regard him as helpless, Jaric said, "I can saddle my own mount."

Kencie shrugged, her face a blurred oval in the predawn mist. "Very well. If you wait, I'll fetch your saddlebags. The rest of your horse's gear is in the tackroom, just beyond the ladder to the loft."

But Jaric could not stay still. The compulsion set upon him would relent for nothing, far less courtesy, and while Kencie retrieved her buckets, the boy hurried on into the stables.

He located the tackroom by touch in the dark; his was the only saddle and bridle on the rack. Aroused by the noise, the Earl's black gelding lifted its head, the blaze on its muzzle visible in the gloom of the aisle beyond. Jaric dragged the tack to the stall, reminded by the damp straw under his soles that his feet were bare. His hands shook with nerves as he caught the horse's halter.

The gelding shied. Leather burned the boy's palms, and the clang of the tether ring startled pigeons from the loft. Driven by necessity Jaric tried the singsong words he had heard in the forges since childhood; yet where his efforts then had failed, this animal responded. Its eye stopped rolling; taut muscles relaxed and the blazed head lowered, nostrils widened in a soft inquisitive snort.

Jaric slipped the bridle over the broad forehead with unpracticed clumsiness, but the horse seemed not to mind. The saddle, with scabbard and sword attached, proved too bulky for the boy to lift above his shoulder. He had to clamber onto the manger just to reach the gelding's back. Kencie returned as he hauled the girths tight and jumped down. Unaware he had stopped trembling, Jaric led the horse from the stall. Kencie buckled the saddlebags in place, covering his silence with a spate of chatter.

"Mother charged you one silver for bed and board. The stablemaster took a half-silver for grain and resetting your horse's shoe. Five and one remain in the purse in the left pocket. I put food in the right, with your cloak." She stepped back to discover Jaric inspecting the near hind hoof of his mount. "Is the shoe set to your satisfaction?"

Jaric released the gelding's fetlock and straightened. "It will pass." His words masked irritation. The work was poorly done. At the tender age of four, the exacting standards of his guardians had been drummed into his head; but without enough muscle to wield the hammer, the boy could do nothing now but regret the stablemaster's ineptness. He caught the bridle and led the horse from the stable, careful not to look back lest his toes get crushed by steel-shod hooves.

The time had come to mount and ride. Kencie hovered uncertainly to one side as the horse splashed through the puddles by the spring. Jaric set his foot in the stirrup while the animal drank.

"Wait," Kencie blurted. She whirled and ran into the tavern.

Jaric paused, and suffered the first tingling warning of the geas for the sake of her request. He braced himself to resist, but Kencie was gone no more than a moment.

She emerged through the entrance to the courtyard, clutching a pair of boots. Fine double-stitched leather was well cut, and trimmed with coral beadwork and fur.

"Here." Kencie pushed the boots into Jaric's arms. "These are yours. Their owner died of fever while lodging at our tavern. Rich clothes don't suit anyone in Gaire's Main. Wager or not, you can't continue to go barefoot."

Jaric reddened, embarrassed by the transparency of his lie, and the vulnerable need behind it. Ashamed before Kencie's generosity, he bent quickly to try on her gift, before she noticed and thought him ungracious.

The boots were ludicrously large. Inches of extra cuff flapped around calves thin as twigs. Jaric bit his lip and stood up. "I'll think of you with thanks at every step." He smiled gravely and granted Kencie the courtesy due Morbrith's court ladies. "May your inn and its patrons prosper well."

He hastened to mount, and the horse sidled, spoiling the grace of his gesture. Kencie caught the bridle, steadied the gelding until Jaric had gained the saddle. As he gathered the reins, she looked up at his face, into sensitive dark eyes, and an expression pathetic with fear.

"You're so small," she said softly, and instantly regretted the words.

Jaric stiffened. Kencie had given the boots because she was sorry for him. Rage tore through him. He had asked for nothing. Anonymity and a scholar's position in a library had contented him perfectly. At a stroke of fate, a sorcerer's geas and a priestess' prophecy had plundered his self-worth, transformed him into an object of pity; now he was dependent upon charity every bit as much as the lame who begged in the gutter.

In taut-lipped silence, he jerked the gelding free of Kencie's hand. With a jab of his heels he sent it thundering out of Gaire's Main on the south road.

Behind him, Kencie rubbed skinned fingers on her apron, sick at heart for the blow she had dealt his pride. Strange, she thought; if not for Jaric's wretched skinniness, she might have admired more than his courage. The hoofbeats faded slowly in the distance. With stoic practicality, Kencie recalled her neglected chores. But as she walked toward the inn, the ancient priestess of the Well shuffled out of the barn and blocked her path.

The woman scratched her belly through a rip in the skins which clothed her, then lifted blind eyes to the lane where Jaric and the horse had vanished only minutes earlier.

"Do ye know?" The hag caught Kencie's sleeve. "The boy won't walk twenty paces in that pair of boots."

The girl's breath caught. She shoved the priestess rudely aside and fled into the kitchen; and not even her mother could coax her to explain why she looked so pale.

*   *   *

The Earl's gelding stretched into a gallop and the rooftops of Gaire's Main soon disappeared behind the curve of the hills. Tilled farmland gave way to thorny scrub and the heat of Jaric's anger ebbed, leaving loneliness. Ahead the road wound through a wide valley, mist-clothed and deserted. Rendered in shades of charcoal under a pearly sky, the land framed him with solitude. Everything he valued lay behind him. The boy shortened rein to slow the gelding's pace, but the animal proved unexpectedly spirited; it flattened its ears and leaned sullenly on the bit. Jaric felt its stride lengthen until mane whipped his wrists and the earth became a blur under its hooves.

The frightened boy cursed and dragged at the reins until his shoulders ached. The animal had already been ridden hard the night he had stolen it. Now, after rest and grain, the gelding was too strong for him; until it had spent its first fresh energy, Jaric could not hope to control it. Weeping tears of frustration, he clung to the mane and prayed the brute would keep to the road.

Distance unwound like clock chain to the rhythm of the horse's gallop. Its hooves struck with a pure and solid ring, raising tiny puffs of dust. The breeze flung mane and tail and Jaric's light hair like a rough caress. Beneath knees that stung with sores, the boy felt the healthy thrust of the shoulder muscles; the animal enjoyed its resilience, and the run through the cool morning became not a threat but a celebration of its own being. Jaric discovered harmony in the beast's simple pleasure; his panic transformed to wild exhilaration. He relaxed his grip on the reins. The horse stretched its neck and went faster.

When the sun's edge sliced above the horizon, Jaric's cheeks were flushed with excitement. He felt more at ease in the saddle than ever before, and as though attuned to the change in its rider, the gelding gradually slowed. With a shake of its head, it dropped to a trot. And struck by disappointment, Jaric lost his nerve.

He pulled the horse down to a walk, happiness marred by the unchanged fact that his body was no match for a spirited mount. The thrill he had tasted now added edge to his misery. With a tearing pang of sorrow, he understood that Morbrith's library could no longer shelter his frailty, or his innocence. For the first time, he felt imprisoned by his physical limitations, and the grief of that recognition branded his soul.

CHAPTER VII

Crossroads

THE ROAD BECAME CROWDED AS the sun rose higher. By mid-morning, Jaric rode through dusty clouds raised by herds of livestock being driven to market. Buffeted by sheep and cows, and forced aside by the fast passage of the post riders, he strove to calm his restive mount. The gelding jigged nervously, ears pricked and neck muscles taut as cable beneath a sheen of sweat. Jaric's back and shoulders ached without letup. Long before noon, the joints in his elbows and wrists developed the shooting pains of stressed tendons. Yet exhausted as he was, the sorcerer's summons granted him no quarter; he must continue, it seemed, until he collapsed.

At length the dirt track from Gaire's Main merged with the stone highway which paralleled the Redwater River to Corlin Town. Here caravans congested the route; the rumble of ox wagons and the ceaseless shouts of drovers made Jaric's head swim. His eyes and nostrils became irritated with grit. The reins skinned his hands to the point where he feared to dismount. Should the horse shy in the tumult, he could never keep hold of the bridle; neither could he reach the food Kencie had packed in his saddlebag. Jaric hunched miserably over the gelding's mane and hoped enough silver remained in the Earl's purse to pay for a bath and a night's lodging in Corlin.

The afternoon wore on. The teamsters joked and grew boisterous in anticipation of the women their pay would buy when they reached the taverns. Encouraged, Jaric glanced ahead. Thin as pen strokes on parchment, the spires of Corlin notched the horizon to the east. Below lay the valley where the barge ferry crossed the Redwater; the road resumed on the other side, shining like ribbon against the dark border of Seitforest. Jaric counted clusters of pack animals and wagons on the near bank. At least four caravans awaited the barge. He wondered whether he could get across before sundown. By night, Corlin's guardsmen closed the gates to protect against the bands of outlaws who plied the trade routes for plunder. Alone and unskilled with arms, Jaric made easy prey for such robbers. Apprehensively, he eased the gelding into a trot.

The gait aggravated his discomfort. Dazed by fatigue, and with his thoughts flickering on the hazy borders of delirium, Jaric failed at first to notice the sting of Anskiere's geas. He crested the hill where the road swung north to meet the ferry, and was suddenly jabbed by an irrational urge to turn down a footpath which branched to the right. He resisted. To abandon the security of a well-traveled route invited disaster. Jaric turned the gelding's head firmly toward the ferry and rammed his heels into its flanks. The horse sprang into a run.

Yet even survival held no sway over the geas which had claimed his destiny. The instant Jaric drew abreast of the footpath, a vortex of force erupted under the gelding's hooves. Wind arose, and a rushing prison of air whirled around horse and rider, forbidding them to pass. The animal scrambled in terror and reared. Blinded by whipping mane, the boy fought to stay astride.

Energy slashed into Jaric's mind. He cried out as the sight

of ferry and road splintered, replaced by a vision of ice cliffs mauled by the endless crash of storm breakers; the air smelled of damp and dune grass, and the sour cries of gulls haunted the sky overhead. Threaded through the melancholy of that place, Jaric sensed the call which summoned him would relent only when he reached that desolate shore; that the blood debt of Ivain had fallen upon his puny shoulders made not the slightest difference. Anskiere's command would stand, whether the boy's suffering brought the wrath of Koridan's Fires, or his life became forfeit. Jaric would go, or be driven haplessly as a leaf in the gales of autumn.

The fabric of the dream parted, leaving Jaric shakily clinging to the saddle. His mount quivered under him, paralyzed with fright. The boy stroked its neck mechanically, while the scent of the sea faded, overlaid by the tang of dust. The turnoff snaked like bleached cord across the meadows which flanked the Redwater, then lost itself in the gloomy fringes of Seitforest. For a rebellious moment Jaric refused to move. A gust fanned in warning through the weeds beneath the gelding's legs. Anskiere's powers never slept. The boy sighed. With beaten resignation, he gathered the reins and pulled the horse's head southeast, away from the ferry and safety. Jaric's face bore the weary stamp of hopelessness, for the geas led him to ruin with all the finality of a calf marked for slaughter.

The horse quieted once the road fell behind. Jaric tried not to look back at the towers of Corlin. Reddened by the lowering sun, the grass tips glistened as if dipped in blood. All too soon the meadowlands ended, and the trail led him into Seitforest.

The slanting rays of sunset dappled the forest with light; Ancient as time, oaks and beeches rose over delicate carpets of ferns. Moss-streaked trunks rose up on either side, massive as the pillars of a king's hall, and the backlit foliage between glowed like lanterns at summerfair. Yet Jaric rode numbed with dread. For all of its bewitching magnificence, Seitforest was renowned as the domain of the lawless; none but the desperate rode its twisted trails without torches and an army of stout retainers. The vast wood seemed to swallow Jaric's presence, and even his horse's hoofbeats were deadened by musty drifts of leaf mold.

In the rosy pallor of the afterglow, a forester clad in dyed leather stepped from a thicket. Ebony hair streaked with white tumbled over the fellow's shoulders. A full game bag hung at his hip, and the bird snares which dangled from his belt swung gently as he paused to stare at the boy on the horse.

"Boy," the forester called softly. "You'd best turn back. Camp beside the ferry, if you'll take a stranger's advice. If you must travel this way, at least wait until you can join someone with a company of men-at-arms. Those who ride alone fare badly hereabouts."

Jaric made no effort to reply. Tortured by the memory of Kencie's pity, he chose not to pause and explain his plight. As he passed, the forester shrugged and ducked back into the undergrowth. Jaric gripped the reins tightly and restrained an urge to call him back.

The trail wound deeper into the wood. Shadows lengthened, until the evening star pricked like a fairy jewel through the leaves. Jaric traversed a chain of open glades, each more serene than the last. But all of nature's loveliness failed to ease the boy's unrest. In the gloom of twilight, the lawless of Seitforest overtook him.

Warned by a furtive rustle in the foliage, he reached for the Earl's sword. The weapon was heavy. Jaric needed both hands to lift it. Even before the blade cleared the scabbard, a man leapt from the brush, gauntleted hands stretched to seize the bridle. The gelding shied and smashed sideways through a clump of bracken. Tossed against the animal's neck, Jaric tugged the sword free. He slammed his heels into the horse in a desperate attempt to ride his attacker down. The man shouted angrily and dodged aside.

The gelding plunged on across the clearing, its reins flying loose. Over the sharpened edge of the sword, Jaric saw more outlaws run from the trees. Several carried clubs. They blocked his escape. Alarmed by their rush, the horse swerved. Its iron-shod hooves slashed through a stand of saplings. Branches whipped, clattering across the swordblade. Jaric fought to keep his seat. Suddenly the bridle snagged on a dead bough. Jerked short, the gelding staggered onto its haunches. Jaric heard a grunt of human exertion. Tough fingers grabbed his collar. He swung the sword. Steel clashed with the metal-bossed wood of a club. The shock stung Jaric to the shoulders and broke his grip.

The blade fell, slithered through undergrowth, and stabbed deeply into the earth. The outlaw yanked the boy from the saddle. Jaric tumbled, his cheek raked cruelly by the rings sewn on his assailant's jerkin. He landed with a thump in the bracken. Torn fronds framed a glimpse of a scarred face, and the rising silhouette of a club.

"No! Please! Have mercy!" Jaric raised his forearm to ward off the blow. Fenced by the rapid, trampling thud of hooves, he heard laughter. The club descended and struck. Bones snapped like sticks. Jaric screamed in agony. With a savage whistle of air, the club fell again. Jaric rolled, and caught a glancing blow on the head. His skull seemed to explode into fire, and he fell into darkness.

The moon shone high overhead when the forester reached the clearing to check the last of his snares. He paused, warned by the stillness that something was amiss. Where night-thrushes normally flourished, he heard only crickets, and by the path fronds of bracken dangled, crushed and torn on their stems. Attuned more deeply to the wood than his fellow men, the forester stooped and studied the ground. There he uncovered a tale of violence; soft moss had been gouged by the hooves of a frightened horse. The predator too left his mark;

the forester traced the heelprint of a man's boot. Touched by a deep anger, his fingers clenched into a fist. Hurriedly, he followed the tracks down a swath of lacerated vegetation, and there found the robber's prey. A boy sprawled face down on a bed of leaves, his naked limbs veined like marble with blood.

Very likely the child was dead. Such tragedies were common in Seitforest. The forester sighed, grieved such brutality had overcome one so small and helpless.

"I warned you, didn't I, lad?" the man said aloud, and around him the crickets fell silent.

But when he touched him, he discovered the child was alive, and several years older than he had first assumed. Gently, the forester explored the boy's injuries. One arm was cleanly broken; a dark congested swelling and a gash remained from a severe blow to the head. The wound would require a poultice. The forester draped the boy with his cloak of marten skins, and cursing the folly of youth, drew his knife and cut a straight sapling for splints. If this boy recovered, he swore by Kor's fires to teach him how to defend himself.

Fine curtains of mist and rain turned the night into ink. Water beaded on the pinnace's seats, and the sails flopped, disturbed by the swell, and teased by uncertain wind. Drenched after five hours at the helm, Emien drew a deep breath. The warm earthy scent he had noticed a moment ago was now unmistakable. Seventeen days had passed since Tathagres appointed him command of the pinnace, and after a second gale and two spells of calm, an unknown islet lay ahead.

The wind veered south. Emien adjusted course, and the mainsheet slapped with a rattle of blocks. Landfall could hardly have occurred at a worse time, he thought sourly. Since the weather had closed in, the watches sailed on compass heading, visibility reduced to a few yards; no stars had shone for several days. By dead reckoning, Emien calculated the Isles of Innishari must be nine leagues distant. But swift currents might have set the boat off course, and here, where archipelagoes strung like beads across the Corine Sea and submerged reefs frequently clawed the waters into combers, an exact position was a necessity.

The breeze slackened. Again Emien caught the cloying smell of vegetation and sand. The shoreline was dangerously near. In the darkness he could see nothing, not even the white ruffles of foam spread by the bow wave; an attempt to beach the pinnace might well spill them all onto the razor fangs of a coral head. Presently, over the squeal of tackle, Emien heard the thunder of the surf off the bowsprit.

Gooseflesh prickled his arms. He might have left his decision too late. The pinnace was almost on top of the island. Emien bit his lip, agonized by responsibility. Drained by exposure, the sailors would rouse too slowly if left to themselves. No leeway remained for mistakes; and Emien knew he could never endure Tathagres' scorn should he fail to bring the pinnace in safely.

He undid the knotted cord which bound his breeches to his waist, then brought it whistling down on the nearest seaman's back. "All hands awake! Second watch, man the oars!"

The pinnace's occupants surged into action. Emien caught the man he had struck, shoved him into the sternsheet. "Take the helm, you, and head up. Into the wind and hold her there."

While the boat swung, Emien pushed his way forward, shouting instructions to shorten sail.

"Boy!" Tathagres called imperiously out of the dark. "What's amiss?"

Emien answered curtly. "Land. Much too close, and on a bad heading. We drop anchor, or risk our lives. The pinnace can't beach on a strange shore at night with safety."

The crash of breakers was unmistakable. Now even an inexperienced ear could detect the suck and boom of undertow dragging over rock. As he bent over the lashing which secured the anchor, Emien felt the bow lift, tossed as the swell rolled over the shoals and peaked into knife-edged crests which immediately preceded a breaking wave.

The boy shouted, frantic with recognition. "Out oars!" They had only seconds left. His blisters tore as he jerked the knots. The cord gave with a slither. "Row! Get lively, you bastards! Row! Or by Kor we'll swim!"

Emien knelt, clutching anchor chain in both hands as the oars rumbled out and bit raggedly into the sea. The pinnace jerked, shoved by the forces of loom and wave. Emien shouted an order. The oarsmen swung the pinnace starboard. A crest slapped her thwart as she turned, and a fringe of spray shot over the gunwale. The craft lay perilously close to broaching.

Yet Emien held steady. Fevered as he was, he made himself wait. On a bottom of rock or coral, the anchor would not hold unless he allowed plenty of scope. This close, the pinnace would be aground by the time the line came taut; breakers would smash her planking in seconds. But patience became torment, with the taint of earth thick on the breeze. Emien gripped the chain. Rusted links bit into his hands as the oarsmen steadied, synchronized, and the squeal of leathers against the rowlocks blended into rhythmic stroke. The pinnace made tortuous headway. Emien listened intently over the slap of the halyards and loosened canvas. The mutter of surf fell slowly astern. Now his judgment was critical; if the anchor did not grab on the first try, the oarsmen must have stamina remaining to pull the pinnace clear once again.

Emien gritted his teeth. The men were worn, sun-blistered, and starved. Exhaustion would overtake them swiftly, and the over-laden pinnace could easily become unmanageable. With a whisper of appeal to the spirits of the deep, he let the anchor go. Chain clanked, dissonant as death bells. Emien strung the line through his hands though it burned him, counting the knots which slipped across his palms. Two fathoms, three, four; at five the rope slackened. The anchor struck bottom.

"Reverse stroke!" Emien payed out more line, made swift

allowance for the depth, current, and consistency of the bottom, then made the rope fast to a cleat. Stressed plies moaned taut as the pinnace swung, pulled short on her tether. Yet Emien knew better than to count the danger past; whether the hook would hold without dragging would be close to impossible to determine with no visible landmark.

Wearily Emien ordered the oars run in. He dismissed the helmsman and the sail crew and permitted the remaining hands to rest at their benches. Then he seated himself beside the lashed bar of the tiller to stand anchor watch. Through the long hours before dawn, he waited in the misty dark, listening to the waves, tuned to the texture of the swell which jostled the hull. Sound and sensation alone would warn whether the pinnace drifted into the shoals which lay only yards from her rudder.

The rain stopped. By sunrise the mist lifted, streaming scarves of rose and gold across skies like mother of pearl. Curled against the stern, Emien hugged his cloak close to his body. A chill prickled the length of his back as daylight brightened, revealing the contours of the land mass so narrowly evaded during the night. The island rose from the sea like a behemoth, ribbed with cliffs and terraced ledges and shadowed by crags which seemed to comb the roof of heaven. Waterfalls unreeled down rocks flecked like ice with flocks of perched gulls. Below, where crescent beaches met the incoming tide, all image of serenity was spoiled. The sea between pinnace and shoreline was slashed into spray by the jagged knuckles of a reef. Emien rummaged in the stern locker for a ship's glass. He surveyed the boiling rush of breakers, horrified to discover how closely the pinnace had skirted disaster in the dark. Carefully as he searched, he saw no safe route to land.

He turned and studied the seaward horizon with the glass. The mist had dispersed, leaving the humped blue outlines of several surrounding islands visible to the southwest. Emien checked his charts, snapped the glass closed, and rose to consult Tathagres.

He found her propped against the mainmast. Her hair was snarled from water and wind, and beneath the tattered shoulders of her blouse the fine skin he had once admired was sunblistered and cracked. Even closed, her eyes were hollowed with dark circles of exhaustion. Emien hesitated, reluctant to rouse her. A moment later he was grateful for his temerity.

Tathagres spoke without moving. "Boy? If you have something to tell me, speak."

Emien flinched, too startled to note her derisive tone. "Lady, we are anchored off the northeast shore of Skane's Edge. Innishari lies seventeen leagues due north, against an unfavorable wind."

Tathagres' lids flicked open, violet eyes narrowed with annoyance. She said nothing, but her silence struck the boy like a breath of cold.

Emien stiffened, knuckles balanced against the brass bands of the ship's glass. No longer the simple fisherman's boy who had left Imrill Kand, he did not tremble, nor did his uncertainty show. "Lady, I would not trouble you without reason. The casks are empty. Badly as the crewmen need water, I hesitate to consider a landing here. If you would step aft, you'll see the risks."

He offered his hand and helped her rise. Weather and starvation had not robbed Tathagres of grace. She moved like a panther, the slender lines of muscle and bone accentuated all the more by her leanness. Embarrassed to discover he could not repress a thrill of desire, Emien let her go ahead. The deckhands also followed her with eyes like hungry dogs. The boy felt a hot stab of jealousy. That moment, he wished Tathagres would command him to sail to Innishari with the casks still empty. Let the sailors row until they shriveled in the heat, Emien thought, unaware that a scant week past he would never have dared to regard his mistress possessively.

Tathagres paused in the stern, a hand posed on the backstay for balance. She regarded the shores of Skane's Edge with a strange and ruthless intensity. Emien chose a place at her side. Absorbed by the tumble of waves over the reefs, he soon forgot his quarrel with the deckhands. The breeze had freshened out of the north, and sunlight jeweled the spume like sequined lace. Yet to a sailor such beauty clothed murderous hazard; between wind and rocks, no safe landing was possible on this beach. Emien knew he had no choice but to sail on and seek a more favorable harbor. The weight of that conclusion oppressed him. That the oarsmen must suffer fresh hardship now filled him with revulsion; the risk of losing even a single life became not sacrifice but intolerable waste.

Disturbed by his conscience, Emien stared at his hands as if the cracked and blistered skin held answer to the dilemma of command. "Lady," he began. Tathagres turned her face toward him, and he looked up, at first unable to believe what he saw.

His mistress wore an expression of joy. Her eyes glittered with a challenge fiercer than any lust. "You will land the pinnace at once," she said firmly.

Emien's jaw dropped. Fear choked the breath in his throat.

"You heard." Tathagres leaned close and spoke directly into his ear. Though she wore no scent, her proximity unnerved him. "Are you fit to command, or do you yield your will like a nursemaid for the lives of the scum who serve you?"

Emien's jaw clenched. Tathagres mocked him; after Anskiere's storm, she viewed his handling of the pinnace as nothing more than sport to amuse her. Now, like a cat grown bored with teasing a mouse, she sought to slaughter the pride he had gained at the cost of his own sister's life. The jest, at such a price, was too bitter to contemplate.

Emien drew breath, heated by deadly anger. "Lady," he said tersely, "you shall have your landing." And consumed by bitterness which admitted neither regret nor compassion, he yanked the knotted cord from his waist. He strode forward, oblivious to the fact another observed his actions even more keenly than his mistress.

Hunched like a great scavenger bird in the bow, Hearvin sat with his hood thrown back, bald head exposed to the sky. In stiff-lipped silence, he watched Emien drive the sailhands to the benches with the lash. Wind eddied the sound, lending the crack of the cord across flesh an unreal quality, distant and dreamlike as the spool pictures the sorcerer had viewed long ago during Koridan's Grand Ceremony at Landfast. To compel the deckhands' obedience, the boy inspired them to fear him more than death by drowning; the result was disturbingly brutal. Hearvin watched with stony eyes, until Tathagres arrived and perched herself at his side, her cheeks flushed with unnatural exuberance.

"You set that boy up to fail," the sorcerer accused drily.

By the mast, Emien cuffed a recalcitrant oarsman. Wind tossed his black hair like a horse's mane, baring wild eyes and contorted lips. He had channeled his frustrated tangle of passions into violence, and the effect was successful. With curses and wild anger, the boy bullied the crew into submission. Tathagres noted their subservience with satisfaction.

"Why?" said Hearvin softly. "No amount of cruelty will keep this craft clear of the reef. That boy has given you loyalty already. What will you gain by breaking him?"

Delicately Tathagres peeled a torn thumbnail with her teeth. "If he fails me now, won't he extend himself to greater lengths to regain my favor?" She smiled, dropped her hand and suddenly sobered. "His loyalty is not enough. For the purpose I have in mind I need his soul as well. Then I will have the weapon to bring Anskiere to his knees."

If Hearvin replied, his words were buried by the rumble as the men threaded oars onto the rowlocks.

Emien barely waited until the action was complete. "Stroke!" He slashed the nearest back for emphasis, then raced to the bow. Hearvin moved aside as the boy uncleated the anchor line. Close up, the boy reeked of sweat, and his skin radiated a feverish heat. The line whipped free. Emien hauled, adding his weight to the efforts of the oarsmen. The pinnace eased ahead. Chain clanked and the anchor splashed clear of the sea. Emien bent to secure it, shouting orders over his shoulder. The starboard oarsmen reversed stroke. The pinnace swung. Her bowsprit dipped, gracefully as a maid's curtsy, and pointed toward the forbidding shores of Skane's Edge.

"Forward, stroke!" Emien dashed aft and ripped the tiller loose. Braced against the plunging deck, he dragged the helm, brought the bow around to the place he had selected. Ahead the water rushed in a dark, angry vee, fenced by gateposts of rock. Emien would have to steer the pinnace through the gap like a raft on rapids. He grimaced, aware of the difficulties. The men must row faster than the current or he would lose steerage; too fast, and the craft would plunge her bow into a trough and pitchpole. The rocks rushed closer. Waves peaked, crashed, and creamed white off the bow as the pinnace closed with the reef. Surf bashed the keel. Vibrations stung Emien's hands as the rudder slammed against the pins. The sounds of human struggle became obliterated by the thunder of the foam. Drenched by spray, Emien flung hair from his face and wrestled the tiller straight. The gap yawned like jaws off the bow.

"Ship oars!" His shout sounded plaintive as a lost child's. Somehow the men heard.

A wave crashed to port. The pinnace yawed. Emien hauled on the helm. Though the muscles of his shoulders and arms burned with strain, he dragged the pinnace straight. Through salt-splashed eyes, he saw a seaman fumble an oar.

Emien shouted, too late. Rock already loomed above them, a buttress of barnacle-studded granite. The oar struck. Jarred against the rowlock, it smashed the man's ribcage. His scream sawed through the hiss of the foam. The pinnace slewed sideways and punched into the stone. Planking slivered; the gunwale burst with an agonizing crack. Emien dropped the helm.

He leapt over the benches, caught Tathagres just as a comber burst like an avalanche over the thwart. Water bashed them overboard. In the last frantic instant before the sea swept Emien under, he clamped his hand in Tathagres' shirt. Then he was tumbled downward. Dark angry waters closed above his head.

Emien struggled to swim. Tossed over and over, he kicked and tried to break free of the current's icy grip. Although Tathagres' thrashing hampered him, he clung tightly to her clothing. He had failed to save Taen; now, with the pinnace wrecked and everything lost except his sworn oath of loyalty, the boy was determined to see his mistress safely ashore.

Water swirled, plunging him deeper. Pressure crackled his eardrums, and his lungs ached. Emien fought, driven by desperate need for air. Suddenly his shoulder scuffed packed sand. The bottom was shoaling. Relieved to find the current had swept him toward land, the boy pushed away the kelp which twined about his body. He caught Tathagres' hair. She had stopped struggling; fearful she might have lost consciousness, Emien twisted, dug his feet into the sea bottom, and shoved off for the surface.

Something sharp grazed his wrist. Stung by unexpected pain, Emien let go. Without warning, Tathagres yanked at the hand still twined in her shirt, forced the boy to release her. Emien broke water, dizzied and starved for air. Foam-webbed water slapped his cheek. In the second before the next wave rolled him under, he glimpsed a reddened gash in the muscle of his lower arm. The wound itself was unmistakable; *Tathagres had knifed him to free herself.*

Stunned, Emien mistimed his stroke. The breaker which bore him shoreward surged, lifted, and broke. Current pummeled his flesh, dragging him like a rag doll across the shapened edges of coral. Clothing and skin tore from his body. Choking, bleeding, and bruised beyond rational thought, Emien sensed the turbulence shift; the wave was ebbing. He flung his good hand down, instinctively sought the bottom. His fingers scrabbled through weed and loose shells, then caught on a rock. He clung until the greedy suck of the undertow relented.

Emien released and kicked hard. His head broke water. He managed a quick breath before the crash of the next comber overtook him. Tossed like a chip in a maelstrom, he was flung head over heels. This time, his knee struck bottom before the wave receded. He stroked with his arms, dragged himself forward, and managed at last to gain the shallows. Around him, the water thinned into a lacy sheet, and slid seaward with a throaty chuckle of sound. Emien crawled, gasping, and collapsed on the damp sand of Skane's Edge. His throat stung. Blood traced patterns across cheek, shoulder, and arm. The flash of wet shells and mica stabbed into his eyes. He closed his lids. Left faint by the sweet rush of air into his lungs, he lay prone, and the boom of the surf masked the sound of footsteps.

He did not notice Tathagres' presence until he opened his eyes. She leaned over him, hair coiled like sodden silk around her collar. Her tunic dripped in his face as she fingered the ornamental dagger Emien had often noticed in the sheath at her belt. Her face seemed neutral.

But when she spoke, her words were edged with anger. "Boy, I will warn you no more after this. No matter what the circumstances, you will never again lay hands upon me without my express command. Should you repeat your late indiscretion, you will suffer far more than a cut as a penalty. *Am I clear?*"

Emien coughed, sickened by the taste of blood on his lips. His arm throbbed, and every inch of abraded skin stung with the fury of the lash. Yet his physical hurts were slight compared with the deeper wound in his spirit. Sprawled where he had fallen on the sand, he voiced an apology. As Tathagres turned on her heel and left, tears mingled with the brine on his face. Once, as a child, he had accidentally fouled a fishnet; his father went over the side to correct the mistake, became tangled, and drowned. Then, Emien had been too small to understand what was happening. Now old enough to act responsibly toward those he loved, he had first failed his sister, then suffered a rejection no reason could console. Motionless on the beach of Skane's Edge, Emien wept for the last time in his life. Henceforth his tears would flow from the eyes of others, he resolved; and the overly sensitive emotions which had always made him vulnerable hardened into a knot of aggressive self-interest never to be released.

The sorcerer Hearvin viewed the scene from an outcrop above the shore, drenched robes flapping in the breeze. His eyes narrowed into slits against the glare as he regarded the boy from Imrill Kand.

"You've misjudged," he said softly, and though Tathagres was not present, she heard. "I fear this time you've scarred the boy too deeply. Who will pay the price?"

Hearvin waited, but Tathagres sent no answer. And because he also was chilled and weary from the sea, he was careless and did not pursue the matter further.

CHAPTER VIII

Skane's Edge

OF THE SEVEN SAILHANDS WHO manned the pinnace from the foundering of the galleass *Crow* only four reached the beaches of Skane's Edge alive. Followed by Hearvin and Tathagres, the survivors chose a dell beside a pool of deep, clear water, refreshed themselves, then slept off the exhaustion of their ordeal.

Emien did not join them. Instead he sought a place farther downstream where willows overhung banks edged by spear-straight ranks of cattails. The brook ran shallow and clean over a bed of rounded stones. Emien knelt and drank deeply. He found the water sweeter than the brackish wells he had known on Imrill Kand, but the improvement brought him no pleasure. Surrounded by the mournful trill of marsh thrushes, he bathed without hurry, rinsed the salt crust from his hair and clothes, and bound his cut forearm with strips torn from his shirt. He was bone tired. His eyes stung with sleeplessness, yet he felt no inclination to rest. Tathagres' hostility had disrupted his confidence, confused his thoughts till they circled in his mind like a pack of dogs balked by conflicting scents. Emien possessed no understanding, only bitterness, and he longed for the harsh life of Imrill Kand intensely. But Taen's death forever barred his return.

Troubled by cherished memories of the beaches where he had scavenged shells as a child, Emien twisted the last strip of bandage into place and tightened the knot with his teeth. The cut beneath was not deep, yet it stung without surcease. A ragged line of blood quickly soaked three layers of linen. The color reminded Emien of the marks his lash had left on the backs of the sailors. On Imrill Kand, brutality of any kind had revolted him; yet the unpleasantness had barely crossed his mind aboard the pinnace. Even now he felt no regret. He had struck the seamen not to punish but to ensure the unquestioning obedience necessary for efficient seamanship.

Inwardly aching, Emien leaned back against the trunk of the nearest willow. The thrushes over his head hopped to higher branches, nervously silent, while he rubbed at his bandaged arm. Emien could not have guessed Tathagres would swim the dangerous shores of Skane's Edge with such ease. Absorbed by his command, he had done nothing but overlook her self-confidence. That was no transgression. His desire to protect her had been right, justifiably human, as her reaction had not been.

A jay scolded on the far bank. Lost in contemplation, Emien traced a finger over his wound. Tathagres had intended no lasting harm; the gash was shallow, running parallel to the muscle fibre, where it would least impair movement. She had *said* she gave him warning, exactly as he had used his lash for laggardliness; *but his sailors were not lazy.* Emien stiffened, chilled by sudden revelation. What if, *like him*, Tathagres had cut to shape him for her own purpose?

Emien drove explosively to his feet. The marsh thrushes startled into flight and vanished with a whir of brown feathers. The stream sounded louder in their absence; yet Emien heard

only the recollection of Anskiere's words the last time he had
seen Taen alive.

"The waters of the world are deep. Chart your course with
care, Marl's son." The Stormwarden had spoken confidently,
as if he already knew how roughly the boy he addressed might
be used. The advice galled for its patronizing smugness. Emien
knew fierce rage. He kicked a stone in a short hard arc toward
the stream. It struck shallows with a splash, and fish fled like
shadows for cover. But the boy saw only the face of the sorcerer
who had angered him. The willows trailed closely about his
shoulders, hedging him like the meshes of a destiny he did not
want. Near to panic, Emien spun on his heel and crashed
through the brush to the beach.

Bathed in afternoon light, the cove was a snowy crescent
flecked with the chipped crystal glitter of shells. Soothed by
the open sea, Emien could almost forget the painful snarl his
life had become. He walked along the tidemark and searched
for the smooth fist-sized stones he preferred for hunting rabbits. The meadows of Skane's Edge were uncommonly lush.
From the size of the droppings in the grass, the boy guessed the
animals were plentiful and plump; easy prey if he chose good
cover. And on Imrill Kand, stalking rabbits with throwing
stones had been his favorite escape from chores which he now
understood were the thankless inheritance of poverty. He had
been right to leave; he only needed space to regroup shattered
dreams.

Tathagres had taught him to question the oath of loyalty
sworn on *Crow*'s decks. On Skane's Edge the boy might be subject to her will; but the Free Isles numbered more than the
souls of Imrill Kand, and the empire beyond was vast. Emien
resolved to learn from his mistress's methods, then strike off on
his own. With or without her, he would exact the price of his
sister's death from Anskiere.

Emien bent and scooped a speckled stone from the sand.
He tossed it from hand to hand, testing its balance and weigh-

ing choices. His oath did not set limits on ambition. Nothing prevented him from playing Tathagres' plots for his own stakes. Emien slipped the stone in his pocket and presently forgot he had ever missed the village of his birth.

The cliffs of Skane's Edge gleamed like hammered bronze in the afterglow of sunset and lengthened shadows tangled beneath the boughs in the wood where Emien ran. He stumbled across a gully. Pebbles scattered beneath his feet, fell soundlessly into moss. The boy recovered his balance, then hurried on, anxious to locate Tathagres before dark. He had lingered in the hills far later than he had intended, but the time was not spent fruitlessly; two rabbits dangled from his belt, each killed by flawless aim. Emien fingered the single stone left in his pocket, regretful the daylight had faded too soon to make use of it. Two coneys would hardly feed seven people; but even these were scant use if he failed to reach the lowlands before night hid the landmarks.

Twilight deepened over the forest. Accustomed to ocean and the open tors of Imrill Kand, Emien felt uncomfortably hemmed in. Silver beeches leaned on either side, roots knuckled like miser's fists in rotted mats of leaves. Twigs clawed his clothing and foliage smothered the sky. No star shone through to guide the boy and the light had all but failed. With an unpleasant chill, Emien realized he might be forced to spend the night alone in the wilds. Even Tathagres' haughty company seemed preferable.

But presently a gleam of firelight twinkled through the branches ahead. The rabbits bumped limply against Emien's legs as he increased pace. His shirtsleeve snagged on a thorn, but the boy plunged on, drawn by the familiar smell of woodsmoke and comforted by thoughts of fresh meat.

Yet as Emien neared the campsite, he noticed the crickets seemed eerily silent. Over the limpid spill of the stream, he heard Tathagres' voice raised in anger. Cautious of her temper, the boy crouched in the bush to listen.

Tathagres spoke, and the tone of her voice made his skin prickle. "Your sovereign appointed you to my service. You'll go where I command. Fool. Did you think I would return to Kisburn empty-handed?"

Her rebuke was directed toward Hearvin. Certain the sorcerer's secretive silences boded ill for Tathagres, the boy crept closer. He hid behind a thicket and peered anxiously through the leaves. Hearvin stood with his back turned, a hooded silhouette against the firelight. Though his reply to Tathagres held no emotion, Emien sensed threat underlying, subtle and low as a scraped harpstring. Already the exchange had evolved well beyond the simple quarrel he had overheard on the pinnace.

"But the King did not send me." Hearvin's sleeve flapped about his bony wrist as he gestured conversationally. "His Grace of Kisburn granted you the service of both his grand conjurers, and in ignorance you lost them their lives. One was my apprentice. He was a slow learner, true enough, but he died meanly, for greed. What can you answer for him?"

Tathagres advanced, taut as a stalking leopard. Gold gleamed at her throat. "*I* lost their lives? For a lackey that's a presumptuous accusation! Kisburn wishes the frostwargs loosed. I desire the Keys to Elrinfaer. Tell me, what is *your* interest? Or do you claim no ambition other than charity? I don't believe you have no alliance at all with the King."

Hearvin did not trouble himself with a denial. His manner seemed unruffled, yet Emien suspected that fury burned like acid beneath his placid exterior.

"I came because of Tierl Enneth," the sorcerer said unexpectedly. This time his voice showed an edge.

Tathagres interrupted. "I'm amused. Do be more explicit."

"That's unnecessary." Hearvin moved. Emien flinched, braced for violence, but the sorcerer only clasped his hands behind his back. "Why belabor the obvious? I've seen enough. You wish the source of Anskiere's power for your own twisted passions. The King's will was simple convenience, and his resources your playthings. From the start, you were unfit to command any of the lives placed at your disposal. I swore no oath to Kisburn. But for reasons of my own I see fit to protect the royal reputation. You shall not return to Cliffhaven. The Kielmark will be subdued by other means, and I forbid you the Keys to Elrinfaer." He lowered his voice, until Emien had to strain to hear. "Seek elsewhere, Merya. I have tested your mettle and found it wanting."

The name made Tathagres pause. The flush drained from her cheeks, and her eyes widened, startled. But the gap in her poise lasted only a second. The viperish look she bestowed on Hearvin sent chills down Emien's spine. She would never accept the sorcerer's authority, he observed. And threatened, suddenly, by the fact that his own fate was entangled with hers, the boy dug in his pocket and closed his fingers over the cool rounded surface of his last throwing stone.

"You speak quite nicely," said Tathagres to Hearvin. "Tell me, can you act?"

She baited him, Emien saw. But the sorcerer also knew guile. He pushed the black cloth of his hood back over his shoulders, and his crown gleamed in the firelight, lending him an air of elderly vulnerability.

"Be warned, woman. I will challenge. If that happens, you'll be sorry for it."

Tathagres sobered instantly. "You meddle. Were you trained by the Vaere? If not, your threats are wasted. I shall return to Cliffhaven. Prevent me at your peril."

Hearvin bowed his head, his stance gone strangely rigid. "You will be stopped."

White light flared at the sorcerer's feet. Emien cringed, fearful of the spell. On Imrill Kand, Anskiere had always known when others watched his work covertly. But Hearvin remained oblivious and Tathagres seemed absorbed, intent as a hawk covering prey. She lifted her hands, touched the golden torque at her throat.

"I regret this," she said. But nothing of remorse showed in her expression. "You might have worked with me and been rewarded." She tilted her chin, then spoke a word to focus her defenses. Sparks crackled across her flexed wrists and caught like frost in her hair.

Hearvin waited, motionless. From hiding in the thicket, Emien saw a second spell flicker to life between the sorcerer's fingers, this one harsh and red, a needle-sharp geometric of light. Since Hearvin's hands stayed clenched behind his back, Tathagres was unaware of any additional threat. Emien dared not warn her; Hearvin would count the boy's life cheaply in this contest of wills. Miserably afraid, the boy huddled deeper into the thicket. He could not so much as call out, even for his mistress' sake.

Tathagres lifted her hands from the neckband and a golden haze of illumination quivered in the air above her palms. Poised like a quartz figurine, she pitched the energy at the sorcerer who opposed her.

Light met light with a tortured shriek of sound. Blinded by the flash, Emien buried his face in his hands. The night air shivered with the harmonics, as if tempered steel struck glass which would not shatter. Over the din, Emien heard Tathagres' shout of surprise. He forced himself to look. Through a glare of unbearable brilliance, he saw Hearvin had loosed his second spell; Tathagres struggled like a fly in a web of shimmering strands. She reached for her necklace. But Hearvin riposted with a curt gesture of his hand. The spell snapped into a spindle, symmetrically scribed as a crystal's matrix. Trapped, Tathagres renewed her attack. The energy she summoned backlashed, and an agonized scream escaped her throat. Emien panicked.

Ruled by terror, he ripped the stone from his pocket and flung it at the sorcerer.

His throw struck true. Hearvin swayed and slowly crumpled, blood on his temple. The spell which imprisoned Tathagres unraveled into smoke. But Emien saw nothing. Sorcery clove his awareness, sudden and bright as lightning, and he pitched downward into deepest unconsciousness.

Emien wakened gradually, his mouth foul with the acrid taste of ash. Water dripped down his neck, and someone shook his shoulder urgently.

"Emien?"

Gentle fingers traced his cheek. The boy stirred, fuzzily aware Tathagres leaned over him, her hands still damp from the stream.

"Emien?"

Her tone of voice might have moved the boy to joy under other circumstances. But with his head aching and his senses confused with dizziness, just opening his eyes was an effort. Speech became more than he could manage.

"Boy, you did well," Tathagres said, her manner more kindly than ever he might have imagined. "Had you not struck Hearvin, I could not have won free so easily."

Emien blinked. Briefly he wondered whether she could have escaped the red spell at all without help. Memory returned with the precise clarity of an etching; Emien recalled the conflict, the stone, and blood on Hearvin's face. In his mind he felt the soft limp fur of the rabbits when he recovered them, still warm, from the grass. Yet this time his prey had been human; revulsion tore through him. He battled a sudden urge to be sick.

Tathagres held him, her touch gentle against his brow. As if she understood his distress, she spoke again, concern in her violet eyes. "You did right, Emien. By your oath of service you had no other choice." Her fingers lingered on his cheek. "You shall accompany me to Cliffhaven. After we deal with Anskiere, we will return to Kisburn. My liege will be told of your courage in defending me. He is no mean King. You shall be well rewarded."

Distressed by the warmth of her praise and unable to escape the sting of his conscience, Emien tensed under her hands. Raised in bitter hardship, he had been taught to treasure life. Appalled to discover how easily he had struck a man with intent to harm, he searched the delicate planes of Tathagres' face with his eyes. She held his gaze. Emien studied her amethyst eyes, all shadows and depth, and complex as weather to fathom. *How alike we are*, he realized, and shrank at the thought. He drew an aching breath. Speech came at last, with difficulty.

"Hearvin," he whispered. "What happened?"

"He is dead." Tathagres shifted, settled herself in the leaves at Emien's side. Her fine hands went loose in her lap. "You killed him cleanly. Kor's Divine Fires, how fortunate you chose a rock! Had you thrown a knife, or any other object crafted as a weapon, the defense ward which grazed you would certainly have taken your life. But a stone could not be traced except by direction. Hearvin was caught off guard. He died instantly."

Emien turned aside, rejecting her approval. Though Tathagres intended comfort, her words wrought only remorse. He had killed. Neither logic nor circumstances would alter the wretched truth; the act was beyond pardon. The details revolted him. The boy gasped, desperately needing to weep. But no tears flowed, and a spasm of nausea wracked him.

Tathagres caught his shoulders firmly. Emien felt the warmth of sorcery in her touch. His retching eased, then stilled, and a queer dreamlike peace flowed over his jangled nerves. Yet not even drowsiness could blunt his need to acknowledge the consequence of his deed. In a voice gone dry and bleak, he said, "That was murder." The word ached in his throat.

Tathagres bent close and sighed. White hair brushed his

face, while her eyes gazed down, lovely as jewels, and for once clear of intrigue. "By the Alliance's charter, yes, you committed murder. But you serve me, Emien. I am subject to none but the King. By Crown Law, Hearvin was a traitor. You shall never come to trial, I swear it. And the sailors will never talk. They shall be sold to the galleys and we will use the silver to buy passage to Cliffhaven." She paused and traced Emien's brow with her fingertips. Her touch brought weariness and his lashes drooped.

"Sleep now." Tathagres' voice softened, blended into distance like rain over leaves. The boy sank into slumber.

"We begin our vengeance against Anskiere tomorrow morning."

Emien slept. Dreams rose and burst in his mind like bubbles from a well's black depths; he saw sun, and sky, and the swells which rose green and mild off the coast of Imrill Kand. His hands were smaller, younger, less callused, and he struggled with a child's strength to stow the soggy brown twine of a net.

"No! Emien, not like that!" Drawn out of memory, his father's voice rebuked him, gruff and annoyed, yet still filled with love. But in the dream, as on the day during his tenth summer, the warning came too late. The net tumbled overboard.

The child started, pulled his hand back, but not fast enough. A coil snared his wrist, whipped taut, and jerked his arm across the gunwale. Wood skinned his elbow. Emien cried out in pain. Yanked off balance, he lunged awkwardly, but failed to recover the snarl of weights before they tripped overboard and splashed into the sea. The drag on his arm increased. Emien braced his weight, tried frantically to tug free. But the twine tightened, hauling him inexorably after the net. He slipped on the floorboards, bashed his side against the thwart. Crying now from hurt and fear, he saw his father lean over him and slash once with the fishing knife which hung always at his hip. The twine fell away, swallowed by the sea.

Emien tumbled limply against his father's chest. Though the man's huge hands cradled him the boy could not stop weeping.

"There, son," soothed his father, impossibly close and warm; his comfort was only an illusion born of troubled sleep. Though the boy stirred restlessly, the dream continued, brutal for its clarity; for Emien yearned to erase this moment from memory. The burden it had left upon his heart was unbearable.

Familiar fingers ruffled his hair. "Little harm is done, child. You're too young for Evertt's work, I know. When he gets well, the net can be replaced. Dry your tears. The weather will soak me well enough without you adding to it, see? I think a squall is coming."

Emien looked up, saw the clouds which rolled like ink across the windward horizon. He sniffed and rubbed his chin on the grimy cuff of his tunic, old enough to understand the loss of a net was no slight misfortune. Illness had kept Evertt ashore for nearly a fortnight and the coppers were nearly all spent. His mother and small sister might go hungry until his father brought in a catch. And now under the threat of storm the sloop's sail must be shortened. Already the loose canvas slapped and banged against the sheets. Emien made a valiant effort to master himself.

His father squeezed his shoulder and smiled. "Good boy. Take the helm, could you? I'll not be long with the sails."

Emien moved aft, rubbing skinned wrists with fingers still stinging from the twine. He perched on the wide sternseat while his father uncleated the main halyard. Gear rattled aloft. The mainsail billowed, nearly ready for reefing, and the boy curled small hands over the tiller. A gust hissed out of the north, raking his hair and clothes. Canvas smacked taut, and the sloop heeled steeply. Spray boiled over the lee rail, ragged as frayed silk. Emien tried to steer, but strangely the helm would not respond.

"Head up!" his father shouted, impatient, for the boat yawed on an unsafe heading.

The boy pitched the sum of his strength against the wooden shaft. He strained until his muscles ached, but the rudder had fouled, caught in the twisted coils of the net recently lost overboard. With tiller stuck fast, the sloop reeled, sails thrashing thunder aloft. Tossed by rising crests, she bucked under cloud-darkened skies.

Emien's father abandoned the reefing. Slapped by fresh gusts, the sloop's patched canvas flogged with a fury no man could subdue; short of slashing the halyards, the choices left were few. Huddled miserably in the stern, Emien watched his father through a moment of agonized indecision. Green as he was, the boy understood; cut the sails down, and without steering, the boat would be abandoned to the violence of the squall. An unlucky wave might broach her, and everything would be lost. But if the rudder were cleared first, the sails could be brought safely under control. The net might be recovered as well. Emien saw his father assess the waves, the wind, and the oncoming weather with experienced eyes. Then he reached for a spare line and knotted it securely around his waist. The older, dreaming boy wished desperately to cry out, to freeze that moment in time and reverse its fatal outcome. His father would dive only to drown, entangled by the nets as the storm's contrary winds jibed the rudderless sloop again and again and again.

Yet the nightmare granted no respite. With cruel clarity Emien watched his father spring over the gunwale, never to surface. The boy screamed, jerked the unresponsive tiller until his palms blistered and split. Blind, bestial panic overturned his reason as the boom and thunder of the squall savaged the ocean. Rain fell in whipping sheets. Winds keened through the rigging, unravelling the whitecaps into driving veils of spindrift. Buffeted by the elements and trapped in stormridden meshes of horror, Emien lost all sense of continuity. The sloop's crude, hand-hewn timbers smoothed under his fists, transformed to the slim lines of *Crow*'s pinnace. Emien leaned over one thwart, nails gouged deep into vanished spruce. Showered by blown spray, he strained to reach a brandy cask which bobbed just out of reach in a trough.

He licked salty lips, shouted. "Taen!"

The cask and his sister's fate were somehow entangled. But Emien's need was not great enough to abandon the pinnace and follow her. In the desperation of his dream, he snatched up an oar and stretched outward, trying to hook the cask and draw it to the boat. But a white tern appeared out of the mist. Ringed by the harsh aura of a sorcerer's craft, the bird dove at his face. Blinding light burst upon Emien's retinas. Then someone gripped his shoulders and shook him painfully. The brilliance vanished, muffled in darkness.

"Emien?"

The boy woke with a start. He blinked, momentarily disoriented. Tathagres bent over him, her white hair enhanced by the pearly glow of dawn.

"You must get up," urged his mistress. "We travel at daybreak."

Emien braced himself awkwardly on one elbow. "I dreamed." He paused to steady the shake in his voice. "I saw my sister Taen floating in a brandy cask after the wreck of the *Crow*. She was under a spell by Anskiere. Could this be so, Lady? Should she be alive I—"

"No," Tathagres interrupted. "You saw nothing but a nightmare."

She released the boy and turned her face away. "Rise at once, Emien. If we're to cross the heights of Skane's Edge before nightfall, we'll require an early start. And I would prefer dinner and a bed in a tavern."

Emien clambered stiffly to his feet, too preoccupied to observe the glint of speculation in his mistress's eyes. He banished all memory of the dream, forgetting in his grief his island heritage, that any vision he had experienced could hold more truth than any word of Tathagres'.

Far south of Skane's Edge and well beyond the farthest archipelago under the Alliance's charter, the cask which had sheltered Taen since the wreck of the King's war fleet at last neared its destination. It rolled gently, unmolested by the surf which broke and creamed whitely over the coast of an islet never marked on any chart. Drawn safely to the shallows by Anskiere's geas, the cask grounded with scarcely a bump. The tern perched on the rim stretched slender wings, and a wavelet arose, curling under its tail feathers. The cask lifted on the crest, and was propelled shoreward, and the water receded, chuckling over dampened sand, its burden delivered to firm soil.

None came to greet the Stormwarden's protege upon her arrival. Breezes rustled through serried tufts of dune grass, and tossed the boughs of cedars whose majestic growth had never known the bite of an axeblade, nor any other abuse of man's invention. The tern hopped to the sand, head cocked to one side. It pecked at the barnacles which crusted the side of the cask. Taen stirred within, roused from her enchanted sleep.

The Stormwarden's spell released her gradually. Protective as a mother's embrace, the warmth which cradled her limbs faded gently away. Wakened by the light which leaked through the bunghole in the top of the barrel, Taen stretched. Though she recalled taking refuge in the cask while Tathagres held her captive in *Crow*'s dank hold, she felt no fear. She heard the boom of surf muffled by the staves, and the solid stillness of the land beneath reassured her.

Taen shifted into a crouch. The bunghole let in a cloud-flecked view of sky, and the smells of tide wrack and cedar. Intently she listened, yet heard no sound but waves and the shrill cries of sand swallows; as far as she could tell, the beach outside was deserted. The girl hammered her fists against the top of the barrel. Barnacles grated, then yielded their grip on the seams. Sunlight flared through a crack and the weathered boards loosened and fell aside.

Blinking against the glare, Taen stood upright and clung to the rim of the barrel. Except that her shift was speckled with mildew, she seemed little the worse for her journey by sea. Anskiere had delivered her from Tathagres' hands, she was certain; her acceptance of his stewardship went deeper than childish faith. In a manner which had disturbed the villagers on Imrill Kand, Taen often perceived things no youngster should have known. She was fey, her peers had accused in whispers. Their taunts had quickly taught her to value silence. Graced by recognition that the Stormwarden had not taken her destiny in hand without reason, Taen braced her elbows against the raw ends of the staves and gazed about.

A tern pecked the sand in the barrel's shadow, but there all sense of the ordinary ended. The islet was as beautiful as a dreamer's paradise, uncanny in its perfection. Daylight shone with transcendent clarity upon beaches bejeweled with crystal reflections. Taen raised her eyes to the spear-tipped ranks of the cedars beyond and felt her skin prickle with uneasiness. She had landed on a northeast shore. Raised where life was tyrannized by the moods of weather and sea, she knew the fury of storms from that quarter. Yet if the trees on this shoreline had ever known the brunt of a winter gale, they suffered no damage. Their symmetry was faultless. The place where they grew seemed possessed by a presence older than man's origins, brooding, silent, and eerily sentient.

Taen's fingers tightened on the barrel staves. She intruded upon territory tenanted by powers which resented mortal trespass; this she understood by the same intuition which had shown her Anskiere's innocence the day Imrill Kand had betrayed him. Now as then she did not strangle her gift with logic as her brother would have done. Though to set foot on this beach was to challenge the isle's strange guardians, Taen swung her good leg over the rim of the barrel and leapt down. The Stormwarden had chosen this site. Confident of his wisdom, Taen was unafraid.

Her movement startled the tern into flight. Light exploded from its wingtips, blue-white and blinding. The energy which bound its form unravelled, whining like a dead man's shade as it fled into the air. Overhead the sand swallows wheeled and dove for cover.

Taen landed, stumbling to her knees in warm sand. A feather drifted where the tern had vanished. Sorry the creature had left, the girl caught the quill in her fingers as it fell. Someone had crumpled it once; the delicate spine was creased again and again along its snowy length. The resonant violence of the act tingled through Taen's awareness; pressured by a sudden urge to weep, she buried her face in her hands. Imrill Kand lay uncounted leagues distant. Reft of all security, the girl longed to be released from the fate Anskiere had bequeathed her. Yet tears were a useless indulgence. Inured to hardship, Taen drew upon the resilience of spirit which had seen her through Tathagres' threats and the horrors of the *Crow's* pestilent hold.

On Imrill Kand, she had felt inadequate, a clumsy child with a lame leg unfit for work on a fishing boat's deck. Forced to remain ashore, she had resented her place with the pregnant women, the arthritic and the elderly. Here at least she could escape the widows in their musty wool skirts who had scolded her often for hasty stitches and girlish pranks; here she did not have to sit silent and straight on a hard wooden chair, knotting tedious acres of netting. No longer must she endure while the gossip of her elders veiled sorrows which Taen sensed but dared never to mention. Steadied by peace she only knew when she was solitary, the girl uncovered her face and discovered her inner sense had erred. She was no longer alone.

CHAPTER IX

The Vaere

TAEN BLINKED, UNABLE TO BE-
lieve her eyes. On the sand before her strode a man little taller
than a grown person's thigh. Clothed in a fawn-colored tunic
and dark brown hose tucked neatly into the cuffs of his deer-
skin boots, he walked with a step as fluid as quicksilver. He
stopped abruptly before Taen. Beads, feathers, and tingy brass
bells dangled from thongs stitched to his sleeves; their jingle
reminded the girl of the chimes which hung from the eaves of
the houses on Imrill Kand for luck against unfavorable winds.

The little man planted his feet. Black-eyed, bearded, and wizened as a walnut, he folded his arms and regarded her with an
intensity made disturbing by the fact her inner awareness detected nothing of his existence. Always she sensed when others
were near.

"Who are you?" Taen demanded, irritable rather than bold.

The creature stiffened with a thin jangle of bells. He ignored the girl's question. "You trespass. That's trouble. No
mortal sets foot here who does not suffer penalty."

"What?" Taen tossed her head, and a black snarl of hair tumbled across her brow. "I was sent here by Anskiere."

"Surely so. Anskiere is the only mortal on Keithland soil capable of the feat. But this changes nothing." The little man drummed his fingers rapidly against his sleeve. Taen noticed his feathers remained oddly unruffled, though brisk wind blew off the sea.

Uncertainty made her curt. "What do you mean? I don't know what land *this* is, far less any place called Keithland."

"Those lands inhabited by men were named Keithland by your forebears." Suddenly very still, the man smiled in grim irony. "You have landed on the isle of the Vaere."

Taen tucked her heels under her shift, sat, and gasped. Had she dared she would have sworn like a fishwife. According to stories told by sailors, the Vaere were perilous, fey, and fond of tricks; few people believed they existed outside of fable. Confronted by a being which showed no resonant trace of humanity, Taen chose to believe. If the tales held true, the Vaere were guardians of forbidden knowledge and also the bane of demonkind; the unlucky mortal who encountered them invariably vanished without a trace, or returned unnaturally aged and sometimes afflicted with madness. For all their perilous wisdom, rumor claimed the Vaere had one weakness; the man who discovered what it was could bring about their ruin.

Stubbornly insistent, Taen rubbed sweat from her palms. "The Stormwarden delivered me here for a reason."

The Vaere disappeared. Astonished, Taen scrambled to her feet. She stared at the empty place where the creature had stood but an instant earlier.

"Did he so?" replied a voice at her back.

Taen whirled, discovered the Vaere behind her, now seated comfortably on the rim of the brandy cask.

Bells clashed softly as he leapt down. "There was a purpose? Well then, we shall find it."

"Find it?" Annoyed by the Vaere's oblique behavior, Taen

scuffed the sand with her foot. "But I don't know how. Anskiere never told me."

The Vaere laughed, and his bells released a shimmering tinkle of sound. "Nonetheless we shall find it. But you must come with me."

Taen stepped back, reluctant to leave the beach. She knew little of Vaerish sorceries, except that they frightened her. The thought of following this peculiar creature to an unknown destination made her distinctly uneasy.

The Vaere sensed her hesitation at once. "I cannot permit you to stay here. Come as my guest or go as my captive, which do you choose?"

Taen swallowed and discovered her mouth was suddenly dry. "I'll come."

The Vaere clapped his hands with a merry shiver of bells. "You are a most unusual child. If Anskiere sent you here, perhaps he chose rightly."

But Taen felt less confident of the Stormwarden's guidance than she ever had previously. As she faced the dark loom of the cedars, she considered changing her mind.

"No. You mustn't." The Vaere stamped his foot with a dissonant jangle. Taen heard an angry whine. Energy suffused the air around her body; her skin prickled, then burned, as though stung repeatedly by hornets. With a startled cry of pain, she stumbled forward. The pain ceased at once.

"Don't lag," the Vaere admonished. He shook his finger at her, and knotted the end of his beard with the other hand. "You must abide by your choice, for the wardspells which guard this place are not forgiving."

The Vaere skipped ahead. Very near to panic, Taen followed up the steep face of a dune. Slipping and sliding as dry sand loosened under her weight, she noticed with foreboding that the Vaere left no footprints. But she had no chance to wonder why. The creature vanished the moment he reached the crest of the dune.

Taen scrambled after, saw her guide reappear at the edge of the wood. Quick as a deer, he darted between the trees. Taen broke into an ungainly run to keep up. She flailed down the slope, then crashed into the cedars on the far side. The wood was dark, a matted interlace of trunks and branches unbroken by any path. Dead sticks clawed at her and her shift snagged on a briar. Yet the Vaere moved without a rustle through the same undergrowth, a faint jangle of bells the only sign of his presence. Taen pursued. All sense of direction forsook her. Sweat pasted her hair against her neck and her game leg ached without respite. Yet the Vaere kept going. The sound of his bells drew the girl onward like the fabled sea sprites whose songs were said to lure unlucky mariners to their doom.

She ran on, through forest so dense daylight seemed to have been forgotten. Finally Taen saw a gleam through the branches ahead of her. She stopped, panting, at the edge of a clearing surrounded by oak trees grown lofty and regal with age. Grass grew beneath, fresh as the growth of early spring, and tiny flowers spangled the turf. No sun shone, only a changeless, silvery glow, like the deep twilight of midsummer.

Before her lay the heart of Vaerish mystery, beside which her own mortality seemed brief and shadowy as a dream. Time held no meaning in this place, and nature's laws seemed usurped by another less malleable power. No frost would blight the blossoms here; nor had winter burdened the limbs of the evergreens with snow for countless centuries of seasons. Taen balked at the clearing's edge, trembling. To step forward was to yield herself to the magic of the Vaere, and no mortal who did so could escape the consequences.

The little man reappeared, seated on a low stone in the grass. A soft glimmer of light haloed his slim form. His beads clinked as sweetly as the wind-borne chime of the goat bells Taen recalled from Imrill Kand as he reached into his pocket and drew forth a carved briar pipe. He struck no flame. But when he puffed upon the stem, smoke twined in lazy patterns around his cheeks. He crossed his legs, blew a wobbly chain of rings into the air, and regarded Taen with sharp black eyes. All urgency seemed to have left him.

"Once a Prince of Elrinfaer paused where you stand now." The Vaere's tone was not unkindly. He blew smoke and continued. "The boy had been delivered here by a mage of great power, who promised he had the potential talent to ward weather."

"Anskiere," Taen said softly.

The Vaere nodded, drew deeply on his pipe, and released three more smoke rings in rapid succession. "Yes, Anskiere. Child, many seek, but few of your kind ever find this place. Fewer still receive the training that only the Vaere can offer. None leave without forfeit. Knowledge, like every thing of power, brings about change. If Anskiere sent you, he did so knowingly. Better you choose with a willing heart, as he did, though he renounced both crown and inheritance, with no more assurance than the faith he held for his mentor."

Taen bit her lip, uncertain how to reply. And in the instant she demurred, the Vaere vanished, leaving only spent smoke rings to mark the fact he had been there at all.

Taen twisted her hands in the limp cloth of her shift. The early brash courage which had first prompted her to follow Anskiere dissolved, leaving her desolate. There could be no turning back. She thought of her brother, recalled how Emien had met adversity with rage and hatred; how Tathagres easily had turned that anger to her own advantage. Taen wondered whether the Stormwarden would use her loyalty in the same manner. If she followed the sorcerer's guidance her choice might later set her against her own kin. But any other alternative was impossible to contemplate. Burdened by sorrow and a heavy sense of loss, the girl chose the way of the Vaere. She stepped into the clearing, unaware the powers which guarded that place had keenly observed her struggle.

Nothing happened. Partially reassured, Taen moved with

increased confidence. Worn by the pain in her bad ankle, she perched on the same stone the Vaere had used and waited.

Silence surrounded her like a wall; the wood sheltered no wildlife, and the leaves remained still as stone in the half-lit splendor of the grove. The fragrance of the flowers lay heavy on the air and the light never altered, blurring any concept of time. Shortly the girl's head nodded drowsily. Instinct warned her not to rest in this place. She struggled to keep her eyes open, but soon, weariness overcame her. Lulled by well-being, she stretched out on the soft ground.

Snared by the magic of the Vaere, she fell dreamlessly asleep as many another mortal had before her. Presently an alien vibration invaded the clearing. A circular crack sliced through the turf where she lay. Blue light spilled through the gap, jarringly bright against the rough bark of the oaks. Slowly, hydraulic machinery beneath lowered the platform of soil where Taen slept, conveying her below the ground. A specialized array of robots bundled her limp form into the silvery, ovoid shell of a life-support capsule which once had furnished the flight deck of an interstellar probe ship. When her body was sealed inside, the lift rose and settled flush with the outside grass. No trace remained to betray the fact that a high-tech installation lay concealed beneath the island.

Busy as metallic insects, servo-mechanisms completed cable hook-up with the capsule, that the girl within could dream in concert with the Vaere. Though her stay might extend for years, she would never discover the nature of the entity which analyzed, nurtured, and trained her. For the electronic intelligence known as the Vaere never disclosed itself to men. Several life forms remained who yet sought vengeance against the descendents of the crew who once had manned the star probe *Corinne Dane*. The Vaere took every possible precaution that those known as demons never discovered how desperately vulnerable was the primary power which guarded mankind's survival. The hope of their star-born forebears must never be lost, that one day this band of castaways could be reunited with their own kind.

Well-versed in the lore of herbs, the forester, Telemark, tended Jaric's injuries with gentle hands and a mind better schooled than most in the art of healing. Yet four full days after the assault by the brigands of Seitforest, the boy had still not regained consciousness. Pale against the coarse wool of the coverlet he tossed, sweating, troubled by delirious nightmares.

Concerned by the lack of progress, Telemark prepared a poultice of ladybush leaves in a kettle and hung it from the bracket above the hearth to steep. If the boy did not waken soon, he would not survive. The forester removed the bandage which bound the cut on Jaric's head. With careful fingers, he explored the extent of the damage. For the third time, he encountered inflammation and swelling, but no broken bone; the wound itself was healing cleanly. The boy's hair would hide the scar.

Telemark sighed in frustration and tossed clean dressings into the pot above the fire. The contents hissed and steam arose, pungent with the scent of ladybush leaves. They would act as a potent astringent, but their virtue was beyond question. If the blow had caused swelling inside the boy's skull, increased circulation to the area could do little else but good. And time now was of the essence.

Telemark lifted the pot from the flames and set it on the settle while the poultice cooled. He regarded the boy on the bed with faded, weather-creased eyes, and wondered anew what desperate purpose had driven one so helpless to attempt passage through Seitforest alone. The lawless who ranged the wood were numerous enough that none of the high-born from Corlin would hunt there. Telemark preferred the isolation; game was more plentiful as a result. But this child, who in his ravings had named himself Kerainson Jaric, was obviously unused to the outdoors. His slight build was more delicate than that of a pampered maid. Yet he had more courage than many men twice his size.

With a regretful shake of his head, Telemark tested the poultice and hastily withdrew a burned finger. He reached for a linen cloth to dry his knuckles, and looked up in time to see Jaric stir on the bed. The forester rose instantly to his feet. The boy raised an arm to his face. The man caught his slim wrist and firmly prevented Jaric from disturbing the uncovered wound in his scalp.

"Steady, boy. Steady. You've suffered quite a bash on the head. The healing won't be helped by touching it."

Jaric protested. His eyelids quivered and flicked open. Telemark swore with relief. With his free hand, the forester caught the oil lamp from its peg and lowered it to the small table by the bedside. The boy's pupils contracted sluggishly under the increased light, and his expression remained blankly confused. He twisted against Telemark's hold, distressed and lost in delirium. But he was conscious at last, which was an improvement. Lucid or not, he could at least swallow broth, and chances were good he would recover his self-awareness.

Once Telemark had served as healer to the Duke of Corlin's mercenaries; he had seen enough head injuries to know that recovery could often be painfully slow. A man might temporarily lose his wits, and Kor knew this boy had been dealt a nasty buffet. With hope in his heart, the forester wrung out the fresh bandages and expertly dressed the boy's wound. Jaric lay limp as he worked, brown eyes fixed and sightless. For many days, Telemark saw little improvement in the boy's condition.

But years in the forest had taught him patience. Where another man might have lost heart and placed the lad with Koridan's initiates in Corlin, the forester continued to care for the boy himself. When Jaric recovered his full strength, he would leave, Telemark held little doubt; any purpose which drove a man into Seitforest alone could never be slight.

* * *

The settlement of Harborside on Skane's Edge was small and ill-accustomed to strangers, far less ones who arrived sun-blistered and barefoot in the town square at dusk. But after a night's rest, a bath, and a fine tavern meal, the townsfolk stopped whispering when Emien's back was turned. Tathagres sought passage off the island the next morning. A merchant brig headed for the ports beyond Mainstrait rode at anchor off the breakwater. Since the vessel was obliged to pay the Kielmark's tribute before passing the straits, passengers bound for Cliffhaven required no change in course. Yet the captain looked askance at anyone who wished business with that fortress of renegades. Tathagres' request met stubborn resistance.

"They're pirates, every one of them a detriment to honest trade," objected the captain.

A bribe quickly overcame his distaste, though Emien felt his fee was preposterously greedy; twelve coin-weights gold apiece would have imported a prize mare from Dunmorelands. But unless they wished to wait for another ship, the brig was their only option.

The ship weighed anchor when the tide ebbed. If Emien regretted the four sailhands traded to the harbormaster for the gold to pay their passage, he did not dwell on the thought. The familiar roll of a ship's deck underfoot buoyed his spirits, and before the ridges of Skane's Edge had slipped below the horizon he asked the captain for work. The brig sailed short-handed. He owned nothing but the clothes on his back, and these were sadly tattered; come winter, he had no desire to rely on Tathagres for silvers to buy a cloak and a good pair of boots.

Four weeks of labor in the rigging fleshed out Emien's starved frame, and the sound sleep of exhaustion gradually eased his harried nerves. Happiest when his mind was absorbed with the simple tasks of seamanship, the boy brooded little. By the time the black battlements of Cliffhaven hove into sight to the northeast, he wished the voyage had not ended so quickly.

The mate bawled out orders to furl sail. Emien swung himself aloft with an oddly reluctant heart. As the anchor cleaved the blue waters of the harbor, the boy felt as if his contentment sank with it. The last time he had viewed these shores, Taen had been alive and no burden of murder weighted his conscience. Now his desire for revenge against Anskiere was complicated by an insatiable yearning for power.

The mate shouted and the deck crew swayed a longboat out. An officer waited to escort the strongbox containing the Kielmark's tribute ashore. Emien slung himself off the mizzen yard and descended the ratlines, certain Tathagres would summon him.

But the longboat departed with no word from her. Puzzled, Emien sought his mistress. He knocked at the door of her cabin, half fearful she would turn him away with his question unanswered. But she greeted him pleasantly, and after one glance at his expression, volunteered her intentions without his needing to ask.

"Go to the captain. Release yourself from service and collect what coin you've earned. Then report back to me. We shall go ashore after sundown, for I've no desire to involve myself with the Kielmark. If we are to succeed against Anskiere, our plans must be carefully laid."

The sun was low in the west by the time Emien returned. Busy with other complaints, the captain had been slow to attend the details of his dismissal and the brig's purser was unavailable until the water barrels and stores were replenished. But silver in his pocket made the boy feel less vulnerable, should his mistress be displeased by his delay.

Emien arrived at her cabin breathless. Tathagres admitted him without complaint, a preoccupied expression on her face. Her earlier garb was replaced by tunic and hose of unrelieved black. Except for the gold torque, she had stripped herself of jewelry, and her bright hair was knotted under a scarf at the nape of her neck.

"I have clothing for you." She waved absently in the direction of the berth. "See whether it fits."

Emien squeezed past, overwhelmingly aware of her in the tight confines of the cabin. Set on edge by his involuntary response, he forced himself to concentrate on the items laid out on the berth. Spread on the mattress were two cloaks, a tunic, and a pair of hose. The garments seemed right. Reluctant to undress before Tathagres, Emien looked up, but the intensity of her mood robbed him of all protest. In silence he turned his back and peeled off his ragged shirt.

"The clothes fit," he announced after an interval. He swung around, boyishly embarrassed, but his mistress paid no heed. She sat before the cabin's small writing desk with her hands clenched in her lap.

Emien took an uncertain step toward her. "Tathagres? The tunic fits just fine."

But his mistress remained unresponsive as a stone statue. Disturbed, the boy moved closer. He peered over her shoulder, and saw that sorcery engaged her attention. Hair prickled on the back of his neck and his hands clenched reflexively into fists. On the desk lay what appeared to be a feather. But closer scrutiny yielded another view superimposed over the first. Above the scarred surface of the desktop, Emien viewed the living image of a cliff side bound by tiered prisms of ice. Gulls wheeled above the heights, their cries faint and plaintive above the boom of the breakers which smoked spray across a shoreline of jagged rocks.

Emien gasped and started back, bruising his elbow painfully against the bulkhead. Tathagres roused at the noise. Absorbed by her own thoughts, she sat silently while Emien rubbed his arm. When she did speak, her words seemed intended for someone else.

"What has he *done?*" Perplexed, she shook her head, then focused on Emien, as though aware of him for the first time.

"We shall find out, I suppose, when we get ashore. Do the clothes fit?"

The boy nodded, decidedly ill at ease. Seldom had he seen Tathagres unsure of herself. Yet if her confidence was shaken, she rallied swiftly.

"Boy, to all appearances, Anskiere has set a seal of ice across the mouth of the cavern which imprisons the frostwargs. All attempts to trace his location end at that same barrier. I am certain he cannot have left Cliffhaven. But finding him may prove more difficult than I expected. We must be cautious." She laced her fingers together so tightly the knuckles turned white. "Should we fall into the Kielmark's hands, reveal nothing. The man may be formidably powerful but he cannot deter me. If you keep your silence, you shall be safe."

Tathagres looked up, and the lack of emotion in her violet eyes chilled the marrow of Emien's bones. "But should you betray my trust, you'll wish your mother had never lived to give you birth."

"If Anskiere escapes, I should feel just as miserable," the boy replied hotly.

"That is well." Tathagres stretched like a cat in her chair and smiled. "Then we agree perfectly. Meet me by the starboard davit at nightfall. The captain has agreed to leave us the brig's pinnace."

Familiar with the captain's fussy temperament, Emien dared not guess how that had been accomplished. As he opened the cabin door, he regretted he had not been witness to the arrangements; no doubt his companions in the forecastle would have given their shirts to know.

Tathagres laughed. In that uncanny manner which always unsettled Emien, she answered as if he had spoken his thought aloud. "I won the craft at cards, boy, but Kor wouldn't have sanctioned my technique. When we reach court, I'll teach you, if you remember to ask."

But the friendliness in her offer embarrassed the boy, and he hurried off without answering.

Taen awoke believing she still lay in the grove amid the oaks. Unaware a machine had taken her into custody, and unable to distinguish the fact that all she experienced since was a dream inspired by advanced technology, she sat up. The Vaere stood on the stone by her elbow. He regarded her in silence and smoke from his pipe twined patterns in the air around his wizened face.

Taen stretched, her mood somewhat cranky. She had worried herself ragged for no apparent reason, and memory of her recent discomfort rankled. "Nothing happened," she accused the creature beside her.

"I beg your pardon." The Vaere stiffened, accompanied by a dissonance of beads and bells. "Quite a bit happened. You were judged, and my kind decided what will be done with your future. Take care, mortal. You are ignorant."

Nettled by the Vaere's superiority, Taen tilted her chin at an angle her brother would have found all too familiar. "I have a *name.*"

"But few manners," the Vaere observed. "I am called Tamlin. I trained Anskiere, and before him the one you call Ivain Firelord. You were sent here because you possess the rare gift of empathy; you share the emotions and feelings of your own kind."

Taen drew breath to interrupt, but Tamlin waved her silent. "You must learn to listen, child. There are demons abroad who would take your life, for your talent threatens their secrets. Without defenses, some among your own kind would stone you, or worse; and lacking control of your gift, since birth you've suffered the unwanted miseries of others who happened into your presence. But the Vaere would change that."

Tamlin leapt off his rock and gestured expansively with his pipe. "These are troubled times. Certain demons have bound mortals to their cause, to the sorrow and destruction of mankind. Did you hear of Tierl Enneth?"

Taen bit her lip and realized the Vaere referred obliquely to Tathagres, whose obsessive desire to usurp Anskiere's powers could be explained no other way.

"Just so," said Tamlin. "Anskiere is the only defender left, since Ivain Firelord's death." The Vaere paused and chewed reflectively on his pipe stem. "Now more than ever before a channel is needed to sound the minds of men. You will provide that link, Taen."

The girl shivered and drew her knees up to her chin. The most powerful sorcerers in Keithland were trained by the Vaere. Nothing of her upbringing on Imrill Kand had prepared her for Tamlin's proposal. As a cripple and a child who had known adult problems at an unnaturally tender age, she felt small and helpless, a mere cipher in the age-long struggle between demonkind and man.

Tamlin blew a large smoke ring, and his bells tinkled as softly as rain onto glass. "You have great heart for one so small," he said gently. "And though you will pay a heavy price for your learning, the damage to your leg will be mended. When you go, your body will have aged fully seven years, though far less time will have passed in your absence. But never again will you limp, and the dreams and aspirations of all mankind will be within your dominion. Because of you, there may be peace for the next generation."

And though she found hope and much cause for joy in the words of the Vaere, Taen bent her head and wept for the first time since leaving home on Imrill Kand. If Tathagres allied herself with demons, then Emien trod the very path of evil; unless he came to his senses, he would someday meet his sister as an enemy.

CHAPTER X

Prison of the Frostwargs

THE OVERCAST OF AFTERNOON broke at sunset. By dark, when the sailors launched the pinnace, Cliffhaven lay like sculpted ebony against a dusky sapphire sky. From the rendezvous point by the starboard davit, Emien studied the view with a fisherman's eye for weather, more irritated than pleased by the change. Clear skies would not favor a concealed landing on a northerly shore.

Chosen for silence and deadly skill with weapons, the Kielmark's sentries would kill for far less cause than trespass. Emien tugged his cloak closer about his shoulders. He distrusted the brash exhilaration which invariably possessed Tathagres in the face of danger. After the disaster of Skane's Edge, the boy hesitated to suggest a change of course. Doubtless the woman would drive him straight at the Kielmark's front gates, should he mention prudence at the wrong moment. Beside his mistress, the sentries were the more predictable risk.

"Are you ready, boy?"

Surprised out of reflection, Emien started. Tathagres

paused at his side, her expression brittle as porcelain and her mood black as the cloth which bound her hair. She lifted a hand unfamiliarly bare of ornament and pointed to the pinnace below. "They're anxious to cast us off."

She swung herself over the railing without waiting for assistance. Cautious of her temper, Emien followed her down the side battens and into the cockpit of the pinnace.

He did not speak until she had settled herself on the stern seat. "If the Kielmark stations guards on his northwest shore, they'll see us when we land." The boy indicated the last clouds which drifted, underlit and pale as knotted fleece above the island. "Moon's rising, and this tub carries bleached canvas. We'll stand out like silver in a coal heap."

"Why not row?" Tathagres pitched her tone to wound. "Or don't you trust me to manage the guards?"

Emien banged open the sail locker without answering. With a bucket like the pinnace, the Kielmark needed no guards on his northwest shore. Lacking four stout hands to man the benches, her oars were useless sticks, and for a craft built as heavy as scrap iron she was clumsily rigged as well. Emien guessed by her lines she would be cursed with a lee helm. The crossing to Cliffhaven promised agony enough without Tathagres baiting him.

Emien dragged a ratty headsail out of the locker and discovered five hanks torn off. He swore then in earnest, for baggy canvas meant the pinnace would point like a lumbering bitch. Bilgewater lapped at his boots, warning of leaks in the hull. Radiating anger, Emien stamped forward to find the jib halyard. If Tathagres had lost even a single coin in her cursed game of cards, the captain had claimed the winning stake after all.

Tathagres leaned against a thwart and watched the boy fuss with the tackle. "Once ashore you can scuttle this boat if you wish. We won't be needing it again."

"For sure?" Poised with halyard in hand, Emien laughed, his

spirits partially restored. "Let it be rocks then, big ones, right through these worm-ridden planks." He did not add that on a lee shore in the dead of night, the rocks might complete their task before the time appointed. At least after Skane's Edge he knew Tathagres could swim.

A stiff breeze blew out of the north and the sails cracked and flogged aloft as Emien made the last lines fast. Later, the clear weather would bring calm; anxious to reach shore while the conditions held fair, the boy cast off promptly. He sheeted in main and jib and the pinnace drew clear of the brig, her lee rail well down and her wake a gurgle of bubbles astern.

The crossing to Cliffhaven began smoothly, marked by the slap of reefpoints in the wind, and the occasional squeal of blocks as Emien adjusted a sail. Absorbed by her own thoughts, Tathagres made no conversation, and busy with the wayward roll of the pinnace, Emien made no effort to draw her out. He maintained his heading, guided by the cold glitter of the polestar, until a rising moon rendered the waves in ink and silver and the island fortress reared up off the bow, notched and black against the horizon.

As the pinnace drew nearer, Emien saw the white glitter of ice partially veiled by mist. Breakers crashed beneath, their thunderous impact warning of submerged reefs; spume jetted skyward, then subsided into foam with a hiss like a hag's cauldron, making any landing there impossible. Yet after Skane's Edge, Emien dared not meddle with Tathagres' intent. Grimly he held his course, helm gripped in sweaty hands, until the bowsprit thrust against current lit like fairy lace in the moonlight.

"We'll land there." Tathagres' voice was barely audible above the boom of the surf.

Emien looked where she pointed. A thin crescent of sand gleamed just east of the cliffs. Though hedged by wreaths of white water, the beach seemed free of obstructions. Properly handled, the pinnace might barely thread through, but timing was critical. Emien hauled in the sheets, shoved the helm down, and let the craft jibe. Wind slammed the sails onto the other tack. Unmindful of the line which burned through his palms, he let the jib run free. The pinnace slewed. Then a wave lifted her stern, and the boat careened shoreward with all the grace of a rock shot from a catapult.

Something moved overhead. Emien glanced up. A spear drove past the mast and thumped with a rattle of splinters into the sternseat inches from his knee.

Emien sprang to his feet.

"Hold course!" Tathagres leaned over the gunwale. Poised like a figurehead against the baroque swirl of foam, she raised her hand to the gold band at her throat and invoked a spell. A bright interlace of lines shot through her fingers.

Dread sent chills through the pit of Emien's stomach. Although he knew Tathagres conjured in defense, her sorceries brought no comfort. Her mastery only forced recognition of the depths of his ignorance. Shamed and furious, Emien steadied the pinnace against the heave of the breakers and loosed the mainsheet. Lines smoked through tackle, and the sails banged overhead. Deafened by the report of soaked canvas, the boy dragged the helm amidships, just as a crest flung the bow skyward. Spray flew, carved into sheets by the rail. Then the craft grounded with a crunch that rattled every plank in the hull. Emien abandoned the tiller and leapt overboard just as a second spear arched overhead, aimed with killing accuracy.

Thigh deep in the flood of the breakers, the boy flung himself against the pinnace. The spear hissed down. Tathagres shouted and a flash of red ripped the air. Barely shy of its mark, the weapon exploded with a snap and a shower of sparks. Then the drag of the undertow flung the pinnace sideways. The next wave would broach her, despite Emien's efforts. He called warning to his mistress.

Tathagres gathered herself and jumped lightly as a cat from the gunwale. She landed without mishap in the surf, just as the pinnace tore free of the boy's grip. Sand grated hoarsely across planking. Then the boat capsized, and the crest of the following wave cascaded over her starboard thwart. Emien watched as the sea boomed and broke, smashing the craft to a snarl of slivered wood.

At his side, Tathagres pulled the cloth from her hair, her mood brittle and dangerous. "Get ashore!" She shoved the scarf roughly into Emien's hands.

The boy flinched as if wakened from nightmare. In the moment his eyes met hers, he caught a glimpse of runes glowing red against the gold band which adorned her throat. Then Tathagres turned away, in haste to reach the land. Emien plunged after, hands knotted painfully in cloth which smelled of ozone. Waves mauled the pinnace's planking like bones at his back. He shivered and bit his lip. There could be no escape by sea now. Wary of his own vulnerability, the boy slogged through the shallows toward a shore defended by hostile men-at-arms. He cursed the fact that he had no sword, nor any training with weapons.

Tathagres walked ahead as if the water was the finest of silken carpets under her feet. Contemptuous of the spears and defended only by sorcery, she paused while Emien caught up, her arrogant air of confidence a challenge no attacker could resist. And yet no weapons fell.

Breathlessly Emien drew alongside. Close at hand, the sheer height and mass of the frozen cliffs overwhelmed him. Yet he repressed his uneasiness as Tathagres leaned close and spoke in his ear. "Stay behind me, no matter what happens. You must not come forward until I have finished with the guards. Disobey me at your peril, for if you stray, I cannot protect you. None who cross my path shall live. Am I clear?"

Chilled and mute, Emien nodded. Gripped by indefinable foreboding, he watched his mistress stride boldly shoreward. She reached dry sand unchallenged, tossed her cloak to the ground, and left it in a heap at her feet. Her hair blew free, and burnished like pearl by moonlight, her skin gleamed against the deeper shadow of the land beyond. In morbid fascination, Emien saw his mistress lift her head and touch the band at her throat with her hands.

Mist arose, translucent as smoke from lit shavings. It twined around her, interlaced like gossamer in the moonlight until her slender body seemed clothed, not in black wool, but some garb out of faery, all shimmer and cling and no substance. The ivory curve of her shoulders, breasts, and hips caught the eyes of the concealed guardsmen, and held them helplessly enthralled. Emien felt as if a great weight crushed his chest. He struggled to breathe. Though the spell was not designed to doom him, still his body flushed and sweated and ached. Numbed by the chill water about his ankles, he beheld the vision of lust his mistress wove to doom the guardsmen, and even as his flesh yearned to possess her, his spirit cried out for reprieve; Tathagres' cruelty knew no bounds. In her hands, man's admiration for woman became a weapon to slay, a terrible tool to implement her powers. When the first guard tumbled from his niche in the rocks, Emien bunched his fingers into fists. Tears spilled down his cheeks. He watched helplessly while a second man fell headlong to the sand below the cliffs.

The sentry's body twitched on the sand and settled finally, grotesque and still as statuary in the moonlight. Nothing moved on the beach but the tireless roll of the surf. Emien roused. Shuddering as if the frosts of winter clenched his bones, he started forward and stumbled to his knees in brine.

But Tathagres was not finished conjuring. She lifted arms pale as bone against the rise of the dunes, and softly, too softly for natural hearing, whispered an incantation. The words pierced Emien's ears like a needle sharpened by longing; loneliness opened like a wound within him, until the woman posed on the shoreline framed his sole hope of redemption. But the song Tathagres sang was not shaped for him. Agonized by her rejection, Emien cried out, tasting salt. Only the bitter reflection of his own inadequacy made him hesitate. Her music became discord in his ears. No portion of his being could bend it to harmony, and the pain of that recognition was more than his spirit could endure.

Emien crouched like a beast in the surf, at first unaware that a third guardsman emerged from the scrub, his fingers clamped around a drawn sword and his eyes dark hollows of desire.

Tathagres arched her body, arms extended in welcome. Drawn by her movement, Emien looked up, saw a stranger approach her with the confidence of a lover. The man's muscles quivered under his leather tunic, and his breath came in labored gasps. He reached out and touched her bared shoulder, and the rapture in his face poisoned Emien with jealousy.

Tathagres bent her head, murmured something into the hollow of the guardsman's throat. His fingers shifted, releasing the sword. It fell and struck rock with a sour clank. The man took no heed of his fallen weapon; discipline forgotten, he smiled as Tathagres melted into his embrace and knotted her hands with fevered passion in the hair which spilled over his collar. The man whispered hoarsely. His arms tightened around her slim shoulders. Driven by lust no human could deny, he sought her lips, kissed her deeply and long. Around him the very air quivered as her spell closed over his heart.

Crazed by frustration, Emien hammered his fists against his thighs. He wept as though his heart would break, oblivious to the waves which broke behind him, sending foam swirling and splashing around his boots. Blinded by tears, he saw nothing as the guardsman's arms quivered and tumbled loose. Only when the man's knees buckled did Emien recognize the snare Tathagres had set to destroy the last of the Kielmark's sentries. Her victim swayed and spilled onto the sand. He sprawled dead in the moonlight; incoming tide lapped at his outflung hands. Horror jolted Emien free of passion. He trembled while Tathagres retrieved the abandoned sword, and her laughter sickened him to the core of his being.

The air crackled, scoured by a brief rain of sparks as the spell dispersed around her. Emien choked, doubled over with nausea. He jabbed his hands to the wrists in icy water, coughing and miserable, until Tathagres arrived at his side.

When his equilibrium did not immediately return, she plucked insistently at his cloak. "I've brought you a gift."

Emien raised his head, discovered the dead guardsman's sword posed above her outstretched hand like a needle etched in light. Though earlier he had craved a blade of his own, the offering appalled him, made him feel less than human. Still he accepted the weapon with unemotional practicality. Tathagres' tricks had eliminated the guards from the beach; but if anyone reported to the Kielmark at the time the pinnace was sighted, their present safety was not secure.

Tathagres snapped as if she heard his thought, "You worry like a pregnant heiress. Get ashore. We have a task before us."

Stung by her scorn, Emien surged to his feet. With his hands clenched tightly around the sword hilt, he sloshed through the shallows. Ahead of him, Tathagres stepped over the guardsman's corpse with barely a pause. Unable to match her callousness, Emien glanced down. Lifeless eyes stared skyward, as if a reason for mortal betrayal lay scribed in the depths of the heavens; the hands lay helpless and open, denied any vengeance for a death which held no honor. Emien regretted the fact that he had lingered. To recognize the guardsman's anguish and not act was to share the inhumanity of the crime.

Shamed by the cowardice, he moved on without stopping to recover the sword sheath and buckler from the body. With the steel naked in his hand, he hastened across the strand, and for one reckless instant longed to bury the blade to the crossguard in his mistress's back. Fear alone stayed his hand. For the guardsman's death, not even hatred of Anskiere could relieve his tortured conscience, and troubled by fresh guilt, the boy hurried into the shadow of the escarpment.

The ice cliffs towered above, terraced against the dark sky. There Tathagres halted and peered upward.

"Wait," she commanded, and set her hands to the gold band at her throat.

Emien leaned against a rough shoulder of rock. Huddled in the wet wool, he propped the sword near at hand and blew on his knuckles while Tathagres cast magic about her like a net. Soft violet light haloed her form, then widened like a corona until it thinned to invisibility. Emien felt a tingle of heat fan his flesh. From the hollow by the dunes, a nightbird startled into flight with a soft whir of wings. Its melancholy calls faded in the darkness, and the warmth of the spell fled with it. The ice radiated cold like the deepest heart of winter. Chilled by more than frost, Emien sifted through the noises of the night, listening for the faint telltale chime of metal which might herald the arrival of a patrol. Should the Kielmark's guards encounter them now, the cliffs would block any chance of escape.

But no men-at-arms arrived. Presently Tathagres stirred. She lifted her head. The magic she had cast forth dispelled with a snap, and for a second the wind wafted the acrid smell of brimstone toward the waiting boy.

Tathagres turned from the cliff. Her brows knitted with frustration, and the gesture she directed upward delineated vivid anger. "The Stormwarden is there, *inside*, and certainly trapped." She chewed her lip, irritated by the discovery. "Boy, fetch my cloak from the beach. I wish to know more, but I cannot risk a deep trance here. This place is dangerously exposed. We must climb higher."

Sullen and silent, Emien collected his sword; at least his mistress had spared a moment to consider caution. The moon hung dead overhead. Shadow spread like soot beneath Emien's boots as he walked back to the water's edge. Ebbing waves had ribbed channels the breadth of the beach. Tathagres' cloak still lay at the edge of the tide mark. Wise enough not to leave unnecessary evidence for the Kielmark's patrols, Emien retrieved the garment and dragged the hem over the tracks marked by his passing. Although the dead guardsmen lay exposed, already stiff, and blatant as a scream of warning to any arriving scout, corpses were more than the boy could bear to handle alone. His weakness made him fretful. Guards would certainly come. Tathagres' confidence made her careless to a fault.

But he mentioned nothing of his uncertainty when he returned the cloak to Tathagres. With a brief nod, she pulled it over her shoulders and tucked her hair out of sight beneath the hood. Then, without asking whether Emien would follow, she began her ascent of the cliff.

The boy set foot in her tracks, his heart hardened like ice in his chest. The sword dragged at his wrist, forcing him to grip with his free hand to steady himself. Cold burned his flesh, bitter as venom, and his boots slipped treacherously, as if apparently solid footing were an illusion born of the powers which bound the ice, hostile to intrusion and dangerous to scale. Emien toiled upward grimly. The memory of Taen in the Stormwarden's arms robbed any threat from a fall; and three dead guardsmen on the beach below diminished the meaning of all else. Now he might feel insignificant as a leaf tossed before the winds of a storm; but one day he vowed his fate would no longer be commanded by the whims of enchanters.

The black wool of Tathagres' cloak veiled her features from view. Emien could not see the smile of cruel satisfaction which curved her perfect mouth. Absorbed by the perils of the climb and dizzied by the sweep of the waves over the rocks below, he never suspected his anger awaited her purpose, volatile as tinder to her hand. By the time Tathagres halted beneath a natural overhang of rock, the expression she presented to the boy was concerned, even friendly.

"We shall pause here," she announced. "The trance I must employ to trace the Stormwarden's presence may last several hours. If you stand guard, do you think you can stay awake?"

"If I sleep I'd freeze." Emien hauled himself onto the ledge beside her, weary and displeased by the place. The terrain was rough, buffeted by wind, and framed by an archway of frozen cascades. Anyone arriving below would sight them easily. Yet the boy offered no complaint, for here where the cold rose like blight from the bared bones of the rock, he would at last know Anskiere's fate.

Tathagres settled herself cross-legged at the juncture of the ledge and the ice. She braced her back against a buttress of stone, touched her necklace with her fingertips, and closed her eyes. This time Emien saw no flare of light. Her spell of summoning took effect with a thin whine of sound, and a tracery like engraving flickered across the band at her throat. The characters glared red against the band's polished surface. Consumed by curiosity, the boy edged nearer.

Careful not to disturb her concentration, he leaned close and examined the ornament which controlled Tathagres' spells. Wrought as a seamless ring, the metal was as thick as his forefinger, and deadly plain when not in use. But now while Tathagres engaged her powers to tap the depths of Anskiere's sorcery, runes blazed, etched in light across the surface of the gold. Emien could not read. But he had seen trader's lists often enough to recognize a scribe's hand; the writing on the band described no human letters. With a sharp chill of foreboding, Emien drew back.

Once on Imrill Kand, a severe storm had washed a bit of wreckage ashore beside the rotted pilings of the fisher's wharf. Emien had been there when the child who found it burned his fingers to the bone trying to pick it up. The object had borne markings similar to those on Tathagres' gold collar. Anskiere had destroyed the artifact the instant he saw it, claiming it bore runes of power no human should know. No villager on Imrill Kand questioned the sorcerer's wisdom; plainly the object was crafted by demons. And though Emien had repudiated all belief in Anskiere's doings, the possibility Tathagres' magic might be founded by the works of Kordane's Accursed had never before entered his mind.

Troubled, he seated himself on a shelf of rock, balanced the sword blade across his knees, and regarded his mistress. Her angry violet eyes were closed. Moonlight rendered her form in silver, lovely as the icon Emien recalled from the shrine by Kordane's Bridge. From the smooth skin of cheek and brow to the finely sculpted wrists resting in her lap, her pose seemed the image of peace and perfection. Wrung breathless by an unexpected rush of desire, Emien clamped his fist on the pommel of his weapon. Surely Anskiere was wrong. Not all demons were evil. Perilous, surely; in ignorance, the child of Imrill Kand had touched their formidable powers and been harmed. But Tathagres controlled similar forces as effortlessly as breathing.

Emien perched his chin on his knuckles, teeth clenched against the cold. Any enemy of Anskiere's was an ally to his cause, a hand to lend impetus toward vengeance for Taen's death. Why should he be troubled to know the source of Tathagres' powers? But the bleak mood which accompanied his discovery persisted.

Emien stared morosely over the sea but saw no horizon. Images of the guardsman's fatal embrace returned and haunted him. Wind pried at his clothing, sharp with the coming frosts of autumn, and the breath of the ice pierced the very marrow of his bones. Poisoned by the knowledge of his own mortality, Emien dreamed hungrily of power. His thoughts dwelt deeply and long upon Tathagres' gold necklace as the moon wheeled across the sky to its setting. If somehow he came to possess such an object, he could be secure from the meddling of men and sorcerers forever after.

Fog moved in at sunrise. It beaded Emien's cloak and lashes and sword hilt with droplets, and coiled like wraiths over the ice cliffs; surf boomed and echoed invisibly off the rocks, eerily amplified. As the first gulls took flight over Cliffhaven,

Tathagres stirred from her trance. In the half-lit gloom while night yielded to daylight, Emien saw her eyelids tremble and open. She stretched, showing no trace of stiffness, a secretive, self-satisfied expression on her face.

Chilled and disgruntled, the boy waited for her to speak. Finally, after seven weary weeks and an unpleasant night-long vigil, he would learn what befell the Stormwarden whose meddling had stolen Taen's loyalty and whose tempest had taken her life. Bitter as spoiled wine, Emien thumbed the bare edge of the blade on his knees. When Tathagres at last met his gaze, he barely curbed an outright demand for the result of her search of the ice cliffs.

His tension appeared to amuse her, which annoyed Emien further. With his knuckles whitened against the chased steel of the crossguard, he glared in furious silence. Like a coquettish high court lady, Tathagres tossed her fine white hair and laughed.

Emien sprang halfway to his feet in a moment of wild anger. Then he realized her caprice was caused not by him, but by Anskiere. Unable to restrain his own fierce smile, he settled back.

"Anskiere is a fool," Tathagres said softly. Above her shoulders the mist swirled like smoke over the blocky spine of the ridge, and for a second weak sunlight struck through, striking gold highlights against the ice. Paler than usual and obviously cold, Tathagres rearranged her cloak over her shoulders. "When the frostwargs wakened, the Stormwarden sealed them behind a wall of ice. But he could not free himself. The ice imprisoned him as well."

Emien raised the sword, saluting her triumph. "Then the Stormwarden is dead."

Tathagres tilted her head, gazed in speculation through the thinning veils of mist. Her reply held dreamlike tranquillity. "He's alive but in stasis, a trance so deep he lies a hair's breadth from death. He cannot last indefinitely in such a state. He believes he will be saved."

Emien lowered the sword, black brows gathered into a frown. He began a vehement protest, but Tathagres stopped him sharply, violet eyes widened with murderous intent. Her expression froze the breath in Emien's chest and he clenched his teeth to keep from quivering like a terrified child.

"The Stormwarden has unleashed his curse upon Ivain Firelord." Tathagres shaped her words with harsh, incredulous fury. "He trusts a geas and a stripling boy to spare him from the frostwargs' ferocity." She laughed again, but her mirth sounded forced, as if some inner plan had been thwarted.

Cued by a leap of intuition, Emien said quickly, "You can't touch him." The thought sparkled resentment.

"I can't touch him, true." Tathagres leaned forward, dangerously rapt. "I don't *need* to reach him. His fate is sealed already, with no help from me. Look, I'll show you."

She reached out and caught the sword. Emien relinquished the weapon, reluctant, yet also determined to share her discovery. He crouched, braced on one fist, while Tathagres turned the blade point downward and scratched a triangle into the ice between her knees.

She rested the tip of the sword on the apex, then touched the worn pommel to the gold band above her collar.

"Ivain's heir is a half-wit weakling." Her lip curled in scorn. "See for yourself."

The lines scored in the ice blazed with sudden violent light, followed by scorching heat as the sorcery took hold. Ragged drifts of steam rose and mingled with the mist. Emien braced his body, mistrustful of the sorcery, yet unable to tear himself away. Before his eyes the ice melted and an image from a place far distant reformed on its surface. Inside a neat, single-room cabin, a boy sat propped in a wicker chair. His body was half buried under woolen blankets, though sunlight spilled warmly through the open window beside him. Framed by a straggle of mouse-colored hair, his features were blanched by ill health and the fingers resting across his knees were fragile as spring twigs. He appeared asleep. On closer examination, Emien noticed the boy's eyes were open but vacant, as though bereft of intelligence. Yet even as Emien watched, the brown eyes lifted. For the space of an instant, the boy in the cabin seemed to focus directly upon him.

Touched by foreboding, Emien flinched and flung back. "Kordane's Fires, who is he?"

Tathagres withdrew the blade with a coarse scrape. The image spattered into sparks. She regarded Emien with a strangely guarded expression and said, "Who? He is named Kerainson Jaric, and he is Ivain Firelord's heir. But he will never survive to rescue Anskiere, even if he did possess a constitution sturdy enough to achieve his father's prowess. The initiation process, the Cycle of Fire, itself engenders madness; Ivain suffered as much. His heir is already damaged, a half-wit, couldn't you see? The Vaere would never accept him for training, and without the skills of the father, Anskiere is doomed."

Emien sucked fresh air into his lungs. Harmless as Kerainson Jaric appeared, something about his presence touched off an instinct of warning. Born and raised a fisherman, Emien preferred never to ignore hunches, however illogical they appeared. Yet his island superstitions seemed foolish beside Tathagres' worldly sophistication.

Embarrassed by his premonition, Emien accepted the sword from Tathagres' hand. An equally heavy weight seemed to settle on his heart. For at last he correctly interpreted the cause of Tathagres' brittle temper; with the frostwargs confined and the Stormwarden beyond reach of her command, she could not claim the Keys to Elrinfaer from her King. The setback galled her. Judging her pique, Emien guessed the powers of her neck band were still no match for the forces which bound the frostwargs behind their bastion of ice. Anskiere had bested her in this contest of wills, even if he had forfeited his own life in the accomplishment.

Unwilling to relinquish his passion for vengeance, Emien searched his mistress for signs of defeat; if she gave up after all he had suffered, he would strike her, though he died for impertinence. But the violet eyes which met his gaze still burned with determination.

"Your Stormwarden, if he survives long enough, shall certainly pay for his tempest." Tathagres' mouth thinned with sovereign cruelty. "The ice cannot protect him forever, this much I promise."

Suddenly Tathagres stiffened. Emien heard a horse stamp and snort somewhere below. Alarmed, he searched the thinning mist, hands clenched on the sword hilt. Hazy sunlight illuminated the beach. Fog still clung to the cliffs, but not for much longer. Within seconds the ledge would be visible to the patrol which approached from below. Emien prayed the bodies of the murdered guards would pass unnoticed.

That moment a man shouted in horrified discovery. Harness jingled and hooves pounded across wet sand. Another man hailed from the ridge above, followed abruptly by the din of an armed company dismounting.

Emien licked dry lips. "We're surrounded," he whispered frantically. Lifting his sword, he ducked beneath the ridge of ice, prepared to defend their position as best he could.

But Tathagres seized his wrist and jerked him painfully to her side. "No. Stay by me." Her nails dug like claws into his forearm. "I am going to tap the powers of Anskiere's geas, use them to pull us out of here. Unless they have archers we are safe."

Trembling, helpless, and diminished once again by Tathagres' superior powers, Emien wrestled to contain his panic. Sweat slicked his back. Clinging to mangled pride, he stood rigid in Tathagres' hold, while she touched her free hand to her collar and began an invocation. The last billow of mist drifted clear of the ice. Plainly visible on the strand below, an armored knot of men clustered around the corpse Tathagres had kissed to his death. Even as Emien estimated their number, the dark captain in their midst glanced up and stared straight at them.

CHAPTER XI

Backlash

"There!" shouted the Kielmark. He raised a muscled arm and pointed at the intruders. Cloaked in black like scavenger crows, a woman and a boy with a sword stood on a ledge of rock seventy yards above the beach. Who they were and what purpose had brought them to Cliffhaven made no difference. Three guardsmen lay dead, most likely of poison; for that crime, they would never receive pardon.

With blue eyes narrowed to slits of anger, the Lord of Cliffhaven commanded his men-at-arms. "You." His gesture singled out a horseman on the fringes. "Ride to the east station and bring back archers." The man appointed wheeled his mount, spurred at once to a gallop. The Kielmark raised his voice over drumroll of retreating hooves. "The rest of you cordon that cliff. Cut off every possibility of escape. When the bowmen arrive, you will close in and take the boy and the woman alive."

The men broke ranks with alacrity, aware their performance

might later be reviewed to the last critical detail. But this once, the Kielmark's concern lay elsewhere. Tense as a caged lion, he paced the tide mark, stooping now and again to examine scattered fragments of planking which once had been a boat. The keel and a few ribs were intact, enough to determine the craft's dimensions. The Kielmark planted his foot on the wreckage, and with thumbs hooked in his sword belt, regarded the corpses sprawled upon the beach. After a moment he spat in the sand and swore with a violence few men ever witnessed and lived to describe.

The boat, an aged, ungainly rig, at least explained why last night's watch had ignored his most urgent directive, that every person who trespassed on Cliffhaven be reported on sight. Probably the three had shirked duty on the assumption such a clumsy craft should carry equally harmless passengers. The mistake had killed them. That much was simple justice, the Kielmark reflected, and he fingered the pommel of his sword in temperamental fury. Though spared the nuisance of three hangings for disobedience, he still confronted the consequence the dead men's negligence had wrought.

The woman and the boy remained on the ledge, pinned in position by the relentless efficiency of the guardsmen. The base of the ice cliffs lay ringed by a glittering half circle of weapons and a full score more men waited on horseback, prepared to ride down any attempted escape through the lines. The presentation was perfect, each man alert at his post with his spear held angled and ready for instant action. Yet the Kielmark scratched his bearded jaw, distinctly unsettled. Where other commanders might disdain to pitch sixty men-at-arms against an unarmed woman and a boy, the King of Renegades acted without a second's hesitation. He deployed his finest company precisely because his trespassers seemed so contemptibly vulnerable.

With the wily patience of the desert wolf, the Kielmark studied the two who had dared trespass his domain. The boy evidently knew no swordplay, he gripped his weapon like a simple stick. The Kielmark dismissed him as terrified and ordinary, turning eyes cold and bleak as glacial ice upon the silver-haired woman who stood at the boy's side. A less careful man might have wasted precious minutes in appreciation of her strikingly beautiful form. The Lord of Cliffhaven searched only for inconsistency which might lend him advantage; and the woman's utter lack of concern jarred him like a sour note in counterpoint. Anyone confronted by sixty men-at-arms could be expected to show distress, but the only tension visible about this woman was in the hand she held clenched at her throat.

Revelation struck the Kielmark between one stride and the next. Arrogance on that scale accompanied none but an enchanter's power; if the woman had slain last night's watch with sorcery, even an armed company could well prove no match for her. Fearful for the lives under his command, the Kielmark sprinted up the beach. Whoever the woman was, she came for Anskiere, but not as his ally; any friend of the Stormwarden's would never have done murder.

"Back!" shouted the Kielmark. He waved his arm at the cliff. "Withdraw from the ice."

The troop captain glanced around, stupidly surprised. Irate, the Kielmark shouted again with an edge to his tone no officer under him dared disobey. *"Pull those men back!"*

White with alarm, the captain barked an order. The formation coalesced, initiated an orderly retreat. And the Kielmark cursed and regarded the woman once again, his great corded fist clenched in frustration around the hilt of his sword.

The jangle of weapons and linkmail echoed and bounded off the ice, threaded through by the rapid beat of hooves. Riders approached, the archers the Kielmark had sent for earlier. He spun to meet them, planted his massive frame squarely in their path. To avoid riding him down, the lead horseman reined back from a gallop with a violence that yanked his rawboned mount onto its haunches. The animal scrambled down the steep side of the dune, and sand showered over the Kielmark's leather leggings as it plunged to a halt scarcely a yard away. The Kielmark sprang forward, snatched the bow from the scabbard at the saddlebow. He grabbed for an arrow while the two score archers summoned from the east station thundered to a standstill around him. Without pause for explanation, the Kielmark shouldered clear of the press, bent the bow, raised it to the woman on the ledge. He aimed for the triangle of bare flesh framed by her black wool collar, and the drift of her fine silver hair.

His target made no move in defense. Her lips parted with amusement, and she laughed aloud at the notched threat of the arrow. A gust eddied her cloak hem. The Kielmark released. His shaft hissed skyward, described a flawless arc across the morning sky. The woman's smile dissolved. She lifted her hand. The arrow deflected, cracked harmlessly into rock, and rebounded in slivers.

"Sorcery!" shouted the captain. "She's a witch!" He raised crossed wrists in the traditional sign against evil, just as the woman touched both hands to the gold which encircled her neck.

Her gesture overturned the elements. Air howled suddenly overhead, as if a dragon had appeared out of legend and inhaled a piece of sky. With a crackle like tearing fabric, the woman and boy vanished as if they had never existed, transferred elsewhere by forces wrenched from the framework of Anskiere's geas. The Kielmark cursed with savage eloquence and flung down the bow.

Backlash struck an instant later as the powers the woman tapped to execute her escape ripped all else out of equilibrium.

Wind screamed off the sea, whined over cliff and dune and beach head. Sucked into a whirling tornado of force, the gale spiraled across the ice cliffs, bashing men and horses from their feet and uprooting trees like twigs. Hammered to his knees, blinded by a maelstrom of driven sand, the Kielmark buried his face in his hands. Somewhere to his right a horse thrashed and a wounded man screamed in agony; but the sounds seemed strangely overpowered. A second later the Kielmark divined the reason. Driven to towering heights by the wind, breakers raged shoreward, crests frayed into spindrift. Icy spray dashed the Kielmark's cheek, proof his shores were presently being ravaged by forces none but a weather mage could subdue. Every man ordered to duty beneath the ice cliffs stood in peril of drowning.

Determined to prevent losses, the Kielmark tore off the sash which bound his tunic and flung it over his face to protect his eyes. The gale harried the cloth, snapped it out of his fingers as he tried to tie a knot. He struggled, too stubborn to quit. At last, protected by his makeshift blindfold, he leaned into the wind and gained his feet.

Weather harried his every movement. Stung by flying sand and deafened by the rage of the elements, the Kielmark battled for each step gained; the effort taxed even his great strength. Never in memory had Cliffhaven's shores been beset by so violent a gale. Aware the entire island might be affected, the Kielmark forged ahead, possessed by outrage. He swore. There would be survivors; but the inevitable waste of men and resources galled him without end.

Laboring into the wind, he blundered into a man's wrist. Encouraged to find at least one of his guardsmen alive, the Kielmark guided the man's fingers to his belt. The wind screamed like a torture victim in his ears, making any word of encouragement impossible. The Kielmark granted the man a moment to steady himself, then plowed forward and sought after another. Soon he had gathered a small band of survivors. The stronger ones lent their efforts to his, and gradually the group gained on the storm and pulled back, away from the rampaging seas and into the scanty shelter of the dunes.

Even there, gale wind shrieked and buffeted their shoulders, sharp and punitive as a lash. Braced on widely planted feet, the

Kielmark panted for breath. He tugged the cloth from his eyes. Six of his finest fighting men crouched in the lee of the rocks, battered and bleeding and half beaten with exhaustion. One of the horse archers had fallen on his quiver when thrown from the saddle; the broken shaft of an arrow protruded from an ugly wound in his thigh. Close to seventy of Cliffhaven's finest men still struggled for their lives, all for a woman's meddling and a guard captain's failure at duty. Now all of Cliffhaven stood endangered. The Kielmark's great hands knotted into fists and his lip curled in a manner which sent chills down the spines of the men who clustered round him. But his voice and actions remained controlled, after the manner of a wolf stalked by mastiffs.

He touched the arm of the man who stood nearest, and even his shout could barely be heard above the din. "Fetch others. Form a chain. And make sure you place the wounded well up on high ground."

The man nodded, rallied gamely to the task. And concerned for the rest of his island demesne, the Kielmark left the hollow with no more delay. Belabored by the elements, he clambered over rocks and thorny scrub to higher ground. There the scope of the destruction the woman's sorcery had unleashed across Cliffhaven became awesomely apparent. Wind roared in from all points of the compass. The Kielmark was now certain Anskiere's powers had been usurped to complete the woman's transfer to safety. A mass of air had rushed elsewhere upon her departure, and the sharp drop in pressure made it plain a gale would follow, fiercer than any tempest. A towering line of squalls spanned the horizon as far as the eye could see. The speed of the storm's approach defied all credibility. Throughout a lifetime of collecting tales, only once had the Kielmark ever heard such weather described, and then by a gouty old salt who claimed to have survived the drowning of Tierl Enneth. Impossibly, a similar horror beset Cliffhaven.

The Kielmark rejected the inertia of despair. He crashed

like a bull through the thornbrakes, and by luck stumbled across a loose horse. He caught the bridle, vaulted astride without touching the stirrup, then slashed the reins on the animal's flank again and again, until its white hide quivered, flecked scarlet. Sped by pain and panic, the animal galloped mindlessly. The Kielmark shouted like a madman and urged it still faster.

Except for a few scattered steadings, Cliffhaven's population lived mostly on high ground. But several families of refugees left homeless by Anskiere's earlier tempest sheltered yet in the warehouses by the dockside; if the sea rose, they would perish. Racing the closing storm as if Kor's Accursed howled at his heels, the Kielmark drove the horse beyond safe limits. He would arrive in time to save his own, he swore by his very life. And he vowed also, for each death and every injury accrued beneath the ice cliffs that morning, the next man, child, or woman who dared set foot on Cliffhaven in the name of Anskiere of Elrinfaer would be put to the sword.

The axeblade whistled through the air and bit cleanly into the center of the old beech stump by the cabin door. Warmed by exertion, Telemark the forester leaned against the woodpile and paused to rake the hair back from his face. The air carried the first piquant chill of autumn, and true to habit, the ground before the woodshed held an untidy jumble of logs to be split before the coming winter. But unlike other years, the pile inside already stood waist high; with an invalid boy under his roof, Telemark took no risk of running short of fuel. His canny forestbred instincts warned that the coming season would be harsh, even for the lands north of the Furlains. Snowfall would be heavy and deep, and wood scarce; but cold weather enhanced the pelts. He could expect good trapping.

Telemark reached once again for the axe, and froze with his fist on the handle. The brushpheasant in the south thicket had stopped calling. Attuned like a musician to the natural rhythm of the woods, the forester listened and swept a glance across the sky to see if a hawk flew overhead. Noisily the brush-pheasant took wing, an odd trait for a species whose best defense was camouflage and stillness. That moment Telemark heard the sound which had startled it into flight.

A high keening gust of air rushed down on the clearing from the southeast, bending the treetops like ripe wheat and wrenching off a whirlwind of twigs and leaves and dead branches. The disturbance resembled no weather pattern Telemark had ever known, and even as his hair prickled with alarm he dropped the axe and sprinted for the cabin.

The force overtook him before he reached the doorway. Wind struck with the impact of a battle hammer. Slammed between the shoulders by the brunt of its violence, Telemark missed stride, tumbled into a rolling fall which fetched him hard against the stone stoop. Bruised, frightened, and half stunned, he groaned and struggled to rise while pelted by a malicious shower of sticks and torn leaves. And above his head, the wind smashed headlong into the door. Leather hinges rent like paper and the latch burst into a fountainhead of sparks. Horrified by recognition, Telemark saw his dwelling assaulted by the powers of sorcery.

Frantic with concern for Jaric, the forester caught hold of the doorframe and dragged himself across the threshold. There he confronted a scene which tore him to the heart. Wind raged like a demon's curse through the cabin's tight confines. Bottles of rare herbs tumbled from the shelves, seasons of careful collecting spoiled in an instant. Tools pinwheeled from their hooks and the polished copper pots from the pantry clattered across the floor, splintering all in their path to wreckage. A meticulous man by nature, Telemark winced and looked beyond the immediate destruction for the boy. The wicker chair lay overturned by the hearth, its stuffed pillows strewn dangerously close to the flames. Jaric sprawled on the floorboards nearby and the blankets which once had covered him flapped like bats across the floor by his side.

Telemark clutched the doorjamb to steady himself. Splintered wood jabbed his palms as the wind buffeted his frame, but the first violence of the assault appeared to be waning. Even as the forester noticed the change, the sorcery set against him dwindled and abruptly died. Ripped from table and shelves and hooks, the belongings he had acquired through long years of solitude lay scattered and smashed in the corners. A pan lid described a drunken circle across the floor, its metallic ring like a shout against sudden silence. Shaking with reaction, Telemark kicked the object to a stop. Then he fell back against the breached security of his wall, and blinked back tears of anger.

Wise to the ways of the world beyond his wood, the forester considered his desecrated home, and knew that the damage resulted from a backlash of power. Somewhere two sorcerers stood in conflict, and a deflection in equilibrium between them had brought ruin through his door because the boy he sheltered was somehow involved. Telemark twisted his hands in his sleeves, pained by the inevitable; no safety existed for Jaric here. Whoever the boy on his hearthstone was, he had enemies beyond the capabilities of any forester, even one who had once served mercenaries in the Duke's army. The decision weighed heavily on Telemark's heart. Yet he dared not keep the boy longer; with sorcerers involved, the peril was too great to shoulder in solitude.

Beyond the door the brushpheasant called, returned to its thicket. Assured the immediate danger was past, Telemark crossed the littered floor and stooped at Jaric's side. Though deeply unconscious, the boy seemed physically undamaged; time would determine whether anything else was amiss. With the stiff-lipped expression he assumed when commanded to snare songbirds for the Duke's menagerie, Telemark gathered the boy off the floor.

With unsteady hands he laid Jaric on the cot in the corner, then paced restlessly to the window. Except for a mangled drift of branches by the shed, the forest stood unchanged, its green depths a balm to the eye after the pathetic wreckage inside the cabin. The shadows slanted only slightly; if he hurried, he could be across by sunset. The town gates closed promptly at nightfall. Much as the forester cared for Jaric, the sooner the boy was placed in the care of Kor's initiates in Corlin, the better his own peace of mind. Without pausing to sort the ruins of his home, Telemark belted on his sword, slung bow and quiver across his wide shoulders, and bundled his charge into a blanket. Then he lifted Jaric in his arms, picked his way around the slivered door, and turned his steps toward Corlin.

The hollow where the path joined the main trail through Seitforest seemed oddly dark for midday. Telemark frowned, hesitated, and shifted Jaric's weight higher on his shoulder. Something was amiss. Overhead the sky was cloudless, but the light which filtered down through the crowns of the oaks seemed strangely murky. The trees themselves stood hushed, undisturbed even by the busy rustle of squirrels in a place where the acorns lay abundant as beach pebbles among the leaves.

Telemark halted at the edge of a thicket, every sense alert. Leftwards, behind a heavy stand of brush, he heard a footfall stealthy enough that even a wild creature might overlook so slight a sound. He laid Jaric at his feet, and with swift, sure fingers, strung his bow. Then he drew his sword and ran it point first into the moss, with the hilt ready to his hand. And he waited.

No common footpad lurked behind the trees. A human would make more noise, perhaps startle the birds and cause the squirrels to scold from the branches; but no disturbance of man's making could explain the eerie dimmed light. Even as Telemark sought the cause the gloom deepened, as if the very stuff of darkness clotted upon the air. Slowly, cautiously, the forester eased an arrow from his quiver. The familiar grip of the bow felt clammy to his palm as he knocked shaft to string and bent the weapon to full draw. Again he waited, motionless, his muscled arms steady as old knotted wood, and his aim on the brush as unerring as if he stalked the shy satin-deer. But with chill certainty, Telemark knew he hunted no animal.

As the shadow darkened around him, he heard a slight sound, nothing more than the sigh of a brushed leaf. And a pair of eyes gleamed ahead, orange as live coals, and as deadly. Telemark swung the bow fractionally. He brought his arrow to bear, knowing his doom was upon him; for the creature he opposed was of demonkind, a Llondian empath whose defenses no mortal could withstand.

Before Telemark could release, a thought image ripped into his mind, words shot through with a white-hot blaze of agony. *'Mortal, place the weapon down.'*

The forester resisted, quivering. Cold sweat beaded his forehead and his streaked hair clung damply to his temples. For the sake of the boy at his feet, he loosed his cramped fingers from the string. The bow sang, transformed by Llondian influence to a note of pure sorrow. The arrow hissed into the brush. In the instant the demon's whistle of anger clove his ears, Telemark saw his shaft rattle through the branches and cleanly miss. Llondian eyes looked up in scarlet accusation. And its anger transformed unbearably into an image sharpened to wound its attacker.

Telemark screamed. He saw the greenery of Seitforest withered, the stately, familiar trees riven from the earth. Blackened roots jabbed at the sky like accusing fingers, and across the vale beyond the Redwater, Corlin Town smoked and blazed; all for an arrow carelessly loosed upon a creature who intended no harm.

There the image ceased. Abruptly released, the forester returned to himself with the echoes of his own cry of pain still ringing in his ears. He straightened, shaking, and saw the cloaked figure of the Llondel poised in the gloom before him. Baleful orange eyes regarded him, and a good deal less steadily Telemark stared back.

"What do you want?" he asked hoarsely, and risked a glance at Jaric. The boy appeared unharmed. But only a hole remained where the sword had rested in the ground. The Llondian took no risks.

'Never you take the young fire-bearer to the blue-cloaks,' the demon sent.

"What?" Telemark spread his hands, palms upward, to show he did not understand.

The Llondel lifted a finger slim and gray as a lichened twig. It pointed to Jaric. *'Never you take,'* and an image of uprooted trees and the smell of burning overlaid the words, sharply defined warning of the demon's powers.

The forester stepped back, unable to contain the desperate cornered fear a songbird knows when the snare closes over its neck. What was he to do with a boy who was shadowed by the meddling of sorcerers, if not leave him with the initiates at Kordane's Sanctuary? To keep Jaric was to risk his death; yet the Llondel's intent was clear. Telemark felt a sensation of well-being brush his mind, plainly an attempt at reassurance. But no man dared trust a demon.

Burdened by a poignant sense of helplessness, Telemark shook his head. "I'm sorry," he said firmly. "I cannot keep the boy. He requires better care and security than I can provide."

The Llondel trilled a treble fifth and moved suddenly, lifting the missing sword from the dusky folds of its cloak. It offered the weapon to the forester, hilt first, with a hiss of aggrieved affront. *'Leave, then.'*

Telemark hesitated, unsure of the creature's intent, afraid if he reached for the weapon he would again be made to suffer.

The demon jabbed the pommel impatiently at his chest. *'Man-fool,'* it sent. *'You take.'*

Careful to move without threat, the forester raised his hand to the sword. But the instant his flesh touched the grip, demon images clove his mind like the sheared edge of an axeblade, and swept away all semblance of identity.

* * *

Telemark saw the forest through alien eyes, but the trees, the sky, and the dusky humid smell of vegetation in his nostrils, were like nothing he had ever known. The wood was a place of dim violet shadows. Long trailing tendrils of leaves arched overhead, dappled by reddish light, and strange animals whistled from the thickets. Yet the vision held no ambiguity of meaning; Telemark understood he beheld the Llondel's home, a place inconceivably removed from Keithland soil.

Suddenly the alien forest was slashed by an aching flare of brilliance. A shrill scream of sound ripped away the image of trees, and Telemark's eyes were seared by the blistering glory of Kordane's Fires as they had shone before the Great Fall. But to the Llondel, the Fires brought not salvation but captivity, exile, and suffering. Shackled by the demon's imaging, Telemark saw the Fires arc like heated steel across the velvet depths of the heavens, then plunge earthward, never to rise again.

His sight went dark. Beset by pain, he breathed air which ached his lungs, dry and thin and cold after that of his home forest. One with the first Llondelei of Keithland, he crawled forth from the wreckage of an engine which lay smashed in the snow of a hillside. The image spun, wavered, blurred encompassing generations of Llondian history. Pinned by an onslaught of incomprehensible realities, Telemark tasted insanity, hopelessness, and a longing for the purple twilit shadow of a homeworld believed lost. His heart ached with a measure of sorrow unknown to the heritage of man. Tears coursed down his cheeks. Just when it seemed the demon would break him upon a wheel of sheer despair, the image shifted.

A man appeared, etched against the darkness. And bound to the Llondel's intent, Telemark beheld the silver hair and the stern sad features of the Stormwarden of Elrinfaer; but the sorcerer's wrists were fettered and his powers dumb, and for that reason darkness closed over the world, never to be lifted.

Savaged by an agony of loss, the forester cried out. And his scream drew fire.

Swept under by a red-gold flood of flame, Telemark flung his hands across his face, but the blaze consumed his fingers, and his vision was not spared. The conflagration raged and spun, fanning outward into a wheel of light. At the center stood a man whose hair streamed over raggedly clothed shoulders like a spill of raw gold. With a jolt of startled awe, Telemark recognized the fine dark eyes of Kerainson Jaric; and the Llondel's image ceased.

Released, Telemark opened tear-soaked lashes and discovered he sat in the wooden chair in his own cabin. His bow and his sword lay at his feet. Shivering with reaction, and half stunned by disbelief, he glanced about and saw that his belongings had been straightened up, each item returned to its place; the smashed jars of herbs stood restored on the shelves, the glass miraculously repaired. Except for the charred ruin of the latch, the backlash, and the Llondel's intervention, it might all have been a dream. . . .

Still caught in wonder, Telemark rose stiffly to his feet, and at his movement, Jaric stirred on the cot in the corner. The forester crossed to the boy's side in time to see the brown eyes open, restored to true awareness for the first time since the injury. Telemark stared down at the boy upon the bed with a mixture of awe and trepidation and tenderness. For incomprehensible as much of the Llondel's imaging had been, a portion of its message was plain; with the Stormwarden of Elrinfaer entrapped, this boy represented the final hope of the Llondelei to end the exile which began at the time of the Great Fall. Never would the demons permit Jaric to fall into the hands of the priests.

Haunted by the mystery of the fire image, Telemark watched the boy's recovery carefully, uncertain what to expect. But Jaric's initial reaction seemed entirely ordinary.

Confronted by the strange confines of the cabin, his hands

tightened on the blanket and his pale brow creased in confusion as if seeking the reassurance of something familiar. Quickly Telemark caught the boy's hand.

"Easy," he said softly. "You've had a tough time since I took you in. Can you tell me how you feel?"

The words did nothing to reassure. Jaric's frown deepened, and he seemed to struggle for speech. At last in a thin frightened voice, he admitted, "I can't remember who I am."

CHAPTER XII

Protégé

TELEMARK GAVE JARIC'S HAND A squeeze of reassurance and reflected that the aftereffects of a head injury could occasionally prove merciful. This boy had ridden into Seitforest harried by powers no mortal could support with grace; he would recover his health more easily without recollection of his immediate past.

"Don't fret." The forester tugged the blanket free of the boy's tense fingers. "You suffered a terrible blow to the head, but time and rest will set everything right, even your memory."

Jaric twisted his head on the pillow. "But I don't even know my name." His gaze quartered the cabin again, as if he searched for something lost. "How did I get here?"

Telemark sighed. "Your name, which you mentioned when delirious with fever, is Kerainson Jaric. And I picked you up off the ground in Seitforest after you were assaulted by bandits. They robbed you of everything, even your clothes, which effectively eliminates any further clues. Since no one seems to have searched for you since, I suggest you winter with me while you recover. You'll be as safe here as anywhere else, and I could use help with the traplines."

Jaric bit his lip, eyes widening to encompass the neat rows of snares which hung from pegs on the far wall. "But I know nothing," he said softly. The admission seemed wrung from the depths of his heart, and the anguish reflected on his features moved the forester to pity.

Telemark framed the boy's face between his palms. "Don't worry. I'll teach you. And in our spare time, you'll study swordplay. That way, when you recall who you are, you'll not get your skull cracked again at the hands of the lawless."

Jaric's expression eased. Encouraged by the response Telemark winked, and was rewarded for the first time by a smile.

For Telemark the following days became a time of discovery and revelation, after so many weeks of caring for a comatose invalid. Though weak and unsure of himself, Jaric applied himself to life with a feverish sense of determination. Watching him re-weave the laces of an old snowshoe, the forester sensed the boy lived in fear of incompetence. The harsh leather of the thongs cut into the delicate skin of his fingers, but Jaric persisted until his face became pinched with fatigue. Still he showed no sign of quitting until the task was complete.

Telemark laid the pack strap he was mending across his chairback and crossed the cabin to the boy's side. "No need to finish the whole task today." He ran his fingers over the weave, and found the firm, careful execution of a job well-handled. "You've done fine."

Jaric looked up, eyes dark with uncertainty. He said nothing, but plainer than speech his expression revealed his distrust of the praise. The boy would finish with the snowshoe though the thongs wore his fingers raw, Telemark observed. With a small sigh of frustration, he let his patient be.

Hours later, when Jaric knotted the last thong in place, Telemark was startled by the sweet smile of satisfaction which lit the boy's face. And it occurred to the forester that for Jaric, who had no recognizable past, the accomplishment represented a major victory.

Oblivious to the fact she actually slept in a capsule deep beneath the isle of the Vaere, Taen dreamed she sat cross-legged in the changeless silvery twilight of the clearing. Tamlin stood opposite her, pipe clenched between his teeth. His red-brown whiskers framed a thoughtful expression.

"I'm thinking you're ready," he said softly, and for the first time Taen could recall, his feathers and his bells were stilled.

She tilted her chin impishly and grinned at him. "You mean you're finally tired of hearing me describe how much that old fisherman dreams about the tavern girl at the docks?" Under the Vaere's tutelage, her skills had grown and refined, and recently, as an exercise, Tamlin made her spend tedious hours tracking the mind of a crotchety fish trapper who sailed just north of the island checking his lines. She *was* getting better, and increased confidence gave her leeway enough to tease.

But levity was wasted effort with the Vaere. "How many pairs of socks does the fellow own? Can you tell?" Tamlin bit down on his pipe and puffed furiously, frowning at his charge.

Taen wrinkled her nose in distaste. "Socks?" With a re signed sigh, she closed her eyes and cast her mind outward, awareness spread like a net across the lifeless face of the sea. At first she felt nothing.

"You're overriding the subject," said Tamlin sharply. "Stay annoyed with me, and even if you manage to locate the old man, you'll alter his frame of reference. Perhaps at that you're not ready at all."

Although Taen had not the slightest idea what she was supposed to be ready for, she curbed her irritation and concentrated on emptying her mind. Her sense of self gradually receded, replaced by a passive quality of waiting timeless as the magic which bound the clearing. Presently, like the tentative flicker of the first star at twilight, she felt the old man's consciousness brush against her awareness. Bent over a reeking bucket of fish bait, his thoughts preoccupied by daydreams of the tavern wench's ample bustline, his mind interested Taen about as much as old woolens in need of darning. But she persisted, threading cleanly through the man's surface awareness in pursuit of his collection of footwear.

The information she discovered startled her to the point where she burst into honest laughter. Opening her eyes, she glared at Tamlin, who maddeningly vanished at once. But by now she was accustomed to his vagaries.

"You knew," she accused the spot where he had stood a moment earlier.

A smoke ring appeared, wavering in the air, and an instant later, Tamlin materialized beneath, frowning in agitation. "Knew what?"

Taen twisted a stray lock of hair between her fingers. "Knew about the socks," she said, and grinned. "The old crow doesn't *have* any. He goes barefoot."

"True enough." Tamlin folded his arms with a rattle of beads. "But that's no excuse for carelessness." And he left her with the image of the fisherman, who scratched his gray head with fingers still slimy from the fish bait, and puzzled to fathom why the tavern girl's fair bosom suddenly reminded him of socks.

"You must practice," said Tamlin, and the sudden curtness in his tone cut Taen's amusement short. The flush left by laughter drained slowly from her cheeks. Her blue eyes turned serious.

"Not the fisherman," she pleaded.

Tamlin paced, his bells a jingling counterpoint to his impatience. "No. You've grown beyond that. I rather thought you should try something more demanding." He stopped short, and sharply considered her. "Your short-range skills are quite satisfactory. It's time to try you over distance. Close relations often make the easiest subjects to start. How would you feel if I asked you to dream-read the members of your immediate family?"

Taen glanced up, transformed by excitement. Although she had dedicated herself heart and mind to the training offered her by the Vaere, the satisfaction gained through her progress had been marred by constant worry for the mother she had left on Imrill Kand. And Emien, when she had last parted from him, had been troubled and desperate with worry for her.

"Your skills are ready," said Tamlin. "But there are perils. I leave the choice up to you."

But the chance to look in on those she loved, and perhaps reassure them of her well-being, attracted Taen beyond caution. "I would try now," she said steadily.

Tamlin shifted his pipe between his teeth and puffed on it, considering her answer. Then he nodded, blew a smoke ring, and vanished, obviously well pleased with his charge.

Taen sat down in the grass, trembling in anticipation. Ever since she had learned her gifts could be controlled, she had longed to contact her home. Now with permission granted she felt strangely apprehensive. What if she discovered all was not well? Yet before the lonely yearning in her heart even fear held no power to sway her. Proud of her place as one chosen by the Vaere, she closed her eyes and began the primary exercises to prepare her mind for her craft.

In recalling Imrill Kand, the first thing Taen remembered was the dusky smell of the peat. Even in summer, fires burned in the smokehouses, curing herring against the long, lean months when boats could be locked in the harbor by winter's storms. Guided by that memory, Taen felt the darkness within her mind shift and part before the reality of another place. Though the deep shadow of evening lay over the isle, she knew her dreamsense had brought her home.

Poised on her gift like a hawk on an air current, Taen hovered over Imrill Kand, startled to find the keen chill of autumn in the air. Lulled by the magic of the Vaere, she had forgotten that seasons would continue in her absence, and the discovery disturbed her. She would return one day, perhaps; but all she knew would be changed. And like a small girl caught in a nightmare, she fled to the house off Rat's Alley for comfort and protection.

Her mother dozed in the wooden rocker by the hearth, sheltered still by the brother who had taken her in since the death of her husband. Beloved work-worn hands lay cradled in her apron, and a familiar curl had strayed from the pins which secured her hair; Taen noticed new lines around eyes already heavily wrinkled by hardship and loss. But the women of Imrill Kand were inured to life's deprivations; Leri Marl's widow had endured her personal tragedies without yielding to despair.

Suddenly uncertain of her control, Taen reached out, tentatively opened contact with her mother's mind. But delicate as her first touch was, she was noticed. The woman's eyes quivered open, blue, but faded now by the first traces of cataracts. Her seamed lips parted into a smile of welcome which changed almost at once to laughter.

"Taen?" Her mother blinked, spilling sudden tears of welcome. Secure in her island heritage, she never thought to question when the sight was upon her; and no vision ever brought more joy than the assurance of her daughter's well-being. "You are safe, I see, Fires be thanked for that." She paused and smiled again, unabashed by the moisture on her cheeks. "Have you seen Emien? I worry about your brother. He was always brash, and quick to resent what he could not change. I fear he bears the Stormwarden no love, child. And that sets sorrow upon me, for Anskiere was like a father to you both."

Taen hesitated, reluctant to share what little she knew of Emien. And mercifully her mother mistook her silence for impatience. "Go, child. Seek your brother. Tell him he is missed, and that *Dacsen* is needed at home."

But the sloop was lost, cast onto the reefs by orders of a

King's man now dead. If the wreckage had failed to wash ashore, Taen could not bear to break the news. Burdened by a sense of her own responsibility, she withdrew from her mother's presence and flung herself headlong into a search for her brother, as if by finding him she could negate the betrayal of his upbringing and the sorrow that knowledge might cause the folk who raised him.

Darkness closed like a tunnel about her. Suffocated by the sensations of distance and cold, Taen struggled to regain control of her gift. Unlike the old fisherman, Emien's mind was hard and bright, a fierce turmoil of emotional conflicts; the pattern was closer to her than any other. No matter how remote her brother had grown, Taen was determined to find him. She steadied herself with a memory of his face, black hair spilled untidily across his brow, his eyes shadowed and wary since the day the accident had claimed their father's life. And light suddenly exploded into existence around her, as if the association opened a connection between them.

Centered by the powers of her gift, Taen found herself looking down on the torchlit arcade of a palace courtyard. Two men circled over the patterned brick beyond the archway, stripped to the waist, and armed with practice foils. In a fast-paced exchange of swordplay, the larger man lunged. His blade clanged against his opponent's guard. The smaller fellow grunted and recovered.

"Mind your footwork, boy," said the larger man, and with a start of surprise, Taen recognized her brother as his partner.

Annoyed by the correction and unaware of his sister's presence, Emien riposted. Linked by her dream-sense, Taen shared her brother's bitter satisfaction as he hammered blows upon his tutor's weapon. The pace increased. Flamelight gleamed on sweat-slicked shoulders as the fighters wove across the courtyard, graceful as dancers in the rhythms of parry and riposte. The sparring was intended for practice, an exercise to develop sharper skills. But merged with her brother's mind, Taen realized Emien fought for much higher stakes, as if the outcome of this simple match held capacity to poison his future. Wrapped in a black web of passion, he fenced as if his teacher were an enemy.

Steel rang upon crossguard with a sharp, angry clamor. Both men gasped for breath. Absorbed by the fiery play of light on the foils, each teased and feinted, seeking an opening in his opponent's guard. And drugged on the wine of her brother's hatred, Taen almost missed the raised hand as his instructor signaled the end of the bout. For one ragged, flickering instant, it seemed Emien would not desist. Then he lowered his foil, and rubbed his damp forehead with the back of his wrist.

His instructor regarded him intently, then collected the practice weapon. "You're getting quite good. With work, you have the potential to be very good indeed. Now get some rest. I'll meet you again tomorrow."

Emien watched the swordmaster depart with narrowed eyes. The praise was a string of meaningless words in his ears. Still oblivious to Taen's presence, he crossed the courtyard and retrieved his shirt and tunic from a bench. Sewn of soft scarlet material, the garments were bordered with black and gold threadwork, with laces at cuff and neck caught by jewelled hooks. Amazed by his finery, Taen shivered as the sweat chilled on her brother's body. He had risen high since they had parted on the decks of *Crow*. And somehow, somewhere, along with his bettered station, he had acquired a hunger for power no training at weapons could assuage.

Numbed by his strangeness, Taen did little but follow as Emien entered the palace. He made his way down a series of ornately decorated corridors and entered a carpeted antechamber. A pair of men-at-arms guarded the doorway beyond. Emien nodded in greeting and crossed inside, blinking in the sudden glare of candles.

The room's furnishings represented more wealth than Taen could have imagined in one place; but after three weeks of life in King Kisburn's court, Emien barely noticed the rare wood, the patterned rugs, or the fine wool tapestries which covered the walls by the casements. He paused with his tunic and shirt draped over his forearm, embarrassed to discover the chamber was not empty.

A richly dressed official stood by the hearth, engaged in animated conversation with a woman clad in ermine and amethysts. Fine gold wires bound her snowy hair and the bracelets on her slender wrists chimed as sweetly as Tamlin's bells as she lifted her head and acknowledged the boy's presence. The official faltered and fell silent, plump cheeks quivering with irritation.

Emien bowed smoothly, as if accustomed to court manners all his life. The easy grace of the movement left Taen uneasy, and worse, the face of the official seemed strangely cloaked in shadow, as if something about his complexion did not agree with the light.

If Emien perceived anything unusual about the person of the official, he chose not to be bothered. "Tathagres, my Lord Sholl, I beg to be excused. Had I guessed the council would end early, I'd have chosen a different route."

Tathagres waved him impatiently past. Painfully conscious of her beauty, Emien proceeded to the suite of rooms which served as his own apartment. There he tossed the rich tunic carelessly over a stuffed chair, summoned servants, and called querulously for bath water. Appalled by the ease with which he had shed his upbringing on Imrill Kand, Taen watched Emien berate the servants for clumsiness and savagely banish them from his presence. Soured by the exchange, he finished his washing in solitude, then poured himself wine and sprawled, exhausted, across the rich coverlet of his bed.

He did not immediately sleep, but lay staring with widened eyes at the single candle left alight on the nightstand. Rest came with difficulty, Taen sensed, and troubled by the unhappy changes court life had wrought in her brother, she decided to engage her gift and bring him comfort. Poised like a dream on the edge of Emien's awareness, Taen gathered her powers into tight focus and spread a blanket of peace over his thoughts. She led him back to his beginnings on Imrill Kand. Enfolded in the soft scent of peat and the sigh of sea wind through the chimes on the rooftree above the loft where he slept during childhood, Emien relaxed. Disarmed by the gentleness of her sending, he slipped into sleep.

Oblivious to the fact that his thoughts were influenced by another, he imagined he stood with his sister on a grassy hillside above the village. Summer breezes fanned her black hair across her cheeks and the gray wool of her shift blew loosely about her while the small brown goats left their grazing and nosed her hands, begging for grain. Taen tangled her fingers in their rough coats, a smile of joy on her face. Watching her, Emien could almost forget her lameness and the innocent vulnerability which had permitted her to believe Anskiere's lies; but now she was dead, drowned in a storm like his father. Never again would she play with the goats in the meadows of Imrill Kand.

Though her memory held nothing but tragedy, in the dream she would not stop smiling. Through the window of her gift, she regarded her brother with eyes of clearest blue and said, "But Emien, I am alive."

Emien tossed on the bed, struggled to free himself from a torment he now recognized as nightmare. Taen had died; Imrill Kand was forever barred to him. Fevered and sweating, he fought the vision of his sister, insistent in his hatred of Anskiere. The dream would not release him; he could not make himself waken.

"Emien, no." Taen's voice battered against his isolation, seductive with compassion. "I survived the storm when *Crow* foundered. The Stormwarden protected me. I am with you now, can't you see? Oh, why must you believe Tathagres' lies? Don't you know she uses you?"

But her words failed to soothe. The kindness Taen intended brought Emien nothing but anguish, poisoned as he was by his own guilt. For if his sister had been preserved at the Stormwarden's hand, every act he had committed in the cause of her vengeance became evil beyond question.

He tossed on the bed, sobbing aloud with misery. "You're *dead*," he accused, and when the image of his sister's presence failed to leave him, his voice went ugly with rage. "Leave me!"

"But why?" Taen searched his face, her light eyes suddenly flooded with tears. "What could make you turn against the Stormwarden who once protected you? Did you believe the Constable, that he murdered the folk of Tierl Enneth? Emien, Anskiere was innocent. *I can show you.*"

Confident of his trust, Taen gathered her skills, assembled dream images to prove to her brother how her gift had enabled her to know beyond question that Anskiere had not caused the drowning of helpless people. She touched her brother's mind with truth, utterly unprepared for the fact that her message brought him nothing but guilt.

Emien's voice split into a raw scream of denial. "No!" Condemned beyond pardon by the vision she wove, he lashed back, set the poisoned dregs of his own warped reason against his sister in attempt to restore the dignity he had lost when he first accepted Tathagres as mistress.

The dream link reversed itself. Caught in the meshes of her brother's passion, Taen felt herself tossed headlong into clouded skies and the savage, storm-whipped seas of a gale. To the battered, emotionally torn mind of her brother, this tempest seemed more than a natural contest of elements. A squall had taken the life of his father. Hammered by thunderous, foam-laced swells, *Crow* had foundered, and above the demented howl of the gusts Emien heard once again the screams of drowning slaves and the cries of his lost sister; and with the pinnace's tiller clenched once more in his blistered hands, he watched, helpless, as the seas stripped the lives of the survivors with passionless cruelty. Soon scarcely a handful remained. Always the sea lurked at his back, a tireless, insatiable enemy. Humbled over and over again by its might, and by the powers of the sorcerer who controlled it, Emien wept in frustration.

Inflamed by the need to retaliate, he raced down a rocky beach on the isle of Cliffhaven. Drawn along by the dream link, Taen felt the icy air ache in his lungs with each breath, through his ears heard the crash as the breakers creamed white against the shore and the shrill calling of gulls. Ahead, cliffs rose like a wall against the sky, lofty stone tiers encased in crystalline sheets of ice. The raw cold of a sorcerer's enchantment reddened Emien's skin, but he felt no discomfort; beyond that bastion of frost lay his enemy, and his obsession for vengeance permitted no rest. He would pierce Anskiere's defenses though he broke his hands trying, and with a separate thrill of horror, Taen realized the glassy abutments of ice imprisoned the Stormwarden who once had protected her from harm.

She tried to break free, to wrest control of the dream from her brother's maddened grasp. She had to know more concerning the Stormwarden's fate. But Emien's hatred was too strong to resist, and her presence itself threatened his existence. Even as Taen reached to manipulate the fabric of his image, her brother drew the sword from the sheath at his side and lifted it high overhead, point poised for a killing blow.

"No!" Taen fell back, spread-eagled against the ice, unable to believe he would strike. "Would you murder your own sister? Emien!"

But the words failed to deter him. Emien seemed not to see her at all, and with a pang of awful horror Taen realized the fury which drove him was directed solely at the Stormwarden of Elrinfaer. Emien would drive the sword home, and never notice she stood in his path.

Just as his wrist tensed to engage the downstroke, a shout rang out down the beach. Hooves thundered like war drums over the sand. Emien whirled and saw one of the Kielmark's mounted patrols bearing down on him at a gallop. Steel sang through the air as he twisted, white-faced and frightened. But before he could ready himself for defense, a force like white-hot magma closed over him, and he felt himself ripped into transfer by the powers of Tathagres' neckband.

The dream link carried Taen along with him. Even with her senses overwhelmed by the rush of strange forces, she heard her brother scream aloud in terror, for the memory of his transfer from Cliffhaven to the palace of Kisburn's court recurred to him only in nightmare. Ripped away from the solid ground beneath the ice cliffs, he felt himself suspended as before, in a place where darkness reigned. The air he breathed held the metallic tang of a blacksmith's forge, and dizzied by its heat, his grip upon his own self-awareness wavered. As if torchlit against a backdrop of dark, Emien beheld beings whose features contained no trace of humanity. While the forces of the transfer held him locked and helpless, the black-skinned, red-eyed visages of Kor's Accursed leered down upon him from a high dais of stone.

Trapped in his frame of reference, Taen also noticed the demons. Powerless to intervene, she stood by as they conferred among themselves, weighing the poison in her brother's soul. And with a horror as great as Emien's own, the girl watched one of the demons rise and point, and pronounce her brother's name as one chosen.

Revulsion tore through her. The dream link unraveled under a lightning burst of negative force, and flung across distance by an explosion of emotional rejection, Taen shivered and woke in the dell on the Isle of the Vaere. Sheltered once more within the grove, she huddled with her arms clenched around her knees. The place seemed less than secure. Taen glanced about her with dream-haunted eyes. Although the link with Emien stood severed, she sensed the resonant echo of her brother's screams as he woke from nightmare on the silken coverlet of his bed in Kisburn's palace.

Never in Taen's darkest imagination had she guessed her brother might stand in such peril, even when fear and anger had sometimes made him cruel. Troubled, she hesitated to confide her findings to the Vaere. Though quick in his perceptions, Tamlin could often be dispassionate concerning events beyond his island sanctuary. If Emien was to be helped, he would require the care and the compassion of one who understood his difficult nature; one who knew, as his family did, that he had never been able to forgive himself the error which tangled the net and began the inexorable string of circumstances which resulted in his father's death.

Alone with her dilemma and confined to the Isle of the Vaere, Taen knew only one on all of Keithland capable enough to restore her brother's trust. Without pausing to ask Tamlin's permission, she gathered the battered remains of her dream-sense around her, and launched her awareness in search of Anskiere of Elrinfaer.

Fragile as fine silk thread, her probe unreeled across the void. Though the Stormwarden's mind had largely stayed closed to her, Taen recalled every nuance of his presence. She searched for the constant rhythm of surf against the beaches of home; the wild, keening song of the first north wind of autumn, and the sure power of the solstice tides; Anskiere was all that and more, changeless as the renewal discovered each year in the gentle showers of spring. Confident the Stormwarden would recognize her, Taen strengthened her sending and presently located a thin glimmer of daylight. Hurrying now, eager to reach her goal, Taen rushed through the gap, into a reality far distant.

She was greeted first by the solid boom of breakers and the sigh of breezes combing windswept heights. A moment later, the darkness parted around her, and her dream-sense ached in the glare of sunlight thrown off the sheer, impenetrable heights of the same ice cliffs she had encountered in Emien's dream. The sight dismayed her. Pierced by the plaintive cries of the gulls, Taen felt daunted by unanswerable sorrow. She surveyed that desolate vista, unwilling to believe her search would end here, in a place of deserted wilds. With the care Tamlin had taught her, Taen focused her dream-sense and sounded the place for traces of life, or any clue which might reveal the Stormwarden's presence.

Almost at once the resonance of Anskiere's power surged through the gate she had opened in her mind. Constant and strong as storm tide, the warding forces he had set forth in that place sang across the channels of Taen's sensitivity. Reassured of his presence, the girl gathered herself and turned her dream-reader's skills to tap the ward's source.

Darkness met her, deep and vast as night, and seemingly solid as a wall. Taen gasped, unable to orient herself. She delved deeper, sought to thrust the suffocating blackness aside and reach the Stormwarden's awareness. But her meager skills would not answer in that place; the shadow refused to part. Tossed about like a moth in a downdraft, Taen floundered and struggled to reorient. But the wards restricted her, making progress impossible.

Taen persisted. Cold savaged her flesh, cut deep into her bones until it seemed her very thoughts would freeze in place. Her dream-sense labored, suddenly burdened by an over-whelming weight of earth and ice overhead. Taen persevered, striving to fathom the hidden center of the wardspell, but it was not Anskiere she found. High and thin with distance, she caught the whistling echo of a cry. Strange creatures lay imprisoned beneath. The eerie harmonics of their wailing chilled Taen even more than the terrible cold, for the sound touched her dream-sense with a feeling of lust and killing beyond the capacity of violence to assuage. Held fast by Anskiere's wardenship, the creatures she sensed could not win through to freedom; but here, at the vortex of his powers, where she should have encountered the Stormwarden's living presence, Taen found silence and frost and the impenetrable stillness of ages.

Discouraged at last she withdrew, returned to awareness of her own body. But the grove of the Vaere seemed strangely comfortless after her sojourn, its unbreakable quiet a constraint upon her ears. Grieved for the fate of her brother and distressed by the loss and the loneliness created by the Stormwarden's absence, Taen bent her head and wept. With her face buried within her crossed arms and her shoulders shaking with misery, she did not notice the thin chime of bells as Tamlin appeared at her side.

He seated himself on the rock by her feet, his forehead creased by a frown. "I warned there might be risks, child." He paused to puff on his pipe. Blue smoke rose and braided on the air currents around his hair, untouched by any hint of a breeze. "Now, why not tell me what troubles you so."

Taen lifted her head, embarrassed by the tears on her cheeks. She dried her face with her sleeve while Tamlin waited with his thumbs hooked in his pockets, his beads and his bells strangely silent in the silvery twilight of the clearing. Slowly, carefully, Taen described what she had experienced of her brother. Her phrases were clumsy and halting, but Tamlin did not interrupt. With bearded lips thinned with concentration, he puffed furiously on his pipe, now and again touching Taen's mind directly to gain a detail left out.

Her tears began again as she described the plight of Anskiere, but she hardly noticed. Tamlin's eyes became piercing and his pipe hung forgotten between his teeth. Yet he spoke no word until she lapsed, faltering, into silence, her tale complete.

"You bring me sad tidings, Reader of Dreams." Tamlin sighed. He raked stubby fingers through his beard and twirled the pipe stem thoughtfully between his hands. At last he stirred, and regretfully studied the tear-stained face of his charge.

"The demons of Keithland grow overly bold, I think. Mankind must not be left defenseless. If the Stormwarden of Elrinfaer is no longer active, your training and your skills become a matter of urgent importance." Tamlin paused as if weighted by an impossible quandary. "After I have held council on the issue, the Free Isles must be warned of the danger. For if I read the matter correctly, the demons prepare an assault against Landfast. There are records there, in Kordane's shrine, which must never leave the care of humanity."

He did not add, as he could have, that much of the burden of mankind's defense might fall on the slender shoulders of the girl who stood before him. Soon, of necessity, she must confront the supreme test of her abilities.

CHAPTER XIII

Cycle of Dreams

LIGHTS FLICKERED LIKE A FIXED swarm of fireflies across the console in the underground installation which housed the Vaere. If some of the panels stayed dark, the autologic and memory banks which once had served the star probe *Corinne Dane* still functioned to capacity. But charged with responsibility for mankind's survival, the computer itself had evolved in a manner her builders never conceived.

The Vaere turned the intricate mathematical functions once employed for stellar navigation toward probability equations. Taen's encounter with her brother showed evidence of a demon's plot against mankind. The Vaere required more data. But with the Firelord dead and the clan priestesses fallen into disrepute, many sources of intelligence had lapsed. Anskiere knew enough to assess the implications of Taen's dream. Yet her failure to find him at the vortex of his own wardspell created complications; the Vaere itself could not penetrate those defenses.

All sophisticated mechanical practicality, the Vaere pursued alternatives, then mathematically simulated the consequences. The numbers turned up negative with persistent regularity. Had the Vaere been human, it would have cursed in frustration. Being a machine, it tallied assets, and considered a fresh approach. The Stormwarden of Elrinfaer could be reached, but only at considerable risk.

In an ocean trench beneath the polar ice cap lay Sathid, the crystals which founded Anskiere's powers. The Vaere could generate sonic interference and rouse the crystals; Anskiere would know at once he was needed. But if, as Taen's dream suggested, he had somehow become incapacitated, the crystals would discover his weakness; they might rise up against him. The Sathid were alien symbiotes which augmented the psychic abilities of a host; when bonded with an intelligent being, the crystals acquired sentience, and an insatiable lust for dominance. Agitated lights raced across the console as the Vaere ran yet another set of probabilities. *Should the Sathid attempt rebellion, how much of Anskiere's resources could be diverted without risking a reversal of control?* Past data held the sole basis for analysis.

An access circuit closed in the memory banks. The Vaere reran the profile of Anskiere's reactions when he had initially bonded with the Sathid matrixes. He had subjugated the first, for wind, without undue hardship. The graphs mapping his physical and psychic stress levels rose in clean, even lines, then tapered back to normal. But the second graph differed. Decades later, the Vaere surveyed a struggle whose outcome was by no means guaranteed. Controlled, the double bond yielded an exponential increase in power. But failure inevitably created a monster possessed by alien passions; Anskiere opted for a Stormwarden's mastery with full knowledge he would succeed, or be killed instantly by the Vaere who had trained him.

His stress rose in steep, jagged lines, spiked high into the danger zone as the new Sathid linked with the first. Both ma-

trixes combined to battle the sorcerer's will. Plunged into torment, Anskiere had held his ground, and eventually battered
the two Sathid into quiescence.

The Vaere juggled facts with electronic accuracy. Should
the Sathid rise up with Anskiere in difficulty, the most optimis-
tic calculation showed his chances were slight; and if he had
raised wards at Cliffhaven to confine frostwargs, he would certainly fail.

Balked by improbable odds, the Vaere abandoned the idea
of contacting Anskiere. With no Firelord left to restrain the
frostwargs, the Stormwarden was no option. With every alternative exhausted, the Vaere considered Taen, whose empathic
abilities held such promise, but whose training was far from
complete. Linked with a Sathid matrix, the girl's sensitivity
would increase to the point where she could tap any human
mind on Keithland for information. Every nuance of the demons' plot would be immediately attainable. The girl was
young, untried, and as yet barely able to command her gift. But
she was also extraordinarily brave.

Reluctantly the Vaere ran a third set of equations. Lacking
her mentor's years of training and preparation, did the girl possess enough resilience to master the bonding process on her
own? Her personality profile was still sketchy; the Vaere had
not mapped her tolerance to stress. But extrapolations based on
her past history yielded figures which offered a slim possibility
of success.

Never in Keithland's history had the Vaere been forced to
make this crucial a decision on such scanty data. The stakes
were inflexibly severe; should Taen fail to withstand the rigors
of a Sathid bonding, if she once lost control to the matrix, she
could not be permitted to survive. Yet logic offered no better
course of action.

The lights on the control panels flickered red as the Vaere
entered sequence after sequence of probability figures. If the
demons' plan was to be thwarted, Taen must master the Sathid

matrix, and achieve the full potential of her gift. Programmed to protect humanity, the Vaere could only ensure her ordeal was handled with optimum chance of success.

The girl rested dreamlessly in her capsule while the Vaere finalized its rigorous analysis. A day later, after pursuing each alternative, it concluded that Taen's self-confidence would become seriously impaired were she to be given last minute instruction. Knowledge of the bonding process would be no help to her.

The Vaere surveyed her vital signs, ran a final check on her health. Unlike Anskiere and Ivain, this child must experience the ardors of bonding ignorant and untrained. If she survived to gain her mastery, she would be physically changed, for the Sathid took seven years to mature. But by applying the principles of the star-drive directly to her capsule, the Vaere would create a time anomaly; she would emerge at the age of seventeen, but Keithland's continuum would have advanced only days by contrast. Once the parameters of the time envelope were set, the girl would be physically isolated from Keithland's reality. No longer could the Vaere intervene in her behalf.

Taen lay peacefully in her capsule, her ebony hair, red lips, and pale skin like the sleeping beauty in the tale from old earth. She felt no pain as the needle pierced her flesh. The Vaere injected a solution containing an alien entity into the vein in her arm; when the Sathid evolved enough to challenge, it would strike when Taen was most vulnerable. In time, the girl would battle her psychic nemesis.

The Sathid spread swiftly through Taen's body. Triggered by warmth and the presence of life, it germinated and groped, instinctively as a newborn child, for awareness of its new host. Impressed by Taen's own character, the Sathid began patterning itself to mesh with her mind. The sensitive psychic empathy of her gift opened like a gateway to her innermost self.

Guided by the Sathid's need to explore, Taen began to dream of her past.

Time meant nothing to the matrix. From the moment of birth to the first acquisition of language, it experienced the girl's memories, analyzing even the most trifling details. Through her memories, it learned to walk, to speak, and to reason. Sharing a stolen tart in the alley behind the bakeshop it discovered duplicity, and from her first lie it gained cunning. Taen dreamed on, at first unaware a foreign entity inhabited her awareness.

Carried back to the age of two, she sat in her mother's lap, playing with shells, while the gusts of an afternoon squall battered the window panes and rain fell in hissing sheets down the chimney. Taen concentrated single-mindedly on her game, uneasy in the strange surroundings of her cousins' house. But Uncle Evertt tossed in his cot, sick with a fever. Her mother tended him while Emien and their father were off fishing in the sloop.

Thunder rumbled overhead, shaking the floor with its violence. The girl cowered against her mother's breast, small fists clenched around her shells. Suddenly, horribly, she had difficulty breathing. Taen choked, red-faced, and struggled not to cry; she had promised to be quiet, and let Uncle Evertt sleep. But the air seemed thick as syrup in her lungs. A sharp, tearing pain gripped her chest. Taen felt dizzy. Tears traced silently down her cheeks and soaked into the neck of her wool shift. And alerted by the quiver in her daughter's body, her mother lifted her up.

"Child, what in Kor's Fires ails you?" She peered anxiously at her daughter's face.

Yet Taen knew no words to explain what her mind envisioned, that her father struggled for his life, entangled in a net under the sloop's dark keel. Too young to comprehend his death, she laid her head against her mother's shoulder and wept. And the Sathid, sensing discord in her life, probed deeper.

Three days later, the townsfolk brought Emien home. Taen heard the scrape of boots on the brick sill of the kitchen door. Men spoke in hushed voices in the next room, and suddenly her mother cried aloud in anguish. Alarmed, Taen peeked around the door, her rag doll forgotten in her arms. She saw Emien standing among strangers, still clad in his oilskins. Her brother's clothing dripped seawater, and he stared with unresponsive eyes at the floor while the men talked.

"We found him adrift beyond the reef," said the tall man to her mother. "The sloop took some damage in the storm, but repairs can be made. The shipwright offered his services for nothing."

Taen saw her mother straighten in her chair. "And Marl? What happened to Marl?"

The stranger shrugged, ill at ease. "Can't say, mistress. Old sharks fair ruined the remains. Your boy knows. But he won't talk."

"Emien?" Marl's widow turned tear-streaked eyes upon her son and opened her arms wide to receive him. But the boy flinched back and refused to meet her gaze. Aware something serious was amiss, Taen ducked out of sight behind the door. She fled the house, crowded as it was with strangers, and sought refuge in the shed behind the goat barn, where the dusty darkness and fragrant piles of hay hid her distress. She lay still. Miserable and alone, she listened between the clink of windchimes and the mournful notes of the pigeons for the boisterous voice of her father returning home. But she heard only the shouts of the village boys sent out to search for her. She would not answer, however frantic their concern. Well after sundown, when the wind blew cold off the harbor and the inn's faded signboard creaked like an old man's rocker above deserted village streets, Taen returned to the house.

The strange men had gone. But her mother's grief tore into

Taen's young mind, feeding her nightmares of ruined hope, and that night her Uncle Evertt started shouting. The Sathid looked on, intrigued, while she cowered behind the linen chest with both ears muffled by winter blankets. Yet even through the wool, the girl heard the relentless slap of her uncle's belt, and Emien's cries of pain. Assaulted through the window of her gift by violence, anger, and misunderstanding, she pressed the blankets more tightly over her face; but the shouting seemed never to end. Punishment only made Emien sullen. Weeks passed. He never spoke of the storm. Only Taen, whose strange perception permitted understanding of her brother's mind, knew he had not been at fault for the loss of his father's life. She was too young to explain. And since Emien also was a sensitive child, the damage quickly became permanent. Nothing would ever amend Emien's distrust of his uncle.

Evertt seemed not to care. He shouldered the additional burden of providing for his brother's family with an islander's dour fatalism. Along with her young cousins, Taen learned to be silent when her uncle returned from the docks, and to stay clear of his boot when rough weather confined the fleet to anchorage. Evertt had always been a brooding, reclusive man; but after Marl's death he spoke little and smiled less. Each of the children tried incessantly to please him, but nothing Emien ever did was acceptable.

Emien stayed aloof from the village boys. Taen, through the rare insight of her gift, became the only person on Imrill Kand to bridge his isolation, until Anskiere came.

The Stormwarden had a way with the boy. Where the villagers saw recalcitrance, the sorcerer looked deeper and recognized loneliness and need. He delighted in Emien's company. After a time, the boy began to tag at the Stormwarden's heels.

Influenced by the Sathid's prompting, Taen dreamed of the year she turned seven. Though still too small to accompany her brother on his jaunts with the sorcerer, she recalled how Anskiere called the wild shearwaters in from the open sea, or dissolved the overcast to bring sunshine. Slowly Emien learned to laugh again, though never in his uncle's presence. His confidence grew in Anskiere's shadow, until at last he managed to tell of the storm, and the accident which had taken the life of his father. The village forgave him. Yet Emien never fully regained his self-confidence.

On a stormy day the spring she turned eight, Taen ran down to the docks to meet the fishing fleet. As silent observer, the Sathid absorbed the pattern of her dream as she threaded her way breathlessly through the alleys behind market square. Wind tore at her cloak. It rattled the loose boards in the fish stalls and tumbled broken sticks and bits of loose refuse across the rain-sleek cobbles. Taen skipped through the gap in the drying racks, salted by wind-blown spray. Today her brother would return home, after close to three weeks' absence.

Taen slowed to a walk as she reached the shore. Exposed to the full brunt of the gale, the storm slashed across the face of the sea, fraying the wave crests into white tendrils of spindrift. Waves smashed hungrily across the breakwater, thudding into the docks with malicious force; the old tarred pilings shook with the impact.

Taen surveyed the soaked planks with trepidation. The weather had worsened since morning. Anxious to locate the fleet, she squinted against the spray and intently surveyed the harbor. Several small boats jounced and yawed at their moorings, the greenish copper of their bottom paint showing like a drunken maid's petticoats. Buried under tattered layers of cloud, the horizon was not visible. Taen saw no trace of the returning fleet. Resigned to wait, she sighed and settled herself in the lee of the loading winch.

A heavy packing crate had been left in the sling. Cords creaked as the wind tossed it to and fro. Irked by the sound and soaked to the skin, Taen huddled under her cloak, attention glued to the horizon where at long last the dark reddish triangle of the first sail sliced the gloom. The rest of the fleet followed behind. Anxious to catch the first glimpse of *Dacsen*, Taen did not notice the blond tassel of frayed rope overhead, where the line securing the crate crossed the pulley.

The first ply snapped with a whipcrack report. Taen started, looked up, and saw the box swing ominously in the sling. But the chill had cramped her muscles and her body responded sluggishly as she started to rise. The crate shifted before she moved clear. Added strain snapped the rope. Iron-bound wood ripped free of its constraints and fell, crushing Taen's slender ankle.

The Sathid matrix watched dispassionately as the returning fishermen found her, barely conscious in the soaked folds of her cloak. They lifted the crate with careful hands, and said little to the brother who carried his sister home. One of the younger cousins was sent to fetch the Stormwarden.

But when Anskiere arrived, he had no magic to mend Taen's shattered leg. He explained as much in a tone subdued by regret, while the gale whipped across Imrill Kand and the wind tore at the shingles with a shriek like Kor's Accursed. Emien watched the Stormwarden gather his gray cloak about his shoulders. Without taking time to speak to the boy, the sorcerer stepped out into the night, letting a gust of rain across the threshold. Within the hour he had calmed the storm enough to send a boat to the mainland for a healer. But Emien had never forgotten the fact that his presence had been ignored.

Taen's convalescence progressed slowly. The Sathid learned patience and endurance through the days she lay abed suffering the pain of her healing leg. The Stormwarden spent hours visiting her and his walks into the hills with Emien were curtailed. At first the boy moped sullenly in the kitchen until his mother scolded him for idleness. Deprived at one stroke of the sister and the sorcerer who were his only friends, he spent his afternoons alone in the meadows and refused to seek other companions. Aware of his resentment but unable to console him, Taen bore her own misery in silence; as a cripple, she could never fully earn her keep in the hard life of Imrill Kand. The fleet would forever sail without her.

While she dreamed through the weary months of recovery, the Sathid deepened its grip on her mind. Slowly, experimentally, it sorted what it had learned and in the first poisoned seed of conflict sown between Taen and her brother, it found the weakness it sought in her character. The girl perceived Emien's shortcomings well enough, but cursed by the clarity of her gift she also understood him. Bereft of the security of her father's love, she would forgive the boy, though his flawed personality caused her pain and destroyed her emotional equilibrium. There the Sathid read potential for conquest.

The matrix probed for more detail. With utmost delicacy it examined every aspect of Taen's relationship with her brother and through that discovered the estrangement created by her loyalty to Anskiere. The Sathid weighed alternatives. While Taen relived the anguish brought on by her brother's rejection of Imrill Kand, it gained maturity. Soon the matrix and the girl's mind became inseparably interlinked. The Sathid's psychic strength combined with Taen's gift of empathy and expanded her abilities to paranormal proportions.

A day came when the Sathid launched the girl's awareness beyond the bounds of her own subconscious. Above the capsule which encased her body, a needle quivered in a meter embedded in the control console set to monitor her life functions. The Vaere noted the deflection and began actively to monitor. The Sathid sought a deeper hold to secure its bid for power. Taen would face her brother in Kisburn's court again; but with the Sathid's psychic strength now linked through her gift, she would learn more of his character than she ever wished to know. . . .

Emien ran full tilt down the corridor leading from the King's apartments, unaware his movements were observed by his sister and an alien matrix. "Wait!" he called after the small blond footpage who raced ahead of him. "You promised."

But the child, who was barely twelve and a recent addition to Kisburn's household, hesitated only an instant, then ducked through the portal which led to the King's private orchard.

Emien swore in exasperation. Though exertion went poorly with his best velvet tunic and fine silk shirt, he put on speed and hurried after. He caught the heavy door panel before it swung closed and sprinted down the steps. Cold struck through his thin sleeves. Dead grass crackled under his boots, stiff with winter frost, as he dodged between the statuary of an ornamental fountain; the basin stood clogged with ice and dead leaves. Emien cursed again, annoyed by the fact he had left his cloak behind. But the boy he chased must be equally chilled, clad as he was in the royal livery.

"Stop!" Emien called. "Do you always keep your word this loosely?"

But the page never slackened pace. Emien caught a glimpse of maroon brocade through the bare boughs of the fruit orchard, and with a scowl of black anger he leapt the stone wall and pursued. Twigs scraped his face as he fended the branches away from his clothes and his breath clouded on the frigid air, but gradually he closed with the child, who ducked like a frightened rabbit into the densest part of the orchard. A scant step behind, Emien reached out and closed his fist in light blond hair.

The page yowled and tripped over a root. Yanked off balance, Emien missed stride. Both boys rammed into the unforgiving trunk of a pear tree.

Scuffed by bark and the sharp ends of numerous twigs, Emien scowled down at the footpage who had nearly caused him to tear his best shirt. "You're a nuisance," he said sharply.

The page lifted his chin, frightened of the older boy but determined not to cower. He leaned against the tree, panting heavily from his run, and refused to answer.

"When does Tathagres go for audience with the King?" demanded Emien. "The lists were written this morning. Surely you've seen them by now. Did you think I gave you that silver for amusement alone?" He caught the page's collar and twisted the cloth cruelly around the child's throat. "We had an agreement. Dare you break it?"

White-faced, the page shook his head.

Emien released his hold, dusted his hands on his tunic. "I thought not." His tone turned peevish. "Fires! It's not as though you were giving away state secrets, or anything. Now give. When does Tathagres have audience?"

The smaller boy swallowed and wiped his nose. "Tomorrow," he said miserably. "Did you have to mess up my tabard?"

"Did you have to run me around the King's gardens?" Emien mimicked. He rummaged in his pocket and tossed a double copper to the ground by the child's feet. "Give this to the maid. If she complains, tell her you were lucky to get off so lightly."

The page regarded the coin with visible reluctance. Although his skin was blue with chill, he waited, shivering under the trees, until Emien had gone. Then in a fit of helpless rage he stamped the coin again and again into the weeds before he returned to the palace.

In her capsule beneath the ground on the Isle of the Vaere, Taen experienced the footpage's humiliation as though it were her own. For the first time since her dream began, she recognized the increase in her ability as a dream-reader. As yet oblivious to her peril, she tested her new powers and found she could skip from Emien's consciousness into the minds of others in his presence. The experience excited her, went to her head like wine. And like the nestling discovering the first use of its wings, she decided to accompany her brother when he went to spy on the audience between King Kisburn and the witch Tathagres. The Sathid did not object. Her response to Emien's cruelty precisely followed the pattern it sought to establish.

* * *

The Sathid and Taen waited with Emien as he crouched in the dusty darkness of the hidden passage behind the audience chamber. Exhilarated by his own daring, he pressed his eye to the small spy hole concealed by the room's ornate decor. On a bet, he had bested the chamber guard three times with practice foils, with access to the passage his claimed forfeit. The guard was an unimaginative fellow; linked with the Sathid's powers, Taen picked up the man's feelings without effort.

Though relieved not to be losing his beer money, the guard had agreed reluctantly to Emien's plan. He could be tried for treason if the boy were discovered. But gambling of any sort was forbidden to the guard, and the boy could cost him a month's docked pay if the captain was informed of their wager. Like many another in Kisburn's court, the guard placed little trust in Emien's scruples; Tathagres' young squire had a look of dangerous ambition about him, and his dicey temper was certainly no secret. He was fast becoming the sort of person nobody wanted to cross.

While the guard sweated at his post, Emien studied the officials present in the council chamber. Only three of the King's advisors were present. As usual, Lord Sholl sat to the right of the throne, bald head tilted behind his hand while he whispered in the royal ear. To the left of the arras stood the court's grand Conjurer, a position held by any of three sorcerers who currently held the King's favor. Tathagres had not yet arrived. As a boy raised to a fisherman's poverty, Emien stared, still enthralled by the presence of the King.

His Grace of Kisburn was slender, stooped, and barely thirty-three. He had a face like a mouse, quick, shifty eyes which missed very little, and a mind whetted to a fine nervous edge. His aspirations knew no bounds. Though he looked like a sickly scholar, engulfed in his heavy robes of state, the idea of conquest obsessed him. He ruled with a quick sharp hand, and if dissidents at court claimed he listened a bit too readily to

Lord Sholl, his Grace the Ninth Sovereign of Kisburn never made foolish decisions. Emien watched with envious fascination as the King shook his head in denial. Lord Sholl straightened in his chair, lips puckered with displeasure. For a moment he looked as if he might speak again. But the King waved his hand impatiently, dismissing the issue, and that moment the doors opened to admit Tathagres. The King glanced up expectantly.

Emien leaned closer to the spy hole, rapt with anticipation. Today his mistress intended to end the long months of waiting. If the King approved her proposal, they would return to assault Cliffhaven with an army, and at long last Anskiere would fall. Taen, as observer, suppressed her dismay. Unless she remained passive, her brother would discover her presence and raise defenses against her.

Tathagres strode boldly into the audience chamber, unencumbered by her usual court finery. Emien was startled to find her clad in a man's heavy riding leathers, boots, tunic, and breeches impeccably brushed and a cloak of dyed wool falling in luxurious scarlet folds from her shoulders. Except for Lord Sholl, the advisors regarded her with stiff disapproval as she bowed neatly before the royal dais.

Tathagres unpinned the brooch at her throat and flicked her cloak over her arm with an air of confidence difficult to disregard. Emien was forced to admire her tactics. In a court entangled with corruption and intrigue, Tathagres abandoned any feminine wiles; with an air of uncompromising directness, she brought nothing to the audience chamber but the sure recognition of her own power. And though custom demanded that the King speak first, her stance gave the impression that she waited for him to petition her for information.

The King leaned eagerly forward, wiry fingers laced together in his lap. "Have you come to tell me your plan concerning Cliffhaven? If not, be brief. My patience is growing short where you are concerned."

Behind the King's shoulder, two of the advisors exchanged surreptitious whispers. With the major war fleet lately smashed to splinters by Anskiere's storm, most of the court opposed further dealings with Tathagres; shipwrights labored day and night to replace the broken ships, but at least a year had been lost to damages. Only Lord Sholl supported Tathagres, and to the annoyance of many he still held the King's favor.

The witch behaved as if the setback never occurred. "If I bring about the defeat of Cliffhaven, our bargain still stands. With the Kielmark fallen, your passage through Mainstrait would stand unopposed and the Free Isles would lie open for invasion. You will deliver me Keys to Elrinfaer tower then, is that understood?"

One of the advisors stiffened at her affront. "With permission, your Grace." The King nodded irritably, granting him leave to speak. "Lady, may I point out that the loss of the war fleet seriously hampers any invasion campaign at this time?"

Tathagres smiled, her fingers still on the folds of her cloak. "When Cliffhaven falls you may replace your ships." She dismissed the advisor with a slight toss of her head, and addressed her next line to the King. "Why not invade the Free Isles with the Kielmark's fleet? His ships are known to be the finest vessels on Keithland. After his defeat, they will be yours to command as spoils."

The King settled back. Jewels flashed on his doublet as he drew a fast breath. But he tempered his impatience before he spoke. "Defeat Cliffhaven? You jest. Without an inside accomplice, it cannot be achieved."

"It can, your Grace. If you give me leave, I can deliver the fortress intact."

"How?" the King demanded, at last unable to restrain his eagerness. To his left the advisors shifted apprehensively in their chairs. Lord Sholl's expression remained impassive, but he toyed with his rings, his hands betraying his anticipation. To Emien, watching, it seemed as if the first advisor to the

King held a stake in Tathagres' plan. But Taen, through the expanded resources of the Sathid matrix, caught the peripheral discomfort of the man's two colleagues; they were very much aware Lord Sholl was party to the witch's schemes, and the idea displeased them hugely.

Having won the edge in her exchange with the King, Tathagres lifted her cloak from her arm and draped it carelessly over the back of a carved chair. "Have I leave to sit, your Grace?"

The King assented with a gesture of annoyance. "How do you propose to take Cliffhaven? Many have tried." He did not belabor the fact that the wreckage of seven royal assault fleets littered the sea bottom beyond the Kielmark's harbor; the former sovereigns of Kisburn had many times emptied their treasuries in attempt to eradicate that den of renegades.

Tathagres arranged herself in the chair with maddening grace, and spoke only after she had settled herself in comfort. "I had other tactics in mind," she opened, as if answering the King's thought. She glanced up at the dais, her violet eyes gone chilly as arctic sunset. "There are those, among Kor's Accursed, who are willing to become your allies. How invincible would Cliffhaven be against a force which included demons?"

CHAPTER XIV

Bid for Mastery

THE ADVISORS SHOT BOLT UP-
right and the taller one banged his fist on the table top with a
crash that shook the candlesticks. "That's madness!"

"You'll bring about our ruin!" shouted the other. "Kordane's Blessed Fires, witch, no man bargains with demons with
impunity. Never in Keithland history has there been a prece-
dent. And may I remind that Kor's Brotherhood will never
sanction your alliance. That would enrage the populace, surely
as tide, quite possibly provoke a revolt against the crown." The
advisor paused for a near-hysterical breath.

But the King spoke before he could continue. "I would hear
what motivates the demons, Lady. Why should they wish to
support us?"

The advisors subsided with a rustle of brocades, their worry
evident, even to Emien who observed still from the peephole.
But linked with the Sathid matrix, Taen could perceive their
minds directly; both men regarded Lord Sholl with a mixture

of panic and admiration. His opinion very likely might spring the King's decision beyond prudent limits.

Taen considered Lord Sholl through Emien's eyes, and encountered the same disquiet she remembered from the first time she followed Emien to his apartments, as if the chief advisor's form were somehow draped in shadow. Although she had not attempted direct contact with the man's thoughts, he glanced up and stared at the peephole, perhaps aware someone observed him. Taen felt Emien repress a shiver of discomfort; the secret passage hid him from view, and probably none other than the King knew a peephole existed in the wall. Presently Lord Sholl looked away and Emien found everyone in the chamber had stilled to hear Tathagres' reply.

"The demons have a grievance with Anskiere." She paused a moment, her eyes distracted, as if she collected her thoughts. But a glance at Lord Sholl betrayed otherwise. Judging by his rapt, predatory expression, Emien would have bet silver upon the possibility the chief advisor was privy to her plans.

Tathagres resumed. "They wish the Stormwarden's death and access to the sanctuary shrine at Landfast. The Council of the Alliance will certainly defend the Brotherhood's interests; they'll not accept surrender, and for that they must fall. Demons have no scruples, every man knows. They'll direct their own campaign if they must. But since your interests lie along similar lines, why not make an alliance and so preserve the isles under a Kingdom overlord? I can negotiate for his Grace. The consequences shall be mine alone, this I promise."

Lord Sholl touched the King's sleeve, leaned close, and spoke into the royal ear. None in the room heard his counsel. But Taen, quickly becoming more adept with her added powers, quite easily tapped the royal mind with no one the wiser for her prying. She overheard the chief advisor's whisper as clearly as if the man had directed his advice to her.

"My King, you must be aware of the ramifications of this. The woman is in league with demon powers and has been for quite some time. Better Kisburn controlled her than leave the option for an enemy to exploit."

Taen detected the fact the King's interest was engaged. As a spoiled product of a decadent court, Kisburn held a suppressed fascination for the forbidden, interlaced like thread through a tangle of morbid curiosity. Beneath the state concerns which framed his desire for expansion, he ached to level Cliffhaven, at last eliminate the Kielmark's humiliating demands for tribute on shipping through the straits. Kisburn also coveted the Free Isles, saw their addition to the Kingdom as vindication for an early and shameful defeat at the council table. Taen picked up enough echoes of passion underlying the royal ambitions to convince her; with very little encouragement, the King could be persuaded to accept Tathagres' proposal, dangerously immoral though it was.

Taen withdrew, distressed by her discovery. With Emien involved, her worst fears would be realized should demons be called into alliance by Tathagres. She could not allow such heresy to proceed unimpeded. Her loyalty to her brother lay too deep. Somehow she would reach him, set him free of Tathagres' influence. Yet even as she resolved to act, the Sathid within her gathered itself expectantly; the trap it had set to bring about her defeat was nearly ready to be sprung.

Beyond the peephole the advisors groped, desperately trying to raise an argument to counter Tathagres' proposal. "You suggest heresy," said the stouter of the two. He clutched his chain of office as if it were a fragment of the Blessed Relic, proof against the works of Kor's Accursed. "How dare you encourage your King to transgress Kordane's Law? The arch priests should have you burned."

Slowly, maddeningly, Tathagres smiled. "Let them try." She paused, and for a single fleeting instant her expression sobered. Only her eyes brightened with the same joyous challenge Emien recalled from the time she had commanded him to land the pinnace on Skane's Edge. In link with him, Taen felt the chills which prickled the length of her brother's spine. But she had no time to trace the cause of his uneasiness before Tathagres resumed.

Her tone was deceptively soft. "The truth is, they dare not lay hands on me."

The grand Conjurer caught his breath, his sallow complexion gone pale. He froze like a painted icon in his seat by the King's left hand and beyond him the advisors fidgeted, suddenly sweating above the stiff cloth of their collars. Taen needed no empathic skills to understand how greatly they feared Tathagres' powers. No man on the dais could touch her with impunity. Only Lord Sholl and the King seemed unconcerned by the woman's implied threat. The rubies in the chief advisor's rings flashed as he laced his fingers together on the table top; his colleagues' discomfort served only to amuse him. And a rushed glimpse of Kisburn's thoughts showed him weighing possible ways of evading the justice of Kor's Brotherhood, should the alliance prove viable. If anything, the added edge of danger in the plan attracted him the more. Now frantic to avert a decision all but complete, Taen turned her Sathid-born talents upon the disingenuous person of the King's chief advisor.

Her probe went amiss. Accustomed to the layered configuration of the human mind, its fixed preoccupation of past memories and learned passions, Taen was immediately baffled by hazy fields of patterns, a snarled confusion of sensation human reason could not sort. The alienness of the images overwhelmed her and she faltered. That instant, something slammed closed around her mind.

Dizzied, isolated, Taen strove to recover her balance. For a second she sensed the shape of the forces which sought to hold her trapped. Their strangeness defied comprehension. Alarmed, Taen tapped her reserves, and with a sharp stroke severed the link. There followed a flurried moment of confusion. When at last her inner vision cleared, Taen found herself restored to Emien's perception.

He crouched in the dust-dry darkness behind the peephole, doubled over by an excruciating pain in his head. Hammered by the effects of a backlash he did not understand, the boy moaned. He pressed a hand to his aching brow. And through the discomfort her own interference had brought upon him, Taen heard Lord Sholl's voice ring out across the council chamber.

"There is a spy present, your Grace. Did you place an observer behind the wall?"

Both advisors exclaimed in surprise, cut short by curt orders from the King. The doors to the audience chamber banged open. And through the jabbing waves of discomfort in his head, Emien realized the feet which thundered down the aisle outside belonged to royal men-at-arms sent to apprehend him. The wave of panic which shot through him disrupted Taen's equilibrium. She had no time to consider her peculiar encounter with the chief advisor's mind before Emien rose, slamming his elbow clumsily against the wall.

"Kor!" exclaimed the Conjurer. "There *is* someone back there."

That moment, the access door to the passage crashed open. Dust eddied against sudden light as guardsmen shouldered through. Emien whirled to run. Almost immediately a mailed fist closed over his wrist. The guard yanked him around, shoved his face toward the door.

"Fires!" The soldier's voice carried an unmistakable note of disgust. "You're nothing but a squire." He hauled Emien out of the passage, but his grip on the boy's arm became slightly less punishing. Frightened but defiant, Emien permitted the guardsman to escort him down the corridor and on through the portals of the audience chamber.

Over the chatter of the advisors Emien heard Tathagres speaking in a tone entirely free of inflection. ". . . My personal squire, your Grace. No, I did not send him to spy. He did so upon his own initiative."

Held pinioned in the grip of the guardsmen, Emien glared sullenly up at the men on the dais. The advisors' agitation had mellowed into speculative curiosity and the Conjurer simply looked bored. Only Lord Sholl regarded Tathagres' black-haired squire with the tireless intensity of a carrion bird, until Emien flinched and turned away.

His Grace of Kisburn tapped agitated fingers against the pearl buttons on his cuff, his expression sour with displeasure. "Take him away," he said to the guards. "I would have him questioned later, to determine whether his behavior warrants a trial."

"No!" Tathagres rose sharply from her chair. Her cloak slithered unheeded to the floor and the clink as the brooch struck the tiles sounded like a cry of distress against the silence. "The boy is mine. None will lay hands on him. I demand that he be released at once."

"You're impertinent," snapped the King. "How badly do you want the Keys to Elrinfaer?"

"How badly do you want Cliffhaven?" Tathagres tilted her head, and with an imperious grace no court woman could equal, touched her fingers lightly to the neck band at her throat.

Between the guardsmen, Emien started. The movement attracted Lord Sholl's attention. His gaze intensified upon the boy, and with an unexpected thrust of force, Taen felt him seek contact with her brother's mind. How the chief advisor had acquired a dream-reader's talent remained a mystery, but his touch was crude. Emien noticed the presence which sought to exploit his thoughts. Hair prickled at the back of his neck. In attempt to disrupt the intrusion, he gasped and flung back against the guardsmen's hold.

The King sat sharply forward, antagonized by the disturbance. But the royal displeasure had no effect upon Lord Sholl.

He brushed past Emien's discomfort, rummaged ruthlessly to discover whether the boy still harbored the source of the touch which had molested him earlier at the council table. Rather than reveal her presence, Taen withdrew, darting like a fish into shallows out of reach. Presently Lord Sholl abandoned his search. But his expression of annoyance bespoke the fact that he would forget nothing until his suspicions concerning Emien were fully satisfied.

"You will release my squire," said Tathagres to the King. "I tell you he is mine. Would you contest me?" She phrased her words politely, but Taen saw into her heart and read murder there. And during the moment the girl tested the witch's intentions, a portion of Tathagres' mind engaged with a presence within the golden band at her throat. Although her body remained standing before the King of Kisburn in the palace audience chamber, her thoughts traversed a vista of darkness.

Swept along by the dream link, Taen accompanied the witch into a dimension of nightmare. Wind arose, buffeting her like the rustle of bats flying from their roosts at twilight. She recoiled, repelled. But the tenacity born of her island upbringing lent the girl strength to overcome shaken nerves. She clung to the contact. Presently the suffocating blanket of shadow dissolved into light, as red as sunrise viewed through thunderheads.

The illumination brightened, flared suddenly to blinding intensity. Sensing the advent of evil, Taen battled an urge to withdraw. Suddenly a wave of savage spite overpowered her. Through the window of Tathagres' consciousness, the girl perceived the demon faces of Emien's dream. Only this time the vision was direct and imminently threatening. Taen held on for her brother's sake. Though blistered by the ferocity of the demons' hatred, Taen reached beyond, to partial understanding of their intentions. Not only did Kor's Accursed grant Tathagres her power, they sought control of Emien as well.

"No!" Taen's horrified protest reverberated through the

fabric of her contact, and snapped the dream link a bare second before Tathagres engaged with the demons. Yanked back to Emien's perspective, Taen felt an unseen force strike the hands which restrained her brother's wrists. The guardsmen shouted and staggered back, releasing their grip. Weapons held no edge against sorcery; deaf to the King's shouted command, the soldiers fled the chamber, unwilling to risk further contact with the boy.

"Don't try my tolerance, your Grace," said Tathagres, unmoved by the commotion set off by her action. The advisors watched, white with alarm, as she bent and retrieved her cloak. "I will await your reply, but not long. My patience, like my time, is limited." And with a nonchalance which bordered on insolence, she motioned Emien to her side and departed.

The boy followed on his mistress's heels, barely able to refrain from gloating. He discovered a bitter, vindictive pride in Tathagres' manipulation of the King, and, inspired by a wish to emulate her skills, he quickly regained his shaken confidence. Taen pulled back, sickened. Peripheral emotions still leaked from the audience chamber, pervading her dream-sense; through the advisors' dismayed affront, she felt the King's appetite for risk bite into her awareness with the cruelty of a spring frost. There could be no doubt; he would choose the demons' alliance, if only to intimidate his rivals.

Taen tempered her distress with a stout resolve. She would stop the corruption of her brother. Trained by the Vaere to dream-read and heartened by confidence in her increased powers, she decided to attempt contact with Anskiere once again. Perhaps now she could call him back to her brother's aid. Except that the instant her young determined heart became dedicated to that quest, the Sathid rose up to prevent her.

The alien matrix pinned her thoughts without warning, then struck a psychic blow which sent her reeling back, stunned and surprised and in agony. At first unaware the entity which opposed her used the same powers she controlled scant seconds before, Taen felt herself plunged back into the mind of her brother, but deeper than she had ever ventured previously. She fell, as if into darkness. And poignant as a minor arpeggio of harp strings, emotions pierced her until her whole mind rang in concert with the boy's unbearable pain.

"Your brother Emien is a cruel man, his deeds unfit for forgiveness," said the Sathid within her mind, its voice framed as her own, or perhaps that of her mother. Laced in the depths of nightmare like a fish in a gill net, Taen tried to raise her voice in denial. But her throat pinched closed and no words passed her lips.

"See for yourself," continued the voice of the accuser, and Taen found herself unable to close her eyes against the vision which battered her awareness.

She saw her brother Emien stride the length of *Crow's* pinnace, a length of knotted cord in his fist. The boat tossed, her bowsprit flung skyward by wave crests which thundered and crashed over the razor fangs of a reef. Emien threatened the rowers in a voice gone ugly with rage. And with the same hand he had used to dry Taen's tears as a child, he lifted his lash and brought it down with all his strength on the helpless backs of his oarsmen.

Taen shouted denial, but her protest went unheard. Blood flowed down the naked backs of the men, spilled in thick drops to mingle with the bilge, while Emien shouted like a madman, sounding more and more like his Uncle Evertt.

"No!" Taen shouted. "It's not true!" But vividly etched by her gift the details said otherwise. The pinnace slammed into rock with a boom that deafened thought. And Taen fell, through a dying man's cry of agony, into darkness once more.

The Sathid pursued, hounding her with remorseless certainty. "Your brother is a murderer, a breaker of the codes of life. Let him be condemned."

Taen whimpered in protest. But through the firelit boughs of a forest glen, she watched Emien select a rounded stone, and with a clean, vindictive throw, end the life of an elderly man. The victim crumpled, lay still in the wilted folds of his black cloak. And stung into action by fierce disbelief, Taen searched the mind of her brother. His memory confirmed the scene she had witnessed, the emotions etched by the remorse of an act best forgotten.

Taen retreated, stunned. Emien was no longer the tormented but guiltless brother she had loved on Imrill Kand. Somewhere, somehow, he had become hardened and insensitive in a manner not even his mother would accept. Wounded by the change and unable to adjust, Taen abandoned herself to pain. And anticipating victory, the Sathid moved to imprison her.

While the girl's will lay passive, it fashioned barriers, using the shattered remnants of her faith. The instant her love for Emien shifted to hatred, her confinement would be complete. The Sathid paused for a moment to gloat. How very smoothly its takeover had proceeded; the girl hardly resisted at all.

Absorbed by her grief, Taen felt an echo of the Sathid's triumph. The emotion rang false. Whether Emien had murdered or not, she could not abandon him to Tathagres' demons. Rededicated to her earlier resolve, her emotions polarized, and at once she recognized the image and the voice to be that of an enemy. Not Lord Sholl; this one knew her, used her mind and her memories against her in an attempt to break her spirit.

Taen struck back. With the anger of the betrayed she smashed through the Sathid's grip, recalled the image of the victim Emien had struck down with his stone. But this time she viewed the completed action and recognized the man in the black cloak as Hearvin, one of Anskiere's oppressors and evil in his own right.

"Liar!" she accused the Sathid. "Who gave you the right to meddle?"

"I need no right," the Sathid replied. "I am a part of you."

And as Taen paused to question the statement, the matrix added, "See for yourself."

Taen focused her scrutiny inward. With every available discipline Tamlin had taught her, she examined the source of the Sathid's intervention and discovered it to be inextricably linked with her powers as dream-weaver, its character a mirror image of her own. The Sathid had spoken the truth; the opponent she faced was herself. Yet because that self had encouraged her to abandon her brother, break the integrity of her upbringing upon Imrill Kand, Taen perceived the matrix to be the dark side to her character, that flawed facet of selfishness which sought to overturn gentleness and love with discontent.

"You see," said the Sathid. "We are one. To oppose me is to deny your own resources."

But words did little to ease Taen's suspicion. To follow the Sathid's logic was to invite the same mistake Emien had made to the detriment of his own self-worth. And as the survivor of misfortune which had left her a cripple in a society where bodily health was a necessity, Taen had already accepted the fact she could never be whole. She would reject the Sathid's proposal though she had to suffer lifelong deprivation. And because she believed its interference to be an extension of her own small-mindedness, she condemned it ruthlessly, left not the smallest quarter for argument.

"I will help my brother no matter what he has done," said Taen firmly.

The Sathid returned with a laugh which bounced demonic echoes across the fields of her awareness. "You're an idealistic fool. Do you truly know the brother you intend to save? I think not. For Emien is becoming someone far different than the brother you grew up with. If you try to help him now, it is apparent by his character he would kill you."

"No!" Taen pulled back, tried to thrust the irritating presence from her mind. But it was part of herself, and inseparable. She found no release from her nightmare.

"If you look, you will see," invited the Sathid.

And challenged by her own self-honesty, Taen sought the measure of its statement. "Show me. But I'll not be convinced by half truths. If Emien is evil, let me see for myself."

Goaded by the Sathid's cold reasoning, Taen sought her brother, sank downward into the limitless wells of Emien's subconscious, through territory within his mind unknown even to himself. She visited a landscape of insecurity. Sensitive to a fault, Emien saw his early years as a siege against the relentless and wounding concerns of his elders; the pressures of survival on Imrill Kand allotted no space for his fears. With only Evertt to share the workload, necessity often forced Marl to ask his young son to shoulder a man's load. Isolated by his perception, Emien hid his suffering, strove to meet expectations too great for a child to master. Life became a ruthless experience, a joyless siege of endurance. He despised the hardship, for it exposed his weaknesses without mercy.

Taen unraveled his personality with utmost patience. Tangled at the core of his being, she found Emien longed secretly to inflict cruelty, as if causing hurt to others might somehow ease his starved feeling of inadequacy. Yet twisted desires alone did not make a criminal. Desperate in her care, Taen searched further.

She traced the emotions underlying her brother's admiration for Anskiere. The Stormwarden alone had breached the boy's melancholy following the death of his father. Taen explored the trust which had grown between the sorcerer and her brother firsthand. The contact initially had been a fragile thing, tenuous as the miracle of birth or a light in the darkness of midwinter. Through the sorcerer's guidance, Emien discovered happiness and laughter and the bright new joy of self-acceptance for the first time. The news of Tierl Enneth and Anskiere's guilt had fallen with the devastation of a cataclysm. The fact that he had given his innermost love to a condemned man whose crimes were beyond human pardon threw Emien into towering, ungovernable fury. All his frail new stability collapsed like sand castles bashed flat by the tide.

The blow of that discovery sheared through Taen's defenses. She experienced the panic Emien had known as he raged, blinded by the brutal solitude of betrayal. Through the dream link, the sister experienced the fear, the horror, and finally the first sour seeds of resentment. For Emien never accepted responsibility for his own unhappiness. If Anskiere had brought down ruin and death with the same powers he had sworn to the protection of Tierl Enneth, all that he lived was a lie. His teaching left Emien vulnerable, another victim for the spoiling unkindness of fate. Driven by a venomous tide of bitterness, the boy wished he had never tasted the illusion Anskiere had brought: that life could reward a man who aspired to develop his strengths, and that security and happiness were things of faith within reach of any who strove. Feeling his contentment slip forever beyond reach, Emien abandoned belief.

Scourged by the sharing of her brother's loss, Taen beheld the birth of his ultimate desire. Emien sought a way to crush the fear which lurked within the darkest center of his being; he wished a weapon, power great enough to ensure that no man nor sorcerer nor any agency of fate's design should ever judge and find him wanting. Never again would he suffer manipulation at the hands of one he loved. For now he trusted no one.

Imprisoned behind the brickwork of an untenable position, his spirit ached for release. Taen perceived that her brother's misery knew no limits and understood none. He could not achieve peace without first acknowledging failure; and goaded by Tathagres' contempt, Emien found it simpler to kill.

He believed his sister had died, drowned without mercy by Anskiere's hand during the foundering of the galleass *Crow.* To accept her as alive, safeguarded by that same sorcerer's hand, was to negate what had come to be the foundation of his existence. And though he did not yet know the extent of the wretchedness his suffering had created, Taen beheld the truth the Sathid had foretold. Emien would murder before he would forgive himself the error of condemning Anskiere, even if the life he took was that of his own sister.

The Sathid poised itself; the moment it awaited had come to pass. The girl's loyalty surely would crumble under the knowledge, and in that instant, when the impact of rejection weakened her, the matrix would achieve permanent dominance over her will.

Taen felt the first stir of the Sathid's expectancy. She pushed it back, sharply and as unreasonably as a spoiled child. All but undone by the loss of her brother's trust, she did not welcome its intrusive sharing of her grief. No logic could console her loss. The Sathid waited with the cold patience of a serpent. It had measured Taen's vulnerability and extrapolated from there, centering its attack upon the one event which would create her greatest distress; the outcome was as inevitable as frost at the end of summer. After years spent judging Taen's character, the matrix anticipated that pain would shortly break her spirit.

But the moment never came. To Taen, daughter of generations of fishermen who had braved the caprice of ocean storms, Emien was not lost until he was dead. If the Stormwarden could not spare her brother, at least he would know a way to alleviate the boy's misery. The girl roused herself. She would seek Anskiere. And pressured by the dogged edge of her determination, the Sathid discovered it had underestimated her capacity to hope.

The conflict now was joined, with no advantage left but surprise. As Taen reached for the power to bridge the distance to the ice cliffs, the Sathid lashed out. It struck with the physical agony she had known when the crate crushed her ankle, its intent to throw her off balance.

Stabbed by a white-hot wave of pain, Taen perceived the Sathid for an enemy. Although it had merged with her mind, its will was a separate entity, and now it stood as a barrier be-

tween her and Anskiere, who offered Emien's sole chance of
deliverance. Dizzied by the savagery of the matrix's attack, she
clung to consciousness with the desperate grip of a sailor cast
adrift on a spar. To yield was to invite oblivion. And having
mastered the torment of injury once before, Taen endured. She
would not give in to torture. She had seen into Emien's
wounded spirit, and death itself could not make her choose the
same self-betrayal.

"I will reach Anskiere." Her words emerged mangled by
suffering, but her intent was fixed. "Set me free."

The Sathid shifted focus, assaulted her mind with a score of
hurtful images compiled from her memory. Taen watched the
houses of Imrill Kand smashed to a snarl of weathered gray
boards by the fury of an ocean storm. The matrix showed her
the same desolation the inhabitants of Tierl Enneth had
known when Anskiere's powers destroyed their homes and
families. Icy gusts flattened her skirts against her knees, ham-
pering her steps as she trod the choked remains of the village
streets. Beneath the slivered beams of her cousins' home, she
discovered the bones of the Stormwarden she sought, knotted
like tide wrack in the tattered wool of his cloak. The skull regarded her accusingly, eye sockets clogged with sand.

"No!" Taen wrenched against the Sathid's hold, forcing the
scene to dissolve. She tried to counter its ugliness with her own
memories of beauty, but the images twisted in her mind, cor-
rupted by the matrix; as she reached for spring wildflowers on
the tors of Imrill Kand, her hands grasped withered thorns.
The warmth of the solstice fires blew away as dust transformed
to stinging sleet, and the small violet shells she had once collected on the beaches at low tide rotted as she touched them.
The Sathid's malice knew no limits. Unwilling to watch everything she loved desecrated by its spite, the girl sought the
coarse mind of the fish trapper Tamlin had often borrowed for
her training.

And as nothing about the fish trapper's existence had ever

been dear to her, the Sathid found no hold to exploit. It hesitated, thrown off balance, and in that instant, Taen's will predominated. Her dream-sense cleared. She saw herself once again through Emien's eyes. He sat, limp and trembling on a bench in the palace courtyard. Tathagres supported his elbow, her expression sharply concerned.

"What happened?" she demanded. "Did you faint?"

Taen guessed at once that her conflict with the Sathid had not proceeded without effect on her brother's mind. Even as the matrix gathered itself for a second assault, she felt the boy's painful confusion, and saw also that Tathagres' sympathy masked deeper feelings, strung like beads on a wire of mistrust. Yet the Sathid allowed no scope to explore further. Like a swimmer rising for a gasp of air, Taen gripped her brother's mind with inarguable firmness and forced speech past his lips.

"I'm a little dizzy," the boy replied. "The guardsmen weren't very gentle when they caught me." And before she released him, Taen cast a veil of confusion over her brother's thoughts, that the disorientation he had experienced following his departure from the King's audience chamber could not be too clearly examined. Then as the Sathid sprang to engage her once more, she dove down through a twisting spiral of space and time to the dockside inn of an island village, where a familiar and boring acquaintance clad yet in reeking oilskins stood beneath a shuttered window, begging the favors of a buxom tavern wench.

The Sathid sensed the fact that its control was slipping. Unprepared for the defensive, it scrambled for strategy, but found nothing in Taen's recollection to suggest her reason for seeking the personality of the fish trapper. Denied any direction, the matrix chose the familiar. In the same manner as it had transformed Taen's memories of the shells and the wild-flowers and the solstice fires, the Sathid fixed on her object of concentration and created the illusion of its opposite.

Taen's opinion of the fish trapper's method of courtship

was precisely defined, no trial for the Sathid to encompass. And the simplistic mind of the fish trapper provided an easy opening. With full command of a dream-reader's skills, the matrix shaped its resistance and altered the fellow's perception.

Standing chilled but hopeful amid the frost-browned stems of last season's herb garden, the fish trapper experienced brief disorientation. The instant his muddled senses cleared, he discovered a spray of seven red roses clutched in his callused hand. Shocked speechless by the sight of flowers in the dead of winter, he noticed the remainder of the Sathid's illusions more reluctantly. For nothing about him was the same.

The mildewed oilskins stood replaced by a cloak of brushed gray felt. His hip-high, fishy-smelling boots disappeared, transformed into soft calf leggings with silver buttons and embroidered cuffs. And the wild red snarl of hair and whiskers which habitually buried the man's neck and most of his features appeared clean and neatly trimmed, revealing an expression of bug-eyed astonishment.

He swallowed twice and raised a trembling finger to touch one of the roses. A thorn scraped his knuckle. Convinced the illusion was madness, he shouted aloud in disbelief.

The noise displeased the object of his passion. Above his head the shutters banged open and the tavern wench thrust her head out, her mouth opened for carping complaint. With its ruse nearly ruined, the Sathid was forced to intervene. It included the woman in its dream spell and extravagantly added a velvet waistcoat to the fisherman's attire.

And finding the suitor beneath her window was not the tiresome pest who brought the reek of cod into her taproom each evening, the woman yelled with predatory delight. Here stood a clean, strapping fellow who obviously had wealth by the look of his clothing; and roses in winter were a luxury no island doxie could expect unless she were courted by royalty. This one never hesitated. She smiled, hiding her broken tooth with her tongue, and swooped over the sill to be kissed. The fish trapper's eyes went wide at the sight of what bounced within inches of his nose. And unable to contain her humor over the fish trapper's ridiculous predicament, Taen burst into peals of laughter.

The Sathid recoiled in dismay. In the spectrum of human emotions, ridicule lay furthest from the cowering dejection of defeat. And having only Taen's upbringing within the harsh environment of Imrill Kand on which to draw conclusions, it understood very little of humor, except that its attempt to intimidate had failed. Flustered, it abandoned the structure of its attack.

Caught with her face half-smothered in the greasy beard of the fish trapper, the tavern wench emitted a muffled yell. She tried to yank back, but the fellow by now had thrust a fist inside her blouse. Bleached linen tore with hardly a pretext of modesty. The woman yelled again, while her suitor stared crestfallen at a bodice stuffed with woolen rags.

The sight reduced Taen to a quivering paroxysm of mirth. In vain the Sathid tried to reestablish its hold; but the comical expression on the fish trapper's face overwhelmed the girl, and her hysterical laughter could not be controlled. Baffled by frustration the matrix withdrew, and above the capsule which sheltered Taen's body, meter after meter quivered and dropped within the green sectors of the dials. The Vaere, standing by, recorded the fact. The girl had triumphed in her struggle for supremacy. Her laughter gradually dwindled to manageable proportions. She had defeated the Sathid and claimed the full command of a dream-reader's powers for her own.

Taen barely paused to acknowledge the victory. The instant she discovered her will was no longer contested, she collected her scattered thoughts. Though every nerve cried out for rest, she called her dream-reader's skills into focus. For Emien's sake she drove outward once more, and sought the sorcerer Anskiere.

CHAPTER XV

Anskiere's Geas

THE ICE CLIFFS REARED ABOVE Cliffhaven's northern headland, white against the dirtier gray of storm clouds. Beneath, voracious winter seas chiseled the spellbound ice into caverns. Spray struck with stinging fury more bitter than any seasonal cold, and the air bit with the brittle edge of an Arctic night. Here, Taen returned to seek the sorcerer Anskiere.

This time she saw the wards, made visible through the expanded awareness of the Sathid link. Shifting curtains of blue-violet light radiated like a corona from the cliff face. Taen traced their energies deep into the earth, layer upon interlocking layer, in search of the Stormwarden's presence. Frost pervaded her senses, enfolded her innermost mind with the white desolation of a snowfall. But the energies which had disoriented her before now parted cleanly. Although the powers Taen had won from the matrix granted no influence over weather, Anskiere's works were Sathid-borne; seen through the lens of her newfound mastery, their structure was comprehensible. And following a pattern intricate as the laces woven by the elderly women on Imrill Kand, Taen unraveled the spell toward its source. The whistles of the frostwargs echoed distantly, with overtones as dreadful as she remembered. But Taen passed them by, untroubled by the crippling fear of her former experience. Soon, at the vortex of the wards, she confronted the cone of silence and darkness which had formerly defeated all her skills.

She paused there to renew her concentration. No cause which held Anskiere confined would be slight. Already weary from her battle with the Sathid, she dared not tap the final ward with less than total caution. Here misjudgment might prove fatal; and a single slip could easily cause damage beyond any power in Keithland to mend. Taen cast forth her dream-sense with a touch of utmost delicacy, and spun awareness like a cocoon around the barrier to sound the most central of Anskiere's defenses.

The configuration she encountered proved to be strangely familiar. Through the expanded perception of her dream-sense, Taen recognized the triple ring of force which once shot blazing bands of light around the wings of the stormfalcon she had released from the galleass *Crow*. But now Tamlin's schooling granted her more complete understanding. The interlace of power shaped the defense wards of a sorcerer's staff; a single touch would kill any being not attuned to their resonance. But Taen sensed a flaw in the structure.

Something about the ward's continuity seemed amiss. Its symmetry stood less than perfect, as if something sometime had struck its harmony slightly out of balance. Taen explored the anomaly with her dream-sense. The wards had certainly been disrupted, if only slightly. Resonance of tampering lingered still, and its nature made Taen spring taut with alarm. Someone with unfriendly intentions had entered here before her. Their passage had left a gap in the defenses. Although Taen held insufficient knowledge to assess the full extent of the damage, she recognized the touch behind the sorcery. Whoever had intruded upon the Stormwarden had been the instrument of Kor's Accursed; the culprit was certain to be Tathagres herself.

Discovery and revelation roused Taen to rage. When the witch had magically transported herself and Emien to Kisburn's court, the powers she manipulated had surely been Anskiere's; she had once tapped his staff to raise the sea at Tierl Enneth. Suddenly frightened for the Stormwarden's safety, Taen thrust her dream-sense recklessly past the wards and sounded what lay beyond.

She encountered Anskiere's awareness, sharp and immediate and demanding as the living presence she recalled when the sorcerer controlled the weather on Imrill Kand, but with one difference. Anskiere slept, his will quiescent, as if he hoarded his resources for a day of awakening yet to come. He seemed undisturbed. Apparently even Tathagres dared not disrupt a sorcerer trained by the Vaere. Softly Taen folded her awareness into the Stormwarden's. So light was her touch that he did not rouse from stasis as she joined with him in his dreaming.

Anskiere's sleep shaped a landscape of broken hopes, sharp with the memory of strife; for seven decades Stormwarden and Firelord had labored, their talents joined to form a single force. Together they had subdued eleven species of Kor's Accursed, and finally undertaken the imprisonment of Keithland's most terrible oppressors, the Mharg-demons from Tor Elshend. Although the two sorcerers had worked, mind within mind, for more years than the life span of most men, Taen found no love between them.

Half buried in the shadows of emotion which cleft the Stormwarden's dream, the girl experienced the venomous, spiteful twists of Ivain Firelord's character. This malice had wounded Anskiere, for he alone remembered Ivain before the Cycle of Fire forever upended his sanity. Anskiere returned such cruelty with sympathy, and once with a trust which nearly proved his ruin. For Ivain had betrayed him at the height of their contest against the Mharg-spawn. The Stormwarden survived and continued alone until he achieved the demons' confinement, but the scarring left by Ivain's malice never healed.

Now Taen beheld the implications of the frostwargs' release; shackled by shared understanding, she saw that Anskiere's life was fully dependent on a Firelord's skills. Tuned to the Stormwarden's aspirations, her dream-sense replicated the decision to release the geas to call the heir of Ivain into service. The choice rebounded with echoes of tragedy. Anskiere fully understood that the boy who answered his summons must someday suffer the fate of the father. No man who attempted the Cycle of Fire escaped its mark of madness. For that reason, Ivain's name was remembered with hatred, though the young man who first accepted his training from the Vaere had been loved for his generosity of spirit.

Burdened by Anskiere's past and by his agonized surrender to the only choice left available to him, Taen tuned her awareness to the spell which shaped his final hope. And since that hope also encompassed the fate of her only brother, she plotted the path of the geas the Stormwarden had shaped to summon the son of Ivain Firelord. The line of force struck out to the northwest, spanning the open sea with the directional clarity of a light beacon. Suspended by the dream link, the girl followed the geas.

Her search began without effort. Guided by the precision of Anskiere's handiwork, Taen sped over the wave crests with the ease of a skipper bird's flight. She traveled unaccountable distance within a matter of seconds, tracking without landmark beneath the flat overcast of the winter sky. Suddenly the spell wavered. Taen faltered. Wrenched by the resonance of violence, she tried to brake her speed. But the geas suddenly exploded around her, its linear progression jagged like crumpled wire into eddies of spent strength.

Overturned by confusion, Taen lost its track. Through a

horrid, stunned moment, she tumbled on the edge of the void, struggling to sustain her contact with the place where the geas disrupted into chaos. Her control gradually prevailed. The dream link stabilized. Oriented once more, Taen drifted exhausted. Below her, the snow-covered roofs of a fishing village nestled closely against the slopes of a mountain coastline. Smoke curled from the chimneys, and through perceptions strangely altered by her dream-sense, she smelled the fragrance of birch logs. A crude road led out of the settlement, its switched-back curves rising tier upon tier up the slope until it lost itself into ranks of stunted evergreens.

Taen scanned the village inhabitants with a dream-reader's awareness. But she found nothing more than the simple thoughts of fisher folk, concerned with the mending of nets and baking bread and fretting over the thickness of the ice which choked the harbor; Taen felt it improbable that the subject of Anskiere's hopes would be concealed among such workaday folk. More likely the heir of Ivain lived farther distant, well beyond the break in the geas created by Tathagres' transfer. Confident of her hunch, Taen abandoned the village, turned her focus northwestward in a direct line from Cliffhaven. Her search carried her across the high drift-bound passes of the Furlains and on through the hill country on the far side, where the trees of Seitforest thrust matted boughs against the winter sky.

There above the bare crowns of the beeches, Taen encountered traces of Anskiere's geas. The pattern was hesitant, visible to her dream-sense as snarled trails of light. It steadied as she progressed, gradually becoming structurally intact. No power coursed across the spell. Like a conduit shattered in midspan, the break beyond the Furlains had disrupted the continuity of the geas Anskiere had designed to summon Ivain's heir to Cliffhaven. But Taen easily read the spell's orientation from the segment which remained. Its path resumed, straight as a draftsman's line across the rolling dells of Seitforest, to end at last in the dooryard of a forester's hut.

There Taen discovered a fair-haired boy about Emien's age, bundled to the neck in furs. His breath frosted on the clear winter air as he grunted, hefting a heavy pack onto the slim frame of a drag-sleigh. By the restless, self-questioning intensity of his thoughts, Taen knew at once she had found the subject of the geas' creation; this slim, unremarkable boy was the Firelord's heir and Anskiere's hope of deliverance.

Bare-headed and with cheeks flushed from the cold, the boy never noticed the presence which observed his movements. He fussed irritably with a knot in the cord he had brought to secure the pack to the sleigh, hampered by gloved fingers and the whipping tug of the wind. Never once did he swear. In silence, he worked the tangle free, his brows drawn into a frown over dark brown eyes. Taken by his single-minded preoccupation with the task, Taen paused, her concern momentarily eclipsed by curiosity. She watched the boy lash the pack with painstaking care. He finished with knots as neatly done as any tied by a fisherman's son.

The door to the cabin banged open. The boy looked up. A tall, lean forester clad in a cape of marten emerged, black hair streaked heavily with white tumbled across his shoulders. He crossed to the boy's side and knelt beside the drag-sleigh.

With the caution of a man bred to the wilds, he tested the tension of the cords. Then he straightened, satisfied, and clapped the boy on the shoulder. "Fine job," he said softly. "Did you remember the striker and flint?"

The boy tapped the pouch at his waist, and although he spoke no word, the shy smile which touched his features revealed feelings of fierce pride. The forester's praise was desperately important to him. Sensitive to the fact that the fate of Anskiere, Emien, and perhaps the well-being of Keithland itself depended upon this boy's uncertain shoulders, Taen reached out to sound his thoughts.

Her entry was silent as an owl's flight and her quarry unsuspecting. Called Kerainson Jaric, the boy carried the mark of a recent and painful injury. He worked as apprentice to the forester, Telemark. A silent, earnest lad, Jaric took desperate care in his craft; he pushed himself ceaselessly, as if to overcome some greater deficiency than the weakness of convalescence. But when Taen sought the patterns of his immediate past, she encountered only emptiness and an anguished sense of shame. To her dismay, Kerainson Jaric possessed no conscious memory of his past or his parentage.

His plight moved Taen to pity. With full command of her dream-reader's skills, she reached to find out why, and experienced a disquieting discovery. Jaric's affliction resulted from the combined damage of a head wound dealt by outlaws and the backlash of Tathagres' interference at the time she had disrupted the geas. The boy could be made to remember. But through one stolen glimpse of the past he had forgotten, Taen understood enough to know that restoration of his memory would be doing him no kindness. Yet lacking Jaric's inborn talent on the opposing side, the demons would surely triumph, Anskiere's imprisonment would become permanent, and the Keys to Elrinfaer would fall into Tathagres' hands. Taen withdrew from the boy in the clearing, troubled by the realization that his peaceful life with the forester was destined not to last.

The instant the psychic net of Taen's awareness resumed normal proportions, the Vaere collapsed the time-differential which governed her, restoring the capsule which enclosed her to Keithland's main continuum. The girl within slept peacefully, her hair grown long and as glossy as the plumage of a raven through the lengthy years of her confinement; her body by now had fully matured. But the cycle of Sathid mastery had exacted a heavy toll upon the girl's physical health. The Vaere found her weight dangerously slight and much of her vitality depleted by exhaustion. Should Taen be removed from the capsule's protected environment in her current weakened state, there would be risk of disease; but her sleep patterns were normal. Rest would eventually restore her resilience.

Yet the months to come would develop the prime factors which determined humanity's survival. The Vaere tinkered probability figures as if fretting. Taen had uncovered new information during her passage into mastery. Merged, the facts shaped a picture distinctly threatening. The Vaere computed a second set of extrapolations and deduced potential disaster from the figures; for it appeared that the demons had dared to meddle directly with human politics for the first time since the crash of the *Corinne Dane*. If Taen's perceptions were accurate, the chief advisor to King Kisburn was almost certainly an alien shape-shifter. That posed immeasurable threat as Lord Sholl's influence could be seen behind the King's heated ambition and his decision to trust Tathagres. The Vaere perceived the entire campaign against the Free Isles as a plot to set the Landfast libraries into demon hands. If the Alliance fell, the heritage of humanity would be irreparably lost.

Lights glittered like stars on the consoles as the Vaere sequenced equations. Now more than ever before, Taen's talents as dream-reader were needed; she alone could challenge an alien shape-shifter and disrupt its influence over the affairs of the men it had selected as puppets. But her mastery of the Sathid also left her vulnerable. The Vaere knew that the frail girl its capsule sheltered would be ruthlessly destroyed should the demons discover her existence. Only two held power enough to protect her; the Stormwarden, still helplessly enmeshed in a defense spell to contain the frostwargs, and the untrained heir of Ivain Firelord.

The Vaere drew conclusions from its calculation with something akin to emotion. Taen would need to spend most of the winter inside the capsule recovering her physical strength. During that interval, she must engage her dream-reader's powers, restore Jaric's memory and drive him over the Furlains to the village of Mearren Ard. Once the boy made contact with the sea, Anskiere's geas should begin to resume its effect. The Vaere balanced the odds and found the margin for error non-existent. Even pressed by the geas' cruel directive, Jaric could not possibly sail for Cliffhaven before spring; by then the armies of Kisburn would already have left for the Straits, with the Kielmark's defeat all but inevitable.

The issue at stake was no longer limited to Taen, or even to the uncertainty of Anskiere's rescue. By the Vaere's analysis mankind's very survival depended upon Kerainson Jaric's potential mastery of the Cycle of Fire. And should Lord Sholl learn from Tathagres that Ivain had left an heir, the demons would hunt the boy down and kill him.

Had the Vaere been human, it might have despaired. The balance of the boy's future rested within Taen's influence as dream-reader and a race against the exigencies of time. For the facts converged with ruthless persistence. Should Jaric fail his inheritance, the demons would achieve their final vengeance against mankind. And the stakes which the Vaere surveyed reflected all the uncertainty of a horse race. Since humanity's preservation lay in Jaric's hands, plainly Taen must send him to the ice cliffs and to Anskiere before Kisburn's armies arrived.

The straps of the drag-sleigh cut deeply into Jaric's shoulders as he yanked it clear of a thicket. Snowfall dusted his hair and melted flakes dripped unpleasantly through his fur collar. Yet Jaric never thought to complain. By midwinter, drifts would lie thick and soft beneath the trees, burying obstacles which now hampered the drag-sleigh's runners. Jaric looked forward to the time when Telemark would lift the oiled frames of the snowshoes down from their peg in the loft. The gap in his memory distressed him less when he had a new task to master.

The forester moved through the snowbound forest with practiced silence. Jaric followed, towing the drag-sleigh

gracelessly over a fallen log. The straps bit into his hands
and runners grated over bark with a dry metallic ring. Once
again the packs snagged on a branch. Snow showered down
wetly over Jaric's neck. He paused to shake the ice from his
shoulders.

Telemark stopped and glanced back. "Here," he said as the
boy labored to catch up. "Let me pull the sleigh for awhile."

Ashamed, Jaric shook his head.

The forester regarded the boy, a stern set to his weathered
features. "Jaric," he said at last, "there are rules a man does not
break if he lives in the wilds during winter. The first is never to
deplete any resource unnecessarily."

Telemark reached out with startling speed and clapped Jaric
on the shoulder. The blow was not rough. But it caught the
boy squarely and painfully on muscles already worn out by the
weight of the sleigh, and he flinched reflexively.

"You're tired." With gentle sympathy, the forester pulled
the straps of the drag-sleigh free of Jaric's grip. "If you push
yourself to exhaustion, who will help me set camp and build
the fire?"

The boy sighed and nodded. He stepped aside while
Telemark tugged the sleigh clear of the log. Although the
man's face was averted, Jaric understood the forester was still
concerned over the fact that he seldom spoke since his recovery
from the accident. Occasionally disappointment showed in the
forester's manner, though he never troubled to mention the
subject.

Jaric bit his lip, watched Telemark haul the drag-sleigh with
what seemed careless strength. Yet his rhythmic stride and the
unbroken swish of the runners reflected more than years of accumulated skill; the man's haste described frustration. Jaric
hated to distress the forester who had granted him shelter and
healing; still, he avoided speech. Words disturbed him, created
interference patterns whose echoes would not be stilled, as if
they represented more than the simple sound of their pronun-

ciation. To speak was to become disoriented, lost in the blackness of the void where memory ended and where the unknown tantalized him endlessly with unanswerable questions. Like a mariner cast adrift in fog-bound waters, Jaric clung to the particulars of the moment. In silence he listened for the marker which would guide him back to the past he had lost.

The weather worsened as afternoon progressed. Blinded by the thickening fall of flakes, Jaric stumbled often into branches and his boot cuffs became packed with ice as he waded through freshly drifted thickets. The terrain grew rougher, sliced by steep-sided gullies and the black unfrozen sheen of running water. Yet the boy pressed on without asking for rest. Telemark halted well ahead of sundown beneath a high shelf of rock. The wind drove the snow in smoking clouds off the exposed crest of the ridge and flakes tumbled, hissing, through the bare poles of a lean-to beneath.

With his back to the rocks, the forester set his boot on the drag-sleigh and leaned crossed arms on his knee. "Do you think you can set up the shelter?"

Jaric smiled, at home with the silent snowbound forest and the prospect of making camp as he never could have been before leaving Morbrith. But no memory of his former helplessness returned to trouble him as he knelt and set his hands to the cords on the sleigh.

Telemark laughed and bent to assist him. "Let me have my bow and two beaver traps. Do you suppose I can lay the traps and bag dinner before you can make camp and start a fire?"

Jaric grinned, yanked off one mitten with his teeth, and tore industriously into the knots.

"Right, then, it's a race," said Telemark. "If you win, I'll begin to teach you the quarterstaff. The wind keeps the snow thin on the bluff. The footing there should be adequate."

The forester unlaced a bundle and pulled forth two steel traps, each with a length of chain ending in a forged ring. Then he strapped on his quiver of arrows, took up his bow and his axe, and disappeared silently into the wood. Jaric barely noted his departure. He unloaded the drag-sleigh with exuberant haste and tugged the patched sailcloth shelter free of its ties. Snow cascaded down his cuffs as he tossed it over the poles of the lean-to, and an icy wind billowed the canvas while he fought to lash the lines to secure it in place. But Jaric was exhilarated by the contest and barely noticed the discomfort. He spread the dropcloth and stacked the supplies safely inside. Then, running and sliding in the fresh-fallen snow, he pulled his mittens on again, seized the straps of the drag-sleigh, and went off in search of firewood.

He returned with a full load, breathless and laughing. Warmed by his exertion, he stripped off his mittens and went to work with flint and striker. Falling snow dampened the shavings. Jaric cupped his hands, huddled against the wind, but the spark fizzled again and again into frustrating curls of smoke. The boy glanced over his shoulder, certain Telemark would arrive at any moment. But when at last he coaxed a small flame from the chips, the forester had not yet returned.

Jaric stacked logs over the blaze with miserly care. Then, elated by his accomplishment, he settled on the empty frame of the drag-sleigh and stretched his boots toward the fire. As the glow of the flames deepened to ruddy gold, the boy listened with every muscle strained taut for the sound of Telemark's step. Snow fell, hissing into the flames like the whispered secrets of ghosts; the birch logs crackled and popped, blackening into ash, while beyond the circle of firelight live branches creaked under winter's burden of ice. The wet patches on his leggings steamed and slowly dried. Jaric pulled his cloak hood over his head and tried not to worry. Often Telemark moved with such quiet that wild animals themselves did not hear him. If he was delayed, chances were the storm had made the game scarce.

But the first logs crumbled into coals without his return. Daylight slowly failed and twilight shrouded the wood beyond the ring of firelight. Jaric rubbed his mittens restlessly across his knees, felt the sting of heated cloth as his leggings pulled taut across his shins. Nightfall was imminent. Telemark should have come back by now. With the excitement of the contest forgotten, Jaric stared off into the gloom and considered the ugly possibility that something might have gone amiss.

The thought caused him great distress, that the only living person he had known since his accident might be threatened. With the wind getting stronger, he dared not sit waiting any longer. Jaric rose and entered the lean-to. He pulled a twist of oiled linen from the supply pack. His hands shook as he wound the cloth around the end of a stick and secured it with wire. Yet he completed the task with the exacting care the forester had taught him, now acutely aware the winter weather would not forgive ineptness. Then he thrust the stick with its linen wrappings into the fire.

The oiled cloth caught and flared, shedding a brilliant wash of light across the campsite. Jaric buckled on Telemark's spare knife, shoved a dry cloak under his arm, retrieved his lighted torch, and stepped beyond the safe warmth of the firelight into the icy blackness of the night.

Snowfall had all but obscured Telemark's trail; only slight, rounded depressions remained of his footprints, and where the brush grew sparsely, drifts had already covered all trace of his passing. Jaric suppressed the temptation to hurry. If he made a wrong turn in the dark, he might never regain the forester's path. And the wind was rising. The torch flame guttered, streaming oily smoke into the boy's face. He blinked stinging eyes, thrusting the stick at arm's length. If Telemark had been injured, there was a very real chance he might freeze to death before Jaric found him.

The boy pushed through a stand of young pines, guided by the fact that the branches had recently been swept clean of snow. On the far side the ground dropped off into a steep-sided ravine. A stand of saplings cast long, weaving shadows by the light of the torch; sheltered by the bank, snowflakes whirled, glittering with diamond-chip reflections. Jaric ducked under the fallen branch. Withered clusters of oak leaves raked his cheek and his boots slid in the uncertain footing. But as he progressed down the slope the wind dwindled; here where the snow accumulated more slowly, Telemark's tracks were more distinct.

Jaric squinted through the storm. Open water glinted at the bottom of the embankment, black against the reflective white of the shore. The brook was wide and deep enough for beaver trapping; the boy proceeded with caution. The ground was treacherously obscured by snow and a misstep could end in disaster. Despite his care, Jaric slithered down the final slope, whipped by the trailing tendrils of a willow tree. The torch threw off sparks like midsummer fireflies as he flailed his arm for balance. His boot splashed into the shallows. The water showed treacherous furrows of current between its bed of snowcapped rocks. Jaric caught a branch and barely prevented a fall. He paused, breathing hard, and waited for the flame to steady. Upstream he heard the faint rush of falls. Telemark's footprints led in that direction.

The boy turned along the stream. He made slow progress. The terrain was icy, crisscrossed with fallen trees jammed in haphazard array against the sides of the ravine. Jaric stumbled clumsily over dead branches. Worse, the torch showed the first flickering signs of failure. The boy cursed himself for neglecting to bring along an unlit spare. Telemark's footprints proceeded through the darkness ahead in a seemingly endless row; if he returned for a fresh light, all of his search might be in vain.

The splash of the falls grew louder. The flame sputtered against the wind, reduced to a sullen red glow. Through the shimmer of falling snow, Jaric made out the densely piled twigs of a beaver dam. The sight encouraged him. Telemark would have selected such a location to set beaver traps. Sheltering the light with his body, the boy hurried anxiously forward. The tracks ended by the edge of an eddy pool. There the ground lay strangely disturbed, as if a pine branch had been used to sweep the snow smooth. Jaric drew closer and saw a freshly cut sapling angled downward into the water's icy depths. He recognized the configuration of a freshly set beaver trap, and gave the area wide berth. The trap itself would be set on the stream bottom, its steel ring affixed to the pole well beneath the surface of the water. But any scent of man's presence would warn off the intended prey.

Stumbling over the uneven ground, the boy worked his way past the dam. The bank on the far side lay smooth and white, unmarred by traces of man's presence. But an exposed band of wet mud showed darkly at the water's edge; the level of the pond had recently been lowered. Jaric frowned and retraced his steps. Probably Telemark had pried a break in the dam, then left the second trap set in wait for an animal to come and mend the damage.

The boy drew abreast of the dam. In the uncertain glimmer of flame which remained of his cresset, he studied the glistening cross-weave of mud and twigs which spanned the throat of the gully. The hole, if any existed, was lost in darkness, and the tangled interlace of branches visible near at hand offered perilous footing for a man with unreliable light. Jaric assessed the situation and saw he had no choice but to return to camp for a fresh torch, then seek a safer crossing downstream.

The realization filled him with despair. He clamped his fingers around the torch shaft and shivered, cold and forlorn in the darkness of Seitforest. The mournful spill of the falls overlaid the higher-pitched sigh of wind through the treetops on the ridge. Jaric hesitated and stood listening, as if by sheer desire he could fathom Telemark's location before the torch died. For an instant his longing was desperate enough that it seemed the forest itself paused to share his pain. Suddenly dizziness claimed him. Jaric swayed, grabbed hold of a tree branch for balance. But the moment of disorientation lingered, and in the dying glare of the torch he beheld the vision of a woman's face.

She was young, perhaps his own age. Hair as black as fine velvet curved softly over her shoulders and her blue eyes regarded him levelly from features set with earnest concern.

Jaric gasped and started back. His hand jerked reflexively, and the torch guttered, nearly extinguished. But the girl's face remained in his mind as if her presence locked his very thoughts in place.

"Do not fear me, Jaric," she pleaded, and the tone of her voice pulled at the depths of his heart. "I appear to you as a dream, but I can help you find the one you seek."

"Telemark?" Jaric spoke loudly, startled by the sound of his own voice. The darkness and wind swallowed his words without echo, and for a second he thought he heard someone calling from the far side of the stream.

"The man you search for lies beyond the beaver dam," said the girl. "His foot is wedged, and he is injured. You must go to him at once."

Jaric released his grip on the tree, took a hasty step in the direction of the dam.

But the girl shook her head impatiently. "No." Her dark hair swirled and her face abruptly vanished into mist, but her voice lingered in his mind. "You must cross farther down. Beyond the first trap you will find stones where the footing is safe."

Jaric roused and discovered himself staring, half dazed, at the surface of the water. "Who are you?" he demanded aloud.

No answer came to him but the sigh of the wind in the branches. Yet above the ceaseless spill of the falls, he was now certain he heard Telemark calling his name. The voice was faint but unmistakable. And if not for the strange enchantress's sending he might have missed it.

Jaric whirled, sliding in the fresh snow. He plunged down the bank. The distance to the eddy pool and the first trap seemed longer than he remembered. Shadows spun and danced under his feet as he moved, and the torch hissed, fanned to temporary brilliance by the passage of air. The crossing lay as the enchantress had promised, a row of flat boulders spanning the dark rush of current like footings of an incomplete bridge. Jaric felt his palms break into sweat, shaken by certain evidence; the woman's sending had been something more than a fancy born of fear and distress. But concern for Telemark drove him onward without time to spare for thought.

Dense brush lined the far bank of the stream. Jaric crashed through, careless of ripping his cloak. His feet slipped often on the steep rocky ground. Jaric slowed, counting his steps to maintain patience. A fall would snuff out the cinder which remained of his torch.

"Jaric, over here." The forester's voice sounded hoarsely above the wind, yet quite close, from a point just down the slope.

Jaric followed the sound, ducking impatiently through a stand of briars. Thorns hitched his sleeve. He yanked clear, thrusting the torch high overhead. And in the faint orange light of the coals, he saw a rumpled form sprawled in the snow.

"Telemark!" Consumed by sudden sharp fear, Jaric slid down the embankment. The forester lay with his foot wedged between two fallen trees and his shoulders propped against a rock further down the bank. The knife left stabbed upright in the ice by his hand, and a white slash in the bark of the near trunk which pinned him revealed a desperate struggle to free himself. But the tree was too thick for the blade to be any help, and bending uphill against the pain of a twisted ankle in the end had exhausted his strength.

"Jaric." The forester smiled, though his lips were blue with cold. "The axe is down by the stream. I dropped it when I fell."

Jaric knelt, tugging the spare cloak free of his belt.

But Telemark frowned impatiently. "Go now," he said quickly. "Find the axe while you still have light."

The boy bit his lip. Tossing the cloak over the forester's

still form, he rose and scrambled down the bank. The axe lay
dusted with snow, its haft partly submerged in the stream. Jaric
retrieved the tool from the water. Its weight dragged unpleasantly against muscles already aching with weariness. Jaric
hefted the axe to his shoulder and took a stumbling step back
up the slope.

That moment the torch went out. Jaric clenched his fingers
around the wet axe handle and wondered whether he had endurance enough to free Telemark and see him safely back to
the campsite.

CHAPTER XVI

Dream Weaver

JARIC KNELT AT TELEMARK'S SIDE, sheltering his friend from the worst bite of the wind with his body. Snowflakes whirled madly past and settled in white patches over the spare cloak which covered the injured man's shoulders. Telemark needed care and warmth and every comfort which could be gleaned from the supplies left in the packs back at camp. Jaric estimated the lean-to lay close to half a league distant, too far to travel without light, and with the storm becoming steadily worse, time was of the essence. The boy wished he could curse the inconveniences of fate. But words stuck in his throat and the raging despair he felt at Telemark's misfortune found no expression but stillness.

Moved by the boy's bleak silence, Telemark spoke from the darkness. "Jaric, many a problem will seem impossible at first sight. You must remember that no man can handle more than one step at a time. The most troublesome difficulty must be broken down into small tasks, each one easily mastered. Any predicament which cannot be dealt with this way will prove your undoing. This is not such a one. Trust yourself. All will be well, and sooner than you presently think."

The advice brought little comfort when measured against the fact that Telemark suffered the continuous discomfort of his twisted ankle. Yet with the same blunt courage Jaric had shown the day he regained consciousness in the care of a stranger, with no past and no memory of self, he placed total trust in the forester. He had nothing else. Either Telemark spoke truth, or both of them risked death by exposure in the stormy winter night.

The forester reached out and clasped Jaric's wrist with fingers already numb with chill. Through the contact the boy felt the deep tremors of shivering which racked his friend's body. He guessed Telemark's calmness was probably a brave facade, for the forester understood the gravity of his situation and Jaric was too perceptive to be fooled.

Whether Telemark sensed the boy's distress could not be told from his manner. "Did you find the axe?"

"Yes." Jaric swallowed. Determined to remain steady, he continued, though words came with difficulty. "I'll make a fire."

"Good lad." Telemark released his grip and settled wearily back on the snowy ground. "The branches on this fallen log appear to be seasoned. Work slowly. Better I wait for warmth than have you slip with the axe in the dark."

Yet Jaric knew the fire must not be delayed for very long. The wind was rising. It rattled through the treetops in heavy, whipping gusts, driving snow before it with stinging force. Unless the boy could shelter Telemark from the cold, and quickly, the forester would slip into delirium and thence to unconsciousness. Jaric selected a dead bough. He hefted the axe, swung it downward with a steadfast stroke, well aware that life depended upon his performance. Steel bit into wood with a ringing thump. The branch shivered and cracked, and snow showered down, sifting wetly over the tops of Jaric's boots. He jerked the blade free, snapped the limb off with his foot, and chopped into another, knowing if he stopped for a moment, weariness and fear would freeze him in place.

He worked with no thought of rest. After a time his movements settled into a rhythm entirely independent of thought. The axe handle raised blisters upon his palms through his mittens, but he felt no discomfort. Exhaustion robbed the sensation of meaning, and his muscles responded mechanically to the needs of the moment. Only after he had accumulated a sizable pile of branches did Jaric lay the axe aside. He scooped a hollow in the drift at Telemark's side, using a stick to scrape the ground clean of snow. Then he hastened down the embankment and returned with an armload of stones, still dripping from the stream. With shaking hands he lined the depression with rocks, stacked the wood in the sheltered place at the center, and at long last set to work with striker and flint.

The storm hampered his efforts. Gusts whirled the sparks away into the dark and scattered the last dry shavings he had brought in his pouch. Grimly Jaric drew his knife and carved fresh ones. Snow settled on his wrists as he whittled, chilling his skin until his bones ached with cold. Telemark had not stirred for some time. Afraid to find the forester's condition grown worse, the boy hunched resolutely against the elements. He struck another spark. This time the chips steamed and caught. Jaric hoarded the flame between his hands like gold. One twig at a time, he coaxed the fire to grow, all but singeing his fingers in the process. Then he draped his cloak over an overhanging branch as a wind break, weighted the hem with two rocks, and bent anxiously over Telemark. The forester lay with closed eyes, unresponsive to the boy's touch.

Jaric spoke, though the necessity stung his throat. "Can you feel your feet?"

The forester stirred sluggishly, his answer unintelligibly slurred. Jaric could only guess at the meaning of the gesture which followed. Cold had begun to slow Telemark's reflexes, and presently he would no longer be capable of rational action.

Cognizant of the fact that the forester's situation was critical, Jaric lifted a brand from the fire. He searched until he located a long sturdy stick, dragged it back, and wedged one end between the logs which trapped Telemark's foot. Then he leaned every ounce of his weight on the farther end. The branch creaked under his hands. Dead bark split, baring wood like old bone in the firelight. Jaric closed his eyes and pulled until his tendons burned from exertion. The upper log shifted slightly, then remained fixed as a boulder. Jaric coiled his body, heaved the stick in desperation. But the makeshift pole only snapped with a crack that stung his palms, with nothing gained but frustration.

Shivering from stress and exertion, Jaric abandoned the stick. He fell to his knees in the snow and feverishly explored Telemark's trapped leg with his hands. His work had not been entirely in vain; the logs no longer pinched the limb so tightly. But the ankle had swollen badly. To drag it free would cause the forester great pain, and could cause unaccountable damage if any bone had been broken.

"The bone's intact," Telemark murmured, aware enough to realize what was happening. "You must tug until the leg comes clear."

But Jaric preferred not to take such a chance. He trimmed the edge of Telemark's boot sole with his knife, and slowly, carefully began to ease the foot free. Gently as he worked, Telemark gasped at the first slight movement. He bit his sleeve to keep from crying aloud as the boy lifted his twisted ankle clear of the logs.

Jaric supported his friend's shoulders, helped him to sit up. The fallen trees offered a reasonable backrest, and while Telemark settled shivering into the damp folds of the cloaks, the boy chafed his limbs to restore circulation. Then he turned to assess the extent of the forester's injury. The leg was not broken. But the flesh was bruised, swollen, and painful to the touch and certainly unfit to bear weight. And the storm was growing more violent by the hour.

"We cannot stay here." Telemark's teeth chattered with cold, and even the slightest speech seemed to tax his remaining strength.

Jaric touched his friend's arm, bidding him to be still. His brows drew into a troubled frown as he considered what should be done next. If he cut a stick for a crutch, the forester could move. But first he must have time to become thoroughly warm. The gusts struck with such fury no brand could long stay alight, and progress through the forest with an injured man would be tortuously slow. Jaric knew he faced a trip back to camp to fetch oiled rags for torches. But he dared not leave Telemark alone until he had cut enough logs to keep the fire going in his absence.

Jaric lifted the axe once more. Although his shoulders and arms trembled from exhaustion, he crossed to the foot of the nearest fallen tree and brought the blade down through the air in a clean, hard arc. Steel struck wood with a punishing jar. The impact left Jaric numbed to the elbow, yet he raised the axe for another stroke, and another. Chips flew, flickering into the shadows. Log by single log, he built a pile of fuel to ensure Telemark's survival, even should misfortune strike a second time and delay his return.

Drifts had piled waist-high between the thickets by the time Jaric departed alone to fetch fresh torches from the campsite. The boy plowed stubbornly through the heavy snow, too tired to feel any sense of his own achievement. He labored all that cruel and stormy winter's night to bring Telemark back safely, unaware he had surpassed, in strength and skill and persever-ance, every limitation he once despised in himself as a sickly apprentice at Morbrith.

Dawn cast a pall of gray through the blizzard by the time Jaric lowered Telemark into the lean-to's shelter. He saw the

forester securely wrapped in furs, then braved the torment of
the wind once more to dig the accumulated snow and sodden
ashes of last night's fire from the pit. The boy dared not rest
until he had laid down fresh wood and covered his handiwork
with canvas, ready for lighting should warmth be needed at
short notice. Then, with his ears ringing with weariness and his
body bruised and shivering with exhaustion, he stripped off his
boots, wet leggings, and tunic. He rolled into his own blankets
and almost instantly fell asleep.

The storm lifted toward afternoon. The sky blew clear of
clouds and the temperature fell, leaving the forest brittle with
cold. Jaric woke to the blinding glare of sunlit snow. Telemark
had risen before him. A pot boiled above the fire and the boy
smelled the enticing odor of brushpheasant and herbs cooking
within. He began to rise, grunting as the pain of stiffened muscles protested his first movement. Brought fully awake by the
sting of his blistered palms, Jaric recalled Telemark's accident,
and the agony of endurance he had suffered the night before.
Alarmed by his friend's empty blankets, the boy pulled a fresh
tunic from his pack and tugged it clumsily over his shirt. He
shoved his feet into icy boots and grabbing the frozen folds of
his cloak he left the shelter.

Telemark sat with his sprained ankle propped comfortably
on a log before the fire. His bow and skinning knife leaned
alongside a bucket of hot water, and a soggy pile of feathers lay
strewn around his feet.

Jaric gestured at the forester's injured leg, a confounded expression on his face. Then he directed a questioning glance at
the cooking pot. "How?"

Telemark laughed. "I threw out grain. Brushpheasant are
lazy creatures, particularly after a snowfall. They'll often risk a
handout from a human rather than scratch for themselves. Are
you hungry?"

Jaric nodded. He settled himself on the woodpile, spreading
the icy cloak across his knees to dry. Telemark watched his

companion's stiff, careful movements with every bit of his former acuity.

"Boy," he said softly. "Wherever you come from, and whoever you were does not count here. Last night you managed a man's work, and did it well. You have every right to be proud."

Jaric stared awkwardly at his hands, afraid to smile, fearful that if he acknowledged the forester's praise something inexplicable might intrude and ruin the moment. He longed to share the strange vision he had experienced by the beaver dam; to tell the forester of the black-haired girl who appeared in a dream to guide him. But the necessity of framing thoughts into words daunted the boy. Before he could manage a beginning, Telemark spoke again.

"You will have to set the traps alone until my leg heals. If I instruct you, do you think you can manage?"

Jaric looked up, brown eyes widened in surprise. Never had he considered the possibility that the forester might trust him to handle traplines by himself. Yet even as he sat, aching and tired, with his features stamped with the marks of last night's stress, he knew he could cope with the responsibility. Whatever his lost past, his work the last night had fully proven his capability.

"I can do my best," he said levelly. For the first time since he had recovered consciousness, confused and nameless in the forester's hut, speech came easily to his tongue.

Though pale from weariness himself, Telemark's stern countenance broke into a smile. "Good man," he said softly. "Fetch me the pack with the traps and I'll show you how we bag marten, silver fox, and ice otters."

Through the sunlit afternoon, Jaric worked in the clearing under Telemark's direction, learning the particulars of the trapper's trade. At dusk he loaded his pack and strapped a parcel of equipment to the frame of the drag-sleigh.

He rose at daybreak. Leaving Telemark to manage the campsite, he set off alone to lay the first of the winter traplines.

Early on he covered only as much ground as he could manage in a single day's hike. But he learned quickly. His confidence grew to match his skill. A week passed. The catch lashed to the drag-sleigh at the end of his rounds increased steadily; by the time Telemark's ankle recovered enough to manage the inner circuit of traps, the boy had progressed to the point where he could choose his own route. The day soon dawned when, with hard-earned pride, he loaded the sleigh with provisions and the spare cloth shelter and set off to manage the outlying territory on his own.

Jaric came to know the winter woods as home, whether under the trackless blanket of new snowfall, or the crisp cold of a diamond-clear sun. During the weeks which followed, he struggled over heavy drifts with the drag-sleigh in tow, day after long day; he chopped his own wood for each evening's fire, and gradually grew stronger. His face tanned from constant exposure to the weather. And the results of his labors filled the drying shed back at Telemark's cabin with the rich smell of curing pelts.

Midwinter's eve came, marked by austere celebration at the cabin. For hours Jaric stared into the fine, smokeless flames of candles made from beeswax, brought out specially for the occasion. If ever he had known such beauty in the past, his mind could not recall it. Silent with reflection, the boy sipped mulled wine fresh from the heat of the fire, unaware the forester studied him intently in return.

The shirts which had clothed an unsteady convalescent last autumn now fell without slack from shoulders grown broad with new muscle. Telemark noted the change but offered no comment. Sturdy and self-reliant as Jaric had become, and resilient as his outlook seemed, the fact he could recall no memory of his past lay like a shadow upon his young heart. Deprived of any knowledge of his origins, the boy lived like a man haunted by ghosts. Every commitment became a risk; each achievement, a footing built on sand.

But midwinter was a poor time to dwell upon somber thoughts. "Come to the shed," said the forester, a glint in his blue eyes. "I have something to show you." He rose and tossed Jaric a cloak from the peg by the back door and the boy followed him out into the night.

Telemark unbolted the shed door, kicked the snow clear of the sill, and tugged the heavy panel open. Jaric waited while the forester pulled a striker from his pocket and lit the candle in the near wall bracket. The flame grew, hesitant in the draft. By its first unsteady light, the boy saw a gleam of new metal on the worktable. He exclaimed and moved closer. There, still shiny from the forge, stood a full set of traps, laid out in Telemark's habitually neat array. Speechless, he turned and faced the forester.

Telemark picked a stray thread from his sleeve, embarrassed by the intensity of the boy's gaze. "I made spares during the time I was laid up. And I was right to do so, it would seem. You know enough now that we can keep two lines of remote traps going. Are you willing?"

Jaric reached out, traced the sharpened jaws of an ice otter snare with tentative fingers. He disliked killing animals; like him, they ran unknowing to their fate. But Telemark was never callous with his craft. He took only what he needed, cleanly and well, and never demanded more for the sake of greed. The forest was his livelihood, also his only love. Even with no past experience from which to draw conclusions, Jaric understood he might never know a better friend. The compassion and the trust represented by the forester's gesture touched him deeply. For a moment he could not answer. Yet the expression on his young face told the forester far more than any word.

The boy would accept the responsibility he had earned. By springtime, he perhaps would have bagged enough pelts to purchase a decent sword and knife. And certain Jaric's destiny did not lie with him in Seitforest, Telemark prayed silently that the boy would have time and the chance to finish the learning he had begun.

A month passed, the forest peaceful under winter's mantle of snow. A fortnight's distance on foot from Telemark's cabin, Jaric settled with his feet to the embers of his campfire. Tired from an arduous day tending traplines and satiated by a meal of stewed rabbit, he leaned back against the trunk of a gnarled old beech while the sky changed from pale violet to the heavy indigo of dusk. The expedition had gone well. The drag-sleigh lay piled high with pelts, including several from the rare six-legged ice otter, whose highly prized fur was beautifully mottled in silver and black. Telemark would be pleased. But morning was soon enough to contemplate the trip back to main camp; for now, Jaric delighted in his evening alone.

Here as nowhere else he felt at peace with himself. Seitforest took on an austere beauty all its own in the dead of winter. Its law was harsh but fair and its silence made no demands upon a troubled spirit. For competently as Jaric managed the responsibilities of his traplines, the gap in his memory tormented him, leaving a hollow of emptiness at the core of his being no achievement could erase. He felt as malleable as soft clay, fitting the mold of Telemark's life, but owning no shape of his own. Jaric had hammered that mental barrier with questions until his head ached with no success. His past remained obscured until even Telemark ceased promising that time would restore the loss.

The boy picked a stick off his woodpile, jabbing at the embers of the fire. Sparks flurried skyward, bright and brief as the blossoms of the night-flower vine, which opened but one hour at eventide and wilted immediately thereafter. The image stopped the breath in Jaric's throat. His fingers tightened until bark bit roughly into his palms. *Where had he seen such flowers, and when? By the time he had regained awareness after his accident, frost had already withered the greenery in Seitforest.*

Jaric shivered. Suddenly inexplicably dizzy, he filled his lungs with icy pine-scented air, but the moment of disorientation lingered. Gooseflesh prickled his arms though he was not cold and his ears rang with a strange singing note like nothing he had ever experienced.

A log settled, scattered embers into the snow with a sharp hiss of steam. Jaric started. He rubbed his sleeves, driving away the chills with self-deprecating logic, until a glance at the fire set them off once more. In the bright heart of the flames he again beheld the face of the woman who had guided his search the night of Telemark's injury. Her black hair was bound by a circlet of woven myrtle; the delicately colored blossoms matched her blue eyes. Since no such vines could possibly be in bloom at midwinter, Jaric knew she must be an enchantress. Her beauty left him utterly confused.

She spoke, and her voice rang oddly inside his head, as if her message originated many leagues distant. "Kerainson Jaric, look upon me and know my face, for I shall return to you this night in a dream. I offer you full memory of the past you have lost; but in exchange I must also demand a price."

Her image wavered and began to fade.

Frantic to know more, Jaric shouted, "What price?"

But his words echoed across the empty forest unanswered and the fire burned as before. Jaric clenched his fists until his knuckles pressed as bloodless as old ivory against his stained leather leggings. The girl's mysterious promise made him blaze with impatience and her unearthly beauty inflamed his mind. Wracked by frustration too intense for expression, the boy wrapped his arms around his knees and stared restlessly at the sky. Stars glittered like chipped ice through silhouetted branches and somewhere above the thickets to the north an owl hooted mournfully. Seitforest remained unchanged in the winter darkness, except that the peace which Jaric found in evening solitude was now irreparably destroyed. Miserable and alone, he threw another log on the fire then bundled his cloak tightly around his body. He diverted the anger he could not express into the motion. Yet no human effort could lift the chill the enchantress had seated in his heart.

Wind arose in the night, pouring icy drafts through the patched canvas of the lean-to's meager shelter. Jaric curled like a cat in his furs, sleepless and tense. With bitter irony he wondered whether the enchantress' sending had been nothing better than an illusion born of his own unanswered needs. His disappointment was so intense that the enchantress' second sending came upon him unnoticed. One moment he lay with his head pillowed in the rigid crook of his arm. The next, his eyes closed and he fell into relaxed sleep.

Jaric dreamed he stood in the center of a twilit clearing. The air was clean and mild, and grasses flowered under his boots. The wintry gloom of Seitforest stood replaced by a towering ring of cedars whose age and majesty held no comparison to any woodland known to mortals. At once the boy knew he beheld a place beyond the boundaries of time, and there the enchantress chose to meet him.

It never occurred to him to feel afraid. "You were long in coming to me," he accused as she stepped into view between the trees.

Her shift glimmered white in the gloom, falling in graceful curves over her slender body. Although the glade remained eerily still, her presence reminded Jaric of music and torchlight and the rustle of fine silk on a midsummer's night. The associations arose unbidden, left him uncertain and confused, for the memories seemed those of a stranger.

"No." The enchantress touched his hand with small warm fingers. Jaric found her nearness disorienting. She gazed deeply into his eyes and spoke as though she shared his most private thoughts. "The memory is your own, Jaric. You grew up at Morbrith Keep. The Earl who rules there often guested great ladies in his hall."

Jaric felt his chest constrict. He forced himself to speak. "Earlier you mentioned there would be a price for my past."

Although the enchantress was a woman grown, a look of uncertainty crossed her features, as if a child suddenly gazed out at him through wide blue eyes. She glanced down, but not quickly enough to hide a fleeting expression of sorrow. Jaric guessed, after the open longing in his tone, that she already knew what his answer would be. Whatever her terms, he would accept; if he did not, the desperation, the loss, and the question of his own identity would eventually drive him mad. It was no fair choice she offered; that she well understood, and the fact pained her. She looked down as if fascinated by the flowers at her feet.

But her discomfort was not great enough to make her lift the restraint she had placed upon him. "The price is this: you will cross the Furlains at the earliest possible opportunity. When you reach the coast and the town of Mearren Ard, your fate will pass into the hands of another more powerful than I."

The enchantress looked up, her expression honestly distressed. "Jaric, I swear by my life. The destiny which awaits you is of crucial concern to those who safeguard the people of Keithland. Anskiere of Elrinfaer is wiser than any but the Vaere. He would not ask your service lightly."

But neither names nor the girl's entreaty held meaning to one who had no past loyalties to bind him. Jaric's lips thinned, a look entirely alien to the frightened boy who had once fled Morbrith Keep on a stolen horse. "I accept," he said flatly.

Although the enchantress had won the concession desired by the Vaere, the victory was bitter. Jaric's decision arose from no feeling of compassion for Anskiere, nor for humanity's endangered existence. He consented only to gain knowledge of his birthright; and better than any, Taen knew the consequences were heavier than he could possibly imagine.

Telemark tossed down his polishing rag, hung the last kettle on its hook in the pantry, and succumbed at last to restlessness. Jaric was a week overdue. Unwilling to admit the depth of his concern, the forester paced the cabin's confines, searching for any lingering trace of untidiness; but he had cleaned, polished, and mended every belonging he owned twice over since his own return several days ago. No more loose ends remained to distract him.

He sighed and crossed to the window. Twilight settled over Seitforest, the gloom beneath the beeches all stillness and indigo shadows between the high crests of the drifts. With midwinter past, the snowfall lay deepest, before the first thaw swelled the stream beds. There had been no severe storms of late; already the sun shone warmer in the afternoons, offering easy weather for travel, even with a loaded drag-sleigh. The trapline Jaric covered had been set over mild terrain, far from any traveled route where outlaws might lurk. The boy should not have been delayed.

Telemark left the window to pace once again, irritated by his own vulnerability. In all other matters he had learned to be fatalistic. The solitary life of the forest suited him; he had no need of companionship. Yet somehow Jaric's earnest desire to excel and the soul-searching depths of his silences had captured more than the forester's sympathy. Telemark roamed past the hearth for the fiftieth time that day; perhaps it was the fact that the boy carried the terrible mark of destiny that had caused him to bestow every protection in his power, even for the brief space of a winter. Few men were unlucky enough to be the focus of a sorcerers' dispute, far less stand noticed by Llondian prophecy. And Jaric was so very human. It was impossible for any man with sensitivity not to be moved by his plight.

Telemark paused again by the window. Night deepened

over the forest and the trees bulked black and twisted beneath a thin sliver of moon. To the untrained eye nothing seemed amiss. But something in the shadows along the path beyond the shed caught Telemark's attention. His fingers tensed on the window frame. He looked more carefully and saw the faintest suggestion of movement. Impatience drove him to act before logic could restrain him.

Telemark ran to the door. He snatched the lantern from its peg, cursing the tremble in his hand as he fumbled for the striker. The first spark missed the wick entirely. The second caught. Without bothering to pull on a cloak, Telemark let himself out into the icy cold of the night.

The lantern cast arrows of light between trees limned by the flash and sparkle of hoar frost. Dazzled after the dimness of the cabin, Telemark squinted, unable to tell whether anything moved on the path. Worry made him stubborn. He refused to consider the idea he might have been mistaken.

"Jaric?" The word died on the air without echo, leaving silence.

Telemark lowered the lantern, overwhelmed by disappointment. He reached for the latch on the cabin door. But before he could let himself in, he picked up the sound he had strained to hear through five uneventful days; a sharp ring as the dragsleigh's runners scraped across the rock by the bend in the path.

"Jaric!" Telemark whirled and crossed the clearing at a run.

The lantern swung, jounced by his stride, and by its flickering light he saw the boy stumble out of the woods, towing a full load of pelts. Nothing appeared to be wrong. Yet as Telemark drew nearer he saw that Jaric, who was usually fanatically neat, looked raffish and unkempt. His cheeks were unshaven. Dark circles ringed eyes which contained a poignant and painful awareness.

"Jaric, what happened?" The forester set the lantern on a stump. He caught the boy in a fierce embrace, as if the solid feel of him might reassure the feeling of foreboding which had plagued him week long.

Jaric clung with a desperate grip, but after a moment straightened up. "I know who I am," he said. The dull edge of resentment in his tone raised the hairs on Telemark's neck. Memory of the Llondel's vision and of the boy's inexplicable destiny gave the man a powerful urge to weep. Instead he grabbed the lantern and gestured back toward the cabin. "Let's go home. You can talk later."

Jaric drew a heavy breath. He leaned into the straps of the drag-sleigh as if the sweat-stained leather was all that held him bound to the earth. "I have a debt, also," he announced.

And Telemark suddenly understood why the boy's step was so heavy. It appeared the fate foretold by the Llondel demon had at last overtaken him.

The forester walked at the boy's side, forcing himself to remain calm. "The tale can wait," he said, sensing reluctance behind Jaric's need to talk.

They stopped together by the cabin's door stoop. Telemark hooked the lantern on a bracket overhead and bent briskly over the drag-sleigh. The lashings had been tied with painful perfection, as if Jaric had tried to negate the inevitability of his future through single-minded devotion to his present craft. The pelts were expertly dressed, not a hair pressed against the grain during packing, and the axe blade gleamed, newly sharpened and oiled to prevent rust.

The boy and I are much alike, Telemark thought, and suddenly bit his lip as he realized how deeply his influence had rooted. Jaric had possessed no past and no self-image except what example his healer had provided him. Now, such a meager measure of stability was all the boy had to stave off the devastation of utter upheaval; the reckoning meted out when Jaric first entered Seitforest had been cruel but just. Before his accident, the boy had been singularly unfit to survive.

With the gentleness he would use to soothe a wounded animal, Telemark spoke. "I knew all along you would not be staying here. But how and when you leave is your choice alone. Until then this cabin is your home." He forced himself to concentrate on the untying of knots as Jaric drew a shaking breath that came very close to a sob.

At that Telemark could not help but look up. Tears streaked Jaric's face in the yellow glare of the lantern. Behind the boy's flooded eyes, Telemark saw agonized self-awareness and the just pride of accomplishment earned through the hardships of the winter woods. But undermining such knowledge lay a hunted, desperate self-doubt, as if some blight from early childhood had arisen to haunt the grown man. For suddenly there seemed very little of the boy left in the person who stood silent and determined at the forester's shoulder.

Torn by unbearable sympathy, Telemark could restrain his inquiry no longer. "How much did you learn?"

Jaric bent and began to loosen the lines with mechanical practicality. "Nearly everything. I know where I grew up and the names of the parents who bore me. I know I am not Kerain's true son, but the get of a sorcerer." He paused, unwilling to mention any name, and seemingly also unwilling to accept it. "That is the reason I left Morbrith Keep, where I was raised. But I know nothing of how or why I came to leave. Nor do I know why I am going; only that I must go."

His fingers froze on the knots. He looked up, meeting Telemark's gaze squarely for the first time since his return. And the forester saw he lived in horror of discovering what other surprises might lurk behind those memories still denied him.

But even Telemark's keen intuition could not guess the full truth; that Jaric's own mother had almost certainly tried to kill him in the very hour of his birth. The other children of the Smith's Guild had never allowed the boy to forget the fact. Kerain's account of his betrothed's crime lay inscribed in the records of Morbrith. As a scribe's apprentice, Jaric had checked the registry for himself and found in the cold words of the

Earl's justice the transcription of testimony alongside the entry which sentenced an innocent man to hang.

The child Kerainson Jaric had grown to manhood without ever coming to terms with the horror born of his mother's rejection. Now posed tenuously at the edge of his first recognition of self-worth, the dream-weaver who guarded the last lost threads of his past demanded that he renounce the only happiness he had ever known in exchange for service to a second sorcerer whose name was linked with four thousand deaths. Pinned between the self-discovery learned under Telemark's guidance and a lifelong feeling of inadequacy Jaric struggled, inwardly deafened by overpowering conflict.

"I must cross the Furlains to the town of Mearren Ard on the coast," he said in a tone stripped of emotion.

The boy's words struck Telemark like the last statement of a man condemned. He caught Jaric's wrist in a forceful grip. "That may very well be. But you'll go nowhere before I have gone to Corlin market for supplies." Jaric's stricken expression caused him to gentle his manner at once. "Come in and get warm. The passes over the Furlains are closed at this season anyway, and a fortnight's rest will serve you well before beginning such a journey."

Jaric nodded. He resumed unloading the drag-sleigh as if all were restored to normal. But by the look of naked relief which settled over his features, Telemark knew the day of parting would be difficult. All he could do was prepare the boy as well as possible. For a start that meant the commission of a good well-balanced sword from the armorer in Corlin. But the forester mentioned nothing of his intention to Jaric.

CHAPTER XVII

Mearren Ard

JARIC PERCHED ON A STOOL OF carved maple, one elbow braced in the sunlight which spilled through the south window of Telemark's cabin. With a freshly sharpened pen in hand, he listed the supplies the forester would purchase during his monthly trip to Corlin market. But the return of his former skill brought him little joy. The familiar flow of ink and the neat incisive script which emerged beneath his nib provided final proof the dream-weaver had not lied about his past; once he had been a copyist in the archives of Morbrith Keep. The certainty left him feeling trapped.

"Add potatoes," said Telemark, pacing between window and hearth in a manner grown routine to Jaric through his months of convalescence. "And lamp oil. That should cover everything."

Jaric dated the list out of habit and laid aside his pen. He stared at his fingers, now heavily callused, and sliced across the right thumb by a scar where an ice otter maimed by a trap had bitten him as he bent to deal a mercy stroke. The hands he studied no longer looked like those of a scribe. Evenings, when the fire burned in the forester's hearth, the past the dream-weaver had unlocked within his mind seemed remote, belonging to a frail sickly stranger whose sleep had been riddled with nightmares of his own inadequacy. Jaric clenched his fists in the sunlight, chilled despite the promise of spring's warmth. At night the dreams and the terrors of that former self flooded his mind, battering away the self-assurance he had discovered at Telemark's side. The boy lived fearful he would waken one morning and discover his earlier image to be the true measure of his worth. All of daylight's logic could not unravel his uncertainty.

"Jaric?" Telemark crossed his arms and leaned against the chimney. "I'll be gone for a fortnight. Be sure the temperature in the drying shed doesn't fall below freezing. I've started seeds in the planting box in the back corner."

Caught with his mind wandering for the fourth time that morning, Jaric nodded.

"Good." Telemark straightened up. He collected the list from the tabletop. "Are you certain you don't wish to come? We could move the sprouts to the root cellar."

"I don't mind staying." Jaric rose as the forester moved about the cabin, gathering together last-minute items in preparation for his trip into town. The boy felt no regret from his decision to remain behind. Although Telemark made no issue of the subject, newly planted herbs would do poorly in the root cellar; with Jaric home to tend the fire, the bottled stores would not need to be moved to prevent freezing and the near circuit of traps could be kept in operation.

Telemark laced up his knapsack and directed a keen glance at Jaric. "You'll be all right alone?"

The boy nodded. He jabbed the stopper into the ink flask and rose to help the forester carry the remaining supplies to the door. Outside the drag-sleigh waited, already piled with pelts. Jaric stood awkwardly aside while Telemark buckled on his sword belt and shouldered his bow. Thieves preyed on the fringes of Seitforest even in the depths of winter and the ice otter fur by itself was worth a prince's ransom. The forester never went to the ferry unarmed.

Jaric watched his friend prepare to depart with strangely mixed feelings. He would miss Telemark sorely. But since his return to the cabin, the enchantress who unlocked the memories of his past had sent no more dreams. If she only appeared when he was alone, the boy wished one last chance to question her before the passes opened; for his recollection of events was complete except for the circumstances surrounding his departure from Morbrith. More and more, Jaric sensed the missing facts were pertinent, that Taen had a reason for withholding them. Since her abilities as a dream-weaver permitted her to cross the mental barriers left by an injury, surely she could also create them at will. And Jaric had reason to suspect he was being manipulated.

Disinclined to linger once the drag-sleigh's load was secured, Telemark left for Corlin. He had barely disappeared beyond the bend in the path before Jaric applied himself to mending the gear he had worn out on the trail. By sundown the boy was determined to demand the reason why his life was of such interest to the sorcerer who had once drowned half the souls of Tierl Enneth.

But the dream-weaver did not appear to him that night nor any time following Telemark's departure. Jaric attended his chores with increasing frustration, convinced some fact of vital importance had been denied him. But his attitude in no way affected his work. He checked and baited the traplines conscientiously while the afternoons lengthened toward spring. The icicles dropped from the eaves of the cabin with a sound like shattering crystal and the stream lost its crust of ice. On the fifteenth day, Jaric returned from his rounds to find the drag-sleigh leaning against the weathered boards of the shed. Smoke curled from the cabin's stone chimney, delicate as embroidery against the reddened sky of sunset. Telemark had returned.

Jaric shouted. He burst into a run, knapsack banging clumsily against his shoulders. The cabin door opened as he reached the clearing's edge and Telemark stepped out.

He caught the boy in a smothering embrace. "Stow your gear quickly and come inside. I have a surprise for you."

Jaric did as the forester bid him. But when he returned to the cabin doorway, he hesitated. The closer he came to the inevitable moment of departure, the more jarring he found each variation from habit; never before had the forester brought anything unusual from Corlin. For one wild instant Jaric longed to rush back into the cold familiar darkness of the shed. But Telemark caught his arm firmly and hustled him across the threshold.

Wax candles burned festively on the table beside the window, but Jaric's eyes were drawn at once by the polished metal which gleamed in the light beneath. A sword, dagger, and penknife lay in a row, the bluish patina of new steel in sharp contrast to the rough boards of the tabletop.

Jaric gasped, his hand motionless on the door latch.

"Go on." Telemark prodded him gently forward. "I had them made for you in Corlin."

The boy crossed the floor as if the planking beneath his feet was thin and treacherous as old ice. Candles struck a haze of bronze highlights through his fair hair as he bent to examine Telemark's gift. The weapons were plain but beautifully made. Every detail bespoke painstaking craftsmanship and the result combined grace and beauty with a chilly sense of effectiveness. Jaric regarded the sheen on the cutting edge of the sword blade and knew at once that Telemark had spared no expense. From blades to crossguards, the set glittered with the watery polish of first-quality steel, and the pommels bore his name chased in silver.

Telemark crossed to the boy's side. "Try the balance," he urged softly.

Jaric glanced up, a stunned expression on his face. He made no move to touch the weapons.

Interpreting his silence, Telemark caught the boy's shoulders in a firm grip. "You earned them, down to the last copper," he said emphatically. "Did you think I had you lay an extra trapline so I could deck my windows out in brocade?"

He released his hold suddenly, lifted the sword from the tabletop, and thrust the grip into Jaric's reluctant hands. The boy stared incredulously, then managed to execute an experimental feint. Candlelight danced across the polished curve of the quillon. The size and weight of the weapon suited him too perfectly for coincidence; Telemark had evidently ordered the blades designed exclusively for him.

Jaric raised his eyes to the forester and spoke directly from the heart. "I thank you. Never in life have I received so fine a gift."

"Well then," said Telemark gruffly. "Don't be losing this one as you did the last."

He turned abruptly from the light, but not before Jaric caught sight of the tears which gleamed on his weathered cheeks. The boy laid the sword aside. Without speaking he threw his arms around Telemark's shoulders. And from that moment both understood he was closer to the father Jaric had never known than any person from his childhood at Morbrith.

Two weeks passed with deceptive swiftness. Comfortably settled into the routine of the trapper's trade, Jaric wished he could forget the price he had promised the dream-weaver in return for his past. But the nights grew inexorably shorter. All too soon Jaric wakened from sleep to the sound of rain hammering against the eaves of the cabin; come morning, he would have to leave Seitforest. Although the weather in the mountains had yet to break, a man traveling alone was best advised to cross the high passes early, before the first caravans of spring attracted bandits to lie in ambush.

Telemark rose at daybreak. He helped load the spare knapsack with journey cake, smoked meat, and cheese, as if preparing Jaric's supplies for a trip to check on a remote trapline. He spoke very little. His face looked drawn and tired. This time the blanket roll and the spare snowshoes would not be returning to their pegs in the loft.

He strapped the knapsack closed with brisk efficiency, then folded his arms and leaned on it, regarding the boy with a look of uncharacteristic gravity. "Jaric, listen carefully. I have something to tell you that I don't fully understand. But I believe it to be important and you may someday find the information useful."

The boy rested the snowshoes against the settle and devoted his full attention to the forester. Slowly, with many a pause for reflection, Telemark related his encounter with the Llondel demon the day he had tried to deliver Jaric to Kordane's Brotherhood in Corlin. He spared no detail, though the memory of his attempt to renounce responsibility for the boy he had rescued from the woods now pained him deeply.

But Jaric accepted the forester's judgment without criticism. "I don't know what the dreams meant either," he admitted after Telemark had finished. He tried to lighten the forester's mood. "When I find out, I'll be sure to let you know."

The boy and the man regarded each other for a long moment, each one aware the moment of departure could not be delayed any further. At last Jaric shouldered the snowshoes. He moved decisively toward the peg by the door where his cloak hung.

"Wait," said Telemark suddenly. He crossed the room, flung open a cedar chest which rested at his bedside, and delved deeply inside. "I want you to have this."

He rose with a cloak of ice otter fur draped over his arm. The garment was strikingly marked, luxuriously thick, and lined with the snowy fur of the forest hare. Through a whole season of trapping, Jaric had never seen such pelts.

"It's much too fine," he protested. The worth of such a gift was something a king might envy.

But Telemark tossed the cloak over Jaric's shoulders, in no mood for listening to argument. "This was to be a gift for my son on his eighteenth birthday."

Jaric's breath stopped in his throat. He had never guessed Telemark had any family.

"Yes, I had a boy and a wife." The forester caressed the silky fur with fingers scarred from years of tending traplines. "They both died of fever while I was on campaign with the Duke's army. That was what made me quit the mercenary's profession."

He dropped his hand, saw Jaric's stricken face, and smiled. "I have long since finished grieving, boy. And it's lucky for both of us the moths haven't made a feast of those furs, for Eleith needs no bride price now. Take the cloak with all my blessing. It will keep you warm when you cross the mountains, but wear it inside out lest some bandit take your life to claim it for himself."

He did not add, as Jaric understood he intended, that the cloak could be sold at need, in exchange for immeasurable wealth. And finding no words for the occasion, Jaric embraced the forester one last time, gathered up his belongings, and stepped out into the slush of the dooryard.

Telemark lingered in the doorway long after the boy had vanished down the path to the southeast. The forester would miss Jaric and wonder often through the coming months how the boy fared; yet he also experienced the immeasurable satisfaction of seeing a task complete. Jaric had come to him helpless, frightened, and injured; he had left with the promise of growth and a future, however difficult his lot. If he never returned, Telemark would remember the boy at the moment he vanished into Seitforest. For although the fate which awaited him terrified Jaric to his soul, still he had discovered the courage to go forward and meet his destiny.

Jaric crossed the Furlains while the icy grip of winter still choked the passes with the cruelty of a giant's mailed fists. He struggled through blizzards which drove the snow in smoking clouds off the peaks. Other times, when the sky shone clear azure above his head, he felt the thunderous boom of the spring avalanches shake the mountain beneath his feet. But Telemark had schooled him well to the art of survival in the frozen heart of the wilds. Jaric reached the far slopes two weeks before the equinox, and from a notch cut between the forested foothills gazed down upon the fishing village of Mearren Ard.

The houses looked like toys after the square battlements and watchtowers of Corlin. Built of logs, with steeply pitched roofs shingled with cedar, the buildings nestled against the side of a hill which overlooked two points of land. A well-protected harbor lay between, scattered with the specks of fishing boats lying at anchor.

Jaric propped his snowshoes against the shoulder of a snowdrift and carefully folded his rich cloak inside his knapsack. Then he set off down the muddy trail, a wry expression on his face. The silver in his pocket would not last long at a tavern, even in a settlement as tiny as Mearren Ard. If the only inhabitants were fishermen, his talents as scribe and his knowledge of trapping were unlikely to be considered worthwhile commodities for barter. Either the sorcerer Anskiere made a prompt appearance to claim the service Taen had promised in the dreams or Jaric would take up sailing; he had no intention of selling an ice otter cloak simply to pay for his bed and board.

The sole tavern in Mearren Ard was all but deserted during the daytime. Jaric stepped in from the dirt track which passed for a street and discovered a cramped taproom smoky from a fireplace in need of a chimney sweep. An ancient man in oilskins hunched over a table in the warmest corner of the room, hands cupped possessively around a chipped tankard. His fingers were hooked into useless claws by arthritis, but the sharp clear eyes of a sailor still gazed from his creased sockets. He looked on with crotchety displeasure while Jaric presented his inquiries to the landlord; but no stranger awaited the boy's arrival. Jaric himself was the first outsider to visit Mearren Ard, by land or sea, since winter had closed the passes. The boy sighed and settled in silver for a room. He had no choice but to seek employment and wait until Anskiere chose to present himself.

The taproom grew boisterous by evening, when the fishermen returned. Having bathed away the dirt left from the trail, Jaric went downstairs, found an unoccupied table, and ordered a meal of spiced chicken. He ate while the smoky air of afternoon became musty with the sea-smell of oilskins drying by the back door. An assortment of men with weather-beaten faces gathered at the bar, their boots strongly reeking of fish. They called the barmaid by name, yet offered no pleasantries; all seemed to have wives waiting in snug cottages, except for the wizened, arthritic fellow who sat still in his corner as if he never moved from his chair.

Jaric finished his meal, conscious of fleeting glances from the taproom's occupants. No one attempted to approach his table. In the gruff, tight-knit society of Mearren Ard, he was an outsider; the men would wait for him to speak, and probably be relieved when he finished his business and went elsewhere. But Jaric had given the enchantress his word he would remain until Anskiere chose to contact him. Although he longed with all his heart to pack his knapsack and return over the Furlains to Seitforest, instead, he pushed the bones of his dinner aside and rose.

The man at the end of the bar looked up. He studied the blond stranger who paused by his shoulder, his narrowed stare that of a man who had spent a lifetime squinting over water, overseeing fish nets and weather and stars for navigation. His manner was not friendly; Jaric's presence was an intrusion, but the fisherman withheld any judgment until after the boy drew breath and spoke.

"I need work," Jaric opened. "Is there any man among you who could use an extra hand?"

The fisherman grunted and set down his ale mug. All conversation silenced around him as he eyed Jaric from head to foot, and the thick drawl of his reply fell against stillness grown dense as an ocean calm. "D'ye sail, then?"

The boy answered with a confidence he did not feel. "No. I'm willing to learn."

Boots scraped on the taproom floor as the men shifted their feet and the spokesman grunted a second time. "What for? Have ye no trade, then?"

Jaric refused to yield to the mistrust implied by the words. "I spent the winter trapping in Seitforest."

"Crossed the passes, then?" The fisherman considered the cut of Jaric's leather tunic, then the well-kept steel of the knife at his belt. "Well, then," he said at last. "Tavish lost a son, onto last summer. He'll be in, soon as he sets his anchor in the harbor."

The fisherman gestured to an empty stool at the end of the bar and turned back to his beer. Any lad who crossed the Furlains alone before solstice was hardy enough company, even by Mearren Ard's rough standards; and Tavish sorely needed a crewman.

Jaric seated himself and waited, uncomfortably sure what the outcome of his request would have been had he lacked the experience of Telemark's teaching. But none of his uncertainty showed in his manner and presently the main door banged open. A burly man with a fox-colored beard stepped in, accompanied by another who was unmistakably his brother.

The fisherman who had spoken to Jaric immediately raised his voice over the surrounding conversation. "Tavish! Got a boy here who wants work. Never salted his boots, but he claims he's come in over the passes."

Tavish stamped the mud from his feet, shaking the planks in the floor. Followed closely by his brother, he crossed the taproom with the rolling gait of a man better accustomed to a sloop's deck than solid land; and Jaric found himself scrutinized once more by two sets of keen blue eyes.

Tavish scratched his beard with thickened, rope-burned fingers. "Crossed the passes, did ye then?"

Jaric nodded.

"Let's see yer hands." Tavish caught the boy's wrists and examined the calluses on his palms. "Won't look so pretty after a season with the nets," he observed.

Jaric said nothing.

"Ye'll do, then." Tavish leaned across the bar and called for the landlord to fill three tankards. When they arrived, he hooked one for himself, passed one to his brother, and slammed the other down in front of Jaric. "Drink up, then. We sail an hour before daybreak. Boat's named *Gull*, and sure's tide, ye'll get seasick. Get over it quick and ye'll share the catch. Fair?"

"Fair," said Jaric. He tasted the beer and found it bitter.

Tavish grinned, amused by the boy's grimace. "Drink on't, then." And he emptied his tankard.

Jaric appeared by the dockside at the appointed hour. Cocooned in an early fog, he boarded the dory with Tavish and his brother, and on the way out to *Gull*'s anchorage, set hands to a pair of oars for the first time in his life. His initial effort was clumsy. With his back to the bow of the boat and the darkness obscuring the landmarks, he had difficulty maintaining a straight heading. But the same perseverance which had endeared him to Telemark and an uncompromising desire to learn soon stilled the dry remarks the fishermen of Mearren Ard customarily inflicted upon a greenhorn. If Tavish resented the loan of his dead son's oilskins to a stranger, he made no comment. For the next three days he applied himself to teaching Jaric the difference between sheet lines and halyards. Even to his impatient eye the boy learned quickly. Come evening the fishermen laid bets on his progress in the tavern. Yet sooner than any of them guessed, *Gull* raised full canvas and left the coastline behind to ply her nets in the ocean far from Mearren Ard.

For a day and a half, *Gull* plowed close-hauled through the swells of the northern Corine Sea, driven by the brisk winds of earliest spring. Foam jetted off the bow, white as combed fleece, and gulls dove in the sloop's wake. Jaric suffered a brief bout of seasickness. Yet he eased sheet lines and changed sail with white-faced determination, never once complaining. Shortly his body adjusted to the toss of a sloop's deck at sea. He stood his first full watch at the helm with a vivid sense of exhilaration, and presently even Tavish's dour brother accepted him as crew.

The nets were drawn in heavy with fish. Jaric pulled twine until his shoulders ached and slept dreamlessly in his berth during off-watch hours. The cold air and the wild expanse of open sea agreed with him, yet the boy took care not to love his new life too much. He knew his time aboard *Gull* could not last. Inexorable as the turn of the tide, his promise to the enchantress must be completed; the sorcerer Anskiere would someday claim his service. Yet the fate Taen had promised came upon him suddenly, in a manner not even she could have anticipated.

Two weeks out of Mearren Ard, Tavish steered *Gull* on a southeast tack. Off watch at the time, Jaric dreamed of restless winds and towering waves with thundering crests of spume. He woke, chilled and sweating, and not even scalding hot tea and a cloak of oiled wool could calm his shaken composure. He clenched icy fingers around his mug, feeling as if some alien presence tugged at his mind. The sensation left him edgy, unable to contain his straying thoughts.

Tavish shouted impatiently down the companionway. Jaric roused himself with an effort. He yanked on his boots and went topside to tend the nets. But the odd sensation which plagued his mind would not relent even in the fresh air above decks. Instead it increased through the morning, until he worked with the muscles of his jaw clamped tight to keep from crying aloud.

Noon came, sunlit and pleasantly warm. Jaric bent over the rail, hauling in the first flopping burden of codfish. Drenched twine dug into his fingers and his shoulders quivered as he strained to raise the laden weight of the net. Suddenly a sharp tingle swept across his skin. Dizziness coursed through his body. Jaric flinched. Stunned by horrified recognition, he recalled a horse and a dusty summer road and a punishing vortex of wind which had once driven him forward against his will. His disorientation deepened, drowning the memory under a singing storm of force. He fought it, even as the net dragged at his wrists; echoing down a tunnel of darkness, he heard Tavish curse in exasperation. Jaric struggled to clear his head. But his vision slipped relentlessly out of focus, and his breath went shallow in his throat.

That moment the air above his head split with a crack like lightning. Jaric staggered, eyes blinded. Power pierced his mind, cruel as the harpoons the fishermen used to gaff sharks. The net slipped out of Jaric's fingers. Cod tumbled back into the sea. Their bellies carved silvery crescents into the green of the waves.

Tavish shouted in anger from the helm. He flung the tiller down, bringing *Gull* into the wind. Patched canvas banged aloft, punched by a freshening breeze, and spray flew in sheets over the bow. But the curses died on the fisherman's lips as he looked up and saw Jaric. For an instant the boy's slim form seemed almost incandescent, haloed by a triple ring of blue-violet light; the image of a bird of prey hovered over his head, tawny gold with feathers barred in black.

"Stormfalcon!" shouted the brother in a tone gone treble with panic.

Tavish clamped the tiller in the brake and bolted forward. He reached Jaric's side just as the boy crumpled unconscious onto the deck, salt-crusted hair fanned like frayed silk over the collar of his oilskins. The fisherman met his brother's eyes above Jaric's still form, his mouth set with rare and desperate anger.

"Knew he was too good to be true, then," he said after a moment. A wave thudded against the sloop's side, tossing spray in the sunlight, and gulls swooped on stretched wings above the main yard. No trace remained of the sorcery which had manifested above the decks barely a moment before; except Jaric lay motionless as death against the aft stay, and no mortal remedy would rouse him.

"Should toss him overboard, then," said the brother.

"No." Tavish was adamant. "We daren't."

But neither of them cared to try more fishing that afternoon. Reluctant to touch Jaric even to move him, the brothers tossed an old blanket over his oilskins. Then they hauled in the nets and headed *Gull* about, setting course for Mearren Ard. Their family had seen a streak of bad luck since the death of Tavish's son last season; they wished no further curse to fall upon them for keeping a lad touched by a sorcerer's powers.

Late in the afternoon, *Gull*'s anchor settled and bit into the sea bottom, once more within the safety of the harbor. The boy still breathed. Tavish and his brother slung Jaric between them on the blanket and loaded him into the dory along with the rest of *Gull*'s catch. After tense debate, they returned to his room at the inn, where they dumped him in a limp heap on the bed. Tavish raised crossed fists in the sign to avert evil sorcery while his brother counted out the coppers Jaric had earned aboard the fishing vessel. They left the coins in a neat pile on the boy's knapsack and left the room, hurrying back to their boat without speaking. But word of the incident spread swiftly throughout the village.

Traders from the south arrived that afternoon, the first to reach Mearren Ard since the roads thawed. The bustle of unloading wagons and preparing stalls for their oxen lent the tavernkeeper an excuse to avoid the boy who lay in his back garret. By the time sunset traced the rooftrees in gilt and copper, the taproom stood packed with the bodies of fishermen come to hear the news brought by the traders. The room grew noisy with talk. But no one mentioned the boy who had fallen ill of a sorcerer's curse on the decks of Tavish's boat. Curious, the traders inquired about the mysteriously occupied back room, but received no reply. For not one villager present dared risk the ill fortune which might result if Jaric's name were spoken aloud.

"Jaric!" Taen's call plunged deep into his mind, reached him where he struggled, overwhelmed by a vision of storm-tossed seas and darkness. "Jaric, let me help you."

But he ignored the dream-weaver's call, no longer dependent upon her knowledge. During the moment Anskiere's summons overthrew his awareness, he had remembered his past in entirety, even to his desperate flight from the Sanctuary tower at Morbrith. Old memories slashed like torturer's knives, tore his last precarious peace to ribbons. The months the geas had lain fallow served only to redouble its power; now reconnected with its intended subject, its forces struck with a resonance far stronger than Anskiere intended. Raging tides of power coursed through Jaric's body. Each second he deferred the call which pulled him southeast, he suffered agony.

Yet this time he endured. With the strength he had learned from Telemark he fought to regain his will. Slowly, carefully, the boy constructed a framework within his mind to bring the punishing directive of the sorcerer's summons under control.

"Jaric, let me help." Taen's image appeared before him in the darkness. The flowers were gone from her hair, and her face was drawn, brows gathered in poignant concern. "Anskiere was to summon you, but not even the Vaere guessed the power would strike so hard. *I beg you, let me help.*"

But wounded by her betrayal, Jaric shut her out. She had known. She had let him sail, aware the geas waited to snare him at sea beyond Mearren Ard. All along she had watched, Jaric realized, but never once had she trusted him with the truth.

"How did I dare?" The enchantress's voice lanced into his mind, sharpened by pain. "I could do nothing but follow the orders of the Vaere. No one intended to hurt you. Believe me."

But Jaric would accept none of her help. Lashed by an unwanted memory of Kencie's pity, he unleashed his frustration against the dream-weaver whose promise had brought him to such torment. Rage burst like flame across his mind. Taen's presence dissolved with a pang of regret, leaving him alone in his struggle. Slowly Jaric knotted the shreds of his self-control back into balance. Power flared and sparked, resistant as cold iron against his will. Yet the boy persisted with the same rugged determination he had shown the night Telemark had been injured by the beaver dam. Gradually he dominated the effects of the geas sufficiently to regain consciousness.

Dull light filtered through a single tiny window. Sunset had passed well into the gloom of evening. Jaric saw that he lay on his bed above the taproom, clad yet in his damp wool tunic. Someone had removed his oilskins, most likely Tavish. But he still wore his boots, and a coarse, fishy-smelling blanket had been left twisted in awkward folds around his body; it bound at his shoulders, making movement difficult.

Jaric sat up. He drew a ragged breath and shrugged the blanket aside, then pressed his hands to his aching head. The geas drove remorselessly against his mind; it required a supreme effort to stay the urge to leave the inn and run blindly down to the harbor. He could not swim the ocean; and the road which led along the coast turned southwest, out of line with the geas' summons. Bereft of alternatives, Jaric dragged his knapsack across his knees. Something metallic fell, ringing across the floor. Jaric swore, and in the half light caught the faint gleam of coins scattered at his feet. The boy interpreted their significance with a heavy sense of sorrow. Here, as in Gaire's Main, the sorcerer's geas marked him; not even Tavish would welcome his presence now.

Heartbroken, Jaric pulled the ice otter cloak from his knapsack. He buried his face in the silky fur, hoping he could maintain control of the geas long enough to buy passage out of Mearren Ard. Then he braced up his courage and rose to his feet. One last coin tumbled from his lap struck the bedstead with a bright, pure clang. Jaric winced. Smoldering with resentment, he slammed the door open. Telemark would forgive the sale of the furs intended for his son's bridegift. But Jaric swore by the air he breathed he would make Anskiere pay for the sacrifice. With his fingers clenched around the hilt of his knife, he descended to the taproom.

CHAPTER XVIII

Callinde

JARIC PAUSED AT THE FOOT OF THE stair. Every sconce had been lit in the taproom, but the increased illumination added little; trestles and roof beams loomed through a blue haze of smoke. The close press of people hampered what ventilation the chimneys provided, and more than one fisherman smoked a pipe as he sat over his beer. The talk was loud, dominated by a black-clad trader Jaric had not seen previously. Daunted by the stranger's presence, the stale air, and a falsely boisterous atmosphere, the boy hung back in the doorway, listening.

"Oh, aye," said the man in black. He leaned back in his chair, stretched like a bear, then bellowed for the barmaid to refill his tankard. His listeners shifted restlessly while he wet his throat. "There's rumor enough from ports beyond the straits. Heard it from a sailor who'd been there. Kielmark's crazy, he said. Tribute won't satisfy him, not since some white-haired witch twisted Anskiere's power about. They say Cliff-haven got smacked by a storm so mean she damned near cracked the light tower in twain. Now every ship bound through the straits gets boarded, assessed, taxed, and sailed fully fifteen leagues on her way, manned by the Kielmark's own. Then she's turned loose and no apologies for it. No sorcerer, says the pirate, damn his arrogance to the Fires, no sorcerer will get close enough to Cliffhaven to meddle with his fortress of thieving renegades, sure's tide."

The trader paused to quaff his ale. He wiped his mustache on his sleeve and resumed. "Can't blame him, though, not entirely. Who'd trust a sorcerer? Not me. I recall my father telling how Ivain Firelord burned a hostel to cinders, all because the roof leaked and woke him from sleep."

The trader belched and rubbed his belly. Beside him a drover with sly eyes added a second tale of Ivain's cruel exploits, and in words framed by the consonants of an eastern accent another man recounted the drowning of Tierl Enneth by Anskiere. Hidden from view beyond the stair, Jaric overheard. He felt suddenly as if darkness itself had reached out and marked him where he stood. Morbrith's archives held testimony enough of the Firelord's mad viciousness. Jaric had read the accounts of those wronged who had appealed to the Duke's mercy for shelter; but the stories repeated in the dimness of Mearren Ard's taproom were colored with human emotion no written record could express. In the rough words of strangers, the boy received his first understanding of the stigma in the fate Firelord and Stormwarden had mapped for him.

"Fires, now, *we* understand." The bearded trader gestured to his audience of fishermen with conspiratorial brotherhood. "Nobody with a jot of sense would wish a sorcerer making spells on folks who lived on his own green turf. That boy will bring no good should you continue to shelter him, there's a promise. But talk can't hurt."

But the trader's expansive suggestion left the villagers close-mouthed as clams. The tension in the taproom suddenly became too much for Jaric to endure. Sobered by the knowledge that he could lose his life should his parentage be discovered, he left the shadow of the stair and entered the taproom, the ice otter cloak clutched like a dead animal between clenched fingers. Quietly as he moved, the nearest man looked up from his tankard and pointed. Heads turned. Conversation stilled abruptly, as though something intangibly evil entered through the door behind the boy's back.

Jaric continued his advance, though the silence unnerved him. Oblivious to the spilled beer which splashed under the soles of his boots, he took another step. The barmaid started and dropped a tin jug. It struck the trestle beneath with a crash that jangled every nerve in the room. The man beside her swore and raised crossed fists in the traditional sign to avert malign sorcery.

Hurt to the quick by the gesture, Jaric stopped. A half circle of wind-burned faces confronted him. Across the length and breadth of the room, not one expression held the slightest trace of welcome. Poised and alone, the boy caught impressions like acid imprints; here a chin jutted aggressively forward and there a veined fist gripped a chair back, spaced between pair after pair of hostile eyes. But the geas granted no quarter. Doomed as a hare before mastiffs, Jaric at last set his request into words. "I need a boat to cross the Corine Sea. I can pay handsomely for my passage. Is there a man among you willing?"

Movement rustled like a sigh through the room, as every fisherman present turned his back. The last bit of color drained from Jaric's face. He seemed a figure made of paper, slight and brittle and pathetically vulnerable. "This cloak would buy an army for a king!" he shouted. "Have you no pity?"

But his pleas stirred the villagers at Mearren Ard not at all. They stayed rooted, stony and stubborn as a fortress wall, even when Jaric flung the magnificent fur down on the nearest table, his cry of disbelief stifled with his knuckles. The geas pressured him with the persistence of a tidal current, near to drowning all reason.

The boy felt his control slip. Anger flared through him. Touched by a trace of his father's madness, he longed to blast the rooftrees of Mearren Ard with flame, until charred beams smoked like blackened ribs against the sky. But the passion ebbed as swiftly. Bitter and trembling and sickened by the vindictive turn of his thoughts, Jaric tossed sun-bleached hair from his face and glared at the backs of the villagers.

"Is there no man present who dares to remember the meaning of mercy?" He spoke no louder than a whisper, but his outraged accusation carried to the farthest corner of the room. "Give me nothing but a boat. I'll find a way to sail her."

"Hey, boy!" The black-haired trader rose from his seat near the bar. Respectably clad in wool embroidered with scarlet, he wore a dandyish beard. Sharp features and slitted eyes lent him an expression crafty as a rat's. "I'd give you gold for that cloak, boy." But the price he named was an insult.

Jaric closed his eyes, anguished by the memory of Telemark's face on the morning he had opened the old cedar trunk and pulled forth his only treasure. The boy's straits were desperate; every man in Mearren Ard knew it. Anyone marked by Anskiere of Elrinfaer had no fate to bargain.

"Boy!"

Slowly Jaric turned his head and located the drover who had addressed him.

The man leaned on the bar, pudgy knuckles crimped around a wine flask. His lips parted with amusement. "Mathieson Keldric has a boat he can't sail any more. Why not ask the old relic if he'd swap his craft for your fancy cloak?"

By the fellow's derisive tone, Jaric guessed the advice was ill spent, a crass effort to poke fun at his predicament. But the geas blazed like magma through his flesh, making each separate moment an agony more terrible to endure than the last. He had no choice but attempt the trader's suggestion.

Jaric's reply fell without echo in the packed stillness of the taproom. "Who is Mathieson Keldric?"

The trader grinned, displaying a jumble of stained teeth. "There, son." And he pointed to the arthritic elder who inhabited the corner table by the hearth, as if he intended to die there. Half crippled by age and disease, the old man was the only villager who had not turned his back on the boy from Morbrith Keep.

Jaric gathered the ice otter cloak from the tabletop and reluctantly moved toward the fireplace. A chair scraped at his back. Someone whispered an obscenity. Evidently Keldric's boat was the butt of a well-worn joke, repeated out of pity for the old man's plight. But Anskiere's summons left no space for inquiry. With cautious steps Jaric approached the corner nearest the hearth. And Mathieson Keldric watched him with eyes the light clear gray of rain pools, his lips pursed in alarm.

Suddenly the old man straightened in his chair. He stared in open-mouthed amazement at a point just past Jaric's shoulder and his twisted fingers flew to his face. *"Callinde!"* He spoke the name barely above a whisper, but to Jaric the sound felt louder than a shout against the blighted stillness of the taproom. Yet none of the bystanders appeared to overhear.

"The trader mentioned you have a boat you might sell." Jaric ran his fingers anxiously through the silver-tipped fur of the cloak. "I have no coin to offer, but perhaps you would consider a trade?"

But Keldric acted as if the boy had never spoken. He gazed unresponsively into the air. His lips moved, but no word emerged. For a moment it seemed he would ignore Jaric's need as the others had, leaving him powerless to answer the geas' terrible summons. The boy swallowed, feeling desperation well up inside him. Pressure beat against his ears, savage as the whistle of air off a stormfalcon's wings, and the threat of unending pain raised sweat on his temples.

"I beg you," he said hoarsely, distressed that his anguish was turned to a public spectacle. "I must have a boat."

Mathieson Keldric stirred. He looked up at Jaric as though

fully aware of his presence for the first time. "Trade? Fer that?" He inclined his head toward the cloak, and tangled white hair fell, obscuring his face. But Jaric thought for a second that the clear old eyes showed a glaze of tears. He started to move away.

"Well, then," said Mathieson Keldric gruffly. "Ye'll have to come to the docks. My *Callinde*'s a lady, straight down to her keel, an' I'd not let her go to a man who never set eyes on her. Fair?"

Jaric struggled to suppress the tremor which arose in his knees and traveled the length of his spine. "Fair," he said softly.

An ugly murmur arose at his back, threaded through by the louder voice of the trader and sibilant whispers of sorcery. Jaric heard; he realized old Keldric's attachment to his boat was legend in Mearren Ard. The fact the man had considered parting with her earned the boy nothing but suspicion from the villagers.

Forced to move before their muttering metamorphosed into threats, Jaric extended his hand toward the old man. He spoke without urgency, his phrases shaped with the courtesy learned at Morbrith's great hall. "Come, then, and perhaps the lady will approve."

The voices grew louder. As the old man pushed himself to his feet, Jaric felt the villagers' resentment rise against him, menacing as the rush of breakers over rock. But Mathieson Keldric's lame old body could not be hurried. He walked with painful, halting steps, steadied by Jaric's arm. Bystanders moved grudgingly aside, leaving a wide berth as the pair made their way through the door.

Jaric drew a deep breath of relief. The night was damp and chill after the close heat of the tavern, braced by the tang of salt. But the cold calmed the boy's nerves. He shortened stride to match old Keldric's limp, grateful for the fog which smothered the lane leading down to the harbor; murky weather at least spared him the accusing observation of the villagers. Soon the last cottage passed behind, lighted windows eclipsed by the black hulk of a warehouse.

Surf boomed distantly off the barrier point and the air smelled sourly of tide wrack and fish. Mathieson Keldric lifted a lantern from a hook on a piling driven deep into the sand of the strand. He fumbled with crooked fingers to manage the striker, but something about the resistant set of his back warned Jaric not to offer help. Although Keldric was ruinously crippled, he was not incapable; Jaric sensed that the boat he needed so desperately to buy was inextricably interconnected with the old man's pride. To interfere even in kindness would offend.

The spark spat against the dampened wick and hesitantly caught. Flame quivered behind panes patterned with crystalline whorls of salt as Keldric raised the lantern. The boy stepped behind the old man onto the wet planks of the east dock. Mist rolled past, breaking like ghostly surf over his feet; it seethed through the black teeth of the pilings, stringing droplets on Jaric's hair and clothing. Keldric moved forward, silhouetted against the fuzzy globe of lanternlight. Through the formless darkness ahead, Jaric saw the gleam of a braided painter, then a high curving prow and the angled line of a headstay. But the rank smell of decayed wood warned him, long before the antique shear of the thwart stood exposed in the lanternlight; *Callinde* was ancient and rotten, and nothing close to seaworthy.

Painfully aware the derelict hull was Keldric's sole treasure, a shrine preserved in memory of the brighter days of youth, Jaric's first thought was not for himself. For one stunned moment he ignored the inhuman wrench of the geas' directive and stared at the elder who waited at his side, gnarled fingers gripping the ring of the lantern with an air of desperate self-sacrifice.

"Why?" The boy searched for an answer in the clear pale eyes. "Why would you give her up, after all these years?"

Mathieson Keldric shrugged. "You've the need in you." He

glanced at his hands and spat. "I can't so much as plane a timber any more, and *Callinde* looks sloppy as a whore."

But Jaric knew there was more. Silently smothering an anger
he could ill afford to express, he waited to hear the rest.

Old Mathieson shrugged again, then glared defiantly at the
young man's face. "Well, then. My wife, I saw her standing at
your shoulder, back there in the tap. Black-haired she was, full
of her youth, and prettier than ever I remembered when she
was alive. Seems the old lady would have it so." Suddenly his
expression changed to worry. "Ye won't want to be changing
her name, then?"

Jaric turned abruptly away, poisoned by sudden revelation.
Taen had intervened, plied her dream-weaver's talents upon a
defenseless old man to help buy him passage. But bitterest of
all was the recognition that he had no choice but accept; the
battered old hull represented his only alternative if he was to
escape the insufferable pain of the geas.

Misinterpreting Jaric's stricken silence, Mathieson caught
the young man's sleeve in a clumsy attempt at consolation.
"She'll bear ye safely, son, my word on't. A grand old lady
Callinde might be, but there's no leak to her can't be fixed with
tools and a sound bit of planking. Ye'll see, then."

Jaric straightened, regarding the old man with clear-eyed
honesty. "Thank you. And no, I'll never be changing her
name." He pulled the ice otter cloak from his arm, draped it
across Keldric's stooped shoulders. "If you'll guide me with the
carpentry, I'll make her new again, sound as the day she was
launched. That's a promise."

Mathieson Keldric thrust his lantern into the boy's hand
and spat on his palm. "Your oath?"

Jaric nodded.

The old man pressed his damp hand to his forehead and
stared at his feet, abruptly embarrassed to have insisted on ritual. "Well, then," he said briskly. "Tools are ashore, and I

sure's tide can't lug them like I did when I was your age. Or did
ye not want to start now?"

"At once," said Jaric. "She ought to be hauled, though."

Keldric grinned. "Aye. That's work for two stout men." He
threw Jaric a look of bright-eyed challenge. "How well can ye
row?"

Jaric smiled back, his frustration partially alleviated. "As
well as I must. Is your grand old lady rigged with oars?"

Keldric answered with a dry cackle of laughter. Aged and
lame and heartbroken as he was, Mathieson was villager
enough to find humor in Jaric's ignorance. "I've a dory, son,"
he drawled, and in the foggy darkness the night before spring
solstice, proceeded to instruct the boy how *Callinde* should be
towed from her slip.

Enfolded still within the capsule of the Vaere, Taen
dreamed she sat in the timeless twilight of the grove. The pale
folds of a silk robe clothed a maturity she had only recently
come to accept as her own, and a basin of carved crystal lay
balanced across her knees, much as it had for the better part of
a fortnight while Tamlin taught her the art of casting dream
images onto the surface of water. At present three companies
of Kisburn's royal troops performed toy-sized maneuvers,
bounded by the confines of the chased silver rim.

To Taen the exercise seemed a frivolous waste of time.
Through her mastery of the Sathid, she could tap any mind on
Keithland at will, then impart her findings through a dream
link with the flawless purity of thought. Causing her recipient
to *believe* he viewed an image within water was bothersome, an
added layer of illusion for which she discerned no useful purpose. Taen sighed, while in the bowl the Grand Warlord-
General delivered a command to his aide. Trumpets flourished,
signaling inspection of troops was complete. Neat squares of
pikemen lifted miniature weapons in salute and the lowering
sunlight of late afternoon flashed against polished blades. Even

to Taen's unpracticed eye the movement described lethal perfection. After rigorous hours of drill the troops were ready for action; Kisburn intended to sail his force to Cliffhaven within the fortnight, and Emien would go with them. Still Tamlin insisted she refine a showy set of illusions designed to add mystery to her dream-weaver's talents.

Touched by sharp anger, Taen tilted the basin. Water sloshed, scattering droplets over the rim. Kisburn's soldiers streamed into a muddle of scarlet and gold, then vanished as her contact dissipated. "Why?" she demanded, though the clearing at present seemed deserted.

Tamlin appeared instantly. His bells jangled in dissonant displeasure as he gestured toward the basin. "It's a necessary defense. The demons would kill you should they ever suspect your true capabilities. Not only are they telepathic, they also recall every memory of their forebears, back to the dawn of their history; fortunately for mankind they evolved no cultural need for ceremony or legend or ritualized religion."

Tamlin folded his arms across his chest, bushy brows knitted into a frown. "Twenty-seven generations have passed since the Great Fall. Through that time, I have cloaked mankind's most precious secrets in the forms of myth and legend. The demons attach no value to such things; they perceive no logic in faith and no reality outside of racial memory. They observe and fail to discover my intent."

Taen remained unimpressed. Tamlin shifted his weight from one foot to the other and irritably jabbed a finger at the bowl. "If your client believes he sees a vision in water, but that image does not exist for other eyes, then the demon who observes will dismiss the incident as mummery, the time-worn, traditional sort of fortune-telling many a common man will spend copper to hear. The demon does not comprehend man's craving to control his future. In this manner your true talent will pass unnoticed."

Taen traced her hand over the carved crystal, mollified by
the tirade. "I'm sorry. I never guessed."

Bells clashed softly as Tamlin seated himself in the grass
opposite her. He rested his chin on steepled fingers and spoke
in gentler tones. "Understand me, child. More of mankind's
heritage than is safe for you to know lies similarly concealed.
Landfast itself has no other defense. To save its records from
the demons, you must trust my judgment. Now engage your
craft once again and show me how Jaric fares."

Taen leveled the basin between her knees, then waited for
the water to settle. She needed the interval to steady her own
nerves more than any other reason. As often as she looked in
on Jaric since Anskiere's geas resumed effect, she had been unable to make peace with herself for his unhappiness; neither
Tamlin's insistence nor Keithland's peril could negate her sense
of responsibility.

Taen closed her eyes and carefully cleared her mind. Despite her trepidations, Jaric's presence flowed easily through the
channel of her talents; through the process of restoring his
memory, she had come to know his mind better than any person living. Her call arose like a bird, sped on the silent wings of
thought to the north coast and the village of Mearren Ard.
With barely a pause for transition, Taen felt the salty tang of
the breeze blow against her cheek, sea-scoured and overlaid by
the pungent smell of spruce. Within the crystal basin an image
bloomed on the water.

In a yard beside a weathered shed, new grass lay sprinkled
like snow with the delicate curls of shavings; there Jaric bent
over a trestle, busily planing a length of wood which would
shortly replace a cracked thwart on *Callinde*'s starboard side.
Linen cloth clung to his sweating shoulders as he worked, and
wood chips speckled his wrists, pale against sunburned skin.
Impressed by the play of muscle in his arms, Taen reflected
that the wenches of Morbrith Keep would probably treat him
to a different sort of teasing were they to observe him now.

But the unremitting pull of the geas and days of constant toil left Jaric too worn to reflect upon himself; plank by plank he labored to restore *Callinde*'s rotted timbers. The discomfort of Anskiere's summons permitted him no surcease, even at sundown when other men sought rest. Jaric worked through the nights by lanternlight, feverish and driven, until his fingers cramped on the tools and his body collapsed from weariness.

Watching the strong rhythmic strokes of the plane across the board, Taen ached to reach out, lend him the peace her dream-weaver's powers could provide. But Jaric would tolerate no trace of her contact since the day he had fallen on the decks of Tavish's boat. Convinced she had used him for her own selfish ends, the boy stayed isolated, though loneliness ate him hollow and his arm trembled with fatigue as he lifted the plane to clear the blade. Shavings fluttered to the ground, pale and delicate as moths. For all his inexperience, the boy handled the tool well; even old Mathieson found little cause for complaint. But the dream-weaver saw beyond competence to the measure of pain which inspired it; Jaric acted out of necessity. He derived no joy from his achievements.

Taen shifted the image, caused the basin's crystal rim to frame *Callinde*'s hull. Whole sections of her starboard side stood stripped of planking, leaving the bared curve of several ribs exposed against the sky. To port, yellow boards contrasted harshly with the weathered timbers of her keel; Jaric had made remarkable progress. Still his craft was days away from launch; Kisburn's army would not wait. Swift as the clouds which hazed the horizon beyond Mearren Ard's docks, the King's ships would cross the sea; even the Kielmark's fortress could not stay demons.

Suddenly a blur of motion flicked across the edge of the image. Startled by its presence, Taen stiffened. She bent closer to the basin, a disturbed frown on her face.

Tamlin rose to his feet with a clash of bells. "Something's wrong," he said quickly. "What do you see?"

"I don't know." Taen focused her attention on Jaric, seeking the source of the shadow which had passed briefly across her contact. Yet the sunlight shone brightly in Mathieson's yard and Jaric worked on undisturbed. Concerned, Taen refined her scrutiny. The fine hands which once had penned copy for a Duke's library were now blistered and raw from handling adze and hammer. Stress had left the boy gaunt and exhausted. Beneath the sun-bleached hair which spilled over his brow, his eyes were deeply circled; but other than fatigue Taen found no mark upon him.

She looked up, defeated. At a loss to explain the intuitive prickle of warning which stirred the hair at the nape of her neck, she said, "I did see something."

"I know." The Vaere toyed with his pipe. "There's a reason."

But he would not say what it was. When Taen pressed for an answer, he simply vanished, and none of the usual cues would call him back.

Left to herself, Taen lifted the crystal bowl from her lap and laid it aside on the grass. Disregarding Tamlin's directive pertaining to the water, she gathered her powers as dreamweaver and with no more effort than daydreaming bent her thoughts back to Mathieson's yard and Jaric. She would watch, she decided, to see whether the shadow which had grazed the edge of her vision returned.

Westerly sunlight cast steepening shadows through the opened sections of *Callinde*'s hull. Sheltered from the sea breeze by the angled roof of the shack, Jaric set his plane aside and with a forester's precision laid a fire beneath the steam box. While the planks heated he took up the adze and began to dress an uncut length of timber. Taen watched the chips fly, pale and silver as flying fish in the failing light. The intensity of Jaric's determination awed her. Unlike Emien, this boy had survived the scarring left by the inadequacy which had poisoned his early years. Hurt and pressured and driven, so far he had managed to continue without striking out in hatred. Taen caught her breath. The comparison wounded. Beside Jaric, her brother's shortcomings stood exposed with devastating and bitter clarity. Taen twisted her fingers in the fine silk of her robe. She must not abandon hope. One day perhaps Jaric might guide Emien to regain his faith in human compassion.

Sunset faded over Mearren Ard. Jaric paused to wipe the sweat from his brow and light the lantern looped to a line on *Callinde*'s yard arm. Keldric's unmarried niece arrived with a basket of bread, smoked fish, and cheese. Oblivious to the invitation in her smile, Jaric thanked her, his manner restrained with the polish of Morbrith's high court. Beneath his courtesy Taen read the raw pain left by Kencie's thoughtlessness. For all his accomplishments, Jaric placed no faith in the change wrought within himself since his accident in Seitforest; although the prettiest girl in Mearren Ard lingered to watch him eat, he misread her admiration for pity. Misery kept him silent. And too shy to breach his solitude without encouragement, the girl twisted her chestnut hair back under her cloak hood and quietly left as she had for seven nights previously.

Jaric dusted breadcrumbs from his tunic and resumed work. Jostled by wind, the lantern turned the yard to a circle of wheeling shadows. Removed from the rest of humanity and merged with the rhythm of Jaric's mallet as he fastened heated planks to the hull with tree-nails of locust, Taen almost missed the transition even as it happened. The boy missed stroke. The heavy fastener's mallet banged squarely into his thumb, splitting the skin. He swore once without rancor, and twisted his shirt cuff over the cut to stop the bleeding. The wound itself was slight. But tired as he was, the pain opened an avenue of distraction; his control slipped. The force of the geas welled up inside him, a whirlwind battling to escape the slender check-rein of reason.

A gust blasted the yard, streaming the lantern flame like blood. Jaric cried out, bent to his knees with his arms cradled against his chest. Wind lashed the hair across his cheek. For one stark instant, Taen saw the black-barred wingtips of the stormfalcon beat in the darkness above his head. Then the vision left her. The disturbance died, leaving only the distant crash of the surf beyond the harbor. Jaric shook himself. He reached for his mallet with the dull mechanical motions of extreme exhaustion; and unable to bear the enormity of his burden, Taen wrenched herself out of contact.

The grove surrounded her with maddening and changeless serenity. Taen clutched the silken robe about her shoulders though she was not cold and with all the urgency she possessed, summoned Tamlin.

The Vaere appeared at once. His hands were unoccupied by any pipe and his bells stayed utterly silent. "You saw the stormfalcon," he said softly.

Taen burst into tears. Irritated by the unwanted display of emotion, she nodded. "How did you guess?

Tamlin seated himself in his accustomed place on the stone at the grove's center. "No guess, child, but a natural law of sorcery. Anskiere loosed an energy, the stormcall you perceive in the shape of the falcon. It built a gale, as he intended, and dissipated, carrying out the ruin of Kisburn's war fleet. Left to itself, the seed of that energy had no direction of its own. Under normal circumstances it would lie fallow until its creator unmade its pattern. But when Tathagres interrupted the geas which summoned Jaric, the break opened what once was a closed loop; a structure created by Anskiere stood out of balance, a circumstance he never intended. For such disharmony would attract and bind any loose ends he might have left lying about: in this case, the stormcall."

Taen twisted the thin silk of her cuff. "What will happen to Jaric?" And Emien, she thought, but did not broach that fear.

A bell chimed as Tamlin shifted position. "The geas and the stormfalcon stand linked. With each passing day the tempest will build. If we are lucky, Jaric will sail before it breaks."

But even without asking, Taen knew. *Callinde* could not possibly be ready in time. She swallowed, reluctant to confront the inevitable conclusion; Kisburn's entire war fleet had been crushed like chaff before the fury of that storm. Tortured by thoughts of Jaric's antique craft being smashed by a thundering avalanche of foam, she found her voice and spoke, hoping the Vaere could silence her fear. "Jaric might never make Cliffhaven."

Tamlin stood up, his pipe suddenly appearing in his hand. For a prolonged moment he puffed in silence, an expression which might have been sorrow half veiled by rising smoke. "He might not. We can do nothing more for him except pray that he will. He is Ivain's son. There is much reason for faith in that."

But hope was not enough to sustain Taen through the days ahead, while Jaric wore himself ragged repairing *Callinde's* battered hull. The gaps in her planking closed with what seemed agonizing slowness. By the time he hammered the brass fittings on the raw new shaft of her steering oar, the flat deadly calm Taen recalled from her time aboard *Crow* had already settled over Mearren Ard. The fir trees stood still and silent on the slopes above the village, unruffled by any trace of breeze; confined to the harbor, fishermen varnished spars and swore at the glassy surface of the sea. And though no man put words to the notion, all thought of the boy struck down by a sorcerer's curse on the decks of Tavish's boat. Talk in the tavern turned restless.

Jaric continued his labors, possessed and oblivious. He threaded new halyards through the blocks of *Callinde's* mast and stitched patches on her torn sails. The calm broke in the hour she was launched. Keldric's niece braved the icy, ripping gusts to make her way to the docks, a cloak of green wool bundled in her arms.

"For you," she shouted, her voice barely audible above the

shrill keening of the wind through the stays. Her comely features were scrubbed and hopeful and her braids were tied with red ribbons.

Jaric scrambled out of the depths of a storage locker, his hair whipped like spun gold against his neck. He accepted the gift with genuine appreciation, but his thanks were stilted with wariness.

"Try it on then, Jaric." Puzzled by his reluctance, the girl placed a freckled hand on his arm.

Jaric flinched from the contact, startled. His dark eyes widened with an emotion the girl could not understand. She stammered an apology and retreated, bursting into a run past *Callinde*'s slip. The boy stared after her, frozen in his tracks. He wanted to shout, to call her back and apologize. But words stuck in his throat. He watched until the girl disappeared while the wind screamed around his head, lashing the wool against his thighs.

"Old storm'll catch you in the harbor," warned Mathieson, shuffling up beside him. "Better to wait her out."

Jaric shook his head. He tossed the cloak into the locker and latched it closed, then untied *Callinde*'s docklines. Canvas cracked like a maddened animal as he raised the main halyard. Clouds roiled above the masthead and angry gusts puckered the water, sending wavelets curling off the steering oar. Old Mathieson spat and bit his knuckle. Only a madman, or the most brave, would put to sea in such weather.

Frail against lowering skies, the boat drew away from the dock. Jaric hauled in the sheets, felt the lines slam against the blocks as wind filled the main. *Callinde* heaved, timber shivering as she gained way. Foam ruffled off her bow. Standing forlorn on the docks, old Mathieson Keldric saw her heel like a lady and run for the open sea.

"*Callinde* keep ye safe," he murmured. The gale parted the fur of the ice otter cloak which clothed his stooped shoulders;

but pelts which would have pleased a prince meant less than nothing to him. With tear-brimmed eyes he watched the boat which had once been his father's grow small and finally vanish, another man's hand on her helm.

CHAPTER XIX

Stormfalcon

MATHIESON KELDRIC WAS NOT the only observer to watch *Callinde* depart from Mearren Ard. On the Isle of the Vaere, Taen bent over the crystal basin, her vision centered with feverish intensity upon the dusky tanbark sail of the boat which tacked across the harbor. Past the headland, waves battered like rampaging cavalry against *Callinde*'s sides, sheeting spray from prow to keel. Jaric adjusted his course for the open sea and Cliffhaven. The steering oar dragged against his arms and the boat bucked and rolled, her wake a boil of froth. Yet Jaric held true to his heading, though *Callinde* seemed little more than a splinter tossed haplessly in the path of the elements.

The point fell swiftly astern. Taen's crystal bowl showed a froth of tumbling whitecaps, *Callinde* a murky shadow blurred by smoking sheets of spindrift. Reminded of the shipwreck and disaster which had traumatized her early childhood on Imrill Kand, Taen chased the contact from her mind.

The water obediently went blank. Although the basin's

chased rim gleamed silver and ordinary beneath her sweating palms, Taen's conscience continued to haunt her. *Had she not interfered, Jaric would be in Seitforest still, safely tending traps with Telemark.* Taen raised the bowl with trembling hands. Her nerves refused to settle. Water dribbled like tears over her fingers as she placed the vessel on the grass by her side.

She had been a coward, she realized. The ordeal of Sathid mastery had carved a mark of horror deep within her mind; left the ugly certainty that Emien would betray those closest to his heart rather than confront the error of his ways. Taen ran her fingers through her long silky hair. She had used Tamlin's plans for Jaric as an excuse, permitted herself to believe the Firelord's heir could restore Emien through release of Anskiere from the ice cliffs. That way she need never confront her brother's twisted nature, might avoid entirely the truth the Sathid had revealed.

Taen stared at her hands. The fingers were longer, shapelier and more graceful than those of the little girl who had first landed on the Isle of the Vaere. She had grown up, but childishly permitted herself to shelter her fears behind the risks of others, even justified Jaric's discomfort for the sake of Emien's need. Now Jaric battled for his life against the force of Anskiere's sorceries. The dream-weaver who had influenced his fate felt shamed.

Taen dropped her hands into her lap. The calm of Vaerish enchantment left her restless. Its changeless security made Jaric's peril more vivid by contrast. Chastened by his stubborn display of courage, Taen saw she could never leave her brother's future reliant on the efforts of others. The possibility the Firelord's heir might fail had forced brutal recognition; she must try to recover her brother herself, even should she forfeit his love in the attempt.

Taen settled herself in the grass and glanced carefully around the grove. The clearing was deserted; Tamlin had not reappeared since his explanation of the stormfalcon's presence, nor did he respond to any call. Left entirely to herself, Taen ignored the crystal basin. For the first time since accomplishing her mastery, she closed her eyes and bent her dream-weaver's skills to Kisburn's court and her brother.

Subtle Vaerish twilight yielded before the hard-edged splendor of a palace ballroom. Candles blazed from tiers of silver sconces, casting brilliant and costly light across gaudily dressed nobles, tables laden with sweetmeats, and a quintet of royal musicians. The King had commanded a lavish celebration to honor the eve of the fleet's departure, and there Taen located her brother.

No trace of a fisherman's origins remained about the young man who perched on the silk cushions of a windowseat, twirling a filled goblet between his fingers. Emien had eliminated his accent; the hand which gripped the wine glass was elegantly uncallused. Clothed in a black velvet tunic with scarlet and gold trim, the boy radiated charm and dark good looks.

Several court maidens clustered about, vying for his attention. But Taen saw that his wit was barbed and his smile self-derisive. Emien found no joy in the ladies' company. That they should waste admiration on anyone who lacked influence and power made no sense to him. He received their flattery with secret contempt and the wine stayed untasted in his glass.

Taen gathered her dream-reader's skills. She had no desire to exert influence on her brother amid a chamber full of revelers, particularly where Lord Sholl was certain to be present. Somehow she must entice Emien to leave. Careful not to disrupt Emien's thoughts, Taen awaited her chance.

A ringletted blond exclaimed coyly. With a toss of her head, she flicked a trailing curl of hair across Emien's wrist. Her ribbons looped in his cuff. Taen seized her opportunity; while the girl's flirting distracted him, she slipped silently into her brother's mind. Emien laughed. He flipped the ribbon away without spilling his wine and returned a witty remark. But his thoughts were far removed from the gaiety of the ballroom,

Taen discovered. In a private chamber, Tathagres and the King held conference, finalizing plans for the demon alliance against Cliffhaven. Later, Emien knew, Tathagres would sit alone before a burning candle, hands raised to the collar at her throat and her mind deep in trance. At that moment she would engage three different races of demons and bind them into service, her purpose to bring down Anskiere of Elrinfaer. Ablaze with desire to possess such power for himself, Emien wished he could be present while she spell-wove.

Taen recognized her opening. With a touch imperceptible as dewfall, she touched her brother's mind and sharpened his inner longing with restlessness.

The fair girl tossed her hair irritably over her shoulder. "Emien! You're not listening."

"I'm sorry." The boy rose and pressed his wine goblet into her hand. "Will you excuse me?"

"You're not leaving, Emien. Not so soon." The girl tilted her pretty head and trailed her fingers along his sleeve. "At midnight there are going to be fireworks."

Emien ignored the girl's touch. Oddly unmoved, he glanced quickly over the ballroom, but found no guest compelling enough to hold his interest. Oblivious to the dream-weaver whose meddling made him bored with the glitter, the festivities, and the young ladies, he pressed past his admirers without speaking. They stared after him in puzzled disappointment as he crossed the polished marble of the dance floor and disappeared through a side door.

The hallway beyond lay deserted, except for occasional uniformed guardsmen standing motionless at their posts. Taen shaped her touch into a compulsion, causing Emien to hasten his steps. His fine calf boots made no sound on the carpets as he turned down a darkened corridor and let himself outside, into the windy blackness of a colonnaded courtyard.

Moonlight shone through polished marble pillars and marked concise geometrics on the patterned tile beneath.

Emien leaned against the door panel, felt the latch click gently shut. Unaware that a sister's compulsion had driven him to seek this deserted place, he shivered in the cold spring air and discovered he was not alone.

A woman waited amid the silvery landscape of last year's rose garden, her robe of light loose cloth rippling in the breeze. A moonstone gleamed on a chain at her throat, and fine black hair lay braided into coils about her head, laced with a wreath of myrtle blossoms. Stunned by her beauty, Emien gripped the doorlatch in astonishment. The night air stuck in his throat.

He raised his eyes to the oval of her face. As he studied the delicate arch of her brow and lips, a strange and haunting familiarity made his heart twist in his chest. *"Taen?"*

The woman smiled. The sweetness of her expression snapped the last thread of disbelief. Emien drew a ragged breath and dragged his fingers across his eyes. Her presence could not be real; only a dream born of wine and rich food. But when he looked again, she came closer, her step strangely wrong, and her body eerily ripened into maturity.

"No, I don't limp anymore, Emien," his sister said softly, as if responding to his unspoken thought.

She moved nearer. The thin silk of her robe swished softly through the grass, leaving darkened trails through the dew. Paralyzed by incredulity, Emien stood with his back rammed against the unyielding wood of the doorframe. Taen's shadow flowed ahead of her, an etched silhouette against the tiles. Two more steps would bring her to his side.

"No!" Emien raised his arm before his face, as if to ward off a nightmare. "Leave me!"

Taen closed the distance, stopped scant inches away. "Why should I go, brother? I bring no harm."

Even with his eyes hidden, Emien felt the warmth of her skin; he could still hear the rustle of silk across her breasts as she breathed. Stirred by the breeze, the skirt of her gown brushed gently against his leg. The boy flinched back, felt the iron rivets of the door bear painfully into his back.

"I never drowned." Firmly, deftly, Taen built the illusion of her presence into her brother's mind. Her voice echoed convincingly through the confines of the colonnade. "What you behold is the truth. When *Crow* foundered, Anskiere delivered me safely to the Isle of the Vaere. By the tales you can guess the rest. I have grown up, Emien. I am no longer lame. And I have discovered happiness beyond any I could have found on Imrill Kand."

Encouraged by her dream-weaver's skills, Emien reached out and touched a coil of her hair. But the warm reality of her served only to frighten him. He hardened his hand into a fist, bashed it with bruising force into the door at his back. His reply emerged half-strangled from his throat. "No."

Taen stared at him, heartbroken. "Why, Emien? Why must you forsake belief? What change has Tathagres wrought, that you find no joy in the news that your sister lives and is content?"

Emien twisted his face away, every tendon in his neck pulled taut with distress. His mouth quivered. Taen sensed the clamor in his mind, felt his thoughts wheel like a flock of startled birds as pride and fear and loyalty warred. She ached, sharing his pain, yet not for an instant did she relent.

"There is peace in honesty, Emien, and forgiveness in understanding. Look to your heart." Gently, Taen pressed against his mind, promising comfort and love. "Abandon Tathagres, my brother, for she holds you in contempt."

The words touched him. Emien spun to face her, his expression darkened with indecision. Taen had spoken the truth, dragged him naked into the light of judgment. Emien gasped. Blackened by the evil of his hatred, he buried his head in his arms and shrank against the door. But his sister's image pursued, engraved like a spell of remembrance against the inside of his eyelids. Her words beat against his ears, bright and innocent as his memory of the goat bells in the meadows of Imrill Kand.

"Mother misses you, Emien." Taen's voice softened, tormenting him with hope. "She mourns your absence more deeply than the death of our father."

The reminder suddenly became more than Emien could bear. He lashed out at Taen's presence in pain and rage and terror. "My sister is *dead!*" His shout rang deafeningly off the stone, sent ugly undertones echoing across the garden.

The defiant note of his rejection shocked Taen like a blow. "You shame your ancestors, brother. Would you betray them as well?"

But Emien had regained his footing, and her plea moved him not at all. "Yes." His voice throbbed with malice. "What are they but a miserable, stinking lot of fools? I will *never* waste myself remembering their useless lives, all drenched oilskins and cod nets. When I have done, their kind, and perhaps even the sea itself, will serve me."

His conviction rang vindictively across the dream link, poisonous as the venom of a snake. Taen perceived the evil in him and the depth of it sent her talent reeling out of focus. She wakened weeping within the clearing of the Vaere. The enchanted silence did little to restore her. The instant she parted contact, she had seen into Emien's heart, and known he chose against her out of greed. Since the first intoxicating taste of power, his hunger had increased to the point where he could not, and would never, give up his desire to rise in dominance over his fellow man. Taen drew her knees against her chest, her head bent with unconsolable grief. Tathagres had done her work well; not even Anskiere himself could recover her brother now.

Emien fled the colonnade, wrenched the door closed against the moonlit garden with a crash that shook the carved lintel. Trembling and sweating, he slammed the bar home, then stood panting, his weight braced against the cold steel. His sister was a small child, dead, *drowned beneath the waves. He had seen* Crow *founder.* The pain of his conscience gradually eased, exposed to logic and reason. His panic subsided. The grown woman who had appeared to him could only be a dream, a profanity shaped by Anskiere's guile and sent to undermine his purpose.

Emien smiled in the darkness. Suddenly exultant, he threw back his head and laughed. Obviously, his presence in Tathagres' plan *meant something.* He had been a fool not to see it. Why else would a sorcerer trained by the Vaere trouble with him at all? The idea consumed him, left him drunk with a reckless sense of importance. Perhaps Taen *had* survived, even told him the truth. If so, she was a creature of the Vaere, robbed of her childhood and used as a pawn against him.

Emien pushed away from the door and strode down the corridor. He was tired of waiting, sick to death of being manipulated. Intoxicated by a savage flood of arrogance, he hastened to his chambers. He would arrange Anskiere's destruction himself. The Kielmark would be too busy with the demons upon his shores to bother with a single man. Ice could be broken; mortal steel could pierce a sorcerer's flesh. Emien blotted sweaty palms on his black velvet tunic. If Anskiere died by his hand, that surely would earn even Tathagres' respect.

Emien stepped confidently into his chamber. The sconces were dark and the air chilly; the chambermaid had forgotten to close the windows at sundown. Leaving the door ajar at his back, the boy fumbled about on the mantel until he located striker and flint. He lit a single candle, then banged the mullioned casement closed, setting the flame streaming in the draft. Emien cursed the flickering light. He knelt beneath the slate slab of the mantel and began to lay a fire, no longer awed by the luxuriously patterned carpet beneath his knees. He had come a long way from the wooden planked cottage where he had been born. Nothing could ever convince him to return.

Emien struck a spark to the kindling and rose. He crossed to the wardrobe, flung the inlaid doors wide. Although the clothes within lay deep in shadow, his fingers moved quickly, sorting rich velvets and brocades by touch. He passed the soft weave of his favorite lawn shirt; this once, finery did not interest him. Instead, he chose heavy linen breeches, a leather tunic, and the sea boots he had purchased following the crossing from Skane's Edge. Preoccupied and impatient, Emien dumped the clothing across the bed and began to untie the laces of his cuffs.

He did not hear Tathagres enter the room at his back. Surprised by his presence, she paused in the doorway. The plain clothing on the bed, and the decisive set to Emien's back did not escape her notice. An expression of rapt calculation crossed her face.

Tathagres waited while the boy loosened his shirt. Then silently, she crossed the floor and trailed slender fingers against the bare skin of his neck. "Emien?"

He started violently, but did not whirl. Tathagres felt fine tremors of tension course through the flesh beneath her hand. But when the boy spoke, his words were controlled. "I thought you had business with the King?"

"It is finished." Tathagres shifted her wrist, caught the silk of his collar, and gently tugged.

Emien faced her reluctantly. Despite his determined restraint, the breath caught in his throat. Tathagres had dressed for the celebration. A gown of white lace clung provocatively to her slim waist; bracelets of gold wire circled her wrists. Threaded by a circlet set with amethysts, her hair spilled like spun glass over bare shoulders. A delicate scent hung on the air about her person. Unbalanced by her nearness, Emien ran an appreciative glance over the ripe cleft of her breasts.

Tathagres saw, and a thin smile of amusement touched her lips. She traced the line of Emien's collarbone with a teasing fingernail. "Why did you leave the festivities? It's very unlike you. Weren't there to be fireworks?"

The query seemed casual. But Emien felt the power behind her words; she could force the truth from him if she chose. Seizing what advantage he could, he feigned nonchalance, and told her of his experience in the deserted rose garden. "My sister Taen came to me in a vision. She may have survived the foundering of *Crow*. If so, Anskiere sent her to the Isle of the Vaere, for she appeared to me as a woman grown." He paused. Tathagres' touch against his skin made him ache. Although his body quivered with desire, he resisted fiercely, aware she used her beauty as a tool against him. "Taen's childhood was stolen from her. I would see the Stormwarden suffer for that."

Tathagres dropped her hand, frowning. Emien stepped back until his calves pressed against the solid wood of the bed frame. With barely concealed defiance, he resumed unfastening his shirt. Tathagres continued to regard him. She toyed with the bracelets on her wrists, elegant features preoccupied by an expression he could not interpret.

"Your sister urged you to forswear your oath of service," Tathagres said at last. She seemed almost wistful. "Is this why you choose to attempt Anskiere's death by yourself?"

Emien disguised a shiver by shrugging the shirt from his shoulders. He tossed the garment onto the bed. "Do you care?"

"Yes." Tathagres closed the distance between them. With her arms relaxed at her sides, she bent her head and laid it against the corded muscle of his chest. "It does matter." Her breath tickled his skin. "Did you not guess? We are fated to work together."

Her presence burned him, released emotions like the raging spring tides. Emien managed a harsh laugh. "In all things, lady?" He caught her slim wrists, lifted them with the powerful grip of a sailor. "Remember, I've seen you kill. *Why did you come?*"

Tathagres did not resist, though her soft skin reddened

under his fingers. She tilted her head, her lips within inches of his mouth. "It is destined."

Her voice held a queer note of sorrow. Jarred by the inconsistency, Emien stared at her. For a second Tathagres' control wavered. In one unguarded instant, the boy perceived she was bound to some purpose whose origin could not be guessed; she offered herself against her inner will. The urge to take her became overpowering. Lust beat like storm surf through Emien's veins. Unlike the sentries murdered on Cliffhaven's shores, he saw he could claim her with impunity.

He loosed his hold, turned her slim hands palm upward in his own. She shifted her weight. A lace-clad hip brushed his thigh. Emien quivered in response, released her entirely. Tathagres slipped her hands around his waist. One thinly covered breast traced a line of fire across his chest as she leaned up and kissed him. For a moment, Emien resisted her pliant touch. Then, with vindictive resentment, he wrapped his arms around her shoulders and pinned her against him.

Passion unfolded like the rush of water over rapids. Plunged beyond restraint by physical need, Emien sank to the bed, bearing Tathagres with him; clothing rumpled beneath their combined weight. The boy tugged at the fastenings of her gown. White lace parted, baring her eager flesh beneath his fingers. He buried his face in her warmth, all reason forgotten. His body trembled as, with skilled and exquisite simplicity, she freed the points of his hose. Emien locked his fingers in her hair. Lost to all caution, he failed to note the bright edge of triumph in her smile as she parted her legs and accepted him.

Their union was consummated swiftly. Flung headlong over a stormy crest of emotion, Emien subsided, spent. He lay back on the crumpled coverlet, his pulse beating languidly in his veins. For a very long interval he did not care to move. Tathagres lay still against him, one arm flung possessively across his chest. Emien regarded her, and saw that she slept. Candlelight softened her, lending her curves the grace of a masterpiece painted on velvet. The boy lifted a silvery lock of hair off her cheek, revealing the unearthly perfection of her features. For all his awe, a thread of calculation wove through the wonder left by his first experience with a woman.

She believed she had used him. Abandoned in sleep with her limbs relaxed against him, she seemed vulnerable as any normal woman; the parted line of her lips emphasized her girlish fragility in a manner Emien found disturbing. There was nothing extraordinary about her. Try as he might, he could not equate the lady at his side with the witch who had raised the whirlwind on Cliffhaven or argued with royalty in the council chamber. The thought occurred to him that the powers she employed might be borrowed intact from the demons.

Emien traced the gold band at her throat with light fingers. A thrill of excitement coursed through his body. The plan conceived on the heels of Taen's visit suddenly seemed ridiculous and inferior; his ambitions abruptly expanded. Now he would bide his time. When the opportunity was ripest, he promised himself he would gain Tathagres' powers for his own. Then would Anskiere of Elrinfaer have great cause to fear him.

Storm waves hammered *Callinde*'s stout timbers and the wind shrieked through her stays with relentless fury. The steering oar dragged at Jaric's shoulders with the strength of a maddened horse. His palms had blistered cruelly. After five days at sea, the ache of stiffened muscles made every hour at the helm a trial of torment. His clothing clung, drenched, to his frame, chafing his skin with each movement. Yet such discomforts paled beside the driving weight of the geas. Jaric sailed with every fiber of his being strained on the thin edge of delirium.

Callinde's compass plunged and rocked in its casing, scrolled needle wheeling as she yawed over the wave crests. Jaric ignored it. He needed no instrument to guide him. Anskiere's summons consumed his awareness and the direction of its call twisted every fiber of his being into alignment. *Callinde* tossed on her heading. The spanker was sheeted too snugly; that the boat handled at all was a tribute to the skill of her designer. Yet Jaric had no energy to marvel upon her virtues. He felt far too wretched to bother adjusting lines. Weariness sapped his vitality; each passing hour, his hold upon the geas deteriorated. With one foot braced against the starboard thwart, he battled to keep his sanity through an unending nightmare of cloudy darkness.

The gale howled steadily on a broad reach; sped by its violence, *Callinde* made swift passage. Barely six days out of Mearren Ard, the beacon of Cliffhaven arose through the gloom above the bow. Jaric scarcely noticed. He steered, blinded by hallucination; at times he saw the stormfalcon's tawny-and-black form hurtling above his head, talons outstretched for landing, and the bluish halo about its spread wings backed by a dazzling spike of light. The vision often lasted hours at a stretch. Disoriented and exhausted, Jaric hoped he could muster the presence of mind to bring the boat in safely. The shore toward which the geas directed him was fast drawing nigh.

The island loomed nearer, jagged and dark but for the orange spark of the beacon in the fortress's topmost tower. Sheetlines snapped and banged against the blocks as *Callinde*'s sails bellied, smacked by contrary gusts. Jaric felt the kick of current against the steering oar, and the earthy scent of wet foliage filled his nostrils. Floorboards rattled underfoot as the boat pitched over ever steepening crests. Breakers hissed off the high curve of the prow, tumbling shoreward in ravening ranks of foam.

Jaric braced his body against the toss of deck. His hands clenched on wet wood as he muscled *Callinde* straight. The roar of water grinding over sand deafened his ears and salt spray dripped like tears from his face. At any instant he might be dashed to splinters on the fangs of a reef, though Mathieson had assured him that a boat with shallow draft would beach safely on strange shores. Jaric fretted, nerves drawn taut as bowstrings. Keldric's faith lent no comfort; not even *Callinde*'s stout keel was proof against submerged rock.

The waves steepened, crested, showering spray over the bow. Jaric squinted ahead through stinging eyes. The boat bumped. Sand grated harshly over wood, and the steering oar jerked, aground. Jaric cried out as the shaft was torn from his grasp. He sprang forward to release the sheets. Loosed to the caprice of the wind, canvas snapped with whipcrack reports overhead. The following wave boomed and broke, lifting the ancient boat. Jaric bit his lip in near panic. But the old man's word proved reliable; *Callinde* rode the rampaging flood of surf like a seal. Her chines crunched into fine gravel and she came to rest at last on the northern strand of Cliffhaven.

Jaric uncleated the halyards and with shaking fingers dropped the canvas. Headsails and spanker slithered in wet heaps across the deck. Then he hauled the mainyard across the wind, secured the sheets, and leapt down into the ankle-deep chill of the sea. The geas clawed at his mind, battering him toward the edge of madness; somewhere on this dark shore, the ice cliffs he had only known in dreams held the fate promised by the Stormwarden of Elrinfaer. But Jaric denied the insufferable compulsion long enough to rig a double set of blocks to a stout boulder in the scrub. Though his hands were raw and his back ached, he warped *Callinde* beyond reach of the breakers and saw her secure from the tide. Not even for Anskiere's summons would he abandon Mathieson's boat to ruin.

The stormfalcon flickered at the edge of his vision as he fetched his sword and dagger from his sea chest. Grimly Jaric ignored it. Delirium was not far off, he knew, but this close to release, he was determined not to give in. Belting his buckler to his waist, he hastened shoreward. But progress was difficult. Dry sand mired his steps, and the first solid ground he had trodden in days seemed to buckle and twist under his feet. Dunes shortly gave way to thornbrakes. Jaric stumbled through the night, cruelly clawed by briars and tripped by roots and rocks.

Suddenly a man shouted, almost at his elbow. "You! Stranger! Halt, there."

Jaric heard a harplike ring as steel cleared a scabbard. He froze. Then someone unshuttered a storm lantern, pinning him in a wash of orange light. Blinded, Jaric threw an arm across his face. By squinting against the glare, he picked out a gleaming hedge of spearpoints and the needle-thin line of a drawn sword; with the sea at his back he was cornered.

A man wearing a captain's collar and badges stepped to the fore. "State your business promptly, else you risk your life."

Raked by the tingling discomfort of the geas, Jaric clung to the frayed remnants of reason. Instinct cautioned him to preserve every possible advantage; he narrowed his eyes to slits, keeping his vision adjusted to the dark. Then, careful to screen his movement behind the brush, he gripped the hilt of his weapon and answered in phrases chosen with the nuance of a court emissary. "I come in peace, summoned here by the Stormwarden of Elrinfaer. I honor your laws, but will answer to him only. Permit me to pass."

"He's for the Kielmark," said the captain abruptly, and gestured to the soldiers. Spear points flashed and lowered, arrayed like the spokes of a wheel with Jaric at the hub.

"Alive?" said a voice from behind.

The captain nodded curtly.

Through an incredulous rush of anger, Jaric saw his request would be ignored; the men-at-arms intended to detain him, by force if need be. And that, abruptly, became a setback his stripped patience could not endure. He shouted, launching himself at the light. Brush clawed his wrists. A spear hissed past his ear, clanged harmlessly into rock. Then his fist smashed into the lantern, tumbling it to the ground. The flame was extinguished, leaving eight of the Kielmark's crack sentries blundering in the dark with their night vision spoiled.

Jaric ducked, bruising his shoulder against a weapon shaft. The man who held it shouted, "Here!"

Behind him the captain snapped an order; someone leapt to restore the light. Jaric drew his sword and dagger, desperately repressing an impending recurrence of the stormfalcon's black-and-gold-barred form. He stumbled over a stick and blundered into a leather-clad arm.

The owner whipped to face him. Confronted by a darting glint of steel, Jaric parried. The blow glanced cleanly off his dagger. But the belling note of swordplay drew his attackers like wolves. Even over the wind Jaric heard the crackle of boots approaching through the brush. He riposted, savage and desperate. The geas sang like a chorus of sirens in his ears, wrapping his nerves in fire. He felt no other pain, even when his opponent's blade grazed his shoulder.

Jaric covered with his dagger, late, but not disastrously. His enemy dropped his sword, clutching a cut wrist. Another swordsman took his place. Jaric lunged. His weapon struck steel with a shock that stung his arm. The impact jarred his concentration for a fraction of a second. Light flashed like lightning above his head; the stormfalcon's image rippled and vanished against the sky. Instantly his position was known to every man-at-arms present. They converged at a run.

"Fires, it's sorcery all over again," someone yelled. "Kielmark'll chew bricks. Anyone want to wager?"

A screech of steel met his offer as Jaric caught his blade in a bind. He wrenched the weapon free. Behind him a spark stabbed the darkness. The lantern flickered, blazed, and shot the brush with sudden shadows.

"Merciful Grace!" Jaric whirled, overtaken. A half dozen sword points angled at his chest, red as blood by lanternlight, and the captain stood with a poised spear at his back. The ending was evident; still, for all their seasoned experience, no soldier present foresaw the final move.

"You'll be my death," the quarry whispered. "I never had a choice."

And with an expression of agonized despair, he rushed them. The captain reacted, barely in time. He lowered his spearshaft and cracked the intruder's head from behind. The blow buckled Jaric at the knees. Sword and dagger flew from his grasp. He tumbled gracelessly after them, into a sprawling heap among the thorn.

The captain stepped quickly to his side, blade drawn and ready to kill. When the trespasser did not move, he kicked him sharply in the ribs. "Get up."

Neither violence nor words raised any response. A gust rattled violently through the brush. But Jaric himself lay lax as a lump of dough beneath the folds of his cloak. At that, the captain yanked the helmet from his head and raked sweaty hair from his forehead. "Fetch the light, boys. He's unconscious."

He sheathed his steel. Shadows danced across the briars as a man brought the lantern. The captain seized the outflung wrist which extended beyond the edge of the cloak and yanked Jaric onto his back. The wind parted the light hair, tossed it back from a profile lean as carved teak. Blood threaded his collarbone above a coarse, handspun collar, and the hands showed glistening patches of raw flesh left from unrelieved hours at the helm.

"Kor." The captain grimaced in disgust. "Whoever he is, he needed landfall here rather badly. Look, will you? He's scarcely grown a beard." The man paused and wiped his palms, as if embarrassed by his duty. "Still, the Kielmark'll want him for questioning. Strap his wrists damned tight. Boy or man, he's caused us nuisance enough for one night."

A subordinate ran to the beach and presently returned with a length of line cut from *Callinde*'s main sheet; he bound Jaric's limbs with thorough caution. Another sentry retrieved the boy's weapons. Then, with characteristic efficiency, the company rolled the trespasser in the storm-sodden folds of his cloak and bundled him off to the Kielmark.

CHAPTER XX

Captive

AFTER NEARLY A FORTNIGHT'S ABsence, Tamlin materialized in the grove with a disorganized flurry of feathers and beads. "Don't bother with the basin," he said quickly. "What has happened to Jaric?"

"Cliffhaven's sentries have taken him prisoner." Taen needed no words to elaborate. Since the day Tathagres upset Anskiere's geas, all Keithland's shipping had felt reverberations of the Kielmark's displeasure. As a trespasser brought in by a sorcerer, Jaric's very life stood in peril. At Tamlin's request, Taen cast her dream-weaver's perception northward with the direct force of a bolt shot from a crossbow. Within seconds her talents resolved an image.

High arched ceilings splintered brisk footsteps into echoes; a guard captain and two subordinates strode the length of a hallway floored with checkered tiles. They hefted an awkward item slung in cloth between them. Taen refined the focus of her perception and the object became recognizable as Kerainson

Jaric, wrapped in his own green cloak and tied wrist and ankle with a length of salt-crusted rope.

The captain turned a corner, stopped, and knocked loudly against a closed door. "Night watch reporting, Lord," he said clearly. "I bring a trespasser from the north strand."

A curse issued from the other side of the portal. Then the latch clicked sharply. Wrenched open from within, the panel swung with a chirp of hinges and the Kielmark himself beckoned the men-at-arms across the threshold. Clothed in a tunic of fawn velvet, he carried no visible weapon; but no man who served under him dared disregard his gesture of ruthless authority.

The guardsmen entered, bringing sand-caked boots and sodden accoutrements onto the carpets of Cliffhaven's formal library. Books lined the walls from floor to roofbeams and the mantel above the hearth was carved of rarest merl marble inlaid with silver knotwork; the air smelled of leather and parchment. A sly-faced trader in russet sat opposite a table half buried in charts. He looked on with curiosity as the men-at-arms carried the prisoner into the light.

"Excuse the interruption," said the Kielmark to his guest. He blotted ink-smeared knuckles on a sleeve already stained, and pointed to the middle of an exquisitely patterned rug. "Dump him there. And pull that cloak off him. I want a look."

The men lowered their burden to the floor. When they tugged the wool from beneath his body, the captive rolled limply onto his stomach; turned toward the firelight, his face seemed that of a starved child. For a moment even the Kielmark stared in surprise. Then with a surge like an electrical current, Taen felt his distrust resurface. The Lord of Cliffhaven bent briskly to examine the unfortunate who had dared trespass his domain.

Taen steadied the dream link, gently widened her touch to include Jaric, then transmitted her findings to Tamlin. "He's unconscious, not dead. A sword grazed his shoulder when they took him. The cut is shallow, nothing serious. The bruise on his head is worse, but not so severe as the injury he suffered in Seitforest."

The Kielmark caught Jaric's shoulder and turned him, astonished to discover the blood streaked across the pale skin of his neck. "He gave you trouble, then! How much?" As he spoke, he tore the boy's collar aside and probed the injury beneath with blunt fingers. "You had better report in full. How did he come here?"

"Alone." The captain's armor squeaked as he shifted his weight. "The boy sailed in, on a ratty antique fishing vessel rigged out with a steering oar, one headsail, a square main, and a right damned clunker of a spanker."

The Kielmark's hands paused on Jaric's shoulder. He looked up, light eyes gone dangerously direct. "He landed *that*, in this storm? Fires! He's a madman. No doubt he attacked you in the same vein of idiocy?"

The guardsmen shrank in the shadows, while their captain gripped his buckler with tense discomfort. Every soldier on Cliffhaven recalled the Kielmark's anger and the oath he swore on the morning the witch left his island besieged by the gale. Sprawled helplessly before the fire, Jaric's slim form aroused no other feeling but pity.

Taen felt the captain's dread through the dream link as he resumed his report. "Perhaps not. The boy came ashore armed but not expecting company. When we challenged him, he claimed to be under the summons of Anskiere of Elrinfaer."

At the Stormwarden's name, the Kielmark froze. Massive wrists flinched taut, straining the fabric of his embroidered cuffs. "Anskiere! By Kor, not again."

Bound by the dream link, Taen caught her breath in the clearing of the Vaere. Overturned by the fierce current of the Kielmark's rage, she dared not intercede, even to secure Jaric's safety. The man's distrust made him unstable to the verge of madness; should he discover his inner mind had been breached by a dream-weaver's powers, his reaction would bear little relation to reason. Careful to preserve his equilibrium, Taen braced herself to drive him unconscious, should he move upon Jaric; but his savage outburst ended swiftly. The Kielmark bridled his anger in cold reason, dark brows laced into a frown.

Taen shivered with released tension as his bunched fists eased, and he motioned curtly to the captain. "Continue!"

The man stared at the rug rather than meet his lord's gaze. "The boy kicked the lantern over, rushed us with a sword and dagger. There came a flash of light; one man claims he saw the stormfalcon's image appear. The rest of us were too busy to notice details. Lord, if the work was sorcery, it harmed no one."

The Kielmark rose with deadly grace. "Did you recover the weapons?"

The request was routine; one of the men-at-arms promptly produced Jaric's sword and dagger. The Kielmark accepted them. Without comment he removed himself to the candelabra which burned on the mantel. Flamelight shed bronze highlights over his dark hair as he bent his head, treating the steel to a lengthy inspection. Sensing him absorbed in concentration, Taen tentatively tried to ease the man's antipathy toward trespassers. With delicate precision, she extended her dream-sense, sent calm to blunt the edges of his urgency. But the Kielmark's mood proved resistant as tempered steel. Taen pitched her powers to the very edge of compulsion, but her efforts seemed futile as trying to stay an avalanche with thread.

Thoughtfully the Lord of Cliffhaven fingered the edge of the sword blade. Then he requested the conclusion of the captain's account, and once the tale was complete, deposited both weapons on the table alongside the green cloak.

"What sorcerer would carry Corlin steel?" he observed drily. "And at the end, when he was desperate, that boy should have cast weapons aside and used magic." Rubies sparkled at his collar as the Kielmark folded massive arms across his chest.

"The boy's name seems to be Kerainson Jaric, unless he stole the sword, which I doubt. It suits him too well for size, and the steel is newly forged into the bargain."

Cliffhaven's sovereign paused, his expression drawn and tense with thought. No man present moved a muscle, and in the grove of the Vaere, Taen held her breath. At last the Kielmark stirred and studied the boy upon the carpet with eyes narrowed in speculative calculation. The captain noticed and relaxed visibly. Had reprimand been forthcoming, the Kielmark would already have delivered it. Unaware such forbearance might have been induced by a dream-weaver's presence, he watched the Lord of Cliffhaven rake his knuckles through his beard and at last deliver judgment.

"Lock the prisoner in the east keep dungeon. He's no sorcerer. But he could easily be connected with one, and a storm-falcon may be the reason for the current foul weather." The Kielmark stepped back to the chart table, preoccupied and irritable. He delivered his final instructions with his back turned. "Call a healer to dress that shoulder wound. When the boy rouses, see that he gets food and drink. Send word to me afterward. I want to question him, but I won't like the delay if he arrives in my presence hungry. Take no risks. Post two armed sentries by the cell and replace those ropes with iron."

The guardsmen saluted. They collected the prisoner from the floor. Still wary of the Kielmark's frame of mind, they removed Jaric from the library with dispatch. The latch clicked under the captain's hand; he swung the door closed with preternatural caution.

But the Kielmark paid scant heed to the trespasser's departure. As he leaned over the topmost chart, Taen felt his thoughts turn jagged with concern. Presently he slammed his fist into the inked outline of Mainstrait, and raised cold eyes to the trader in russet. "I don't like your news. It makes no sense. *Why would Kisburn send a force consisting of three ships against Cliffhaven?* There must be a missing factor." His tone turned grim. "I had better learn the answer before this gale lifts. If troops sailed at the time you suggest, the only thing holding those ships from running the straits is this hell-begotten west wind."

For long hours, the sovereign of Cliffhaven glared at the charts. He brooded as if his question waited to be read in the parchment under his hands, while on a table at his back the abandoned folds of Jaric's cloak dripped salt water onto his priceless carpet.

Taen dissolved the contact and directed a stricken appeal to Tamlin. She avoided speech, choosing to clarify Jaric's situation directly through her talents. Unaware that the boy sent to his dungeons was Anskiere's sole hope of release, the Kielmark permitted Jaric to live on the chance the gale was connected to his presence. As long as the motivation for Kisburn's aggression remained unknown, he needed the storm to aid Cliffhaven's defense.

"Jaric is in jeopardy." Taen searched the seamed brown features of the Vaere for some trace of emotion. Finding none, she elaborated. "I cannot control the Kielmark's actions from a distance. His will is much too defined."

She did not need to emphasize that Jaric's imprisonment could not have occurred at a worse time. His resilience had worn away through long days of passage; the moment he recovered awareness in the Kielmark's prison, the pressure of the geas would resume with intolerable force. Denied the freedom to appease its pull, Jaric might well lose his reason.

Tamlin puffed stolidly on his pipe, motionless. Smoke curled through his mustache and eyebrows and lazily circled his beaded cap. "You must go to Cliffhaven," he said simply. "There is no other alternative."

Taen sprang to her feet. She upset the crystal basin in her haste, and water soaked the grasses in a silvery flood. "How can I? The crossing would take days, and I have no boat."

The grove's enchanted silence swallowed her distress without echo. Tamlin blew a smoke ring; his feathers hung without a quiver in the still air. "I can send you in a matter of hours, never doubt." He lifted the pipe from his teeth and regarded his charge with unwavering black eyes. "Free Jaric if you can. But you must promise one thing in return: leave the island before Kisburn's ships breast the horizon, else risk your life as forfeit. Tathagres knows of your mastership; and Lord Sholl the shape-shifter has sworn to achieve your ruin."

Taen stared at her hands, pricked by apprehension. Often during training she had resented her confinement; now the grove which preserved the heart of Vaerish mystery seemed a precious and peaceful haven, far removed from the strife of mortal realms.

"Do you understand?" said Tamlin sternly.

Taen nodded, fighting an unreasonable urge to weep.

"Kneel, then." The Vaere gestured at the grass, his pipe oddly missing from his hand.

Burdened by responsibility she could not refuse, Taen did his bidding. The fate of Jaric and Anskiere and perhaps all of Keithland rested on her shoulders. She trembled, feeling bereft of courage, while Tamlin raised his arms above her head. Bells shivered in the air as he clapped his palms together. The grove whirled and vanished; Taen's senses were riven from her, and she plunged headlong into night.

The capsule which housed Taen was designed for mobility, though it had not traveled from its cradle for close to a quarter century. Switches tripped and closed in the Vaere's vast data-banks. Mothballed machinery responded. Systems powered up in preparation for launch to Cliffhaven; electrical impulses flickered through circuitry as instruments checked operational. Servo mechanisms unsealed the capsule and labored to ready Taen's body for consciousness. Her limbs were clothed in a dream-weaver's robes, made from cloth which had no visible seam. The colors ranged from misty gray to blue-violet as light played across the folds and hem, cuffs and collar were bordered in gold. As a final touch, a robot pressed a circlet woven of myrtle over her dark hair.

Despite painstaking adherence to the details of a mythology the Vaere itself had originated, its plan held a serious flaw. The capsule was a clearly identifiable relic from the *Corinne Dane*'s support systems; derelict, it could never have remained functional so many generations since the crash. Demons possessed eidetic memory, passed on intact through each generation. Should the capsule be sighted during Taen's landing, the enemy might discover evidence that the Vaere still survived. If that occurred, the computer's presence would be hunted more fervently than Landfast's records. But no other option remained if Taen was to reach Cliffhaven in time to help Jaric. Mechanically dispassionate, the Vaere wired a detonation cap into the guidance systems. With luck, Taen would debark unobserved and the capsule would not be noticed until the self-destruct signal fired off the explosive. The Vaere entered Cliffhaven's coordinates with unerring precision. Following one last check on the drive systems, it sequenced the capsule for ignition.

Deep underground, on an islet mantled by a trackless wilderness of cedar forest, a silvery object shot from a tube hidden beneath the surface of the sea. It sliced through the water with a muffled whine of turbines and blazed northward, scattering a trail of phosphorescent bubbles in its wake.

In the still hour before dawn, an ear-splitting bang rattled every pane in the casements overlooking Cliffhaven's harbor. Roused from his sleep, the Kielmark leapt out of bed in a ferocious temper. Cloud-racked skies glowed dull orange beyond his window, silhouetting the roofs of the warehouses against the landing. Naked except for his ruby torque, the Kielmark bashed open his chamber door.

"Fetch the saddled horse and bring it to the west postern!" The sentry posted in the corridor vanished down the stair.

Without further delay, the Kielmark grabbed breeches, boots, and swordbelt from his bedside. He bolted from the room without pausing to dress. Time enough to don clothes while he waited by the postern for his mount, which at best would be an interval of seconds; every hour of the day or night, one horse in Cliffhaven's courtyard stood saddled and bridled, ready at an instant's notice.

The Kielmark sprinted across the outer bailey, sword sheath and belt buckle clanging between his knees. The glow above the harbor had already faded to dull crimson. Cursing, the Kielmark yanked his breeches over his thighs. A shout hailed him through the mist, punctuated by the staccato ring of hooves over cobbles. A groom appeared running; a hammer-headed gray trotted beside him on a leading rein, its stirrups already swinging free.

"To me!" The Kielmark grasped mane and vaulted astride before the animal came completely to a halt. Abandoning his boots in the courtyard, he clapped bare heels to his mount, sent it careening into the gale-torn darkness beyond the gates. He took the stair beyond at a canter.

Shod hooves rang like hammers striking sparks from the stone at each stride. The Kielmark yelled, flicked the reins on the horse's neck and recklessly made it gallop. At the first bend in the stair, he whirled the animal off the path and plunged downslope amid a bouncing rattle of rocks. Brush lashed his arms and thorn branches raked his bare toes; but the Kielmark made no allowance for discomfort. He reined his sweat-soaked mount down twisted streets to the dockside barely a minute after the blast.

Scattered clots of wreckage tossed in the bay; flames streamed like banners, lining the wavecrests a bloody red. A semicircle of guardsmen cordoned the shore, surrounding a solitary figure in wind-whipped robes. But the soldiers held their weapons pointed down at the sand, and their discipline in the presence of their commander seemed queerly lax. The

Kielmark grimaced with displeasure. He drew his sword with a stupendous ripple of muscles, slammed the horse with his heels, and drove it, sidling, straight for the lines.

Angry enough not to swerve for the men who dove clear of his mount, he bellowed against the storm. "What passes here?"

But the answer became apparent the moment he broke through the cordon and pulled the horse to a halt. A woman stood on the strand, alone and weaponless. Her hair fell dark as starless night about her shoulders and a mystic's wreath of myrtle twined her head. By the flowers and the unearthly sheen of her blue-violet robes, the Kielmark recognized her for a dream-weaver. The guardsmen's behavior did not stem from carelessness; snared by the enchantress's influence, they struggled to lift weapons grown strangely unruly in their grasp. Sweat sprang along the Kielmark's brow. His great wrist trembled with the effort of keeping his own sword upright, for it suddenly seemed too heavy for his hand.

Anger tore through him. Two incidents of sorcery in the same night utterly stripped him of tolerance. In a tone of killing fury he addressed the woman who had dared turn her enchantments against his men. "What brings you here? Answer quickly. Your presence is most unwelcome."

The dream-weaver regarded him with an expression of clear-eyed appeal. "This night you took a prisoner, one Kerainson Jaric. I am here to ask his release for the safety of your realm and all Keithland. You must not detain him. He is Ivain Firelord's heir and his obligation is urgent."

Taken aback, the Kielmark lowered his sword. That the slight blond boy brought in by his guardsmen could be Ivain's son was a development he could never have anticipated. The fact explained much. The Lord of Cliffhaven lowered his weapon and braced his wrist upon the horse's neck; unsheathed steel clanged against his stirrup iron as he leaned forward.

"Who sent you?" he demanded bluntly.

The dream-weaver shouted to make herself heard above the

crash of surf. "Tamlin of the Vaere, the same who guided An-skiere to mastery. If you wish the Stormwarden unbound from the ice and gone from your shores, Jaric alone can accomplish the feat."

The Kielmark swore. He straightened in the saddle, jabbed his sword into its sheath with undisguised irritation, and ex-tended his hand to the dream-weaver. "Come here. I'll negoti-ate nothing without a roof to break the wind. Do you drink wine?"

Taen shook her head and tentatively stepped forward. In-terpreting her approach as acquiescence, the Kielmark urged the horse ahead to meet her. He bent, caught her strongly in the crook of one elbow, and swung her up into the saddle ahead of him. Black hair whipped across his bare shoulders as he reined the horse about. With a gesture he dismissed the guards, then set off up the slope to the fortress.

Taen perched uncomfortably on the edge of a stuffed chair in the Kielmark's study, her robes arranged to hide the hands clenched whitely in her lap. The Lord of Cliffhaven paced like a wolf before the hearth, shirtless still, a cut agate goblet in his hand. He sipped his wine and treated the dream-weaver before him to a long unpleasant scrutiny.

He stopped without warning and spoke. "You are younger than you look."

Taen watched the flamelight flash and sparkle in the rubies at his throat. "The Vaere sent me only in dire need. Cliffhaven stands in greater peril than you know."

"Indeed?" The Kielmark's eyes narrowed. He waited a lengthy interval for a reply but Taen volunteered nothing. Day brightened slowly beyond the casement, dusting highlights like faery silver through the hair on his chest.

At last the Kielmark said, "You'll gain nothing through seeking to bargain with me."

Taen met his threat with brazen honesty. "My kind don't

negotiate. Lord, if I wished to manipulate, I would do so, *without your consent if need be.*"

The statement struck a nerve. The Kielmark slammed his goblet down on the window ledge, splashing wine across his knuckles. The girl in the chair flinched, but did not retract her admonition. Poker straight in her gold-trimmed robes, she held her silence while the servant who had brought the wine rushed off for towels and an ewer of water. The Kielmark dripped on the tiles, oblivious. Though the girl seemed guileless and vulnerable, the myrtle wreath and the robe only came to those trained by the Vaere. At her own craft, this childwoman held as much power as Anskiere.

The manservant returned and after a glance at the Kielmark's face began mopping spilled wine without fuss.

Taen confronted the Lord of Cliffhaven with disquieting assurance. "I would rather deal directly with you." Her restraint seemed genuine; and inspiration for her following line was borrowed from his innermost heart. "The Stormwarden of Elrinfaer holds you in highest regard. In his stead, I bring you warning. Kisburn seeks conquest of the Free Isles. Cliffhaven controls the Straits and so thwarts an ambition now turned to advantage by Kor's Accursed. The demons desire Landfast. Through the machinations of Tathagres, they will support the King against you."

The Kielmark jerked as if he tasted poison. The flush which suffused his features sent the servant scuttling backward from the room. "Fires! He *dares*, does he?"

His fury struck Taen's awareness with the splintering force of a mallet. Taxed beyond previous limits, she strove to maintain control. "Lord, listen carefully. You must abandon Cliffhaven and evacuate your following."

The Kielmark's demeanor turned vicious with rage. Seeing his hand reach for his sword, Taen drove to her feet. Power radiated from her person and her voice became forcefully cold.

"Lord, heed me. Time is precious and words are wasteful. Look, I will show you."

She spread her arms, loosed the full force of her mastery upon him. Tuned into sympathy with her will, the Kielmark had no choice but stare into the ewer. Images bloomed in the water. Through interlinked chains of circumstance, Taen led him on a journey which began in Kisburn's secret council chamber and proceeded through the debate-ridden governance of the Free Isles Alliance to a forester's secluded cabin beyond the Furlains. In dreams the enchantress showed him Keithland's most poignant weaknesses; of Cliffhaven's strategic importance, she spared nothing. Twisting the Kielmark's emotions into her pattern, she stung him first with a King's thorny ambitions; ruled by her touch, the Kielmark tasted the greed which had transformed a fisherman's guilt-ridden son into a pitiless pawn, knew the cruelty of the woman who had instigated the change. Battered in turn by a sorcerer's geas, he suffered the storm winds of an ocean crossing and Jaric's lonely hours at *Callinde*'s helm. Taen granted no respite. Shifting her image yet again, she drove him deep beneath the ice which buttressed Cliffhaven's northern shore. There the Kielmark heard the bloodlust-crazed screams of the frostwargs; he felt the last desperate hope of a sorcerer treasured like a brother in friendship.

"Free Jaric," said Taen. Her words reverberated relentlessly within the Kielmark's mind. "If you do not, everything you value will come to ruin."

She released him with calculated abruptness. The water in the ewer lost its sheen of visions, became ordinary and clear once more. The Kielmark started. Restored to his own awareness, he discovered tears on his face. "You place me at extreme disadvantage," he said softly and reached for the carafe to refill his goblet.

Suddenly a thunderous knock sounded upon the door.

"Lord!" A captain with looped brass earrings stuck his head inside. "Come quickly. There's trouble with the prisoner!"

The Kielmark dropped the carafe. It smashed shrilly on the tiles as he ran full tilt for the door. He wrenched the panel open, jerking his head for Taen to follow. The captain continued his account as they raced the length of the corridor.

"The boy roused screaming. Tore the skin off his wrists trying to break the fetters. The healer had dressed the swordcut and gone, and the guard could find no reason for the prisoner's distress. Lord, he rose to summon help. His second on duty opened the door and nearly went blind from a discharge of sorcery." Panting for breath, the captain finished his report. "The guard got thrown from his feet. He bade me inform you that he saw the stormfalcon appear in the cell. Now a wind rips through the keep like a hurricane let loose from its moorings, and not a man dares to go near."

The Kielmark pounded the length of an arched hallway, shouting over his shoulder to Taen, "Can you help?"

Breathlessly, she replied, "If Jaric still has his reason, yes."

The Kielmark whirled. Without breaking stride, he caught Taen in his arms for the second time that morning. Bunched against his shoulders with no more dignity than a bolt of cloth, the enchantress felt his powerful stride lengthen until the guard fell tiredly behind. His fingers bruised. But concerned for the Firelord's heir, Taen barely cared. She endured the sprint to the keep without protest, her dream-sense ranging ahead to reach Jaric.

Contact loosed a flood of terror and pain; and a searing, untameable torrent of power whose intended course had been balked. The force built with each passing second, turning inward against Jaric's spirit with the wanton destructiveness of a cyclone. He had no will left to break, Taen saw. In a moment of shared horror, her control wavered. The geas surged across the dream link. For one agonized instant she knew the full scope of Jaric' suffering. The impact made her gasp. Untrained to handle such a terrible influx of energy, her connection dissolved, leaving her limp and disoriented in the Kielmark's arms.

Taen raised her voice above the noise. "My skills are useless until we reach Jaric."

The Kielmark nodded curtly. He leapt down a short flight of steps and crossed an open courtyard. Rain howled over the roofpeaks, slashing the hair across his brow. Taen's light robes became soaked within seconds. Gusts screamed across the yard, battering shutters and doors with insane violence. Yet the Kielmark would not be daunted. He ran on, until the keep loomed through the downpour, a fixed silhouette against skies churning with clouds. With his head bent against the elements, he ducked beneath the shelter of the arch and kicked open the keep's double doors.

Inside, the rain ceased, but the rush of air became deafening. Slammed by the drafts which eddied up from the dungeons, the Kielmark set Taen on her feet. He wrapped his arm about her shoulders; sheltering her with his own great bulk, they descended the stairwell. Step by labored step, he hauled Taen to the cell where Jaric lay.

The door had been battered open. Harsh white light blazed from within, spilling glare off the rough walls of the corridor. The damp air carried a whetted edge of ozone. Through dazzled vision, Taen caught a glimpse of giant wings, feathers barred in black and tawny gold. The blast of the gale drowned her shout. She clung to the Kielmark's wrist and pointed. But the man had seen the stormfalcon's presence already. He nodded, his profile lined in light above her head, then shouldered stubbornly forward. Wind hammered at his balance. Sweaty fingers bored into Taen's flesh as he reached with his other hand and hooked the grilled iron above the cell door.

Taen's face was buried in his shoulder as he strained to cross the threshold. She felt his muscles strain and quiver under her cheek. But the wind funneled through the narrow opening with the fury of a cataract, making headway impossible. The

Kielmark leaned down and yelled into the dream-weaver's ear, "When you reach him, hang on."

Taen nodded, whipped by strands of her own loosened hair. She felt the Kielmark's arm bunch briefly against her back. Then he flung her bodily against the might of the storm, through the door and into the cell.

Blinded by the brilliance of the sorcery, Taen stumbled to her knees, then tripped headlong over a limp body. Lost to all sensation, Jaric failed to react. Unable to see, Taen groped. Her right hand bruised against chain. Links gouged her palm, cutting the skin. She twisted and caught hold. Wind shrilled past her ears like the scream of a torturer's victim. Taen resisted its force. She slid her hand up past the fetter and seized Jaric's wrist. Her fingers dug into flesh gone dangerously cold and slippery wet with blood. Taen knew anguish at the discovery. While the stormfalcon's wings lashed the elements into primordial fury above her head, she steadied her talents to dream-send.

"Jaric!" Her call was desperate and her touch unerring; still her cry of compassion raised no response. Taen flattened herself against the stone at the boy's side and caught his face between warm hands. Then she sharpened her will like a weapon and thrust into his being, dream-weaving a shelter for the beleaguered mind under her touch. Quickly, surely she cast a barrier across his thoughts which the geas could not penetrate. Isolated, the pinpoint concentration of its powers began to dissipate.

The painful brilliance of the enchantment flickered, then disappeared, taking the stormfalcon's image with it. In darkness, Taen wove her bastion tighter and stronger still. The wind dropped to a sigh, winnowing her robes about her ankles. Slowly she sat up and eased her cramped muscles. Jaric still breathed beneath her hands, but his mind held no glimmer of self-awareness.

Something metallic clinked in the doorway. A spark flared,

revealing the Kielmark's square features in the glow of flame; a lantern stood braced between his knees, and he was frowning. As the illumination steadied, Taen returned her attention to the Firelord's heir who lay sprawled across her knees. Both wrists were abraded from thrashing against the chain; his eyes stared sightlessly from his pale face, and fine sun-bleached hair fell over Taen's wrists, matted into tangles by wind and salt. Confronted by his physical presence for the first time, Taen was startled to find he was smaller than her initial impression in Seitforest. She brushed his brow with careful fingers. Jaric did not stir; beneath the sodden linen shirt, his skin felt icy as death.

The light brightened and boots scraped stone at Taen's elbow. She glanced up, found the Kielmark standing over her with the lantern. His cold eyes were fixed intently upon Jaric.

Taen answered the Kielmark's thought before he spoke. "I don't know. Perhaps I can restore Jaric to consciousness, but the geas touched him brutally and your handling was just short of inhuman." She touched the chains with distaste. "These must be removed directly. Then I will do what I can. If you bear this boy any pity, provide horses and escort, that he can reach the ice cliffs as speedily as possible."

With uncharacteristic tolerance the Kielmark refrained from comment. Sovereign within his domain, he would take no orders, even from a dream-weaver trained by the Vaere. Too late Taen regretted the tactlessness of her demand. If he crossed her, she wondered whether she could influence him at all, volatile as he was, and savage to the point of unpredictability. With the breath stopped in her throat, she awaited his decision.

Still studying Jaric, the Kielmark knelt. He drew a key from his belt and caught the steel which bound the boy's wrists. The locks sprang with a sharp click. The Lord of Cliffhaven removed the fetters from his prisoner with strangely disturbing gentleness. Taen sighed in relief. Her fingers unclenched in

Jaric's hair, and she bent as if weeping over the boy's slack form.

The Kielmark tossed the chain to the floor. He stood then, waiting with ill-concealed impatience for the jangle of echoes to fade. "Do you know? The boy is small, but exceedingly tough. He might just have what it takes to master the Cycle of Fire."

With that he thrust the keys back into his tunic and regarded the dream-weaver who had invaded his island. Wind had torn away her myrtle circlet; black hair rippled across her shoulders, twisted untidily into elflocks. "You have great courage," the Kielmark added thoughtfully. "I think you have earned yourself horses and escort. Beyond that I cannot help. I have an island to defend."

But far removed from mortal hearing, Taen did not absorb the meaning of his words; she had pitched all her concentration into her craft from the instant Jaric's fetters were released. Her touch ranged deep. Digging for one thin spark of awareness in the limp flesh under her hands, the dream-weaver did not see the Kielmark set the lantern at her side. He departed quietly, leaving her unaware he had discarded prudence entirely. Stubborn as sea-battered granite, the Kielmark intended to fight Kisburn and his compact of demons. While he lived, the fortress would not be surrendered.

CHAPTER XXI

Ice Cliffs

LOST IN A SHADOWLESS VOID near the borderlands of death, Jaric felt a current intrude across his isolation. He recoiled sharply. Unwilling to face any more pain, he lay motionless as the flatfish, which settles on the sea bottom to escape the sharpened jaws of predators.

But the presence would not depart.

"Jaric!" The name pierced the core of his silence and shattered into echoes, each one a pledge of compassion. The call promised peace in a world he had been driven to forsake; it also offered healing. But memory of the geas' lacerating pain lingered like an open sore. Jaric dared not trust. Behind bars, locked in fetters, the voice would bring nothing but ruined hope, like the dream-weaver who had once betrayed him. Anskiere never forgot, never forgave; his geas could grant no reprieve.

"Son of Ivain!" The cry raised a flicker like light rays fractured by water. With weary desperation Jaric sought to drown the glimmer in darkness. His effort was battered aside. Images surged across his mind. They harried him in his solitude. Denied all rest, Jaric cried aloud. The presence broke through, flooded his mind with joy so pure he could have wept.

Sunlight broke into jewels on the surface of a river where a small boy sat with a fishing line. The child was himself and the moment a treasured memory from boyhood. The vision shifted without warning. Snow fell in Seitforest, each flake more intricate than patterned lace against the dark wool of his mittens; in a circle of lanternlight by the shed, Telemark regarded the pelts piled on the drag-sleigh. "You never give up, Jaric. I admire that in a man." The forester added praise for the fine woodsmanship of a boy who had never before trapped an ice otter.

Outside of dreams, Jaric winced in shame. He longed for the anonymity of Morbrith's archives, but sanctuary was denied.

"Firelord's heir!" The cry raised echoes of despair and the horror-ridden vision of Morbrith in ruins. But the Llondel who had originally framed the warning with images now was dust, bled to his death by an Earl's cold steel. Jaric knelt amid streets choked with bones. He shouted denial; but his anguish was ignored.

"Kerainson Jaric!" The call built to a crescendo of accusation, paired by a vivid view of Mathieson, who grieved alone on a wind-whipped landing, hands knotted in his collar of magnificent fur.

"No." Jaric shuddered. He rejected the vision's unbearable implication, that he was unfit to have demanded such sacrifice and all who had aided him acted in vain. Punished to respond in his own defense, Jaric stirred. His lashes quivered and he opened his eyes, to find that in truth the pain was gone.

His mind cleared of visions. The dream-weaver who once restored his past sat with his head cradled in her lap. But the shining black hair Jaric remembered lay snarled across her shoulders, no longer crowned with flowers. Her pale eyes were swollen from exhausted tears. The hands which gripped his shoulders trembled, warm in contrast with the damp stone floor where he lay.

"By the Vaere," Taen said softly. "I thought I had lost you." Her smile held such sweetness it stopped the breath in Jaric's throat.

A lantern burned by her knee. Beyond its yellow glow Jaric saw windowless walls and bars, and nearby a brighter gleam of steel chain. He touched his wrists and by the sting of torn skin discovered his fetters had been removed.

"The door is open also," the enchantress said.

Jaric sat up, eyes widened with sudden sharp mistrust. Once she had deceived him, and let him sail into suffering on the sea beyond Mearren Ard.

Taen caught his sleeve with firm fingers. "Ivainson, no."

The sound of the name made him quiver. Jaric's mouth flinched in remembrance of another older pain.

The enchantress released him and sighed with sorrowful regret. "There is a difference between pity and caring. Try to believe me. The last thing Kencie intended was to hurt you. I speak for myself also. The Vaere misjudged very badly concerning Anskiere's summons."

With evident discomfort, Jaric tugged his sleeves over the raw patches on his wrists. Taen had just interceded in his behalf; quite probably saved his life. "I'm sorry. You didn't have to come after me."

"I did." Taen rubbed at her own skinned elbow and ruefully smiled. "The rest doesn't matter. Can you ride? I can subdue the effects of the geas a limited time only, and the storm attached to your presence continues to build. We must go and ask for horses without delay."

She rose expectantly. For a long moment Jaric stared at the broken skin of his hands, his expression stiffly unreadable. Taen waited without probing his thoughts. Unlike Emien,

Jaric did not turn vindictive or angry when fate twisted his life into knots.

At last he raised his eyes to her face. "I'll go," he said warily. "Do you suppose you could convince the guards to return my weapons and cloak? They were gifts, and the loss of them troubles me."

But the request became unnecessary. When Taen and Jaric emerged from the keep, both horses and Jaric's confiscated blades awaited, along with five of the Kielmark's guardsmen to escort them to the north shore.

Whipped into sheets by the gusts, rain slashed across the cobbled yard, abrasive as driven sand. The gale had worsened; it hammered horses and men with unremitting fury. Even inside the walls, the angry thud of surf against the breakwater slammed the air like the thunder of the Great Fall itself.

Jaric collected his sword and dagger and mounted a gray with an ugly head. The horse pawed restively as he gathered the reins, hauling against his hold with ears flattened against its soaked neck. Jaric took the pull in his fingers, trying to spare his lacerated palms. Unlike the morning he had fled Gaire's Main, he was no longer too weak to master the animal under his knees. Yet the discovery yielded little satisfaction. His body might have changed, but the sickly boy who once copied manuscripts could not be reconciled with the man who left Telemark's cottage in Seitforest. Neither the one nor entirely the other, Jaric wrestled endless uncertainty, for every aspect of his life had been shaped by the sorcerer's geas which had upended his will at Morbrith Keep. As Jaric rode out of the courtyard in the company of the Kielmark's guards, he wondered how he would feel when he arrived at the ice cliffs and confronted the Stormwarden at last.

Rain pelted in opaque sheets over the Kielmark's escort as they reined to a halt above the crest which overlooked Cliffhaven's northern shore. Gusts whined through the dune grass, and the crash of breakers against the beach head added deep throaty undertones to a storm still ominously building. Sopping and miserable, the riders sat with hunched shoulders and the horses stood with tails tucked against the wind, snorting the salt taint of spindrift from their nostrils.

One of the guardsmen touched Jaric's elbow and pointed toward the sea. "Over there," he shouted. "You'll come to a sandy beach. Just past where it breaks up into rock, you'll find the ice cliffs."

The surf broke too high on the strand for horses. Jaric dismounted and passed his soaked reins to the guardsman.

"We'll wait for you," called Taen. A small determined figure on the Kielmark's great chestnut, she shivered in robes dulled silver-gray by the damp.

Jaric nodded but did not linger. Uncomfortable with sympathy from strangers, he hastened down the bluff to the strand; the guardsmen who stood vigil on the ridge faded behind. Rain traced icy runnels down Jaric's collar, and eel grass hooked his ankles at each step. But, anxious to complete his journey, he felt no weariness. Presently the dunes gave way to packed sand; close at hand, the grinding boom of waves became deafening. Jaric ducked smoking drifts of spray, his cloak bunched over the hilts of his weapons to keep the salt from the steel. Fifty paces beyond the bluffs he reached a jagged stand of rocks. Glistening in the rain, stone rose like buttresses against the sheer face of a cliff; incoming breakers battered at the base, spouting geysers of foam.

Left no semblance of a path, Jaric splashed through shallows, hurried by the rush of the following breaker. He jammed his boot in a cleft and swung up onto the nearest formation. He dared not look down. The sea sucked and thudded bare yards under his boots, twisting ropy tendrils of weed through the fissures; a man in the water would quickly tangle and drown. Even if he fell clear, current would drag him under like a rag.

Jaric hauled himself onto a narrow ledge. Waves sheeted spray over his back. He crept forward, fingers gouged by barnacles. Yet he dared not move without handholds. Gusts slapped at his clothing, sharp with unseasonal frost. Ahead loomed the ice cliffs. But only when the ledge broadened beneath his feet did Jaric notice the view.

The seas rose beneath, green with lattice marks of current; then crested with a roar that punished thought and broke, hurling foam against steely bastions of ice. Awed by the breadth of the cliffs, Jaric glanced up. But the structure soared upward, obscured by coiling wraiths of mist. He inched across a crevice. The cliff shelved beyond, cut like a road across the face of a precipice. Beyond lay a steep drop to the sea. Breakers battered beneath with the force of primordial creation.

Jaric moved cautiously toward the brink. Pebbles rolled under his boots, bounced outward into air and vanished. He took another step and another. Sorcery flashed, sudden and blinding as lightning overhead. Wind gusted through the defile and built to a screaming rush of sound. Certain the geas had broken free of Taen's protective barrier, Jaric cried out. He flung both hands over his face, prepared to be ripped into agony by Anskiere's implacable summoning.

But the storm died. Wind dropped, weak as a spent breath; the rain ceased. After the violence of rampaging elements, the land seemed deadened under an eerie and unnatural silence. Jaric lifted his head in wonder. Surf still broke over the reefs below; but the wave crests unraveled into foam and subsided, no longer flayed to tatters by the gale. Mist eddied over the defile. Trembling in the midst of calm, Jaric watched the storm dissolve around him.

Storm clouds tore asunder and sunlight cast a mantle of gold across Jaric's shoulders. Peace claimed him. Breezes whispered through his hair and a single black-barred feather drifted down. Jaric caught the quill as it passed. He turned its knife-edge length between his hands and wondered what should be done with the seed of the stormfalcon's power.

"Keep it safe, Ivainson Jaric," said the wind.

Jaric started. He stared wildly about, but the rocky escarpment remained empty as before and the ice beyond as majestically desolate. The voice could only be sent by the Stormwarden of Elrinfaer, who had wrought the stormfalcon's pattern and set the geas of summoning upon him. Before apprehension could defeat him, Jaric gathered courage and spoke. "I have come in accordance with your bidding. Dare I ask what purpose brought me here?"

"You are the Firelord's heir," the wind replied.

Exposed on his shelf of rock, Jaric could not know that deep within the fortress of ice Anskiere of Elrinfaer roused from the deep sleep of stasis. Guided by the stormfalcon's feather, his mind ranged to a ledge beyond his confinement, where a young man with earnest brown eyes awaited his fate.

Jaric shivered as the Stormwarden's presence encompassed him. Aware his person was being assessed, he knew a moment of cynical amusement; the Stormwarden of Elrinfaer would find nothing but a starved, sunburned youth with tangled hair, slight stature, and a talent for fine penmanship; small reward for such stupendous expenditure of effort. Bitterness deepened the lines of hardship around Jaric's mouth. No doubt Anskiere would conclude he had been mistaken to summon him at all.

But the wind swirled, sharply snapping his cloak hem. The break in the clouds widened. Slanting sunlight touched the ice across the fissure, firing the crystals like prisms. As a prison, the structure was awesomely beautiful; also more permanently secure than any dungeon created by man. Struck by sudden poignant sorrow, Jaric realized the Stormwarden of Elrinfaer was no longer master of his fate. He depended on outside help for his rescue.

The fact sparked a painful reminder of Jaric's earlier inadequacy. Trapped by despair, the boy struggled to define what surely was evident. "I am useless to you, sorcerer. I have no power to assist your deliverance. My father resented your hold upon him. He died swearing his debt would stand unpaid. I survived through another man's sacrifice, and I remain ignorant of any heritage of Ivain's. Let me go. I possess no means to help."

The wind whispered mournfully across the rocks. "Power is your rightful inheritance. The heir has potential enough to surpass his sire. But this you must discover for yourself. I did not call you here to force that choice."

"Then why?" Jaric's shout echoed in wild anguish off the face of the cliffs. "Why summon me at all? Why not leave me at Morbrith or Seitforest and let my days pass in peace?" He waited through dense and implacable stillness. For long minutes it seemed he would receive no reply at all.

"You were called through the debt incurred against me by Ivain," said Anskiere in the voice made of wind. "As his heir you are bound to undertake a task in my name. Complete my bidding and you are forever free of obligation. This I promise: should you succeed in the task, you shall gain everything you desire."

Jaric swallowed. His heart felt heavy as lead in his chest. Memory of the tales repeated in Mearren Ard arose unbidden in his mind. Anskiere was seldom mentioned without a curse and Ivain's name was forever linked with cruelty. Small, uncertain, and exhausted, Jaric feared the madness engendered by the Cycle of Fire more than death itself. Still, he summoned the dregs of his pride and phrased the question he most dreaded to ask. "What is the task?"

The wind subsided like a sigh. "You will recover the Keys of Elrinfaer and hold them safe until they can be returned."

No mention of the Cycle of Fire; Jaric took a deep breath, startled by the simplicity of the demand. The Keys to Elrinfaer lay in Kisburn's possession, within reach of mortal means; once returned to Anskiere, Jaric never need concern himself with the

Vaerish mysteries which had ruined his father's mind. Ivain's debt charged him to complete but a single feat.

The sunlight shone more kindly over the black granite beneath his boots. Raising his eyes to the ice cliffs, Jaric knew a moment of puzzled regret. "What of yourself?" His question echoed across the chasm, rebounding off the rock. "Would you demand no rescue from me?"

But the winds did not answer. The sea boomed, changeless as time against the reefs below the cliffs. Slowly, disbelievingly, Jaric waited. But Anskiere offered no reply but silence. At last, with a shrug Jaric turned away from frost-locked cliffs and retraced his steps to the sea.

By the time Ivain's heir gained the beach, Anskiere drowsed within his prison of ice and rock. Troubled by the whistles of frostwargs, he dreamed of a prophecy told by a Llondel master seer. "It is given thus," the demon had said, repeating from flawless memory a piece of his heritage from a generation past. His alien tongue struggled to shape human words. "The fourth ancestor of my mother's sibling sighted a future. She saw there seven times seven Llondelei and a yellow-haired son of Ivain Firelord. Then her sight became colored with warning. Guard the boy's life, for should he recover the Keys of Elrinfaer intact, he will also master the Cycle of Fire. And then shall men and Llondel rise from Keithland on Koridan's blessed Flame, to live in peace in the heavens."

While Jaric climbed the bluffs above the dunes, the prophecy receded from dreams to memory. Anskiere of Elrinfaer settled once more into sleep, in hope the Llondel seer proved accurate. Just before he crossed the border of dreams into stasis, the Stormwarden caught the fading echo of a laugh; but whether the mirth was Ivain's or Tathagres' or a reflection from his own imagination, it was impossible to guess.

* * *

Jaric gained the summit of the bluff, startled to find the guardsmen dismissed. Taen remained, along with one other. Mounted on a huge black horse, the Kielmark himself gripped the reins of the gray Jaric had left with the guard captain. By bearing alone, no man could mistake the sovereign of Cliff-haven, though his cloak was cut from plain maroon wool and weapons and mail were ordinary. Perched in a saddle of leop-ard skin, his watchful eyes reflected chill like glacial water as the heir of Ivain stopped by his stirrup.

Jaric greeted the Kielmark with the courtesy due an Earl; unkempt as he was, he bowed with practiced grace. "Lord, I ask leave to sail. Is my boat still where I left her, or has she been impounded?"

The Kielmark ignored his request. Motionless on his tall horse, he studied the young man with all the imposing arro-gance of his reputation. "What do you know of Anskiere?"

Jaric's chin lifted at the sharpness of the query. Brown eyes met blue with a shock of surprise; the boy had not expected to be balked. His resilient show of spirit sparked instant reap-praisal by the Kielmark.

Jaric answered with cool impatience. "Perhaps instead I should ask the same question of you, Lord, for I desire nothing beyond recovery of the freedom I have lost. The Stormwarden summoned me through the curse set upon my father. The debt demands I complete one task in his service. Once again, I ask leave to sail from your shores."

The Kielmark's horse sidled irritably against the gray as his hand jerked the bit. "What was the task demanded of you?"

Jaric spoke in near defiance. "I must recover the Keys to El-rinfaer. Would you prevent me?"

"I don't need to." The Kielmark flung the gray's reins into the startled hands of the boy.

Taen gave a small cry of dismay. The Kielmark immediately wheeled his horse to face her. She had been weeping, Jaric no-ticed, or perhaps arguing. Her cheeks were pinched and white and the set of her jaw seemed far more determined than the situation warranted.

"Consider again, Lady." The Kielmark grinned with wolfish delight. "The Keys are in the possession of his royal Grace, the King of Kisburn, who moves against me with an army of demons. It takes no dream-weaver's talent to guess what would happen to any son of Ivain's, should he risk an encounter in that antique joke of a fishing boat."

Taen tugged the mare's bridle, her mouth compressed with affront. She chose not to reply. But maddened by the Kielmark's wounding words and the fact his own fate was at issue, Jaric stepped in front of her horse, prepared to intercede in her defense.

The Kielmark softened his tone. "I think you have no better alternative, daughter of the Vaere. I offer you fair bargain: allied with your talents, Cliffhaven has a chance against this threat of demons. Give me the number they send against me and dream-weave a cover for my men. In return I will deliver your shape-shifter to his gods and the Keys of Elrinfaer to Jaric."

Taen spoke without moving. "Lord, I have told you. My kind never bargain."

"Very well." The Kielmark shrugged, his expression bleakly forbidding. "Remember your choices." He jerked his reins from the mane beneath his hands and booted the horse around. Over the boom of surf against the shore he added, "Boy, you are free to sail. *Callinde* is warped to the south dock in my harbor. Take her and go with my blessing."

"No!" Taen twisted in her saddle, her face pale but composed. "I will stay. For Jaric's sake only, I do as you ask. But if you fail, may the Vaere curse your name to the very gates of hell. They promised my death if I disobeyed."

"Lady, no!" Jaric caught the mare's bridle, shocked by the sacrifice she proposed. "You must not risk yourself for me!"

The Kielmark ignored his protest, a wild light in his eyes.

His stallion stamped the ground, punching great marks in the turf, but he kept his seat easily and his lips drew back in a great shout of laughter. "Kor's Fires, woman, I'll whip Kisburn into the harbor." He sobered with startling speed and glared over the taut line of the horizon. "My captains will think me sea-crazed when they hear what I propose. But my plan will work. *There will be no surrender here, not while I can prevent it. And so long as I live, you and Jaric will be safe, my oath as sovereign upon it.*"

The vicious pride in him brought tears to Taen's eyes. To the bitter edge of death the Kielmark's word would stand. But Tamlin's warning lay heavy on her mind as the man kicked his mount to a gallop. He vanished over the dunes to the south while Jaric stood like a man stunned by a blow. No power on Keithland could call the Kielmark back and change his mind.

Five days after Anskiere's second storm loosened its grip over Cliffhaven, King Kisburn's three warships entered the narrows of Mainstrait. The wind blew yet from the west, a misfortune which made the captains irritable; forced to beat every league of the way in ships overloaded with troops and supplies, passage had been grindingly slow. And with Kor's Accursed on board, the sailors muttered and started at every order, making signs against evil even while they worked aloft.

Except for Tathagres, only one man of *Morra's* company remained at ease in the presence of demons. Disdainful of the stuffy cabin he shared with two lieutenants, Emien lounged on the foredeck with his back braced against the rail, a woolen cloak draped over the wood beneath his elbow. He felt peculiarly unclothed without the accustomed weight of sword and dagger at his belt. But since the Gierj-demons could raise no power in the presence of iron, not a man aboard the flagship bore arms. *Morra* had been stripped of anchors and chains, and fitters had replaced every scrap of steel gear with parts made of brass. She carried ballast of sand specially for the passage across the straits.

Denied the security of their weapons, the soldiers huddled below decks, nervously whispering. Their uneasiness moved Emien to scorn. After long delay, Cliffhaven lay just two leagues off the bow. The vindictive hatred Emien felt for Anskiere far outweighed any distrust of the demons brought along to achieve the Kielmark's downfall. Eager for the first stage of conquest to commence, the boy leaned over the rail beneath the rising angle of the headsails.

The breeze freshened, funneled between the gapped peninsulas of the straits. *Morra* sailed with every stitch of canvas pinched tight. Emien squinted at the wavelets and cursed; the tide had recently turned. Ebbing current would shortly reduce their headway nearly to naught.

The captain called for a leadsman to sound the depth, that the ship could be run to the limit of her draft on each tack. *Morra* ghosted close against a craggy head of land which loomed black and forbidding beneath a lowering moon. At least the light lay in their favor, Emien reflected sourly. Any ship set against them would be exposed like an inked silhouette against the silvered face of the sea. That the Kielmark would attack was certain; the Thienz demon had promised it.

The Thienz itself stood propped against the mizzenmast just aft of the helm. The stern running lamps were unlit; but in the reddish glow of the compass lantern, Emien picked out the dim outline of grinning toadlike lips, slitted eyes, and the crested headdress which adorned the creature's crown.

The leadsman's line splashed beneath Emien's perch. In a clear voice the man sounded the mark; five fathoms, then four, then three. The bottom was shoaling rapidly. The captain signaled and the boastwain shouted, "Ready about. All hands, man sheets and braces!"

The quartermaster spun the wheel. The boatswain called orders over the crack of canvas and tackle as *Morra* swung into the wind. Sails ruffled. Sailors heaved on the sheets. With a squeal of blocks, the lines banged taut and *Morra* laid onto her new tack. Downwind like an echo the following ship repeated the flag's maneuver. Excitedly, Emien searched the sea beyond the straits. The Kielmark's ambush lurked in the darkness ahead; alone among Kisburn's men, the boy was curious to see how the demons would send them to slaughter.

Suddenly the Thienz stiffened. Its massive head lifted, blunt face trained forward like a bloodhound tracking an elusive scent. But the Thienz did not pause to sniff the breeze. Half blind by daylight and utterly lacking a sense of smell, it possessed empathic sensitivity more developed than any Sathid-linked talent trained by the Vaere. From a position nine leagues distant, it sounded currents no human could perceive, and reliably listed the position, numbers, and attack plan of the Kielmark's defending fleet. Emien fidgeted in smug anticipation. The renowned Lord of Renegades had no chance against them at all.

The captain fretted behind the quartermaster's shoulder. "Do you sense anything?"

The Thienz whuffed through its gills, noncommittal. But its pose remained tautly attentive. Emien strained to overhear as the captain addressed the mate on watch. "Fetch Tathagres. The Gierj should come on deck. If perfect timing exists for attack, this must surely be the moment."

The Thienz stretched its gillflaps and croaked. Beaded ornaments gleamed upon knotted wrists as it lifted the appendage which passed for a hand and pointed. "Ships, twelve to port, seventeen to starboard. They are signaled by watchfire from the island yonder, and now captains hoist canvas. They will round the points on both sides and bear downwind in a line. They hope to engage us and board."

Metal jingled in the companionway. Clad in ornamental mail wrought of silver and a tunic of dyed leather, Tathagres stepped lightly onto the quarterdeck. She smiled to the captain, who plucked nervously at his beard. "They play straight into our hands, don't you see?" With provocative grace, she hooked her scarlet cloak on a belaying pin and regarded the six creatures which swarmed across the deck at her heels.

Ropy, lean, and blackened like clotted shadow in the darkness, the Gierj-demons scuttled round her boots. Their eyes glowed pale and lambent as sorcerer's candles. Emien shivered despite his interest. Of ten demon races left unbound, the Gierj were most dangerous. Spurred feet scraped against planking as they moved, furtive and quick as weasels, and formed into a circle. Their bodies appeared to melt into a single form as they lowered narrowed heads into a huddle.

"Distribute jackets to the crew," said the captain to the mate. The sweat on his brow was not entirely raised by heat; his thick hands trembled as he accepted his own cloak from the cabin steward.

The Thienz whuffed loudly and barked. Tiny as toys, the Kielmark's first ships rounded the massive shoulders of land up the straits. Emien snatched up his cloak. Wool prickled his skin as he pinned it snugly about his neck. But watching in starved anticipation as the ships rounded the point, the boy forgot to scratch.

The Kielmark's captains maintained position with seamanship unequaled the breadth of Keithland; precise as clockwork, each vessel swung before the wind for the run down the straits. Lacking a ship's glass, Emien could only guess their size and rig; visible only briefly, the enemy craft jibed neatly and steered just inside the shore, for a few brief minutes escaping the backlit cast of the moonlight. Once clear of the land's shadow, they came head on in formation. The outline of the first ship became hopelessly muddled by those following behind.

Emien smiled. Against human foes, the Kielmark's tactics would be powerfully effective. Yet with Gierj on board, the enviable skill of his crewmen served only to aid his defeat.

On the quarterdeck, Tathagres licked pale lips. Bracelets clinked on her wrist as she touched the captain's arm. "They make it easy for us," she said, amused by the man's discomfort.

"Closely bunched, those boats will burn like Koridan's Fires, you will see."

But her complacence felt misplaced to a man who had twice battled the wiliest sea dog on Keithland and been defeated. The captain anxiously checked the heading over the quarter-master's broad shoulders time and again.

With the wind in their favor, the Kielmark's fleet bore down with startling speed. Tathagres plucked her cloak from the rail, cast it over her shoulders with languid grace. The Gierj began to chant. The leadsman called the three fathom mark over an unsettling quaver of sound. Men dashed to the sheets as Morra came about once again. Emien crossed the forecastle and settled against the starboard rail. Slowly the ship clawed away from the shoreline. The demons' incantation rose and blended into a single flowing note which set Emien's teeth on edge. No longer could he pretend to be comfortable with the creatures on Morra's quarterdeck.

"Captain, shorten sail and heave to." Tathagres stepped into the circle of demons and carefully fastened her cloak.

Sailhands swarmed up the shrouds to reef canvas. The Gierj chant ascended in pitch, ringing across the sea like a discordant shrilling of flutes. Emien covered both ears with his hands and wondered how men in the shrouds could bear the sting of that inhuman sound.

Tathagres spoke in an alien tongue from the quarterdeck. The Thienz replied, gestured with scrawny arms, then lowered its bulk down the companionway. No longer were its powers of observation required; lined up like sheep for slaughter, the Kielmark's ships sailed to their doom.

The Gierj shifted pitch. Their song flung screeching discord across the waters. Inured to their presence, the grizzled quarter-master swung Morra's bow into the wind and steadied the helm. The flagship drifted in the current, balanced like a moth in a draft, while enemies closed on both quarters. The wail of the Gierj warbled, abruptly descended and became a bare whisper of sound. Tathagres placed her fingers lightly against her neck-band. She spoke a sibilant word and around her the temperature plunged into winter.

Air burned with startling cold in Emien's lungs. He gasped, knifed to the marrow by chill so intense his cloak stiffened like paper across his shoulders. Hoarfrost traced the ship like crystal in the moonlight, whitening rail and rigging and wheel; the quartermaster's mustache sprouted a rim of ice. Still the temperature fell. With fingers numbed and noses reddened, men blinked frost from their lashes.

The Gierj's song wavered and broke upon the air. Tathagres raised a stiffened arm to the advancing lines of ships. The temperature dropped yet again, bringing the terrible cold of Arctic night. Ropes cracked like old bones and timbers moaned as ice strained the wood. A sudden aura of sorcery blazed around the Gierj. The faces of captain and quartermaster shone blue and their breath plumed against the dark. Tathagres raised her arms. Energy shot like lightning from the Gierj-demons' midst and broke in a blaze of light over her palms. Emien squinted, but the spell grew too brilliant to bear.

He shielded his eyes with his hands. The Gierj's chant ceased, choked off in midbeat. A high, ululating cry burst from Tathagres' throat. Power exploded from her fingers and the night split with a peal like thunder. *Morra* drifted placidly, cloaked in ordinary shadow. But beyond her forestay Emien saw fire burst like the wrath of Kor across the Kielmark's advancing ships.

Flames speared skyward, pinwheeling sparks and debris across the surface of the sea. In the space of a single instant, every enemy vessel was transformed to a raging inferno. Above the crackle of blazing timbers, a barrage of agonized screams rebounded down the straits as Cliffhaven's defenders perished at their posts. Emien gripped the rail with sweating hands. The scope of the demons' destruction left him awed. Confused by elation and a sickened sense of horror, he watched, rapt, while twenty-nine ships burned to the waterline.

Unnoticed beneath the companionway, the Thienz pressed finlike fingers to its face, delicate psychic senses overpowered by the discharge of energy. Blinded to its own element, it rocked and moaned in discomfort, while the cold traced rims of frost about its gills. On the quarterdeck Tathagres stood poised like a cruel marble goddess while the Gierj stirred and scratched at her feet. They turned lean faces up the straits, dispassionate eyes reflecting the ruinous conflagration their powers had unleashed. The living stood motionless on *Morra's* decks while the fires up the straits roared and snapped and at last subsided into smoke.

On the foredeck Emien shivered. His mouth curved with surly desire. No mortal on Keithland could withstand the forces summoned by the Gierj; the Kielmark would be brought to his knees like a child and even Anskiere's great bastions of ice would soften and dissolve into the sea. The screams of dying sailors no longer troubled Emien's ears. If he could defeat Tathagres, the powers of demons would be his to command.

CHAPTER XXII

Fallen Lord

LED BY THE FLAGSHIP *MORRA*, Kisburn's fleet of three cleared Mainstrait, contested by nothing but current and wind; if the vessels were forced to tack often to avoid the smoking snarls of wreckage which drifted across their course, none of the captains complained. The fact that the Lord of Pirates had been defeated on his own waters seemed impossible to believe; yet in the gray dawn, beneath a mottled cover of clouds, *Morra* and one companion vessel anchored in Cliffhaven's main harbor utterly unchallenged. The third was sent on patrol to watch for attack by sea.

Emien leaned on the quarterdeck rail, eyes trained intently on the dockside. The bronze penknife he had lately used to pare his nails lay forgotten between half-clenched fingers. He glanced up as Tathagres paused by his side. Still clad in the mail and tunic she had worn the previous night, she appeared fully refreshed. Her appeal quickened the breath in his throat. But this once Emien had no mind to indulge his desire.

"There are no ships at anchorage, Lady." Carefully

noncommittal, the boy returned his knife to his wallet. "When we last put in with the Stormwarden there were upwards of thirty, and by sailors' accounts the Kielmark never slept with less than two score vessels on moorings."

But Tathagres awarded the comment even less concern than the possibility survivors might have swum ashore from the encounter in the strait the previous night. Posed with perfect grace against the rails, she studied the stone corners of the warehouses which usually housed tribute, as if expecting something.

"There," she said suddenly and pointed.

Emien looked. A shirtless figure raced through the alleys toward the harbor, a white banner streaming from a pole in his hand. "That's a trap," the boy said, surprised into rash words. "The Kielmark ran a man through with a sword once for objecting to the fact he had no white for surrender among the ensigns aboard his ships."

"He still doesn't." Tathagres smiled with pleased satisfaction. "What you see is a strip cut from a bedsheet. The Kielmark had no part in the matter, I assure you. My Thienz informed me an hour ago; it seems the Lord of Renegades has at last fallen victim to the lawless. His own men have betrayed him. We are about to be invited through the main gates and there the Kielmark himself will be delivered to us in chains."

Emien bit his lip in disbelief as the shirtless man leapt into a longboat, propped his makeshift banner in the bow, and cast off. Oars winked like matchsticks against leaden swells, then drove in rhythmic strokes toward the flagship.

"Why?" he said. "Why now of all times?"

Tathagres shook her hair free of its jeweled comb and loosed a bright peal of laughter. "A spy brought word of the Gierj-demons. The sentries on duty in the tower watched their companions burn in Mainstrait last night." She pricked Emien's arm lightly with the prongs of the hair pin. "Don't fret over the remaining ships, my love. Cliffhaven is ours. With the

Kielmark hostage, any captains who remain loyal will be easily managed."

But her attitude was too confident, Emien thought. Like the time Tathagres had murdered the guards by the ice cliffs, her air of reckless assurance grated against his sensibility. Yet he followed when she called the captain on deck to receive the longboat. Certain of her one true weakness, he wondered when he would have the opportunity to exploit it.

The chains which operated the front gates of Cliffhaven clanked across the winches. Heavy steel-bound portals swung wide and thumped against the walls, raising small puffs of dust. From his place to the rear of the King's advance guard, Emien heard a raucous scream of laughter backed by the incongruous notes of a flute. The Grand Warlord-General bellowed an order; the column began smartly to march. But the soldiers ahead had to clear the span of the arch before Emien gained a view of the courtyard.

A score of leather-clad men danced and cavorted in the open; others looked on clapping, all of them drunk except one. Chained by the wrists to the ring which normally tethered the saddled horse, a huge man knelt in their midst, his muscles knotted in wild anger. Blue eyes followed King Kisburn's entry with murderous intent. With a shock of disbelief, Emien recognized the Kielmark. The man's hair was filthy with dust. Flies buzzed about a gash above one eyebrow. The flagstone lay speckled with blood under his knees and the steel links dripped red from a swordcut across his forearm. But Emien observed that the men who had betrayed the legendary Lord of Renegades to defeat were careful to celebrate beyond reach.

The King commanded the Warlord-General to transfer the prisoner to the great hall. The flute player trailed off into silence and the dancers stilled to stare. Each recalled times when the Kielmark had killed for less. Five men moved cautiously from the lines, followed by the spokesman who carried the flag of surrender. Emien licked sweat from his lips. It seemed impossible that Cliffhaven could fall with no struggle after twenty years of dominance; countless bitter forays had ended in broken ships each time Keithland's rulers tried to break the Kielmark's stranglehold over Mainstrait. Yet nothing appeared extraordinary about the flag-bearer. With a snarl of hatred, he lowered his pole like a weapon and jabbed it savagely into the pit of the Kielmark's stomach. The man's body doubled, and he retched, gasping helplessly for air, while soldiers rushed in and unfastened the chains from the ring. They jerked the Kielmark to his feet.

Emien shivered in the morning heat, distressed that a ruler of such stature could suffer common vindictive abuse. Deeply shaken, Emien trailed the royal party down vaulted corridors.

Solid stone felt suddenly unsound beneath his boots and marching feet seemed to rattle the very keystones in the arches. The most defensible fortress on Keithland could not stand against human treachery. Sapped by growing insecurity, Emien passed between the gaudy trophies which littered Cliffhaven's great hall. His eyes saw none of the wealth. He chose a seat to the left of Tathagres, his thoughts trained with fanatical clarity upon the gold which circled her neck.

Guards sprang at the King's command. The chamber reverberated with the scrape of furniture as men cleared space for the prisoner. Seated in the Kielmark's own chair, Kisburn watched with fascinated satisfaction as his men hauled the Lord of Renegades onto the open floor in front of the dais.

The guardsmen tugged his chains, holding him spread-eagled and helpless before the royal presence. Prisoner regarded captor with a level glare of hostility. The Kielmark's chest heaved in great whistling gasps while blood dripped from his wrist, splashing scarlet stars on the marble. He waited in silence for the King to speak, but whether from stubborn pride or incapacity, no man present could guess.

"For a man who has terrorized shipping, your harbor seems

strangely deserted." Kisburn stroked the leopard skin on the chair with lean ringed fingers, an expression of overweening satisfaction on his face. "Where did you send them?"

The former Lord of Cliffhaven grinned. "To the backside of hell, for all the good it will do you."

Guardsmen wrenched at the chains and his shoulders jerked. In a burst of fury the Kielmark yanked back. One of his tormentors slipped, crashing sideways into a basket of alabaster pears. The container overturned. Fruit shattered with a shrill ring of sound and a spray of sparkling chips scattered the tiles. The guardsman cursed and clawed to maintain his balance. For an instant his chain fell slack; the Kielmark insolently wiped the blood from his brow, smearing his sound wrist scarlet.

But his gesture of bravado was spoiled by a vicious rejoinder from the flag-bearer. "He lies, your Grace. The ships left last night, packed to the crosstrees with cowards. Most of us served Cliffhaven against our will, and others didn't fancy getting burned alive like pigs."

But the King seemed unconvinced. His jeweled arm lifted, gesturing to a halberdier. The man reversed his weapon like a quarterstaff. Six feet of studded beech rose and descended and the Kielmark's smile vanished with a gasp. The flag-bearer laughed, backed by sudden ugly silence. The halberd's steel-shod butt carved arcs in the air as the guardsman raised his weapon for a second blow, then a third.

Emien shrank in distaste from his place at Tathagres' side. He barely heard the reply which emerged half-strangled from the Kielmark's throat. The King responded with evident displeasure. Chain clanked. The halberdier closed once more, and fresh blood spangled the floor.

The play of petty emotion across the royal countenance raised hackles on Emien's neck. In all probability the flag-bearer had told the truth; but in vindication for past dishonor, the King was unwilling to quit. The boy felt his stomach twist; linked with revulsion came cold fear that one day the man in chains would be himself. Harrowed by vivid imagination, he saw accusers lined up to condemn him, his drowned father closely followed by mother, sister, and the sailors he had abused on Crow's pinnace. Beyond stood four deckhands sold to the galleys on Skane's Edge; these were joined by the King's youngest page boy and a fat leering guardsman he had cheated into subservience at cards. Each blow that fell upon the Kielmark made Emien flinch and sweat.

The officers soon tired of the sport. Only the King remained unsatisfied. The abuse continued, ascending in violence until furnishings rocked and scattered before the halberdier's obedient enthusiasm. Repelled to the verge of nausea, Emien pressed his palms to his face. And spurred by her squire's discomfort, Tathagres stood up.

Light from the windows sparkled over white mail as she picked her way around the overturned rungs of a chair. "Your Grace, the prisoner is no longer a threat to our position. The Thienz assures it. And with the Kielmark hostage, any captains who remain loyal can be controlled. The Gierj will gain you ships in time, but not if you waste the opportunity."

The halberdier straightened over the Kielmark's sagging form, uncertain. At last, with a wave of bored acquiescence, the King ordered the sovereign of Cliffhaven removed to the east keep dungeon.

The victim staggered badly as the soldiers dragged him from the hall. Shocked by his halting progress, Emien squeezed his eyes closed. A steward mounted the dais with a tray of wine and poured glasses in celebration of the victory. The Warlord-General issued orders to complete occupation of the fortress. The flag-bearer volunteered to close the boom across the harbor; he left with a junior officer and two guardsmen. The remaining troops were dispatched, some under orders to search the town and a few to stand watch in the anteroom. Boots tramped across rumpled carpeting and a blood-spattered expanse of marble with casual disregard; the Kielmark's legendary might was broken. His conquerers answered orders with a cheerful swagger, certain of fame and spoils.

Once the light tower was manned and the town proved deserted, servants arrived and straightened the disarranged furnishings. Emien paid little notice. Concerned with his own thoughts, he lingered when the Thienz was summoned. While the Warlord-General, Lord Sholl, and Tathagres seated themselves on the dais with the officers to conduct their council of conquest, the fisherman's son from Imrill Kand watched on the sidelines, plotting his mistress' downfall.

Motionless where he had fallen when the guards flung him through the door, the Kielmark sprawled face down in the same stone cell where he had lately imprisoned Jaric. Bruised, bloodied, beaten, he did not budge, even to ask for water. The King's guardsmen secured his chains and locked the door. Gloating over his defeat, they left him in darkness without bothering to post any sentry.

An hour passed, then two. Metal scraped faintly beneath the floor. A length of flagstone shifted, raised, and a stealthy whisper issued from a tunnel beneath. "Lord?"

Chain rattled as the Kielmark stirred. He turned his head and spoke through cracked lips. "No guard."

"Fires!" said the man in the hole. "They're fools, then."

The Kielmark offered no comment. Eager hands levered the stone aside and a man emerged, blindly drawing candle and striker from a pouch at his belt. Light bloomed beneath his fingers, revealing the intent features of the man who had played the flute in the courtyard. Still reeking of ale, one of the dancers climbed out after him, armed to the teeth and dangerously sober. He drew a key from his tunic, bent over the Kielmark, and swiftly unlocked the fetters.

Crusted cuffs fell open. In slow painful stages, the Kielmark rolled over. His expression hid very little. Cliffhaven's two wiliest captains looked on with concern and wisely offered no assistance as he sat up. Even by the weak flicker of candleflame, they could see things had gone badly. The Kielmark's ribs and shoulders were crisscrossed with mottled welts; his back was little better. To touch even in kindness would only increase his discomfort.

One of the captains swore.

The Kielmark looked up. His eyes shone baleful and pale beneath eyebrows matted with dried blood. "Did the signal arrive from the straits?"

The flute player raked dirt-streaked fingers through his hair. "Nine dead, a score and four with burns major and minor and the rest of the lot lying about in the brush, croaking like frogs, their throats left raw from screaming. But watching, they said, for your banner in the tower." He paused, suddenly contrite. "Are your ribs intact? You weren't exactly acting after the bit with the flagpole. Corley says he only followed orders, Lord, but there's a wager going round that you'll break both his legs."

The Kielmark grunted. Split lips parted across his teeth. "I'll settle for the Kingsmen's heads," he said bluntly. "On with it, then."

He pinched out the candle. Darkness dropped, hiding his suffering through a terrible interval while the captains lowered him into the tunnel.

Beneath the high vaulted arches of Cliffhaven's great hall, the Thienz coughed through its gills. It leapt to its feet with a shrill scream of warning and suddenly staggered, a crossbow quarrel bristling from its throat. Knocked backward by the impact it fell, smashing through the rungs of an ivory-inlaid globe stand. Keithland rolled across the rug and the chamber erupted into chaos.

"Treachery!" shouted Lord Sholl. He dove behind his stout oaken chair just as the tapestries slithered into heaps, revealing arrowslits cut through the stone walls behind. A storm of shafts flickered past the arched windows. The royal chief advisor rammed face-first into oak, pinned by an arrow through his back. The Grand Warlord-General slipped to the floor beside him, his mouth stretched wide in surprise. The advisor's flesh crumpled before his eyes, melting into a form not recognizable as human; but sorcery blazed above the dais, dazzling his vision before the change was complete. He died still wondering whether a demon had shared his salt.

Shielded by the crackling blaze of Tathagres' conjuring, Emien crouched in terror, while on the dais around him the royal council members slumped in their seats, struck down by enemy arrows. Since the Thienz's first cry, his mistress had leapt to her feet, her hands clenched over the band at her throat. She raised a crackling arch of light over the King. Any shaft which touched it exploded into sparks. But the rest of the arrows hissed to their marks with grisly accuracy; in seconds, Emien, Kisburn, and Tathagres became the sole survivors amid a slaughtered circle of officials. Yet she dared not relax her defenses. The archers continued to fire.

"All is not lost," said Tathagres urgently. "Help get the King to safety."

Unearthly reflections flickered across her face, spangling her jewels in light. Immersed in her wardspell, Emien felt currents of energy tingle across his skin. Ozone stung his nostrils. Suddenly exhilarated by his narrow escape from death, the boy caught the royal wrist and urged the stunned King of Kisburn to rise.

"You must walk, your Grace." Tathagres gestured toward the anteroom. "Outside I can summon the Gierj. Hurry."

The King rallied scattered wits. Shafts banged and clattered across the marble floor, deflected by Tathagres' sorcery. Seizing the chance for survival, Kisburn permitted Emien to hustle him down the dais steps. Tathagres followed on their heels, still conjuring. The attackers switched to spears. Energy crackled and whined overhead, devouring wood and steel with seemingly endless appetite. The party crossed the hall at a run.

Carnage met them before they reached the door, as guards posted in the anteroom belatedly acted in their King's defense. Men charged in disciplined formation, shields raised over their heads. But the tasteless opulence of the Kielmark's decor was designed to foil attack. The lines broke into muddled knots as men dodged between tables and chests. A lampstand toppled with a screeching crash and swords tangled in statuary. The archers slaughtered rescuers at leisure.

The King shouted and extended his arm toward an injured officer.

"Prevent him," Tathagres said quickly. "We can't stop here."

Her violet eyes raked the King with ruthless calculation; she meant the King no kindness, Emien observed. He gripped the royal tunic with bruising force. Thin shoulders jerked under the velvet. Emien knew a thrill of excitement. Never before had a man born to power suffered discomfort at his hands. He shoved the King toward the door. Kisburn stumbled gracelessly forward. Emien followed, stepping callously on the fingers of the officer who thrashed on the floor. With Tathagres a step behind, he plunged through the arch into the anteroom, beyond range of enemy weapons.

The heavy iron-bound panels beyond were closed, *barred from without*, cornering them like mice in a culvert. Emien whirled. He yelled warning, just as the archway leading to the hall exploded in a burst of red light.

Tathagres spoke through the glare. "Move aside. *Hurry!*"

She intended to break the doors with sorcery. Emien dove clear, dragging the King by the collar. The spell blazed at his heels. Shadows streaked the anteroom floor, spattered across with sparks, and the panels sagged on their hinges. Wood and steel unraveled into smoke, rendered ineffective as the weapons set against them in the main hall. But when Tathagres followed the King through the gap, she lacked her usual lithe grace. Use of sorcery taxed her, Emien realized; the discovery pleased him.

If her powers were limited by ordinary human endurance, he wondered how long she could continue before exhaustion made her careless.

A guardsman sprawled dead before the doorway, the handle of a throwing knife sunk between his shoulder blades. Tathagres saw him and stopped. With enemies about the fortress and no time left for etiquette, she spun and faced the King.

"Where are your personal chambers? Take me there quickly. Your Grace cannot be properly defended in the open."

Reliant upon her protection, the King answered at once. But Emien noticed she kept one hand poised on her necklace as if she expected resistance. When the Warlord-General's aide ran into the corridor, a score of guardsmen at his heels, her expression showed open annoyance. *She regarded them as interference,* the boy deduced. With the conquest of Cliffhaven thrown into question, Kisburn's men were allies no longer. Tathagres intended to claim the Keys to Elrinfaer by force.

The aide saw the corpse. He skidded to a halt with a rattle of mail and gear and saluted smartly. "Your Grace, the enemy has closed and barred the main gates of the fortress. Archers fire on the courtyard. We've had to move the company inside."

He paused, breathless, and waited. But without the advice of Lord Sholl and his council, the King seemed strangely indecisive. He made no effort to assert himself as Tathagres intervened.

"Forget the gates. There's been an attempt on your sovereign's life. The Warlord-General lies dead." She jerked her head at the charred ruin of the doors to the main hall. "You, guards. Block this entrance." To the aide she added, "Fetch reinforcements. There must be passages behind the walls. Purge them if you can. You will receive further orders after I have seen your King secure."

The King accepted Tathagres' judgment without question. He dismissed the aide and fled in the direction of his chamber. The Kielmark's fortress proved a maze of stairs and angled passages. Winded after his rush from the main hall, Emien halted with Tathagres and the King before a brass-studded portal. Two of Kisburn's personal honor guards flanked the entrance, vigilant and alert at their posts.

Tathagres' aggression softened like steel under velvet. She waited with poised patience while the guardsmen saluted their sovereign Lord, then stepped smartly aside to admit him. Tired, shaken, and wheezing, the King leaned heavily on the latch. The massive panels swung open, revealing a wide chamber richly carpeted in scarlet and gold. Kisburn hastened to a side table where a tray waited with a bottle of wine from the Kielmark's private cellars. Ignoring the gold-rimmed goblet, he raised the flask to his lips. Fine crystal rattled against his teeth as he swallowed and his fingers marked sweaty prints on the flask.

A choked-off cry made him start. The king whirled, dribbling wine down his chin. Beyond the opened doorway, Tathagres lowered one of the honor guards, dead, across the corpse of the first. She straightened with wicked intent, pulled the heavy panels closed, then placed her back against them.

From the side, Emien saw her grip the latch until her knuckles blanched against the brass. Fatigued at last by her sorceries, she used the doors more to support her weight than to forestall attempted escape.

But her eyes stayed cruelly alert as she regarded her prey across the airy expanse of the chamber. "Get me the Keys to Elrinfaer, *your Grace*." She turned her shoulder to the wood, one hand raised to her necklace. "Or shall I force them from you?"

The King dropped the wine. The flask toppled across the tray and shattered, spattering glass over his gold-bordered tunic. A stain darkened the carpet under his boots as he gaped in astonished disbelief. Tathagres had betrayed him; Emien made no effort to contain the elated laughter which arose in his throat.

Jolted by the sound, Kisburn recovered a shadow of his

royal propriety. He shook his head, wine-streaked fingers clamped over the table edge. "But the Chief Advisor assured me—"

"Lord Sholl is dead," Tathagres interrupted. Amethysts flashed as her fingers jumped against her neckband. *"Fetch the Keys."*

Why does she hesitate? Selfishly eager, Emien wondered. Usually his mistress flaunted power, taking pleasure in intimidation and superiority. Emboldened by the thought that Tathagres might be tiring, Emien hoped the King would resist, compelling her to react until exhaustion lowered her guard.

But the murders in the council had shattered Kisburn's confidence. Deprived of the support of Lord Sholl and the Warlord-General, he lacked the backbone to fight. Emien looked on in disgust while his shoulders sagged, as if the gem-crusted chain of office which circled his shoulders suddenly grew too weighty for him to endure.

"I will yield you the Keys." Kisburn blotted his brow on his brocade cuff and glowered at the woman who blocked the chamber door. Robbed of dignity by defeat, his tone turned querulous. "I hope you have decency enough to leave after this. For your sorceries and your demons have brought my kingdom to the verge of ruin."

The King pulled a ring from a chain at his belt and crossed the room. Sullen and slow, he knelt before the heavy steel-bound chest placed beside the hearth.

"Go with him," said Tathagres to Emien. Her voice held a brittle edge. "Be certain he tries no tricks. The Keys of Elrinfaer lie in a box of black basalt. You will know it by Anskiere's seal set in gold on the top."

Emien obeyed, feigning nonchalance. While Kisburn unlocked the chest and lifted the lid, the boy glanced furtively at Tathagres; her attention appeared absorbed by the King, who reached with jerky, uncertain motions and shuffled among the contents in the chest. Emien sidled closer. Careful to hide his movements, he raised his hand to his belt, closed his fingers over his knife, and pretended to peer over the King's shoulder. Slowly, nervously, he inched his blade from its sheath.

"Here." Kisburn straightened, a cube of dark stone balanced across his palm. The symbol of Anskiere's mastery was inlaid in shining gold on its polished surface, a stormfalcon centered within three concentric circles. To Emien, the seal promised power, permanent escape from the sovereign tyranny of sorcery. With a rising surge of triumph, he seized the royal shoulder and sank his dagger upward to the hilt in the soft flesh of the King's lower back.

Royal blood flooded warmly over his wrist. The King cried out, twisted, and sank in agony to one knee. Anskiere's box slipped from loosened fingers. Emien caught the object, felt its solid corners gouge his skin. Too late he noticed the cube possessed neither seam nor catch. If the stone contained an object of power, he had no time to search for the secret. With the hair rising at the nape of his neck, Emien straightened and faced his mistress.

Tathagres stepped clear of the doorway, both hands in contact with her neckband. Her murdered ally writhed in agony on the hearth, but she made no effort to help him. Slim, straight, and savagely beautiful in her silver mail, she met her squire's defiance with dangerous fury. "Fool," she said coldly. "Give the Keys of Elrinfaer to me."

Taen cried out from the depths of dream trance. Sweat dampened her brow and she twisted against Jaric's hands. He held her shoulders firmly, preventing her from thrashing against the gritty wall of the cavern. The tunnel which led from the east keep dungeon was narrow, hastily constructed, and shored up with scraps of timber and undressed rocks. Sloping gently, it opened into a muddy cave whose entrance lay hidden behind an outcrop above the harbor. There by the light of a single lantern a wizened healer cleaned and dressed the

Kielmark's abrasions with old, careful hands. Throughout the disturbance, his touch on the wounds stayed neat and sure, and if his salves were astringent enough to make Jaric's eyes water, the King of Renegades ignored the sting. Like the Firelord's heir, he sat hunched and still, attention fixed with unwavering intensity upon the dream-weaver who sought news of the trap which closed over King Kisburn's attack force in the fortress above.

Taen shivered and abruptly opened her eyes. In a voice which trembled with shock, she said, "Emien has murdered the King. He wishes Tathagres' death also and has seized the Keys of Elrinfaer on the chance their powers might prove useful against her. As yet Anskiere's sorceries are beyond his ability to master."

"He's ignorant." The Kielmark fretted as the healer wrapped a fresh bandage on his forearm. "The Keys have no purpose except to preserve the wards over Elrinfaer Tower."

Taen offered no reply. Suspended once more in the dream link, she sagged against Jaric's shoulder. But the tension did not smooth from her young face as she merged her consciousness with Emien. Her hands remained clenched in her lap. The Firelord's heir stroked tangled hair from her brow, unhappily aware the Keys' recovery might now cost Taen's brother his life. More than ever before, Jaric wished he had insisted the dream-weaver leave before Kisburn's assault as the Vaere had directed.

But Taen remained unaware of the concern which troubled the Firelord's heir. Absorbed by the mysteries of her craft, she heard nothing as the Kielmark swore and excused the healer with an irritable flick of his wrist. Bound to her brother, she stood in a room paneled in gilt and cedar, the chilly weight of the Keys to Elrinfaer Tower poised between sweating fingers.

Tathagres confronted Emien by the doorway, both hands clenched to her neckband. "I warned you, boy." Though her tone was harsh with threat, she seemed strangely reluctant to engage sorcery and attack. Taen expanded her focus, seeking the reason; she caught the elusive flicker of something similar to fear in the woman's violet eyes.

But fatigue made Taen sloppy. Her dream search brushed Emien's frame of reference, tripped it slightly out of balance. The boy also sensed Tathagres' hesitation. Suddenly brazenly unafraid, he laughed and crossed the floor, treading fragments of glass into the carpet. Taen drew back, alarmed. But Tathagres watched her squire's approach without anxiety, cold calculation on her face. She did not shrink as he stopped, so close he hedged her against the brass-rimmed wood of the door frame. Neither did she flinch as, with a smile of insolent malice, he twisted bloody fingers in her hair and kissed the angry line of her lips.

Although her fingers never left the band at her neck, Tathagres softened slightly under his touch. Only when the boy stepped back and presented the Keys of Elrinfaer with exaggerated courtesy did she relax and lower her hands.

Tapped into dream link, Taen felt satisfaction flood like ice water through Tathagres' thoughts. *The boy could still be managed.* Relieved she would not need to contest him for possession of the Keys, she glanced toward the fireplace. The King lay dead by the andiron, his opened mouth pooled in blood. He could no longer be used as a hostage to threaten cooperation from the men-at-arms; to escape the Kielmark's trap she would need sorcery and help from her demon allies.

Taen dissolved her contact before the idea finished forming in Tathagres' mind. Once the witch engaged her sorceries, the link might reveal a dream-weaver's presence. Unwilling to risk notice by the demons, Taen wakened in the earthy darkness of the cave. She sat up, weary to the point where even her bones ached.

"Well?" The Kielmark knotted the ends of the bandage across his wrist, using one grimy fist and his teeth. He paid no heed to the healer's wince of annoyance. "What did you find?"

Taen met his impatience with words stripped bare by exhaustion. "Kisburn is dead. Tathagres has the Keys. She intends to depart for Elrinfaer at once, with Emien."

The Kielmark crowed loudly and grinned at Jaric. "We have her boxed. Every gate in the fortress is barred from the outside and covered by archers in concealment. The fleet arrives with reinforcements by afternoon."

"No." Taen shook her head, desolate in Jaric's arms. "Archers cannot stop her." She drew a quivering breath and qualified. "The witch calls upon the Gierj even as we speak. The instant the melding trance is complete, she will draw upon their power and transfer."

"She won't get away with it." Linen parted with a coarse scream of sound as the Kielmark tore away the excess bandage. With single-minded disregard for his stiffened, abused body, he surged to his knees and scrambled across the cave to the brush which screened the entrance. There he grabbed the bow which waited in a niche already strung, and nocked an arrow with a streamer affixed to one end. Scarlet flecks soaked the bandage as he flexed his wrist and drew.

The Kielmark aimed high and released; the arrow leapt outward in a long steep arc, streamer trailing like a comet's tail across the overcast sky. The shaft slowed, almost hesitated midflight, then plunged earthward with a rush. Behind the Kielmark's bulk, Taen and Jaric watched it fall, cognizant of the fact that the signal sentenced brave men to die. The arrow commanded the first stage of the attack to retake the harbor; but the fleet which should have supported the strategy had yet to breast the horizon.

CHAPTER XXIII

Elrinfaer

TATHAGRES ENGAGED THE POW-
ers of the Gierj-demons and Kisburn's private chamber dissolved in a shower of light. Red-orange sparks streaked across
Emien's vision and vanished in a scorching blast of wind. Unlike the earlier transfer from the ice cliffs, the boy felt a bucking
lurch. Sorcery whipped his hair into snarls as he tumbled
through air and darkness. He landed gasping beside his mistress on a beach laced with stinking strands of kelp.

Emien looked up, disappointed. A glance showed them still
on Cliffhaven; but outside the fortress walls just a stone's
throw from the dockside. Bruised and winded, Emien struggled to his feet. Sand dribbled out of his cuffs as he straightened his swordbelt and extended his hand to Tathagres.

She accepted his help with none of the acid unpleasantness
he remembered from Skane's Edge. The sorcery of the transfer
had taxed her. Her delicate features were drawn and pale under
a light sheen of sweat. Tremors of fatigue passed through

her as she gripped Emien's arm. She stumbled to her feet as if the demon's powers had left her slightly dazed.

Emien watched like a starved cat, fingers inching toward his sword. Yet Tathagres rallied before he gathered the nerve to exploit her weakness. She swept a rapacious glance across strand, warehouses, and the line of the horizon beyond the boom which closed the harbor, and thought rapidly.

"Find a boat quickly and get us to sea." She flicked sand from her hair with an arrogant toss of her wrist. "To transfer to Elrinfaer I must merge again with the Gierj. This cannot be attempted within reach of men-at-arms."

Whether she referred to Kisburn's men or the Kielmark's pirates made no difference; both sides would carry steel. Emien complied without argument. Outgoing tide creamed over a breakwater fifty paces to the south. Beyond, the shore lifted into rugged bastions of rock too steep for safe anchorage. Northward past the untenanted jumble of dockside taverns and shops a wharf extended beyond the corner of a warehouse. Black against leaden clouds, an angular assembly of spars and rigging reared above the shingled roofs.

Emien pointed. "There."

Tathagres nodded. Together they ran over sand still packed from the tide. The beach ended, shored up by a breakwater of granite. Emien caught Tathagres' elbow, steadying her as she climbed over rocks crusted with barnacles. A push would tumble her onto the jagged stones below. Since she intended a transfer to Elrinfaer, Emien chose patience. Pressed flat against weather-beaten boards, he hurried past the warehouse. The boat lay tied thirty feet out on the pier. She appeared unguarded. After a hasty glance at her lines Emien saw why, and swore under his breath. The boat was aged and ungainly. Yet her planking showed signs of recent repair and she still looked fit to sail.

Tathagres shared none of the boy's annoyance. Although she appeared peaked and tired, she spoke before he managed any complaint. "The boat must serve. The Kielmark has cleared his harbor of everything else."

"Let's hope he was thorough." Emien grimaced. "If that relic sails at all, she'll go clunky as a farmer's wooden bucket."

Suddenly a shout rang from the alley behind the warehouse. Steel clanged, announcing a rapid exchange of swordplay. Out of time to seek options, Emien caught his mistress's elbow and bolted for the dock. The foolish old fishing craft was surely preferable to getting trapped like rats on the shore.

Emien leapt across three feet of water onto the port gunwale; an engraved plaque beneath his boot named the craft *Callinde*. Leaving the docklines for Tathagres, Emien dove for the mess of rope at the base of the mast and uncleated the main halyard.

Callinde rocked sharply as Tathagres followed him on board. Without looking around, Emien hoisted. The heavy yard rattled up the mast, unfurling a patched square of sail. "Cast off," he said tersely, and whipped the line onto a cleat. "Let the stern off last."

Tathagres ducked forward, shadowed by canvas as Emien raised the jib. Wind caught the clew, snaking lines across the deck. The boy dug aft beneath bunched acres of spanker for the knots which lashed the tiller. His hand slammed into floor boards and he cursed. Antique to her last fitting, *Callinde* came equipped with a steering oar.

Line splashed into water and the high curved prow swung free. Tathagres raised the spanker as Emien slashed the stern line with his sword. *Callinde* drifted from the wharf, sails flogging aloft. Emien dove for the sheets, dragged them hissing through the blocks. Canvas fell taut with a whump; the old craft shouldered on starboard tack across the bay.

Emien hauled on the steering oar, eyes trained forward. Kisburn's two ships lay moored to leeward; water stretched ahead in an open line to the sea. Emien felt his hair prickle at the base of his neck.

"Mistress!" He bent to see past the spanker and discovered her kneeling by the mast. "The boom is gone from the entrance of the harbor."

Tathagres hurried to the gunwale and looked out. Her voice came back above the crash of spray beneath the keel. "Kielmark's work. The flag-bearer must have turned coat again."

A deep rumble sounded across the bay. Emien glanced aft, distressed. The entire seaward side of a warehouse slid open to reveal stone crenelations inside. Two catapults reared behind and the barbed bolts of four loaded arbalests glittered through notches cut in the wall.

"Sail!" Tathagres' voice broke. "If they loose any bolts on us, I can manage."

Emien dragged *Callinde* straight—and shouted. One of Kisburn's ships had launched a longboat. Drawn by the frosty gleam of Tathagres' hair, six seamen bent over the looms, driving their craft straight across his path. Emien adjusted lines and tried frantically to coax more speed from his sails.

The first of the arbalests released. But *Callinde* was not the target; the bolt whined overhead and drove with a plume of spray into the waves off *Morra*'s stern.

"They aim to disable the Gierj!" Tathagres leaned over *Callinde*'s thwart and shouted to the officer in the approaching longboat. "Return to your ship and man your weapons. Defend the demons from steel!"

The officer saluted. His oarsmen reversed stroke, turning the longboat aside. Emien corrected *Callinde*'s course. Another quarrel tore through the air, followed by a third which grazed through *Morra*'s mooring ropes. The men at the arbalests would shortly perfect their aim, and over the splash of *Callinde*'s passage Emien heard the sour clank of the winch which cocked a catapult.

Tathagres crouched beneath the gunwale. "I'm going to summon the Gierj and pull us out before the enemy spoil their powers with steel. Make for the open sea. Whatever befalls, I must reach Elrinfaer with all speed."

Tathagres settled against the mast. She bowed her head on crossed arms, her hands in light contact with her neckband, and slipped gradually into rapport with the demons. Emien steered against rising gusts, irritated to discover how soft he had grown during his months at court. *Callinde* tossed like a wayward horse over the crests, wrenching his shoulders without mercy. Emien hauled her straight and bitterly cursed her designer. *Morra* fell slowly astern. Carried downwind, the keening chant of the Gierj-demons pierced through the rush of the wake. In a moment, his mistress would focus enough power for transfer. Frustrated by the speed of her magic, Emien hoped *Callinde* would end on a reef.

That instant the first catapult launched with a crack. Emien whirled, saw a dark line writhe in an arc across the sky. His joy abruptly disintegrated. The enemy fired chain shot. Steel links wailed through the air and splashed with a geyser of spray a scant yard shy of *Morra*'s bowsprit. Disturbed by the brief proximity of the steel, the Gierj chant dipped and leveled. Emien cursed in earnest. Iron in any form disrupted their powers; one strike to *Morra*'s rigging would cripple both flagship and demons.

Screened by the brush at the lip of the cave, the Kielmark sprawled on his belly, a brass-banded ship's glass focused on the harbor. Glad not to rely on Taen's talents for information, he watched soldiers delivered ashore by enemy longboats as they rushed in black lines for the warehouse. In a moment the men who manned the embrasure would be under attack. The whistle of the Gierj-demons shrilled across the harbor, eerily ascending in pitch. Unmoved as a boulder, the Kielmark counted attackers and calculated. The catapults had maybe three minutes to set their range.

An arbalest released. Steel rushed through the air, banged

soundly into wood. The Gierj wavered and fell off pitch. The Kielmark lowered his glass and grinned boyishly at Jaric. "They'll have her," he said. "Quit sulking."

Jaric did not answer. Tense and still by the Kielmark's side, he fingered the blade of his unsheathed sword and tried not to think while Mathieson's boat drove steadily seaward, her sails curved taut to the wind. Taen had tried vainly to ease Jaric's discomfort since the moment Emien had slashed the docklines. The possibility the Keys to Elrinfaer might slip beyond reach troubled the boy less than his oath to Keldric that *Callinde* would be treasured and kept safe.

"Well, don't rust your fittings with tears," said the Kielmark. But his harsh face reflected sympathy and the Fire-lord's heir did not weep. "If we don't get flamed by Gierj in the next minute and a half I'll loan you *Troessa*. She's faster than *Callinde* and rigged for quick handling."

A catapult cracked from the warehouse. The Kielmark jerked the glass to his eye in time to see a sharpened length of chain snag *Morra*'s headstay. Steel whipped in an arc, slashing among tarred line, and the foretopmast jerked, angled brokenly forward. Chain slithered to the deck; and the Gierj chant unraveled into dissonance.

Tathagres cried out sharply from her trance. Sparks crackled across her knuckles and winked out. Flung back against the mast, she lay still, her throat bared to the sky and her hands slack by her sides. Emien could not tell whether she had died or was only unconscious. He dared not leave the helm to check.

Ragged shouting broke out astern. The roof of the warehouse which housed the weaponry burst into flame, smudging the sky with smoke. But the catapults launched still, their aim corrected and deadly. More chain shot scythed through rigging, leaving a trail of wreckage. Sailors died trying to clear the steel from *Morra*'s gear, while quarrels from the arbalests pocked her paint with scars. The Gierj were crippled; their chant rose into ragged wails of pain and tailed off into silence. By the time the men-at-arms overran the warehouse and fought the crew who manned the arbalests to a standstill, the entire forward section of the ship stood riddled with bolts. To remove the steel and deliver the demons from agony would require a crew and tools and hours of time.

Emien looked away from the harbor, his face a mask of disgust. The deckhands feared the Gierj; the confusion set loose by the Kielmark's ruse would grant them excuse enough to upset discipline. *Tide against a sand castle*, Emien thought, reminded of a bitter expression from boyhood. Kisburn's officers would never set *Morra* to rights. He had no choice but sail for Elrinfaer alone.

Callinde breasted the waves, steady despite her mulish lines. She reached the headlands of Cliffhaven's harbor faster than the boy expected. He glanced toward Tathagres. Sprawled like a porcelain doll on the floorboards, she showed no sign of consciousness. Emien licked salty lips. He might easily knife her as she lay helpless. Once he stole the necklace, he could at last bring vengeance on Anskiere.

Confident of his plan, Emien turned *Callinde* into the wind. The boat wallowed, jostling Tathagres' limp form. Emien ignored her, rummaging in a locker until he located a ship's glass. This time he would not be balked by carelessness. Bracing his foot on the thwart, he lifted the glass to his eye and swept it across the sea to check whether Kisburn's patrol ship lay in his path.

But the horizon was not empty as he expected. Etched like scrimshaw against a taut band of sky stood a line of masts, each flying the sea wolf blazon of the Kielmark. A wave lifted *Callinde*'s prow. Water broke with a hiss of foam beneath her keel as Emien crossed to the opposite thwart and trained his glass to the south. Ships approached from that quarter also, nearer still, and with the wind behind them. Carrying every stitch of canvas, the Kielmark's fleet returned to defend their island.

Emien collapsed the glass with a snap and sprang back to the helm. *Morra* and her sister ship were doomed. Caught in the path of two fleets, Emien's sole chance was to turn west on a reach and sail for the open sea.

The boy flung his weight against the oar. *Callinde* answered and headed off; wind filled the sails with a bang, jerked her into thirty degrees of heel. The cant of the deck tossed Tathagres limply into the bilge. Emien had no time to drag her clear. To port a brigantine peeled away from the pack and steered northwest to intercept him.

Unlike a tiller, a steering oar could not be lashed to hold a fixed course. Emien cursed the fact while the sky off the bow darkened under an angry rim of cloud. Squalls threatened. A prudent sailor would shorten sail. But to heave to, even to reef canvas, would cause him fatal delay. Gusts whistled through *Callinde*'s rigging. Spray rushed in sheets over the bow and the steering oar clunked and twisted under Emien's hands, difficult to control with so much sail aloft. He clenched his teeth, watching through slitted eyes as the brigantine closed on *Callinde*'s port quarter. Raindrops slashed his face. Emien hoped the storm would hide him. He raised his head and shouted crazily at the sky. Clouds opened and *Callinde* drove, reeling, into the opaque flood of a downpour.

Emien laughed and threw his shoulder into the oar. From where he stood at the helm the headsails where lost in murk. He headed off, saved from pursuit by gray curtains of rain. Rope burned through his fingers as he eased the lines, setting *Callinde* downwind to run with the squall. The Kielmark's fleet could never locate so small a quarry in such poor visibility; once the weather eased, he could put about to Elrinfaer where the power he ached to possess waited to be claimed.

The rain ended at midnight. Wind shifted to the north and clouds scudded across a burnished quarter moon. Needles of reflection gleamed over the wave crests as *Callinde* rolled on a broad reach, her wake a chuckle of foam astern. Cliffhaven had long since vanished behind the horizon. Secure enough to rest, Emien hauled the steering oar with chilled fingers. The headsails backed with a whispered flop. Hove to, *Callinde* drifted, silent and alone.

In the aft locker Emien found a rigging knife. He slipped it quietly from the sheath and tested the edge with his finger. The steel was well honed. With the blade poised in his hand, the boy crept forward. Tathagres lay sprawled on her back, white tunic stained from the bilge. Her face seemed girlish and innocent in the moonlight. Tumbled hair sparked like frost over wrists so slim that Emien could encircle them easily with the thumb and forefinger of one hand. The mail over her breast glittered faintly. Disappointed to find she still breathed, Emien stole closer, fixed with predatory intensity upon the thin gleam of gold at her neck.

He stepped into shadow under the sail. Suddenly his foot turned on the ship's glass, left against a stay. Brass clanged loudly into wood and Tathagres opened her eyes.

Emien froze. He buried the knife in his cloak with a whispered curse and bent with feigned concern.

Tathagres regarded him, chilly awareness in her violet eyes. She spoke with languid unconcern. "Oh yes, you're very clever." Her smile held stinging viciousness. "But I fear not clever enough. We are pursued."

Emien drew a frustrated breath. "I lost the brigantine in a squall line."

"No." Tathagres sat up, her expression haughty beneath tangled hair. "Not the Kielmark," she said. "Your own sister would stop you now. Taen follows in a boat built for speed. Are you going to sit here waiting for her?"

Emien jerked. Steel quivered in his poised fist.

Unsurprised by the knife, Tathagres laughed with wounding scorn. "Fool. We lost Cliffhaven because Taen gained a dream-weaver's mastery from the Vaere."

Emien's expression lay in shadow. But he listened; the hand which held the knife steadied until moonlight traced the blade silver against the darkness. Waves slapped *Callinde*'s sides, jostling her tackle aloft. Tathagres judged her moment and resumed.

"Your sister blinded the Thienz, tricked us all with illusion so the King would walk into a trap." The witch delivered her final line with calculated malice. "She intended you to die with them, Emien."

Breath hissed between his teeth. Coiled dangerously on the edge of action, the boy lifted his head and looked northward. Faint as a spark, a light gleamed on the horizon, too orange to be mistaken for starlight.

"The boat's name is *Troessa*," Tathagres added. "She was granted by the Kielmark as a reward for the ruin of Kisburn's men. Put up your knife. Else Taen will reach Elrinfaer before us and perhaps take your life."

The blade flashed and lowered. Emien drew an uneven breath. Wrung by unreasoning rage, he spun on his heel. Returned to the helm, he jabbed the rigging knife into *Callinde*'s sternpost. Then he grabbed the steering oar with a wrench that slammed the fittings and turned the boat southeast. Sails cracked taut against the blocks. The starboard rail lifted as *Callinde* gathered way and headed toward Elrinfaer once more.

Highlighted like a cameo in the moonlight, Emien's profile was a mask of hatred as he steered to thwart the same sister he left Imrill Kand to save. Lost to his rage he paid little heed to the woman who watched from the shadows. Tathagres studied her squire, aware of his lethal edge. She smiled again, well satisfied. The boy would wait to murder until morning when he delivered her to the rock where Elrinfaer Tower rose from the sea.

Tathagres settled back and closed her eyes, hands curved protectively over the black cube of rock which preserved the wards of Elrinfaer. After dawn the purpose of her demon

masters would be accomplished; yet strangely as she drifted
into sleep her limbs twitched as if her dreams held a nightmare
of horrors.

The night wore on. Even Kor's Accursed did not guess that
Taen's talents sheltered another man from notice. Ivainson
Jaric bent with dogged courage over *Troessa*'s helm, his blond
hair gritty with salt. Yet swiftly as the Kielmark's ketch could
sail, Emien was the better seaman. Evenly matched, both boats
plowed through the waves toward Elrinfaer.

The wind slackened to a mere whisper out of the north and
by dawn fog smothered the coast, dense as oiled wool. Steering
Troessa one-handed, Jaric reached across the cockpit and
snuffed the lantern which had lit the compass dial through the
night. Taen lay in the bow, collapsed in exhausted sleep, her
hair spilled like a snarl of weed over her shoulders. Slim hands
pillowed her cheek against the mild roll of the boat.

In the half light Jaric could almost forget how thin she was;
mist obscured the marks of fatigue beneath her eyes, softening
the angles where the bones pressed sharply against her skin.
The defense of Cliffhaven had worn her, body and spirit. For
three days straight she had spun interlocking veils of illusion
over the island, concealing the Kielmark's intentions from the
Thienz while men fashioned facsimiles of brigantines from
derelict hulls and half-rotted fishing vessels. She had engaged
her talents in the very presence of demons, brashly sending and
receiving messages from the Kielmark to his captains. All that
she achieved was out of loyalty to Anskiere. The thought made
Jaric feel inadequate. At the dockside when *Troessa* departed,
the King of Renegades had sworn Taen an oath of debt, his
surly features traced with tears.

Asleep, her dream-weaver's robes soiled with dirt and salt,
she seemed a fragile child. Nothing about her appearance suggested a Vaere-trained enchantress; innocent features reflected

no trace of the courage which enabled her to pursue a beloved brother as an enemy.

Sailing under a dank layer of fog, Jaric regarded the girl who had started out a lame fisherman's daughter from Imrill Kand. In her unremarkable beginning he found proof that strength could arise out of weakness. The realization lent hope that someday he might discover confidence and master his lot as Firelord's heir.

An hour passed, then two. Mist clung dense as eiderdown over the face of the sea. *Troessa* ghosted forward by compass heading alone, and over the creak of her gear Jaric heard the distant boom of breakers. Unless their course had been spoiled by current, the shores of Elrinfaer lay ahead.

Taen woke from sleep with a sudden cry of alarm. She threw herself at the bow. "No! Emien, no!"

Jaric leapt forward, caught her slight waist. His hands tangled in long dark hair as he dragged her back, shivering and weeping in his arms. "Taen, what's wrong?"

Sails ruffled overhead as *Troessa* swung pilotless into the wind. Jaric cradled the enchantress against his shoulder and ached for the power to shelter her. Surf crashed, nearer and more distinct, over Elrinfaer's unseen shore. Taen looked up with anguished eyes. The dream link which woke her to nightmare ripped out of control and swept Jaric into rapport.

Possessed by ice-edged hatred, Jaric gripped *Callinde*'s thwart. She lay beached on the cream sand of a cove, her sails left carelessly sheeted. Yet the mishandling of the boat did not trouble him, since the emotions he experienced were another's; following the slender white-haired figure of his mistress, he leapt ashore in Emien's boots, fingers clenched round the haft of an unsheathed rigging knife.

Deadly, silent, he coiled his body and sprang. Steel gleamed in the fog. Consumed by poisoned triumph, he raised his arm and buried his blade to the crossguard in the woman's defenseless back.

Tathagres staggered and fell, pale hair scattered across un-marked sand. Her beautiful features twisted in agony as Emien tore her collar aside, reaching with bloodied fingers for the band of gold beneath. He caught the necklace, twisted fiercely. The metal proved hollow; it crumpled and split, spilling dark liquid over Emien's knuckles. Scalded by caustic reaction, his skin blistered and bled. Emien cried out. He jerked back, just as something *other* stabbed his mind like hot wire.

The contact broke. Wrenched back to *Troessa*'s gentle mo-tion, Jaric stared in horror at the dream-weaver who lay against his shoulder.

Surf boomed loudly, dangerously close. Taen heard, push-ing free of his hold. "Sail!" she said frantically. "Tathagres is dying, and Emien has the Keys."

Jaric stumbled over *Troessa*'s stern seat and threw his weight against the tiller. The ketch swung, maddeningly sluggish. Her canvas ruffled, flopped, and drew taut in the wind. Sudden thunder shook the air. Wind sprang up. A gust tore shrilly through the rigging and *Troessa* jerked sideways onto her thwart.

Taen clung gamely in the bow. With small desperate hands she clawed the jibsheet free. Canvas banged, frayed to tatters by the gusts. Spray dashed madly over the bow. Half-blinded by salt, Jaric fought for control of the helm. Ahead the mist streamed and parted. Hard alee lay a shoreline of terraced rock, and the windowless spire of Elrinfaer Tower raised like a spoke against the sky.

Troessa lifted, flung on the crest of a breaker. Jaric leaned forward, jerked her leaded swing-keel up into its casing. The wave broke with a rush, hurling the boat toward the shore. Jaric caught a hurried glimpse of *Callinde*, pressed flat on her side against a white crescent of beach; then Taen loosened the mainsheet also. The boom swung, blocking his vision. But Jaric needed no sight to confirm the small still form which sprawled beyond, under the edge of the rocks.

Troessa grounded with a scrape. Taen leapt the bowsprit and splashed calf-deep into the cold flood of the sea. Jaric followed. Foam swirled over his boot tops as he yanked a line from the bow. Emptied of weight, the light boat slewed sidewards as the following wave crashed around her rudder. Jaric leaned into the rope, grateful not to be wrestling the heftier bulk of *Callinde*. By the time he crossed shallows to the tide mark, Taen had gone on ahead.

Lightning laced the sky and thunder rumbled. Jaric thrust his hands into *Troessa*'s forward locker and pulled out dagger and sword. Wet leather sloshed against his feet, which became caked with dry sand as he ran up the beach. Ahead, lit by a savage flash of lightning, he saw the dream-weaver crouched over Tathagres' crumpled form.

"Stop Emien!" she shouted over the rising fury of the elements. "I'll stay with her."

Jaric hesitated. Dwarfed by forbidding rocks, he touched his sword hilt with uncertain hands, and wondered what Telemark had felt when he had killed as a mercenary in the Duke of Corlin's army. The thought raised every self-doubt which had poisoned his childhood at Morbrith.

"Go!" Taen's plea was a ragged peal of anguish. "Emien seeks to break the wards over the Tower."

Thunder slammed the air. Jaric shivered. With short sharp motions, he unsheathed sword and dagger. He discarded swordbelt and scabbards in the sand and sprang toward the rocks. Once in Seitforest he had surpassed his limits when Telemark's life lay threatened; now to spare Taen the horror of confronting her brother, he would face Emien with steel, and stop him if he could.

Taen watched through a blur of tears as Jaric vanished up the slope, torn by the insufferable fact that his success depended upon the loss of her only brother. But now was no time to indulge in useless emotions. Mastering herself with iron bravado, she mustered her powers as dream-weaver and centered her thoughts on the woman beneath her hands.

Tathagres lay on her side, hands outflung and still. Her bracelets had carved half moons in the sand under her wrists, and grit clung to her back and shoulders, darkened by spreading blood. Emien had withdrawn the knife and an ugly reddened tear showed through tunic and mail beneath. Taen brushed back a silky fall of hair, baring features whose pale delicacy remained beautiful, even approaching death. For all her Vaere training, Taen could do nothing to save her. But for the sake of her brother, she sent her dream call into the faltering mind beneath her hands.

"Merya?"

Tathagres' lids trembled and opened, baring violet eyes to the sky. Wax-pale lips trembled and almost smiled, for the name Taen used was that given by her mother. Blackness leached through her mind. With a sigh of painful weariness, Tathagres gave in to the ebbing tide; the memory lapsed.

Dream call wrenched her back. "Merya! What has Emien taken?" Desperate to know, Taen caught the fading image of a forest where once a father had forbidden a small girl to play. But the child disobeyed. Laughing, breathless, Merya skipped under the trees on the edge of summer twilight, enticed by the notes of a flute. But the musician ran merrily ahead, ducking through thickets and branches, perpetually out of reach. Suddenly darkness claimed her. Kor's Accursed fitted the collar to her neck, and thereafter she served as Tathagres, her human family forgotten.

Taen clamped her will around the threads of deteriorating life. She forced a desperate question. "The collar. Did it hold crystals from the Sathid?"

Merya/Tathagres quivered. Thoughts flurried like sparks in shadow as she strove to answer the dream-weaver's call. *Emien, warn Emien.* The collar's legacy was misery; woe to the mortal who touched it, for his will would serve the powers of

Kor's Accursed without hope to the end of life. *Warn Emien*, Merya sent, but her breath stopped before the message was complete.

Left no answer but the limitless night of the void, the dream-weaver shivered, wakened to grief and poignant revelation. Freed by death, the woman's peaceful pose suggested the humanity she might have had if her life had been her own. Taen saw that she and the child Merya were more alike than different. Each had been gifted since birth with sensitivity deeper than most human perception. Sheltered by Anskiere, Taen had been sent safely to the Vaere. But Merya, and now Emien, had not been as fortunate.

Lightning snaked across the rocks but no rain fell. Taen raced over sharpened outcrops of shale. Wind rattled the branches of scrub and thorn and thunder shook the ground under her feet. Certain the disturbance in the weather was caused by Emien's meddling with the wards, Taen climbed with desperate haste.

She paused, searched the barren heights, but saw no trace of Jaric or her brother. She engaged her talents to seek, but her dream search was overrun by churning fields of power. The wards over Elrinfaer were stronger than any sorcery in Keithland, Tamlin had said. The Mharg-demons confined there were dangerous enough to destroy all life. Now Emien tried to free them.

Taen plunged over a rise. Breath burned in her lungs. Forbidding against cloud-racked skies, Elrinfaer Tower dominated the ridge beyond a boulder-strewn ravine. Blue-violet light flared across the heights and lightning lanced the ground, set off by discharged energy as the Keys set forces held stable for centuries into flux.

Taen ran, buffeted by a heated backlash of air. Over the rumble of thunder she heard a thin chime of steel. She swerved toward the sound, oblivious to the briars which ripped her

shins. Sped by understanding of Merya's possession, she battered her way up the slope. If Emien had succumbed to the
powers which had claimed Tathagres, Jaric's fine scruples
would prove no match for the black hatred of Kor's Accursed.

Taen dodged past a leaning boulder and crashed into brush
on the far side. Steel flared through the branches, lit by a flash
of lightning.

Thunder drowned the clang as a dagger glanced off a sword
edge. Jaric staggered off balance and caught the riposte on his
crossguard. Emien advanced. Faced in reality by the willful evil
of the brother she had loved on Imrill Kand, Taen stopped,
unable to react.

But Jaric recovered. Slighter, faster, he managed a feint and
sprang clear. Gravel slithered under Emien's boots. He parried
Jaric's dagger, then thrust. Steel screeched, stopped against the
crossed fence of his opponent's blades. Emien leaned, tried to
break the bind with brute strength. Jaric threw him off.
Through the savage exchange which followed, Taen saw the
match was not even. Neither boy was experienced. But Emien
had eight months training under Kisburn's royal swordmasters;
Jaric had spent most of the winter tending traps in the snowbound wilds of Seitforest. Emien lunged. Jaric missed the
parry, twisted, and crashed shoulder first into a thorny clump
of brush.

Lightning flared at his back. Blinded, Emien slashed on
angry impulse. Branches sheared beneath his sword. Jaric
tripped and went down on one knee, close enough that Taen
heard him gasp for breath. Emien smiled with inhuman triumph, sword angled for a killing thrust. Too late, Taen gathered her power to prevent him; emotion shattered her
concentration. Her powers faltered, blocked.

Emien's sword leapt outward. Jaric jerked, desperate. Sticks
clattered over steel as he wrenched his dagger up to guard.
Metal belled on impact. Emien's blade snaked into air, de-

flected above Jaric's shoulder. Right arm extended, Jaric pulled but could not free his sword from the brush. Finding his opponent helpless, Emien crossed his dagger over his quillon and bore down with both hands.

Jaric resisted, tendons whitened in his left wrist. His muscles trembled with exhaustion, no match for his enemy's weight. The crossed tangle of steel lowered, creeping with inexorable finality toward his neck. Lightning flickered, illuminating the instant of Emien's victory. Knuckles blackened with burns pressed downward past Jaric's cheek. Taen saw the marks; with horror-ridden certainty she looked at her brother's face and there found savage, unreasoning cruelty. The demons had claimed him irrevocably.

Torn by grief, Taen cried out. The brother she had loved on Imrill Kand would have died rather than betray his own kind. Released by terrible mercy, she rallied her powers and struck.

Emien screamed and staggered back. Steel grated, sang, and separated. Jaric surged to his feet, his sword free at last. He sprang, prepared for resistance. But Emien crumpled to his knees. His weapons slipped from nerveless fingers and clattered, ringing, onto stone.

Jaric lifted his sword to his enemy's throat. Taen rushed in and grabbed the black stone which encased the Keys of Elrinfaer. With Anskiere's service accomplished, Jaric hesitated.

Taen sobbed in anguish. "For Keithland's sake, strike quickly."

But Jaric saw no threat in the frightened boy beneath his sword. Desolate in his despair, Emien wept uncontrollably. He appeared broken and pathetic in defeat. Jaric flinched in empathy. For a fraction of an instant, he wavered. Emien dove under his blade and fled. He crashed through the scrub and vanished into the darkness.

Taen gathered herself to follow.

But Jaric threw down his sword and caught her in his arms. "Leave him. What harm can he do?"

And drained beyond all endurance, Taen clung to the comfort of his embrace. Let the Vaere decide her brother's fate. She could no longer bear to pursue him.

Epilogue

SAND CRUMBLED UNDER THE Kielmark's boots as he paced the edge of the tide mark on Cliffhaven's north shore. In late afternoon, while his captains celebrated at the fortress, he had gone walking alone on beaches at last free of enemies. His great bow hung at his shoulder. Lonely winds ruffled the hair across his brow as the Kielmark paused to breathe the ocean air, his indomitable pride tempered by sorrow. The victory had been bitterly won. Many fine men had died for no better purpose than the demons' desire to seed discord.

Slanting sunlight struck fiery reflections on the ice cliffs which reared above the sea. Defense against frostwargs and haven for a friend, Anskiere's sorceries still remained a magnet for trouble. Drawn by the inconsistency, the Kielmark squinted and saw a slender figure hooded in gray which crouched at the crest of the ice. A Llondel demon perched on the Stormwarden's stronghold, orange eyes lifted in challenge.

The Kielmark swore and unslung his bow. With no regard for danger, he nocked a broadhead and drew.

The Llondel hissed warning.

But reflexively intolerant of trespassers, the Kielmark aimed and released.

The arrow arched up, a splinter of gold in the sunlight. Following its flight, the Kielmark felt his thoughts explode into images; but the retaliation sent by the Llondel faltered, twisted awry by irrepressible joy. The vision of dismembered ships and a harbor overrun by strangers became muddled out of focus, overwhelmed by other, stronger tidings intended for the Stormwarden of Elrinfaer.

Doubled in discomfort on the sand, the Kielmark saw a wide vista of ocean. There *Callinde* sailed, the lighter, leaner *Troessa* in tow. Seated at the helm with Taen against his shoulder, Jaric steered for Cliffhaven, the Keys of Elrinfaer safely reclaimed.

When at length the Llondel released him, the Kielmark straightened. The demon had gone. But the wind sang a less minor pitch as it swept the rungs of the ice, and the sea broke sparkling like jewels over the rocks beneath.

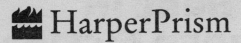
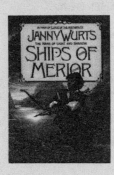

WRATH OF GOD by Robert Gleason.
An apocalyptic novel of a future America about to
fall under the rule of a murderous savage. Only a
small group of survivors are left to fight — but they are
joined by powerful forces from history when they learn how
to open a hole in time. Three legendary heroes answer the
call to the ultimate battle: George S. Patton, Amelia Earhart,
and Stonewall Jackson. Add to that lineup a killer dinosaur
and you have the most sweeping battle since *THE STAND.*
Trade paperback, 0-06-105311-2 — $14.99

THE X-FILES™ by Charles L. Grant. America's
hottest new TV series launches as a book series with
FBI agents Mulder and Scully investigating the cases
no one else will touch — the cases in the file marked X.
There is one thing they know: The truth is out there.
0-06-105414-3 — $4.99

THE WORLD OF DARKNESS™: VAMPIRE—
DARK PRINCE by Keith Herber. The ground-
breaking White Wolf role-playing game Vampire: The
Masquerade is now featured in a chilling dark fantasy novel of
a man trying to control the Beast within.
0-06-105422-4 — $4.99

THE UNAUTHORIZED TREKKERS' GUIDE
TO *THE NEXT GENERATION* AND *DEEP SPACE
NINE* by James Van Hise. This two-in-one
guidebook contains all the information on the shows, the characters, the creators, the stories behind the episodes, and
the voyages that landed on the cutting room floor.
0-06-105417-8 — $5.99

HarperPrism
An Imprint of HarperPaperbacks

PR-001